ANGELKIN

JANE STEIN

First Edition

PAGE PUBLISHING, INC.
New York, NY

First originally published by Page Publishing, Inc. 2019

ISBN 978-1-68456-026-4 (Paperback)
ISBN 978-1-68456-028-8 (Digital)

Printed in the United States of America

To my mom, for encouraging me to read
and nurturing my gift to write.

CONTENTS

Chapter 1 7
Chapter 2 25
Chapter 3 34
Chapter 4 45
Chapter 5 60
Chapter 6 79
Chapter 7 91
Chapter 8 110
Chapter 9 131
Chapter 10 145
Chapter 11 164
Chapter 12 180
Chapter 13 194
Chapter 14 203
Chapter 15 211
Chapter 16 224
Chapter 17 232
Chapter 18 243
Chapter 19 256
Chapter 20 267
Chapter 21 278
Chapter 22 290
Chapter 23 299
Chapter 24 308

Chapter 25 324
Chapter 26 339
About the Author 356

CHAPTER 1

Anthea Black didn't think it was funny. She never thought it was funny. And she usually had an exceptional sense of humor. Her friends since elementary school, Sarah and Caroline, knew that she didn't find it funny; however, they always thought it was hilarious. Just because it always happened the same way. It was dependable, just like clockwork. Both of them knew that their friend Anthea had about a five-minute shelf life with any new guy she met, especially when they found out what she did for a living. It was not as if they took bets on how long before the guy politely jumped ship, bailing on Anthea, but they loved to hear the clever excuses that the men made up. They both found some of them quite inventive. For that simple reason alone, Anthea avoided dating, especially any sort of double dating that involved her friends. Caroline and Sarah both knew that—that was why they flat out lied to her this evening to get her out of the house and back into the dating game. To them, it was a game, but to Anthea, it was always something more. The lie was the only reason Anthea had agreed to go out with the girls this evening. They were supposed to go bowling.

Dressed casually in black jeans and a turquoise blouse that matched her eyes, with her dark-auburn hair down in soft curls for a change, she was ready for some beer, fries, and time with the girls. It wasn't often that she had a night off, and there was no way that she would have agreed to expend that precious time on such a lost cause, a speed-dating club. She had to admit that the club was in a very nice part of town not far from where she lived and worked, so close she could have walked home if the girls got rowdy, if not drunk. If her friends thought they could casually slide it by her that they had passed the bowling alley and pulled into the club parking lot with idle chitchat and questions, they were mistaken. Anthea's eyes narrowed, and her scowl was legendary as the car engine died, the silence in the small confined space almost deafening. Sarah and Caroline turned in their seats and regarded her with guilty expressions on their attractive faces. Sarah was short, with curly blond hair, warm brown eyes, and an almost-too-perky personality. Caroline was tall, with an athletic build, cool blue eyes, and naturally dark, almost black, straight hair. She was even more stoic than Anthea. Emlyn, Anthea's brother, once joked that the two girls were friends with Anthea because it rounded out the blond, redhead, and brunette trio. Anthea hadn't really wondered about their motives until now. She didn't care to be lied to, even if her friends thought it was for a good cause, romance.

"Don't be mad," Sarah cooed, voice quivering slightly, as if she expected Anthea to pull out a blade and slice her in two. Although they knew what Anthea did for a living professionally, there were aspects of their friend's life they were oblivious to, and at times, she seemed downright dangerous, as if she were another person entirely. Anthea's gaze was narrow and frosty, Caroline would say downright steely.

"Asking me not to be mad makes me realize you knew that I would be," Anthea remarked with a heavy sigh. She leaned back in the car seat, considering flipping them off before jumping out of the car and walking home. There were only so many times that she could take this kind of meddling from women who were supposed to be her friends. She had been with them through their marriages, divorces, change of jobs...but when it came time for them to reciprocate, to be there for her, it often wasn't in the cards.

"Well, at least she hasn't given us the finger," Caroline remarked dryly, opening the door.

Cool night air circulated through the car, but it wasn't going to cool Anthea's anger.

"Look, Thea, you are the only one of us that hasn't been engaged or is engaged or has been married, and to be perfectly frank, I don't see any prospects for your future." Wow, that was blunt. "Not to be cruel, you understand."

Thea's jaw tightened just slightly as she regarded Caroline. This from a woman who had been married numerous times, and her friends panicked at the first mention of Vegas. She probably had a parking spot reserved at one, if not many, of the chapels there.

"Sarah and I have given this a lot of thought, and we aren't really sure why men don't find you attractive. You have a very viable personality. In fact, you have this wonderful innocence about you, some cloak of optimism that men are drawn to, at first. As far as your looks go, you could be a beauty queen, creamy skin, dark, burnish-colored hair—natural, I might add—and those eyes, while I think they should be frosty too often to match your personality, are a lovely Caribbean blue."

Thea met her friend's gaze; it had taken a lot for Caroline to list her attributes as she saw them.

"I didn't realize you both had taken inventory," Thea remarked dryly as Sarah opened her side of the car door and stepped out into the night. She glanced around the parking lot, eager to delve inside and see what men were waiting to be swept off their feet by her mighty personality.

"It's just your damn job," Sarah remarked, uncustomarily swearing.

"So you drag me here to meet men because you think I'm not whole without one?" Thea asked as she, too, opened the door and stepped out into the cool air, hoping it would ease her anger. It helped only slightly. "Can I ask what makes you both experts on the dating scene? You, Sarah, engaged more times than you can remember, but never marrying, and Caroline heading for another walk down the aisle?" It wasn't often that she fought back with words, but tonight was marking the end of a quiet and pliable Thea.

"Don't be bitchy, Thea. We know you wouldn't come if we asked you to, so we lied. Suck it up," Caroline remarked curtly.

"All the men you meet are deadbeats," Sarah replied with a pert giggle at her pun. After all, the Black family had been in the mortuary business for as long as their town could remember.

Caroline rolled her eyes at Sarah as she watched her friend bounce across the parking lot toward the double doors of the club.

"You, my dear, have an old soul, and you aren't old." Caroline curled her arms about Thea's shoulders, guiding her toward the entrance, as if she thought she might escape their grasp and run racing home. She knew Thea that well, that her friend was truly considering ditching them. "I know if Emlyn thought we were hurting your feelings in any way, he would skin us alive, but you can't be stagnant."

Sarah stood at the door to the club, her back holding it open, and already she had a drink in her hand with one of those tiny pink umbrellas. That wasn't a good sign. Thea realized that this evening was more for her friends than it was for her; she could, in essence, suck it up, though. She didn't have to like it. She could put up with it for one evening and then reconsider her options. She sighed, stepping past Sarah into the dim light. Immediately scents assaulted her nostrils. There was the smell of flowers in the air—she recognized a few of the arrangements from their florist shop. There was the heavy scent of cologne, the sound of clinking glasses, and the lighting, which appeared to be quite dim. It took a moment for her eyes to adjust, and she figured, for most, the dim light might be a blessing. But for her, it was an annoyance. She didn't like shadows.

"See? Not so bad," Sarah remarked with a glimmering smile.

"I know you both mean well, Caroline, and I appreciate your efforts, but—"

Thea's retort was cut short by a bouncy blonde in a well-meaning suit who sashayed up to them, her smile electric white. Thea thought she might go blind from the glare.

"You must be Ann," she said a bit too sweetly. Did the girls have to pay for this? *She wondered.* They might want to consider a refund. Most people who knew her called her Anthea, her closer friends called her Thea, but no one called her Ann.

"Anthea," she corrected, only slightly annoyed, as the hostess curled her iron claws around Thea's arm, shuffling her away from the safe camaraderie of her friends into a dimly lit dining hall. Overhead lights were replaced by candlelight. It did have a nice ambience, but then again, so did their family's funeral home. Thea quickly scanned the cozy dining room, ignoring the bar area, noticing only the women were seated at tables, a few with drinks in hand, others with appetizers, waiting patiently for the influx of men to be let loose among them. Candlelight flickered over the polished wood tables. Some women were in fancy dresses, others in suits, none of them dressed like Thea, ready to go bowling. Thea glanced at the name card that rested on the table nearest her, wondering just how long her friends had been planning this outing. She plopped down in the booth, back to the wall, face toward the windows and doors. At least she had a decent table. Sarah and Caroline were already sitting at the bar, chatting away with the staff, eyes floating over the room in anticipation. Although most humans would not be able to pick up their conversation among the din, Thea could. And maybe that was the problem: they were just both humans, so they didn't concern themselves with things that lived in the shadows. Listening to their murmurs, she figured they seemed to think she was prime real estate, even dressed the way she was. Thea sighed. She would give them ten to twenty minutes, and then she was out of here, whether they drove her home or not. She rolled her eyes as both her friends gave her the old thumbs-up sign, as if they thought her prince charming would waltz through the door. Thea signaled for the waiter just as a chime lilted over the room. Thea ordered a cream soda just as the first gentleman slid into the seat across from her.

This just wasn't going to be her night.

Thea managed a polite smile and a handshake. Greg was an accountant at a large law firm downtown; he had a pleasant smile, had a dimple in the chin, drove an Audi, and looked at her with anticipation. Greg thought she was hot; it was the red hair and those blue eyes, and she would look great on his arm, he figured. So she wasn't dressed to kill. Casual was sexy too. Thea could feel Greg sizing her up as she sat across from him, soda in hand. Emlyn would say that his adopted sister wasn't bad to look at; she had good height at five seven, slightly athletic in build, but with too much bosom to be called slight. Her complexion was clear and creamy, with a smattering of freckles, but what he thought was even more appealing was that she could defend her honor using either a gun or knife, not that her friends would know. It wasn't something you shared on a first unexpected date.

"So, Anthea, great old-fashioned name there. Sorry I didn't give you a chance to chime in. What do you do for a living?" True, it had been quite a monologue; Thea just sat patiently, nodding and trying to look interested. Thea smiled. It was a dangerous smile that usually gave Emlyn the start of a headache and made him want to run for the hills because something was always up. Now was the moment to make her move.

"I'm a hair, makeup, and clothing consultant."

Greg's face brightened. "That must be fascinating. Work on anyone famous I'd know?" Greg asked, sounding jovial.

"For the dead, Greg. My family owns Black Funeral and Crematory Services, Blacks Flower Shop, and the Black Chapel. I work at the mortuary."

It took a moment for the information to register. His smile quivered slightly, and he glanced at his watch. Thea thought a moment as she considered an answer to his question.

"Yes. Actually, you probably know Jean Merrybel. She was that retired actress who died last week. I worked on her."

Thea watched as Greg shifted in his chair uncomfortably, still trying to keep his smile plastered on his face. He could have collided with the moon the way he rocketed out of the chair when the chime sounded to switch partners. Thea sighed, that devilish smile on her face, Sarah and Caroline glaring at her, concerned that the plan was unraveling. Their moment of triumph had passed, and now she was starting to enjoy herself.

After Greg came Thomas, a mechanic; Zack, a consultant; and Corey, a salesman, each extremely interested in her until she discussed her career choice, then it was as if she had the plague. Thea had finished her soda and decided she had had enough rejection for one evening and was just getting ready to leave. In fact, she was just beginning to stand when another man decided to valiantly sit at her table and give it a shot. Thea seated herself, brushed off her pants, adjusted the pendant beneath her blouse, and managed a patient smile, glancing at, not a man, but rather a male vampire. Thea managed to hide her surprise. At the beginning of the chime signaling the start of musical dating, the room had been filled with only humans. What on earth would a vampire be doing in a speed-dating club? With her best poker face in place, she looked at him sitting all *GQ*, in a dark-gray suit, no tie, across from her, with an amused smile on his face. His dark hair was neatly cut, his blue-gray eyes twinkling in the candlelight. Most humans couldn't tell supernatural from natural, but Thea could. It was a game supernaturals, or sups, liked to play. He played human well, but she played uninformed, innocent little human well, too. It wasn't that she knew the names of all the bloodborn or vampires in town, but she did know most of the regulars by sight. This one gentleman was new in town.

Arkin Kane was a new vampire in a strange town, and since his arrival, he had spent various evenings visiting hot spots in the city, observing. It was a simple strategy: First wave entered the city and collected intel. If the information looked promising, then the second wave established a place for them to stay and shored up their security. And then as third wave, he joined them. It was the quickest way to define the pulse of the city, mingling not with his kind but with humans. There would be time to mingle with his brethren later. In all the centuries he had been alive, he had to admit, this was his first time at a speed-dating club, and it was interesting to watch as humans tried to learn as much as they could about one another in so little time. Then again, they were mortal; they had such little time. It was quite a course in psychology, and Arkin had chosen to watch it all by sitting at the bar, toward the back of the club, out of the way of the serious daters. He had watched the women filter in, primping and preparing themselves for the onslaught of eligible men. Everyone attending was human, except for himself, and he doubted anyone would have guessed that he wasn't human. It was the commotion at the door that drew himself to a blonde, brunette, and redhead, and it was obvious that the redhead was not happy to be there. She looked underdressed for the venue, but she could be wearing a sackcloth and still look utterly devastating in it. Arkin frowned as he regarded this woman. There was something decidedly different about her, and considering his age, he had had his share of identifying quickly friend or foe, human from nonhuman. The problem about living immortally, as it were, was that if you met someone who reminded you of someone else, it often colored your judgment. Faces, mannerisms, even voices could take you back to someone you loved, someone you hated. It was hard not to make a snap decision about someone. The simple fact was that this woman didn't remind him of anyone he had met before.

He shifted on the stool, eyes watching as men approached and plied their charm to her. She had met each with a polite and patient smile. She looked suitably interested, but it was the wicked grin that caught his attention most when she finally revealed what she did for a living. Arkin refrained from a chuckle. No wonder the men were so uncomfortable around her. As the last young man stood, he noted that she stood, ready to leave. No, he couldn't have this before having a bit of fun with her himself. It was high time he entered into the fray. Dressed in simple gray slacks, a well-fitting jacket, a white shirt, no tie, his shoes highly polished, he approached that table. She was just getting ready to leave when he appeared before her. She glanced up to look at him expectantly. "Blue eyes" were an understatement; they were clear blue, and not frosty cold, but warm. There was something about this woman that wasn't entirely human, he thought. She smiled with a slight sigh and seated herself. It was Arkin who gestured to the waiter for another of whatever she was drinking. He knew by the smell it was nonalcoholic, a soda perhaps. He leaned back in the seat and gazed upon her, thinking that the more he looked at her, the prettier she became. And that throat, even hidden behind the collar, was oddly sexy.

"Anthea Black, or so your place card says. A very nice name. I am Arkin Kane, but my friends call me Arkin."

Thea wondered what his enemies called him. Vampires, as humans had mistakenly called them, weren't often seen in such obviously human places. Though the masses of humans knew they existed, they tended to ignore anything they didn't understand. Thea understood all too well. She shifted slightly in her seat, the chain from a necklace beneath her blouse glimmering in the candlelight.

"You seem like an absolutely charming woman. I can't see why men are avoiding you in droves," he commented with a chuckle. Oh, he was good at acting human, and Anthea was going to try like hell to pretend that he was. A fleeting thought fluttered across Arkin's mind as he looked hard at her. Did she know he was a vampire? He had the feeling that she did, indeed, know. How utterly delicious, he thought.

"Are you more daring than the rest, or did someone bet you to come and sit with me?"

"No one dares me to do anything. I am here on my own initiative to see how it is that you scare these eager men away." His voice had that come-hither quality, his diction perfect. Thea bet he was well over two hundred, maybe even older. He might have had a slight accent, but he seemed to fight the urge to use it. She had to admit, he was the hottest-looking thing in that club. Looking just past him to Sarah and Caroline, Thea could see their mouths hanging open, eyes just as wide. They were giving her that go-for-it look, and Arkin was trying hard not to show his amusement.

"So tell me, Anthea Black, what is it that makes weaker men run from you?"

"I work in a mortuary. I work directly with the dead. I thought I would get that out of the way up front in case you suddenly had another appointment, you know, like someone had died, or your dog was sick, etc. So is there somewhere else you have to be?"

Arkin smiled and chuckled. "I need to be right here, and someone has to do your job, don't they? And that is what all the fuss is about? Really, men need to man up."

Thea shrugged as he sat opposite her, casually relaxed.

"Well, if I said I was into forensics, that might have seemed reality-show romantic. Most men aren't squeamish as a rule, but they don't like their women to be stronger than them."

"Are you stronger than most men?" Arkin asked, curious as she ignored the question.

"So what do you do for a living? And what brings you to a speed-dating club? I have to say, you don't look like the type. You look as if you could whistle and women would come a-running. Or is that why you are here? You had to duck into the building to hide from all the women chasing you?"

"And what type does come to a club like this?" he asked with an arched eyebrow.

"Not someone as attractive as you, but I'm sure you know that. You look as if you could walk the runway overseas as a male model or appear on the cover of *GQ*. I am getting a lot of glares from the other women around the room who seem to have their eyes only for you. You aren't actually with the speed-daters, are you?"

"Well, it would be ungentlemanly to leave you without someone to talk to, so I volunteered. I am new to the city and just thought I would enjoy a night out. Are you here because you can't get a date? I find that very difficult to believe."

"Even after seeing all the men run from me? You are too kind. I am here because my friends lied to me. I thought I was going bowling."

Arkin chuckled. "Ah, that explains the casual clothing. Although I find you look highly attractive and a lot less desperate, dressed as you are. Were you just getting ready to leave?"

"I had just about had enough of the small talk and the fake excuses. I like what I do, Arkin. We have a large family business, and someone, as you say, has to do it."

"People often forget the necessities in life. They think about what is good and forget and try to ignore the bad. I applaud your steadfastness."

She smiled, inclining her head. "That is very kind of you. I have made a lot of friends in this city, and I have lost friends as well."

"You like living here?" he asked, voice almost hypnotic.

"I have been here all my life, but things do change, and not always for the better. There have been upsets in the power structure of the city, and that causes rifts, suspicions. It can be hard to reconcile who is best for what has to be done."

Arkin shifted in his seat. Oh, yes, she knew exactly what he was. He wondered how she knew. He was old, but he was a perfectionist when it came to mimicking a human. There had been young vampires who hadn't even been sure he was one of them. To say that there had been an upset in the city was an understatement—the vampire interest in this city was fractured, and they were in danger of a civil war.

"But someone has to take the reins and do it, don't they? I commend you and your family. I would love to stop by and have a tour of your facility."

She laughed now, honestly, head tilted back and that wonderful throat bare. This strange fascination with a woman he had only met was odd, indeed.

"Thank you for the laugh. Truly, no one has ever asked for a tour, but then again, you did come over here and talk to me and you have lasted longer than five minutes. My girlfriends will be totally impressed."

"But I have kept you. You were leaving, weren't you?"

"I was, Arkin. It is rare when I get a night out, and I hadn't planned on spending it this way."

He was surprised that she wasn't tempted to stay and talk to him, but he knew as soon as she stood up, there would be another woman eager to take her place in the booth. And if she wasn't staying, neither would he.

"I am sure your girlfriends meant it to be a good experience for you. Then again, there are some women who feel they don't need men to be complete. Are you one of them?"

"I don't think so, Arkin. I just can't find anyone to spend any time with me to find out. But work keeps me busy, and as I said, I have friends. I'm not so sure that Sarah and Caroline are the friends I need to continue seeing. I think we are moving in separate directions."

"That happens. You have grown past them, seen things they can't imagine, done things they would be shocked at." There was a tender, expectant silence at the end of his sentence, Arkin meeting her gaze. Oh, yes, she was familiar with his world, perhaps protected her friends from it. He stood as she stood, and she extended her hand.

"Thank you for at least making it an enjoyable evening."

"Are your friends all right to drive you home? They look a bit under the weather due to drink."

She chuckled again as he walked her away from the table, female eyes following him with adoration.

"They don't look ready to leave, and most clubs have taxis on call. It is a two-man service, off-duty police officers, one to drive them home and another to take their car as well. They will be fine." Thea drew a long, deep breath, eyes scanning the shadows that skirted the parking lot as they stepped into the night. She was pretty certain that Arkin wasn't alone; he had friends somewhere, and no one was that confident or courted such danger in a strange city.

"And how are you planning on getting home? I have a car."

She met his gaze and had absolutely no plans on taking him up on that offer.

"Nice of you to offer, but we only just met, and trust is a rare commodity with me. I am in walking distance of where I live. I am quite safe."

"I would not assume that you can't protect yourself, but as a gentleman, it makes it hard for me to let you go so easily."

Anthea turned and gently touched his cheek. "I appreciate someone looking out for me, but I already have a brother, Arkin. And I don't think I could think of you in that way."

He opened and then closed his mouth, watching her walk off through the pools of light that dotted the parking lot and inched over into the street. He would let her get so far ahead of him and then follow just to be certain. This was a better evening than he could have hoped for.

To any other vampire, Marta would have been silent, just a hush of breath as she approached, but to Arkin, he knew where she was and turned to greet her with a satisfied smile on his lips.

"I take it your research went well?" Marta asked dryly, her dark hair cut sharply around her face with a razor. She was also dressed like her master, in gray, looking very businesslike, her business danger.

"Pretty little thing, but I don't think she is entirely human. I don't get that weak-blood vibe from her."

"I would bet you that she knew what I was, though she didn't let on. Very interesting." His eyes were still following Thea's retreat. Marta regarded her master with cool interest.

"I take it you found her to be intriguing? You have been singularly focused on the city since we arrived. This is the first time you have…you are going to follow her, aren't you?"

Arkin smiled and shrugged, looking past Marta at his other two children, Jackson and Lang, waiting in the dark-gray sedan.

"She is walking home alone. It would be ungentlemanly for me to let her do so without an escort, even if she isn't aware of it."

Marta nodded, trying to keep a smug smile off her lips. It had been a long time since Arkin had found anything this interesting, and if they were in for a fight to take the city, why not be happy for a bit now? Later, there would be time for tears.

It was a lovely evening for a walk. The air was crisp, the moon almost full, so it added light to the shadows that were hidden from the overhead streetlights. It was less than a mile to the house she shared with her brother when they were in the city working. When they were off the clock, they preferred their large country house, which sat on more than twenty acres of land. It had a wraparound porch and swing. That, to them, was home. As she walked, Thea was keenly aware of her surroundings, especially when the crowds thinned out and all she heard were the soft pat of her shoes on the asphalt. It was that chill running up her spine that told her she was not alone any longer, that she was being followed, and it was the sourness in the air that confirmed who was doing the following. In the short alleyway, brick walls making the small space seem confining, it was Thea who turned and glanced at the opposite wall, finding the glittering eye of a vampire settled on her.

"Pick," she said, voice low so that she wouldn't be overheard. "Out for a walk, are we?"

Pick adjusted himself across the brick wall that he clung to, coming lower to the ground, his claws clinging to the rough surface. He had dark hair, shiny with something, sallow features, and predatory eyes. A cold chain glittered around his neck beneath a worn brown leather jacket. He might have been attractive if he weren't so mentally fucked up. His eyes narrowed as he realized that she had known that he was behind her. That pissed him off.

"Overconfident walking around in the dark, Black, considering our lord and master of the city is no more."

"Yardley may not be around, but tradition still stands. It states that I remain untouched, Pick. Would you want to go against the writings? I have served this city well as a witness. My death or injury would not look favorable upon you."

He hissed at Thea. She sighed, reaching up casually to lay her right hand on her shoulder. She didn't want a confrontation. It wasn't that she didn't want to fight; no, she was up to taking Pick apart. What she didn't want was to reveal herself, shear away that innocence that everyone believed she had. It was a false halo that death didn't touch her, or maybe that she couldn't be tainted by death.

"You have seen too much witness, you know too much, and that in itself is dangerous. Everyone wants your death, but no one wants to do it."

Thea was very still, eyes watching Pick carefully as he swayed, hanging on the wall across from her. There was just enough light from each end of the alleyway to see him clearly.

"I didn't realize I was so unpopular," Thea remarked softly, eyes twinkling in the dark.

"Lure men in with your eyes, woo them with your silence, and pretend to be human, but we know you aren't. We feel you aren't."

"Too polite to ask, are you?" she asked, body tensing as she sensed a change in Pick's demeanor.

She really didn't want to do this, but it didn't look like he was going to leave her a choice. She would have to draw on him, and to keep her secret, she would have to kill him. It was a leap through the air straight at her, right arm reaching out for her throat, claws sharp, but before she could draw out a weapon, Arkin was there in front of her, his hands around Pick's throat. A sharp crack rent the air as Pick's head sort of lulled to the right, Thea realizing that Arkin, without even so much as an effort, had broken Pick's spine. Arkin let the limp body slide out of his hands. It hit the asphalt with a thud. Light danced off his gaze as he regarded Thea with interest. She wasn't on the ground, cowering. She wasn't hysterical, screaming at the top of her lungs. Instead, she met his gaze fully. There was more to her than meets the eye.

"I believe this is just one reason you should have taken me up on my offer to drive you home," he remarked, gently putting his hand on her shoulder, guiding her farther down the alleyway. He left the body where it had fallen and was surprised when she didn't look back. "How far to your house?"

"About two blocks," she answered, voice calm, no hesitancy, no questions, just a stillness that frightened him a bit. "I guess I should say 'Thank you.'"

"Then I guess my reply should be 'You're welcome.' Who was that?"

"Pick. In case you didn't notice, he didn't like me."

"I didn't hear his reasons, but I question his taste. No questions for me?"

Thea shook her head, turning her gaze back down the street as they walked along beside each other. It amazed him that she could just ignore what happened and not ply him with questions. Odd.

"I don't think I will be bothered again," she remarked, quite sure of herself.

"You were almost bothered to death. I'll see you to your door. You seem remarkably calm for someone who was almost attacked."

"I'm not the kind of girl that falls apart so easily. I can do that later in the privacy of my own home. Don't think that little feat of strength bought you something, Mr. Kane. I am capable, don't think that I'm not."

"I didn't say that you weren't. In fact, I rather think you are, and that intrigues me, Ms. Black."

"Don't let it keep you up at night, Mr. Kane," she quipped with a sigh. He had saved her in more ways than one.

Emlyn glanced up as the decorative front door opened. Funny, he didn't hear a car drive up, but of course, Polly, their golden retriever, had her tail wagging so fiercely he knew it had to be his sister. Em frowned as he watched his sister kneel before their pooch, scrub her ears, and then hug her. She was a great therapy dog, and this evening, it looked like his sister needed therapy. Thea stood, walking into living room, leaned against the doorjamb, and slowly slid down to the floor to cross her legs. Polly immediately lay down next to her, as if providing comfort, her head on Thea's knee.

"You okay? You didn't bowl an 89 again, did you?"

She took her hands away from her face and glared at him. Emlyn was about six one, around Arkin's height. He was muscular, with short dark hair and hazel eyes with flecks of gold dancing about, or so various ladies had told her. Em had a great smile, an empathetic voice, and took his job as her brother seriously since he was an only child. He flipped off the TV, leaving the plush La-Z-Boy for her side. He sat on the polished wooden floor and regarded Thea, hand resting on Polly's back.

"Let me use my magnificent powers of deduction. Something happened and you walked home."

"My, we are brilliant this evening. We didn't go bowling. Instead, the girls felt the need to take me to a speed-dating club."

Thea could see Emlyn's jaw tighten as he leaned up against the entertainment console.

"I'm sorry for that. I don't know why they think that they have to intervene in your life. You are happy, aren't you? You do have enough to fill your time, if only they knew."

"That's just it, Em. They think they are doing it for me, but really, it's for them. They think they are being good friends, but in fact, they are pissing the hell out of me. I don't get that many free evenings where I don't have to dress up a corpse or deal with supernatural shit."

"You don't have to explain to me, but maybe you need a break from your friends. I mean, last month, they gave you that personal massage unit. Cheeky, if you ask me, although you didn't. I'm sorry that your evening was a total loss."

"Well, actually, I did meet someone new, a vampire."

Em frowned slightly, trying to get his head wrapped around her statement. He knew it was a bad habit to call them that, but just between his sister and him, it was all right.

"A vampire was at a speed-dating club?" he asked, an odd look on his face.

"Not participating, but observing."

He shook his head, frowning. It still didn't make any sense to him.

"What do you think his endgame is?"

"I don't know, but he wasn't the only one following me. Pick was stalking me as well. He said some not-so-nice things before he attacked me. Arkin Kane saved me from having to defend myself and kill Pick. I would have done it if we were alone, but somehow, I knew that Arkin was too much of a traditionalist to leave me to the dark shadows as it were. I was about 80 percent sure he was following me."

Em opened and then closed his mouth. "So let me summarize your evening. No bowling, but speed-dating. You were picked up by a strange vampire, and he killed Pick defending you."

She nodded. "Nice summary," she added as she slowly got to her feet. Em stood, following her into the kitchen.

"You didn't answer my question as to why you think he is here."

She frowned at her brother as she opened the fridge. He reached out, scratching her along her back, receiving a satisfied purr. He smiled as she shifted under his tender ministrations.

"Thanks. I needed that. Look, I'm not a vampire psychologist. I wouldn't work with them if I didn't have a choice, but supernatural things sort of gravitate toward me, you know that."

"Yeah, I learned it the hard way when you turned thirteen," added Em, leaning against the counter, arms across his chest. He fell silent.

"All I can tell you about Arkin Kane is, he is more than nice-looking. I did ogle him a bit, turned down a ride home, he followed me to make sure I was safe, killed Pick, and if he is any kind of player at all, he is going to have to work to get this city in shape."

“He has to go through seven other vampires, either kill them or charm them into submission, to get this city under control. And between you and me, I wouldn’t want the city, but he could do it.”

Thea nodded a she stood up, an apple in her hand.

“From now on, it is just you, me, and work, whichever kind of work comes my way. I can’t afford to get mixed up in things, and you know what I mean.”

“I know what you mean, but sometimes it doesn’t matter what you want. You are like a paranormal black hole.”

She rolled her eyes at him.

“A very lovely paranormal black hole,” he said. “Look, when we finish our shift this week, we can go out to the country for a few days. I think you could use the quiet solitude. You know, get out there and stretch.”

Thea nodded. “Thanks for being concerned.”

“You aren’t usually this upset by things. The girls just don’t get it, and sometimes I think they are jealous of you but they can’t put their finger on why.”

“Pick, before he died, sort of intimated the same thing, innocent little thing, not human, he said.”

“Yeah, well, he was right about that,” sighed Em.

CHAPTER 2

It wasn't difficult to find what people popularly called the Black Block. Apparently, the Black family owned an entire city block that contained the mortuary, florist, chapel, and on the other side of the block, in the residential area, a home. It was said that they were open 24-7, catered to all types of clients, cultivated interns, and young summer help. It was also said that at the center of the block, behind the buildings, was a lovely, parklike commons area to comfort those who needed to grieve or to enamor those who were to be married. On the whole, they were well-thought-of among humans as well as the paranormals, though Arkin hadn't asked around purposefully, nor had his team. Information just trickled to them naturally. Anthea Black could normally be found in the mortuary, so that was where he was headed the following evening. He wanted to know what would provoke an unstable vampire like Pick to attack her. Granted, she seemed human, but all his senses said that she was something else, something he couldn't quite put his finger on that told him there was more to Anthea Black than his eyes could see or his senses could comprehend. That and he was curious as hell.

Arkin pushed open the right double door and entered a very serene environment that was filled with flowers and soft background music. He was promptly met not by Anthea but by a golden retriever who wagged her tail and sat neatly with her paw up, waiting for a handshake. Arkin chuckled as he bent down and shook the paw, patting the dog on the head. He glanced up, finding Thea standing behind a very sturdy wooden desk, a large vase of multicolored flowers off to the side near the phone, which sat across from the computer. Her hair was curled up in a soft bun, her clothing a gray suit with lavender tank beneath the jacket. She had a very soft smile on her face.

"Come on, Polly, come and sit," she asked gently.

"She is a lovely dog."

"She is a therapy dog. Many who come in here are in pieces. She doesn't care who you are or why you are crying, she just gives comfort," she said. "It's nice to see you again, Mr. Kane. How can I be of service to you? Did you come for a tour?"

Arkin stood and then stepped forward quicker than an average human would, and Thea didn't blink; she didn't even seem concerned or step back in fear. Odd.

"Can we drop the pretense? You know what I am."

It was not a question, and yes, she knew he was born of the blood.

"Are you a hunter, an enforcer?"

Hunters were men and women who killed paranormals, in the beginning for no reason, just because they were considered inherently dangerous. However, they grew into a more law enforcement role, humans having to feel that they had a hand in the safety of their own kind. They did the killing, not so much the catching or the keeping. Emlyn was one of those daring young men.

Arkin watched as Thea reached up into her blouse and drew out a gold pendant. It was a very old symbol, in shapes of a knot, or so most people would assume, the meaning more important that the emerald-cut diamond resting in the center. Arkin relaxed as he reached over to touch the warm amulet. His fingers gently brushed her flesh.

"You're a silent witness," he murmured reverently. "For how long?"

Thea looked at the pendant. "Since as long as I could listen and remember. My parents started me young," she remarked simply.

"So...that does explain why Pick might want to kill you if he were twisted enough to fear for their secrets," Arkin muttered to himself.

"No one has questioned my skill or loyalty, Arkin," added Thea, tartly taking the pendant from his hand, tucking it back into her blouse. Arkin sighed, wishing his hands could follow it.

"No offense is meant, Thea. I just wanted to understand why you seemed comfortable with me and didn't go to pieces when Pick confronted you. Did you know I was following you?"

"If you are a traditionalist, yes, I had an inkling that you might. Did I know Pick had a vendetta? No. Is that why you are here, to ferret me out?"

Arkin smiled, taking her hand and kissing it gently.

"No, it is as you suggested for that tour."

"I am sure, by now, you have heard it called the Black Block? The center of the organization is the mortuary and the services we offer to all races. To our left is the marketing area and display room. Toward the back is where we do the actual work. To our right is the door leading to the viewing area, should our client decide not to use the chapel. That chamber looks out over the green commons resting between our buildings. That door there leads to the chapel. It is non-denominational, weddings, blood risings, it is safe for you to enter if you needed to. We can dress it up or down depending on the need of our client. On the far left of the block is the florist. We have our own greenhouses out of the city. Everything you see in here is supplied by our floral department." Thea buzzed the intercom and asked for someone to sit at reception. An Asian man, dressed in a very well-tailored black suit, nodded to them both as he arrived. Arkin followed her back down the hallway toward the viewing room that was tastefully decorated, Polly following silently behind them.

"Do you do most of your business during the day?"

"That depends on which sort of business. At the hour of the wolf, many die. We pick up the body from the home, or the coroner, depending on the circumstances."

Arkin glanced out into the commons area lit attractively by lanterns. Thea opened the French doors that led out onto a brick patio.

A fountain bubbled in the distance as Polly bounded past them, barking into the night. She headed straight for the house across the commons and ducked into a doggy door.

"I am assuming that's where you live? It is either that or your dog has a side job as a burglar."

"Yes, one who wants her belly rubbed and anything you might be eating. My brother, Emlyn, and I stay there when we are working. All three of our businesses run 24-7, and if one doesn't have anything scheduled, we coordinate."

"But you work on the side as a silent witness."

Thea nodded as she gestured toward the decorative wooden benches. Polly reappeared with her ball. Thea took it and tossed it about the grounds.

"We have a good staff. They can get by without me. But lately I haven't been needed. But times do change, and maybe I will be needed again."

"I am sure you will be again. Can I ask a favor of you?" he asked, curious.

She met his twinkling gaze. "You can ask. I can't say that I'll be able to provide the favor."

"Fair enough." He smiled a small smile. "As you know, I am new to the city, and I would really like to speak to someone here born of the blood about what has happened with our race. Is there anyone you trust that I can speak with?"

Thea was quiet a moment, tucking a stray strand of hair around the shell of her ear.

"You have to have other friends than those who tried to get you a speed date."

She chuckled lightly. It was a pleasant sound, he decided.

"I have a wide array of friends. Most humans don't realize that, but just because I can think of someone doesn't mean that he or she will speak with you. You are a stranger."

"Doesn't killing Pick buy me anything?"

She chuckled. "You got in my good graces by doing him in, but it might cause you some problems with your own race if they find out that you were the one who took his life. He wasn't well-thought-of, but he was someone's to protect." She thought Arkin didn't look all that concerned.

"I quite understand. Do the best you can for me. Here is my number." Arkin pulled out a light-gray card with his name and cell number only on it. That garnered a bit of a smile. She bet he didn't give it to just anyone.

"Are you always this enigmatic?"

"Isn't that what humans want us to be? I would be in your debt if you could find someone for me to speak to."

Thea tossed the ball again to Polly standing gracefully. "I will give it some thought. But understand that if my friend agrees to meet with you, you are not to harm him or her. I know this city is on the edge of a meltdown, but I'm not going to put anyone at risk."

"You have my word, and on my honor, that is still something I believe in. And I hope you will as well."

"Many of you do. That is one thing that I find charming about your race."

Arkin smiled, taking her hand. "There are many things I find charming about you. Call me, Anthea."

Thea watched as Arkin followed the pathway toward the ornate wrought iron gates aside the chapel. He disappeared under the hanging ivy. She glanced down and found Polly with her ball in her mouth, tail thumping the brick.

"Go get your leash. It's time for dinner."

Polly darted off back across the green as Thea turned, finding Emlyn leaning against the open French door. His expression was thoughtful.

"So that was our intrepid Arkin?"

"It was, and he asked me to put him in touch with someone who could bring him up to speed on the city."

"What's to tell? It is falling apart, and no one wants to deal with the vampires and they stay clear. And if he's smart, he would as well. You tell him that you are a silent witness?"

"Yes. That answered some questions for him."

Polly nudged Thea's leg, the red leash hanging out of her mouth, dragging behind her.

"You are going to Edden's for dinner?"

"I thought I would kill two birds with one stone, dinner and ask the favor."

"He's a good guy. He probably will talk to the tall, dark stranger. If this Arkin is going to stay, he needs to know what he is getting into. If he isn't someone that they know and respect up front, they will fight him every step of the way."

"It's his fight. I just watch and listen."

Emlyn watched as Thea bent down and hooked Polly's leash to her pink polka dot collar.

"He's good-looking in a model sort of way. Old, I bet as well."

"I don't ask, and they don't usually tell." Thea frowned at her brother. "Why? What is on your mind?"

Emlyn shook his head. "I know, to most people, you feel human. We both know you aren't quite 100 percent."

She snorted as she started to walk across the grass, her brother following. "Don't you think I know the dangers, Em? Why do you think I hide it from everyone and I tried to hide it from you? Not successfully, I might add. But then you are an exceptional person and didn't exactly freak when you discovered I wasn't what you always thought I was. You just asked a bunch of questions I couldn't answer."

Em chuckled, kissing his sister on the forehead. "Go eat, I'll watch your back. When he finds out how screwed up everything is, he's likely to leave, and your crush on him will wane."

She rolled her eyes at him. "Attack, Polly," ordered Thea as Polly wagged her tail and danced around them.

"Traitor."

* * *

Edden glanced up when the bell on the front door chimed invitingly. He smiled as he caught sight of Thea walking Polly over toward their usual booth next to the bar. A soft dog bed rested on the floor beneath the table, where Polly could curl up. He glanced at his watch.

"You're right on time."

Edden had been born an Irishman. Anthea wasn't sure when that was. He had dark-red hair and sparkling hazel eyes. His tavern was a hangout for the paranormal crowd, though occasionally, a brave human wandered in. Emlyn and Thea were regulars.

Thea unbound her hair and shrugged out of her jacket. She stretched out of her shoes, setting her feet on the cushioned booth seat across from her. Edden's was only a block away. With food in hand, Edden brought her standard fare for a Friday, cheese and broccoli soup, a salad, and of course, an ice cream concoction. Polly got a chew toy to keep her occupied. Edden slid into the booth across from her, watching Thea eat with amusement. He had met Thea when she was just coming into her teens. He had been slated as a bodyguard for her when she was summoned to witness, and they had become friends. Edden gently set her feet on his lap, massaging her lavender toes through her stockings. She sighed. It was the one way he knew that he could make her relax, plus she had cute feet.

"I don't eat anymore, but you make me wish I could with all those yummy noises you are making."

"Don't ever let Everett leave. He is the best chef. That's why the changelings come in. His steaks are legendary."

"Glad to hear that we can please you." Edden refrained from talking shop; he wanted to know if she knew that Pick was dead. They knew it was a matter of time before someone ended his life, and his so-called overlord, Garrick, would be looking for the blood-born who did him in. She met his gaze.

"You want to talk but you don't want to upset me. What's on your mind?"

"How do you read people like that?"

She shrugged, taking a gulp of her Root Beer.

"Pick is dead, and Garrick will want the culprit."

Thea didn't comment.

"But you already knew he was dead."

"Yes, because I am the cause of his death. Pick threatened me, and before I could take his life, I was rescued just like a damsel in distress."

Edden frowned. "Who?"

Thea dotted her lips with her napkin. She leaned back and regarded Edden. "Someone new to the area I just met. His name is Arkin Kane. Pick was concerned that I knew too much and, since Yardley wasn't around to protect me, thought I was an easy target."

Thea watched as Edden waded through his memories. He shook his head. The name didn't sound familiar. "I don't know him. Where did you meet?"

Thea cleared her throat. "If you promise not to laugh at me, I'll tell you."

"I would never laugh at you," he added honestly, hand to his chest over his heart.

"You did in the past." Thea sighed. "I was duped into going to a speed-dating club, and he was there, observing. He was amused by the fact that no human male seemed interested in hanging with me."

"And he followed you home to see that you are safe? What does he look like?"

"Tall, about six one or two. Dark hair, neatly cut. Clean-shaven, dark blue-gray eyes, fit, not like a Viking, but he has some strength and age on him. He wears gray a lot, or at least the two times I have seen him. He came to me this evening and asked if I had a friend who was born of the blood that he could speak with about the state of the city."

Edden shifted in his seat, gently setting aside her feet. Edden leaned on the table in thought.

"I told him I would ask but no one was under any obligation. I would never put you into the crossfire...you can think about it and leave me a message if you are willing to speak to him. It's up to you."

"You think he is a player?" Edden asked softly.

"On this board or elsewhere?" Thea asked. "He took out Pick. He will have to face Garrick, and we know that Cordelia has the hots for Garrick. He could be opening a whole can of whoop-ass on himself."

Edden chuckled. "Could I take him?"

"Polly could take him." She laughed, gently touching his hand. "I told him that he better not threaten you, or I would take care of him."

Edden shook his head with a smile on his face.

"What, you don't think that I could?"

Edden knew that there was something different about her. He, like others, thought it might be magic in her blood. He had seen her at work, as both a mortician and a silent witness, and she excelled in both. He knew she meant what she promised, but he wouldn't want to see her hurt or dead because of him.

"I know that you could. Eat, I'll think about this Arkin Kane and leave you a message if I agree. If I speak with him, I will want you here with me."

She grinned.

"As if you could keep me away," she quipped.

CHAPTER 3

Thea had never been much of a morning person. In fact, she resembled the walking dead until she had something warm to enliven her. Em was used to that scary look as she shuffled her way into the kitchen, groaned as she poured herself a cup of tea, and blinked her eyes open. She glared at the screen on her phone.

"Expecting a call?"

"My other business as witness." She stifled a yawn, walking on autopilot to the table and chair.

Em shook his head. He had been up and dressed for at least half an hour. "Still this Arkin lad?"

"Lad?" she asked, taking a long, deep sip of warm tea. She sighed, curling her foot up under her, as she sat in the chair.

"He is old, Em. I wouldn't call him a lad, but yes. He asked me to set him up with someone he could talk to, and I thought of Edden. Edden said yes."

"Most humans wouldn't understand this or even want to know, but this city is in peril. I don't think I want to be in the middle of a vampire civil war."

"Maybe he wants to stop a war. But you are right, I am only hooking them up. Edden said yes. He wants us to meet him at eight o'clock at his place, SoulFires. I'll call Arkin and let him know, and after that, I'll try to bow out politely."

"You have tried to bow out before and always get drawn back in. You're just too damn good at what you do." Em meant that too.

"Blame it on our folks," she answered as he stood and kissed her on her forehead.

"Do what you have to. I have your back."

"You always have, and believe me, there isn't anyone else I would trust with it."

"Consider me the wind beneath your wings, sis," he remarked with a chuckle.

Thea sat for a moment in thoughtful silence before calling Arkin's number. As with most vampires she had known, he had a daytime man, or secretary, whatever, take the message politely. She was sure she would see him this evening.

Thea showered, changed into a presentable navy suit, managed to tame her hair, and then slapped on a tinge of makeup. With purse over her shoulder, she walked across the commons toward the mortuary. Matt would already be manning the front desk; he had texted to her that he had updated her calendar. There was the Grant lad who had died in a car accident. His face would need some reconstruction. There was Mrs. Howard, who had passed of cancer and wanted her friends to remember what she looked like, hair and all. That was just for the first few hours. You never knew what the day would bring. Also scheduled for the chapel was a service for Mr. Appleton. The florist shop had three orders for weddings, one funeral, and one reception. They were all working today.

It was around noon when Matt buzzed the prep room. Thea was hands deep in Kimberly Parker, who had been murdered, rather gruesomely, but her parents still wanted to have an open casket. It wasn't so much the face as it was making her look whole. Thea was glad that the bastard who did this was dead, with so much silver in his chest.

She hit the intercom with her elbow, Matt stating that she had company waiting for her in reception. Thea washed up, shed her lab coat, and stepped out to greet whomever it was waiting for her. Thea was slightly surprised to find Caroline and Sarah standing in the reception area of the mortuary. When Matt had called back into the prep room and said that she had company, she had not expected her two friends. She stepped out of the workroom and met their rather-thoughtful expressions. She glanced at her watch and realized that they were probably on their lunch break from work. Caroline had never seen Thea not look presentable, even in gardening clothes. She had an air of importance about her, and it struck Caroline that maybe she and Sarah were a bit jealous. She seemed to always look just so, not a line on her face, almost perfect. Sure, they all had important jobs, they were comfortable as far as money was concerned, but even with the men that she and Sarah had, they never quite garnered that feeling that Thea had been blessed with.

Thea smiled softly, face filled with curiosity.

"Hey, what's up?" She had never seen them in any of her businesses except the florist shop. Most avoided the mortuary as if it had the plague.

"We were wondering how you got home the other night?" Caroline asked. "The last thing I remember, you were seated across from a really hot guy. Did you go home with him?"

"Tell us you did," bubbled Sarah.

Thea sighed and shrugged. "Just for edification, I didn't go home with him, and that really hot guy was what you two call a vampire, though I would never say it to their face. *Born of the blood* is the correct term, though I know you don't like to think or talk about things that aren't human. You two were busy drinking, didn't seem like you wanted to leave, so I walked home."

"At night after sitting with a vampire?" Sarah asked, sounding ridiculous. "For someone who seems to be pretty bright, that wasn't really very smart."

"I felt pretty safe, and I didn't have far to go. Was that what you wanted to know?" she asked, losing patience.

"No. We wanted to know if you were still mad at us," Caroline asked, voice low, in case she thought they could be overheard. "I can hear it in your voice that you still are."

"I don't like to be lied to, and I don't want to spend what few times off I have doing something I don't want to do. I thought it was a girls' night out. I didn't think we would be trolling for men. I don't need a man to make my life whole. Right now, I have more on my platter than I know what to do with," answered Thea firmly. "I'm sorry if that offends you. I know that we have been friends since we were kids. I'm not sure what bound us together then, but sometimes those ties that bind unravel, don't stick. Maybe we are moving in opposite directions. You two are very safe in your own little human world. You don't deal with anything you don't understand. I do, my parents did, so we are different in that regard. And I'm sorry if this hurts your feelings, but this is how I feel right now. I'm not mad, just disappointed, I guess."

Caroline nodded. You could feel the frost growing between them. Sarah frowned, not certain what was happening. "You think you are better than us because you haven't been divorced, because you haven't broken as many hearts as Sarah?"

"I haven't had the chance. My life is work, Caroline. You know that. I started in this business the first summer I turned fourteen. I haven't looked back. We worked for every ounce of coin that we had. Nothing has been given to me, and as far as men go, you two are much more adept at the luring than I am. One day I might run into someone that kindles a fire, but until then, I don't need my friends looking for me."

"We quite understand, Anthea," Caroline said as she wrapped her arm around Sarah and pulled her toward the door.

"So now I take it you are mad at me? If you can't tell your friends what you honestly think, then I'm not so sure we are friends." Thea stood, watching the door close behind Sarah and Caroline, the brightness of the day replaced by the comfort of reception.

"That went well," she commented out loud to no one in particular.

"Sorry about that," said Matt, flushed slightly as he stood at reception. He had been an intern two summers ago and excelled at his work. He was hired while he finished school. He was also a shifter, a leopard. "I thought maybe they were here to invite you to lunch." She chuckled, shaking her head. "So no, huh? How about I order us a pizza? You have to eat."

"Yes, I guess I do. You know what I like."

Matt nodded, running his hand through his blond hair and hitting speed dial. At first, the drivers were a little freaked coming to a mortuary, but they got over it. He hoped Thea would get over the slight from her friends. She was a great person and had seen more things, more awful things than her friends could dream.

With the shadows growing longer, sun beginning to set, the change of shifts at the mortuary began, leaving Thea free to meet with Edden and Arkin. She checked her reflection in the mirror and started the walk away from work toward one of her favorite places, a place she was revealing to Arkin. It was still slightly early, but tradition dictated that she wait for Arkin and then enter with him since he was bringing her in as a witness to his discussion with Edden. The laws, she knew them almost as well as Em did, though he knew them far better and their subtle nuances. Thea seated herself on the bench outside the tavern and watched the world walk by. It was true what she said to Sarah and Caroline—they truly had no idea. They lived in their own little human world and didn't look beyond what the world could offer. If she had a choice, she might have chosen to be so close-minded, but her adoptive parents had been Hunters early in their day. They didn't hunt any more, though; in fact, they had faded out of the world, not exactly hiding from enemies, but having let everyone think they were dead. That way, they could find the peace they craved. Thea glanced at her watch as the streetlights flickered on. Her mind turned back to when she had first met Caroline and Sarah, wondering now what had made them friends. They had been children then, and they had clung to her as if she were a life raft in the open sea. They had chosen her.

"I apologize that I am late," Arkin said as he stood next to the bench. It was dangerous not to notice what stepped out of the dark, and Thea had been lost in thought. She glanced up and found him in gray once again, his hair slightly damp and shirt partially buttoned. She rose, shouldering her purse, and touched his shirt, buttoning the two stray buttons casually as if she had always known him and he had given her leave to touch him.

"I was slightly mussed. Had to change at the last minute." Arkin reached over and opened the door for her, and they stepped across the threshold into Edden's tavern. Thea wondered absently what had mussed him.

Edden stood at the back of the tavern, eyes on the door, gratified to see that, at last, they had arrived. He was beginning to wonder. He thought about taking something to eat out to Thea as she waited. He knew she would be waiting for this new blood since she was his witness to this conversation. Edden looked over Arkin hard, as if trying to divine some purpose. He was attractive and old, so old Edden wasn't sure he could define his age. Edden watched as Arkin stopped Thea. He pulled a bobby pin from her hair, smoothed back the stray strand, and then tucked it back snugly to her head. It was an intimate gesture that made Edden wonder just what Arkin wanted from his friend. Thea turned, smiled, and waved at Edden. She wove her way through the other patrons, stopping at her usual table. She stood between both vampires.

"Edden, owner of this fine establishment, may I introduce Arkin Kane. Arkin, this is my friend Edden. He was kind enough to speak to you this evening. Shall we sit?"

Arkin sat on Thea's right, Edden on her left, and she pulled up a chair at the end of the booth without faltering. She tucked her purse under the table by her feet.

"You hungry, Thea?" Edden asked as he gestured. "How about roast beef, a salad, and cream soda?"

"That sounds perfect, Edden. Thank you for thinking of me."

Two glasses made of dark crystal were brought for him and Arkin. There was no need for Thea to know what filled the brim; they all knew it was blood. Arkin nodded his thanks as they continued to sit in silence.

"Thank you for your hospitality."

Edden shrugged, but it was nice to be recognized. Sometimes people just assumed courtesy.

"Can you tell me how this city ended up in such a mess?"

Edden leaned back in the booth and considered the question. "About six or so months ago, it came to everyone's attention that children, between five and seven years of age, were missing. There had been eight in number. The community at large didn't know the cause. It could be a number of things, a slavery ring, sacrifices, organ thefts... We didn't know what was happening, so we formed an interspecies task force. Hunters, enforcers, everyone was on the look out to solve this thing, and when it came down to it, when we finally found the hideaway, two of the children were still alive. Yardley was there. Some believed he had found the hideout on his own and was trying to negotiate with the mixed group of murderers to be the hero. Others believed he was in on it. Needless to say, it was a free-for-all. When the dust settled, he was dead, leaving a rather large gap in the city's hierarchy. Three others tried for the so-called crown, and they were all killed, so now we are splintered by territory like gangs. Everyone else is sitting back, waiting to see what will happen. We aren't that many that we can afford to lose just one of us if we play by the rules. The factions drove out many of the really good people."

Arkin glanced at Thea, who nodded as she took a bit of her open-faced roast beef sandwich.

"Does she always eat like this?" he asked, curious.

Edden nodded. "And she keeps her figure. She must have the metabolism of a hummingbird," he said. "So if you decided to take the city, you would have to go through seven of our so-called leaders, either by killing or coercing."

Arkin took a sip of his warmed blood. "That would be five."

Edden and Thea frowned.

"No, I think that would be seven. I know our so-called fearless leaders. There is Garrick, Tasha, Terence, Asao, Margaux, Ulrich, and Cordelia."

Arkin smiled patiently.

"I don't mean to differ with you on this point, but there are five. It started with Pick. I killed him because he attacked Anthea. At that time, I didn't know that she was a silent witness, which makes his actions all the worse. Since Pick was under Garrick's protection, I brought the body to Garrick with an explanation. He attacked me, and I killed him. His territory, as you call it, is now under the watchful eye of my colleagues."

Edden glanced at Thea, who was trying politely to eat her meal and not comment on the wow factor of what was being said.

"Cordelia, apparently, was in negotiation with Garrick as his bride and took offense to my killing him. She sent four of her men to kill me. They and she are dead. If you can't do the deed yourself, you don't deserve to hold your territory. That was the reason I was late. I had to freshen up and look presentable to be seen in public. So my count is considerably lower. I had no intention of killing them at that time, but they sought a forceful way to solve their disagreement with me."

Edden blinked a couple of times and shook his head in amazement. Arkin could see that Edden was impressed, though that wasn't the idea. Thea was more subdued, her expression hard to read.

"I apologize for correcting you. You have the count right, then. You sit there and tell us so calmly about these attacks...I applaud your stamina."

Arkin inclined his head.

"I also wonder what you do for an encore."

Arkin chuckled. "I didn't walk into this city to fight. I came to see what shape it was in and how dire the circumstances are. They are dire indeed, and it cannot continue like this."

"And you intend to make the necessary changes?" Edden asked casually.

"It would be me or someone else, and though I have just told you I have killed two of our kind who were in power, I am more benevolent than some. As we move forward, I will have to have a silent witness available."

"Both Anthea and I would be delighted to be of assistance to you," mentioned Edden.

Thea, sitting right at the very table, quiet, was mildly surprised by Edden's sudden friendliness. Arkin was dismayed that Edden would just include Thea like that without asking her. Then again, she was a silent witness. Then again, it could be the entire world was trying to set her up with someone appropriate for her to date, and if there was time now, Arkin would not be averse to that idea.

"I thank you in advance for your service and for being friends with Anthea. I have a feeling that she is in need of them."

"Hey," Thea said, annoyed.

Arkin smiled. "I'm not the one who threw you to the speed-dating wolves."

Thea nodded. Too true.

"Do you believe, Edden, that the rest of the temporary leaders will be as defensive?"

"Asao is practical and, I believe, would welcome someone else taking the reins. He would prefer not to have the headaches. Tasha looks to see what she can gain. She likes men. Be wary of her getting her claws into you. She likes to think she is irresistible. Ulrich will want to know what you can do for him, and Margaux prefers business as usual. Terence is sharklike. He waits until he sees a weakness and then pounces. We, however, are not the only supernaturals in the city. You will have to reassure the others that though we are in disarray, it won't spread to them or our mutual interest."

"I appreciate that quick synopsis, Edden," remarked Arkin thoughtfully.

"Can I ask how many colleagues you brought?" Edden asked as Arkin, seeing that Thea was finished with her meal, gestured for her to stand. Arkin smiled, placing his arm around her shoulder.

"All of them."

How cryptic.

Arkin escorted Thea out of the tavern and onto the sidewalk in a leisurely stroll. It was a nice evening. The sky was relatively clear, and there was a crispness in the air. He had his arm wrapped around hers and walked street side, his eyes glittering in the pools of light overhead, his watch ever vigilant.

"You don't think less of me because I had to kill, do you?"

What an odd question.

"Honestly, I don't know what to think of you. It was a free-for-all when Yardley died. There were some fights that were draws, where everyone walked away and nursed their wounds. There is more to you than meets the eye."

"I'll take that as a compliment," Arkin said, smiling slightly. "Can I call on you when I need assistance?"

"I am at the service of anyone that needs me and neutral as ever."

Arkin pushed open the small gate at the front of the house. It screeched in protest. “I shall try not to disturb you too much at work.”

“That is very thoughtful of you. I have to admit that although I was opposed to speed-dating, I did meet someone interesting.”

Arkin chuckled as he walked her down the path, up the steps, and to the door. It was Em who opened it, smiling politely. He didn’t even wait for her to touch the doorknob. There was a moment of male staring, the whole alpha thing. Thea just rolled her eyes in annoyance.

“Emlyn Black, this is Arkin Kane. Arkin, this is Em, my brother.”

Arkin extended his hand to Em, who took it politely. Em then said, “A pleasure to meet you. Thea has told me about you. Welcome to our city.”

“I am hoping it will be my city soon. Your sister has been a great help.”

“She does what she can, though I don’t like putting her in harm’s way.”

“I can assure you that when she is with me, her safety is my main priority.” Arkin gave a short bow, leaned up, and kissed her gently on the cheek. “Until we meet again.”

Em curled his arm around hers and drew her into him, over the threshold, and into the house. He closed the door, giving her a glowering look. Her eyes narrowed as she stared back.

“What? Edden was with us the entire time, and it wasn’t a date. Besides, he offed Garrick and Cordelia, so I would be cordial to him. He isn’t someone I would make an enemy of, Emlyn. Do you hear me?”

Em leaned hard against the door. His expression was worth it. “Really?”

“Would I lie to you? Others maybe, but not to you.” Thea tossed her purse aside, removed her shoes, shrugged out of her jacket, sighing in relief. “And what is it to you if I want to date him?”

“You’re not serious?” he asked, amazed.

“No, I’m not, but don’t give me that look unless you want me to get into it with you. Do you follow me?” she asked pointedly.

"All the way to the kitchen. Just to let you know, Tasha called."

Thea growled.

"She wants to place another order, but she wants you to go, not tonight, but tomorrow."

Thea set the water on the stove, turned around, and regarded her brother.

"You know I don't mind going there, but she always wants to try to startle me with her men, with her clothing, their clothing, or lack thereof, or their extracurricular activities."

Em gave her that pouting look with those puppy-dog eyes. He didn't want to go either.

"Fine," she added with a sigh. "I want a longer weekend at our country house. I feel the need to be left alone."

"I gotcha. Anytime you want to go." Em leaned against the doorjamb, arms folded across his chest. "Did he really take them out?"

"They attacked him, and he has the right to defend himself." Thea flopped a tea bag into her teacup. "You are a hunter. You know that better than I do. I wouldn't want to tangle with anyone of them if I had a choice, but I have a feeling he brought enough of his people to handle this situation."

There was a small smile crawling across her brother's face.

"That is a sinister smile."

"Yes! Well, just thinking. It's about time some of them were put in their place. Yardley didn't like to rock the boat."

"Arkin has the get-out-of-the-boat-and-swim-if-you-aren't-going-to-help-paddle attitude."

CHAPTER 4

It was all Em's fault. He had just stepped out of the house for a moment, leaving the door partially open to recover the paper sitting on the porch, when Ms. Claire Finster sneaked into the foyer and proceeded, at the top of her lungs, to call for Thea. Em hissed as he closed the door, finger to his lips.

"She is still in bed, Ms. Claire. What can possibly be so urgent that you barge in and try to wake Thea up?"

If Ms. Claire heard the reproach in Em's voice, she didn't acknowledge it. Ms. Claire was about seventy-five years old and dressed as if she had just stepped out of the fifties, which included a set of pearls. She dyed her hair a dark brunette, always upswept into a bun. She had brown eyes, penciled-in eyebrows, and a round little face. She also was a self-proclaimed psychic. She had episodes or so, she said.

"Barge in, Emlyn Black. The door was open!" she snapped.

"The door was pulled, too, so I could retrieve the paper. I didn't expect visitors."

Ms. Claire gave him the once-over; he was wearing gray sweats and a black T-shirt. "I should say not dressed like that. I need to see her. I need to see your sister. I had a premonition."

Em tried not to verbally groan. Out of all the visions she had had over all the years, three were correct, and most people in the paranormal community chalked those up to luck. People humored her and, on the whole, tried to be nice, but there were limits. Anthea had enough on her plate without a message from beyond.

"Why don't I take the message for you and then tell her when she wakes up?" Em set the paper on the hall table and tried to curl his arm around hers to turn her around and draw her slowly around back toward the door. "If she has any questions, she can call you."

"I'm awake." Came a grumble from the top of the stairs. Out of the shadows walked Thea, her hair wild about her head, but her body wrapped demurely in a flannel robe. She didn't look fit for visitors.

"There you are, girl. Come down here at once and have a cup of tea while I tell you about my vision."

Thea managed a polite smile. There was no use arguing. She glanced over at Em, who was being hustled into the kitchen. Thea followed, shuffling into the warm room, and plopped down in the chair, leg beneath her. Ms. Claire turned her attention to the slightly dazed young woman.

"You know, Anthea Grace, you would capture men's attention if you looked more ready for the day. You look like Satan himself dragged you out of bed."

Thea bit back a retort. "Ms. Claire, I don't expect any man to be seeing me look like this. I sleep alone."

Her eyes brightened. She patted Thea's hand. "What a good girl you are."

Em cleared his throat, trying to keep from laughing. Ms. Claire didn't seem to think that he looked as bad as his sister, nor was there a comment made about his selection of bedmates.

"Why don't you tell me what you saw or heard?" Thea asked in hopes to make this a short visit.

Ms. Claire nodded, a very sudden, serious expression encompassing her face. She set her clutch purse on the table and met Thea squarely in the eye.

"Something dark is coming this way. It is looking for you."

Thea sat still as Em slid her teacup to her. Thea's fingers curled around the cup for warmth. She had wanted at least another hour's sleep, especially if she was going to have to see Tasha this evening.

"Is that all you know?"

Ms. Claire frowned. Why couldn't visions ever be complete, with a narrator or subtitles? "It's a male presence. It's coming this way, and it's looking for you via a spell," repeated Ms. Claire.

"And it's dark," added Em softly.

"Yes, a dark presence. I am thinking that it means you harm."

Thea took a sip of her tea and nodded politely. "I can see why that would be upsetting to you, Ms. Claire. I do surely thank you for coming here to warn me."

Ms. Claire looked at Thea, as if trying to discern just how serious she was taking this pronouncement. "Take it seriously, my girl. Get a gun, get a bodyguard, maybe you could even hire one of those nice vampires or shifter chaps to watch over you. I hear they are hell when it comes to a fight."

"I'll keep that in mind," Thea answered as she watched Ms. Claire stand, Em offering her his arm. She smiled a thank-you at him before casting one more backward and serious glance at Thea. Thea stayed where she was seated until she heard the door shut. It was a great way to wake up.

"I am so sorry. I just stepped out to get the paper, and she plowed right in here."

"No big deal, Em. I'll get even with you some other time." Thea closed her eyes and leaned back in the chair.

Em cleared his throat as he stood by the coffeemaker. "So what do you think of her vision?"

Thea ran a quick hand through her hair and sneered at her brother. "Really? You believe what she is telling you, us? The entire prenatural community knows that if she has any talent, it is hit-or-miss at best. She has been way wrong way more times than she has been right. We only listen to be polite. No one wants to hurt her feelings."

"True, and you did a good job of listening, though she didn't have much to say." Em sighed as a small smile crept across his sister's face. "What's so amusing?"

"I could plead to Arkin to watch my frail little body. He hasn't a clue about Claire and her inability to predict." She looked coy.

"You like him that much?" Em asked cautiously.

"I'm joking, though he is smoking hot." Thea stood, ambling out of the kitchen and toward the stairs. If he weren't a vampire, she was certain Sarah would be pursuing him. "When do I have to be at Tasha's?"

"She said around eight."

Thea nodded, heading back up the stairs, not giving Claire's prediction a second thought, her mind on the softness of her bed.

* * *

Sunflowers filled the front entryway of reception, brightening the room considerably. Thea herself was wearing a chocolate-brown suit with pretty russet shell, her hair pulled up into curls on her head. It was closing in on noon, and so far, she had handled twelve phone calls that ranged from bookings for the chapel to questions about cost of coffins. There had also been two questions about the urns that they had in stock. Thea had guessed they were possibly for what remained of Garrick and Cordelia. If they garnered any followers at all, they would want to see them at rest. There were plenty of superstitions surrounding the dead. She also had arranged two bodies for their funerals this afternoon. Em was just as busy, and the sales room had two possible clients. Carver had just stepped out of the back room, returning from a pickup for cremation. That was one person who would not need Thea's services. Carver was tall, lean, once having played basketball. He had dark eyes but a friendly smile and close-cropped hair, military-style.

"Did you look at today's date?" he asked Thea.

She glanced at the desk calendar.

"Didn't Rosa say that her grandmother thought she was going to pass today?"

Rosa Moldenhaur's grandmother was what she called sensitive; as long as Rosa had known the woman, she had had a remarkable hit rate, but for her family only. She didn't seem to see beyond that veil for others. Thea had made note of it in the system. It was supposed to be sometime in the evening.

"You're right, she did say she thought she was going to pass today."

"You have everything ready for her, don't you?"

Thea nodded to Carver. "I visited a week ago and collected her clothing, picture, and after the viewing, she wants to be cremated."

Carver nodded. "I'm sure you know by now that Ms. Claire was here early this morning, looking for you. She had a vision." Carver was trying to keep the amusement out of his voice.

"She came to the house. Yes, something dark is coming my way. I hope he is tall, handsome, and wealthy as well."

Carver chuckled. "I hear you are going to visit Tasha this evening. You want company?"

Thea grinned. "Just so you can see how scantily clad she is? No, I'll be fine. I think I have all the brochures. She usually orders the same things, coffins, but this order might be slightly different," Thea remarked, thinking out loud to herself.

She sat for a few moments, pondering on that thought. Yes, with Arkin in town, her needs might change. She shook off her troubling thoughts, realizing Carver had returned to the back room just as the sandwiches were delivered. She and Em would have about half an hour for lunch before they had to attend to the funerals. It was going to be a long day.

* * *

It wasn't exactly called the red-light district, but that was what she and Em called where Tasha lived. It was an area predicated on liquor and lost souls, including those who wanted to find comfort in supernatural abilities. Normally, she wouldn't have considered going to that side of town alone, but with the onset of Arkin killing Pick because he threatened her, she felt she was okay. Also, she was driving a hearse. The locals found it very amusing. They had a fleet of vehicles, vans for the florist, limos for the chapel and mortuary, and then their own private cars. Thea arrived at seven forty-five. She liked to be early, and you could never depend on the traffic being normal. The high-rise where Tasha was ensconced was nestled between three dance clubs, a spa, and two taverns. The neon alone was blinding, and the noise almost deafening, but Tasha felt it was all in good taste. Her motto was "Give them what they want." Apparently, they wanted tacky. The hearse itself was enough to announce her arrival; she didn't have to show ID or anything to security at the door, and instead, she breezed right in and to the elevator. There were eyes on her everywhere. She had gotten used to it, though. In the reflective surface of the elevator, Thea smoothed her hair, adjusted her jacket, and prepared herself for Tasha. In all fairness, Thea was early, so she settled herself in the entryway, on the black leather sofa, near a vase of lilies. She sat comfortably for about twenty-five minutes until her phone buzzed.

"Anthea Black."

It was a prediction extraordinaire. Rosa's grandmother, Maria Louisa, had passed just as she predicted, and Thea had promised to be the one to take care of her body. Rosa was doing well; after all, it wasn't a surprise to her, because she had truly believed in her grandmother's power. Rosa had also called Maria Louisa's doctor. Everything would be in order just as Maria Louisa wanted. It was truly amazing.

"I'll be right there." Thea stood, smoothed her skirt, and walked over to the security that stood at the double doors, glowering sufficiently to scare anyone who might want to pass those hallowed doors.

"Please tell Tasha I had an emergency. I will return if possible." Thea managed a politely deferential smile as she left the vampire world behind and headed for 375 Applewood Street.

It was a three-bedroom Cape Cod–style house, with front porch and geraniums in pots by the steps. The lights were on, lending warmth to the shadows that enclosed the house this evening. Rosa sat patiently waiting on the front step, rising as Thea pulled up to the curb. Thea stepped out of the car, shrugging out of her jacket, and opened the back hatch. Rosa came up to her and hugged her for comfort, sniffling slightly in her ear as she tried to hold back the sadness and the tears.

"I'm sorry, I should have been prepared for this. She told me this would happen, and I truly believed, and damn if she wasn't right,"

Rosa whispered. "I shouldn't have said *damn*. She would have fined me a quarter for swearing." Rosa chuckled lightly as she parted from Anthea's warmth. She tucked a stray strand of dark hair behind her ear.

"It's okay. As much as we try to prepare, death is still hard to accept. Why don't I go in and pay my respects to your grandmother?"

"My brothers aren't home, and Doc Etner isn't here yet. Can you lift her and everything by yourself?"

Thea winked at Rosa as she pulled out the gurney. "I'll manage. After all, Maria Louisa was counting on me, right?"

Rosa nodded, leading the way into her grandmother's neat and tidy room. Maria Louisa lay peacefully on her bed, the covers tucked under her arms. She had congestive heart failure and knew it was just a matter of time, and she knew that date and time, being intuitive and all. So far, she was the only member of her family that seemed to have that gift. She claimed that they had Gypsy blood. Rosa lingered at the door, chewing on her thumb expectantly. Thea gently tugged the blanket back as her phone buzzed on her hip. It was Em.

"Tasha called. She wanted to know where you are. You were there and then you were gone."

"She kept me waiting, and my time is just as important as hers. I'm here with Maria Louisa."

Em sighed. "She finally passed, huh? If people were taking book, they would have won on this premonition. Let's do this. I'll meet you in the mall parking lot. We can trade cars. You need to head back to Tasha's."

Thea gritted her teeth, annoyed. Tasha always seemed to think that life revolved around her. It didn't.

"Fine," Thea replied, annoyed. She hung up, turning to eye Rosa standing at the door to the bedroom, eyes locked on the bed. "Let me close the door. I won't be long."

Rosa would have normally been right. Thea might have had a problem with the body, but there was more to Thea than met the eye, and though many paranormals couldn't put their finger on what it was that mingled with that sense of humanness about her, she was more than human. Thea gently closed the door and then secured

Maria Louisa on the gurney. They had already discussed what she was going to wear and how she wanted to look. She had been well prepared. It had been a warm summer's day. They had lemonade on the back patio and talked about death. On the whole, Thea had found it refreshing.

There was a soft knock on the door that let Thea know that Etner had arrived. He was a tall lean man, looked more like death than a doctor, but he also trusted that Maria Louisa had the sight. He trusted that she had passed peacefully. He had a touch of fey in his background, though he might never admit it. He had the ability, though limited, to define whether a person died of natural causes or by murder. He occasionally worked with paranormal police; human cops didn't always trust what they couldn't understand. That was why Thea remained hidden.

"Ms. Black. Timely, I see."

"Dr. Etner."

Thea stepped aside so that Etner could look over the body. There wasn't much to see, and just as she thought, he quickly signed the certificate that it was death by natural causes and motioned for her to get on her way. Etner had long wanted to get ahold of Thea, be her physician. He, too, apparently liked a mystery, to define what he couldn't quite understand. But she politely declined. She, like her brother, would stick to her old family general practitioner, who thought better than asking such probing questions. He, like every other human, thought that she was one of their own. Thea wasn't going to shatter that perception.

By the time Thea had steered the body out into the dark, it was after nine fifteen, and there were some folks gathering on the street to say their last goodbyes. There were murmurs, a few women crossing themselves, as if they could keep evil at bay. Maria Louisa wasn't evil; she was just gifted. Apparently, Rosa's brothers hadn't believed their grandmother and taken off for the night. Rosa wouldn't let them forget their desertion. With a last hug to Rosa, Thea was off to meet Em in the nearby parking lot. Though she didn't like to abandon Maria Louisa, Tasha demanded that they meet, and they could always use the order and generosity even if Tasha was a bit of a diva. Thea had no trouble finding her brother; he had parked beneath a pool light and was leaning up against his Camaro. Although it looked black in the shadows, in sunlight, it was a deep blackberry. She was surprised that he had brought his personal vehicle and even more surprised that he was going to let her drive it. It was his classic baby. She pulled the hearse up alongside him. She pushed open the door and met her brother's twinkling gaze.

"Was she very pissed?" Thea asked, curious. "Not that I care."

"No. She just wanted to know where you had gone. One moment you were there, and the next you had vanished. Kale stepped out to welcome you, and poof. I explained the situation to her and offered to come in your stead, but you know her." Em shrugged.

"She likes her games. She likes to embarrass me. She says I turn a lovely shade of red," stated Thea, sounding tired. She shifted her purse and valise on her shoulder. "Keys are in the hearse. You brought your car. You are letting me drive your car? Who are you, and what have you done with my brother?"

He snickered, tossing her the keys. She caught them deftly. He leaned in and kissed her on the forehead. "Want you to be safe, little sister. After all, I have heard that there is something dark coming for you."

If that were true, she should have been driving a tank.

Thea rolled her eyes, watching him gun the engine of the hearse and drive away. With purse and valise in hand, she climbed into the Camaro, knowing that as soon as she turned the key, the music would be blaring. She was surprised when she found silence. This once, Em understood her mood; the silence would give her time to prepare, because she, in truth, wasn't in the mood for games.

This time around, Kale was waiting at the main building's double doors, a grin on his handsome face as he watched her approach. He looked like an ad for sex, almost too gorgeous to be real. In some ways, he reminded her of Arkin, whose attractiveness was more subtle, smoldering. And why was she even thinking of him? Kale held open the car door for her. He was dressed in black jeans and a lipstick-red shirt. If he had horns and a tail, he could be the devil himself. This clothing made him look dangerous to any heart, for either gender. He had dark hair and dark eyes, with a dimple in his chin. He could be an old-fashioned movie star, and might have been at one time. The blood were so long lived.

"Evening to you, Ms. Anthea Black," he said suggestively.

"Kale," she responded as he held out his arm for her.

"I have to say, you look very sharp this evening, all business. You also look a bit tired."

"Long day," she answered shortly.

"You know, if you were looking for someone to date, you could have come to me. I don't want your money. I don't care about your job. We could have a wonderful time together."

Thea met his twinkling eyes as they passed through the lobby and stepped into the elevator. She wasn't surprised that he had heard about her ill-fated evening at the speed-dating club. When the paranormal community had their eyes on you, there wasn't much they didn't know or couldn't find out. That was what made her secret all the more important to keep.

"I was there against my will, Kale. Besides, if I were going to date you, I would want you to sign a nondisclosure agreement and contract with you for a year so I have your complete and undivided attention. I hear you can be quite the player."

His eyes widened slightly as they arrived at the top suite. He was intrigued.

"You have thought of this, haven't you?" he purred, pleased.

"I think most of the girls who see you think of it," she answered as she walked away from his side toward Tasha, who was standing in the center of the room looking like pure sin. To say that Tasha liked men was an understatement—she devoured them. And this open room, decorated in white, black, and bright red, showed off her adornments nicely in front of a backdrop of the stars and glittering city. As always, she was dressed in a lacy black negligee that left little to the imagination. She was twenty-five, at least that was the age she looked when she passed, with dark curly hair, bow-like lips, caramel-colored skin, and an innocent expression that really didn't fool anyone who knew her well. She was grinning at Thea, her arms spread wide.

"There's my girl! Why don't you take off that awful jacket and your heels? Sit back and relax as we do business." Instead of gesturing Thea toward a chair, she gestured her to the back of a young man on his hands and knees. There was a soft silk throw over his back. Kale touched her shoulders, offering to take her jacket.

"You can't argue with her," he murmured sexily.

Thea shifted out of her jacket as a young man scrambled to take off her heels. She dropped several inches in height as she joined Tasha by the glass table. She lowered herself onto the soft, silky folds that covered the young man. She checked her balance before setting her purse aside and pulling her e-tablet out of her valise. It had always been this way since the first time they had met, Tasha showing her men and women off, maybe hoping that Thea would break down and join them, hoping to catch a glimpse inside her soul. Tasha would have a long wait. While Thea had been stunned at the beginning how openly sex was displayed, she had recovered enough not to let it bother her again. It was just the price of doing business with Tasha, and she did a good business with the Blacks.

"Have you eaten yet?" she asked, concerned.

"I'll eat later. It is slightly late," Thea remarked as Tasha snapped her fingers.

"Salmon sound all right?"

Thea brightened.

"And a cold mug of root beer?"

Thea smiled, inclining her head as Kale moved to stand behind his mistress. Thea met Tasha's chocolate-colored eyes and saw her pout.

"You were here and then you left," Tasha remarked coyly.

"I apologize, but someone I gave my word to died, and I was honor-bound to see her body away from her resting place."

That was something Tasha could understand.

Thea jumped slightly as someone touched her feet. She looked down through the table at a young blond man who was kneeling under the table and began massaging her feet gently.

"We aim to please," Tasha remarked as she slid a piece of paper filled with her curlicue writing. This was going to take a while.

Thea logged on to the website, trying to concentrate on work, though Tasha was staring at her with those dark, twinkling eyes.

"So I hear you went to a speed-dating club," she remarked casually.

"It was a misunderstanding. My friends thought I needed a life. Is this three of the black and two of the hunter green?"

Tasha nodded.

"You want one in that bright candy apple red?"

"It's for a friend," she answered casually. "I hear you have met a new blood-born."

Thea tried harder to concentrate on her task. She was good at multitasking to a point, but Tasha was pushing her.

"Yes," she remarked curtly.

"Arkin Kane. Funny, I don't remember anyone by that name," Tasha said. "Would you like Kale to rub your back while you work?"

Thea glanced up, meeting Tasha's gaze.

"No, thank you. I don't mind my feet but would prefer not to have my back rubbed."

"Ticklish, are you?" Kale asked jokingly.

Thea didn't answer. The mug of root beer was set next to her e-tablet. She took a long cold drink of it and sighed. Tasha laughed.

"You can take down your hair. I don't mind if you are relaxed. I haven't worked in centuries, but I remember how tired it could make you. And though you are currently taking my order and most of our interactions are business, I consider us casual friends."

"I don't want to appear unprofessional. You want three urns in the black and gold, two in the pink marble?"

Tasha sighed. She was a hard woman to read, this Thea. "Yes. So what is he like?" she asked demurely.

Thea handed Tasha back her piece of paper. "We have everything in stock except the red coffin. It is on order and should be here in a day or so. As usual, it will be delivered directly to you."

"Comfortable, are they?" she asked, curious.

"Yes, very. They have good support for your back. Doesn't compress any sensitive spots."

Tasha wasn't surprised that Thea knew the answer to the question. She had probably tried out the stock just to be able to answer their questions. Clever girl.

"You didn't answer my original question," cautioned Tasha.

"You mean Arkin Kane? You could ask him yourself. I am sure he would be happy to meet with you." Thea shifted on the back of the young man. It was not the most comfortable seating arrangement. "He is like Kale, very handsome, traditional, and competent."

"Well, I should say so, considering he killed Garrick and Cordelia," stated Tasha with a slight frown on her face.

"They attacked him, and he has the right to defend himself," remarked Thea firmly.

"And what did he see Edden about?" Tasha asked pointedly.

The salmon was slid in front of Thea on a black-and-white plate.

"This looks tasty. Mr. Kane asked me to recommend someone trustworthy to speak to about the state of the city. Edden's schedule is more open than yours, and historically, you don't see anyone so new to the city without first understanding their wants and needs. You are wary."

"I am at that, so I forgive you," replied Tasha, mollified.

"That is gracious of you." Thea fell silent as she ate, trying to ignore the tingling in her feet. It was a generous order, so it paid to be on Tasha's good side.

"So what do you think his agenda is?"

Thea ate the last of her salmon and rice, draining her root beer, sliding her feet from the gentle hands of the blonde to fold them up beneath her skirt on the back of the young man.

"I am sure he wishes that he could just arrive and stay without any confrontation, but everyone will want to talk to him. If he is staying and wishes to clean up the city, he will either have to talk his way into it or kill his way into it."

"Do you find him so magnanimous?" she asked, polished nails tapping on the table, her body tense.

"I don't find him anything, Tasha. He was in the speed-dating club, observing. He found me because the human men didn't dare sit with me and he was amused. I have no power over what he does or how he does it. You know as much about him as I do. I think he has a genuine want to tidy up the mess that is this city. I think he would try to ensure that businesses excel and expand, but I don't think he would patiently brook any sort of dissention. I am a silent witness. If he calls me into negotiations, I will go, but there is nothing beyond that."

"You don't find him attractive?" Kale asked, curious.

Thea gracefully stood up.

"I am sure he is drawn to you. After all, you do have that small inkling of not being totally human."

Thea pulled on her jacket, slipped her feet into her heels, and picked up her purse and valise. "I have input your order. What is in stock, Tasha, will be delivered tomorrow as, of course, your standard orders for fresh flowers. If there isn't any other business for us to discuss, I will take my leave. After all, it is late for us humans."

Kale and Tasha were silent as they regarded her. Her chin was slightly raised in defiance, her expression hard to read. Tasha always thought she might have a sliver of fey in her, but never had Anthea given her any confirmation. It was a curious mystery that they had discussed among themselves. Whatever it was made her alluring, like a flame collecting moths.

"I take it you are dismissing yourself from my company?"

Thea managed a small smile, meeting her stern gaze. "I like you, Tasha, I really do, despite the fact that you seem to want to embarrass me by inviting me into your home with men barely dressed, and a few times men and women in the act of having sex. What is it about me that makes you want to destroy my innocence?"

"Maybe because it has been a long time since I felt anyone with that feeling of lightness, of goodness around them. Maybe for the same reason your friends try to take you to a speed-dating club. You aren't living, Anthea."

"My life may be short, Tasha, but it is my right to live it the way I want. Do these men, your shows, make me hot and bothered? Of course they do, but they don't make me respect you any more than I already do. You have lived a long life. Maybe you were like me to begin with. Maybe sometime in the past century, you just became more jaded…I need friends who like me for who I am and the choices I make, not who try to remake me the way they think I need to be."

"You heard that something dark is coming your way," Kale remarked softly.

Thea smiled at him. "Yeah, I heard, and I'll deal with it when it arrives. If you will excuse me?" Thea turned on her heels, walking to the door to leave Kale and Tasha behind. She didn't look back as she entered the elevator, the foyer, and stepped out into the night. She drew several long breaths in hope it would cool her ire. It hadn't. What had gotten into her? She had no idea, but it felt damn good to speak her mind.

Em realized it probably wasn't a good time to speak to his sister. She came walking into the house, heels clicking on the floor, muttering to herself as she tossed off her purse, her valise, and headed up stairs. He would not disturb her tonight, but tomorrow morning, French toast might be in order, and some hot tea. Tasha could be hard to handle. It didn't help that everyone was curious about his sister, not impolite, but damn curious. To those sensitive, he appeared to be perfectly human. She appeared to be human with a mix of something no one could put their finger on. There was a good reason, and it wasn't any of their business.

CHAPTER 5

Thea knew that Em had sensed her anger last evening, leaving her alone to stew or curse, because breakfast was sitting on the table and he was looking at her with those sympathetic eyes. She smiled gently in way of an apology.

"If you look like that at all single women, you could have more dates than you can handle."

"Hey, I see Susan, Heidi…I have sort of a life," he added half-heartedly.

"We have a good life," Thea responded. "Thanks for taking care of Maria Louisa last night. I'll get her all dressed up for her family. She will be beautiful."

"What got you so out of sorts with Tasha last night?" he asked, curious.

"The usual, which, for most people, would be unusual," sighed Thea. "You know I understand how hard it is to hide in the proverbial closet. I feel sympathy for those who have to feel the need to stay in, but I do have things to hide, and it can be hard to ignore the constant questions or pushing."

"She is nervous. After all, Kane is in town and totaled two of her compatriots. She can, I am sure, expect a visit from him, and I don't think her sexuality will change his mind on how he sees her," added Em.

Thea thought as much, but it was nice to have confirmation. "How very true. It might be quite a reckoning for her coddled psyche."

"Look at you, using big words before breakfast," Em said, chuckling. "Get showered up. Another day, another corpse." Em winked. Sometimes if you didn't laugh, you cried, and it always ruined your makeup.

* * *

It was past time for lunch, and the morning had been extremely busy. Maria Louisa's friends and family had filtered into the chapel to say their goodbyes. The majority of Tasha's order was shipped out, and flowers were being brought in for the small evening wedding. Thea was looking forward to a leisurely lunch, but that wasn't to be. She glanced up from her desk in the prep room to find Matt staring at her with an odd smile on his face. Her eyes narrowed.

"What's up? You have an odd look on your face," she commented.

"I have been asked by the Council of Seven to invite you to lunch. Even though it's past noon, they would still like to meet with you."

Thea laid her head on her desk, banging it softly.

"I already said I would bring you."

"You know, I could just fire you."

Matt held out her dark-gray jacket and purse apologetically.

"And don't give me any of this 'But you are a silent witness' crap."

"Okay," he muttered as she shrugged into her jacket.

Thea glanced in the mirror to repair her hair. "I should have guessed this is going to be a long day." Lately, they all seemed to be long. She really needed a vacation from life.

"I'm sorry, but they have questions," Matt replied contritely, and truthfully, he was wrong to promise her appearance before speaking with her. He just got lucky that she agreed.

"Doesn't everyone?" Thea responded, exhaling.

The Council of Seven, as they called it, was a mixed bag of shifters, or, more precisely, changelings, since they changed to other creatures, genders, and races, that adhered to the law and made sure others did as well. Thea knew she wouldn't be seeing all seven of them; she also knew that with the vampire or blood upheaval, they were waiting around to see what was going to happen next and if they should interfere. They didn't want to get in the middle of another race's fight, but sometimes you didn't have a choice, especially if you thought it might spill over into your life or businesses. The one thing Thea did know was that she wouldn't be seeing Copper; they didn't get along. Copper didn't like Thea and couldn't articulate the reason. Thea thought it was that little sliver of herself that wasn't human. Copper didn't seem to like mysteries, and nonhuman men seemed to like Thea.

Matt parallel-parked in front of a rather high-end French restaurant. Thea glanced at him. Apparently, this wasn't going to be a hot dog kind of lunch.

"I told them that if I got you here, they should at least feed you well."

Thea refrained from a smile, following Matt into the restaurant. The maître d' didn't need to be told whom she was seeing; Thea was promptly taken to the back corner of the restaurant, to an elegant table where Perry sat, waiting. Perry was a good-looking man. He looked blue-collar, good old boy, but that was only the facade that he had erected. He had light-blond hair, with a moustache and goatee. If he had dark hair, he might have resembled Lucifer. He had hazel-green eyes and wore nice jeans with a jacket.

He stood as she approached and smiled politely. "I see Matt was able to talk you into meeting with me."

"He invited me to lunch. He didn't say anything about you being here," Thea remarked tartly.

Perry hadn't wanted to accept her as a silent witness, and so she did her best to see that he ate his words with pleasure. Thea seated herself, set her purse aside, and laid the napkin on her lap. She ordered a sweet tea. Perry looked at Thea, and if he thought he could intimidate her, he thought wrong, and that annoyed him.

"So why am I having lunch with you?"

"All business and blunt to boot, I can deal with that," he responded. "Okay, we heard you met the new guy."

"You mean Arkin Kane?" she asked as he nodded. "So has Edden, for that matter."

"But Edden isn't one of us," Perry remarked.

She shook her head as she met his gaze. "I'm not one of you, as you so rudely impressed upon me in our earlier visits."

Perry cleared his throat. That had been a mistake. "You are correct, but I mean to say he is not human. I value your opinion and would like for you to set up a meeting between the Seven and Mr. Kane. I realize you don't have all the particulars like where he is staying, what he plans to do in the city, so we thought we would meet with him. You don't have to be there, unless he insists."

Thea ordered the coq au vin.

"I can't even guarantee that he will want to see anyone, but I can call and leave a message. Will that be sufficient?"

"Yes," Perry answered with a sigh.

"Were you afraid I would say no?"

Perry smiled, shrugging. "In the past, you and I haven't always agreed on having you around. You have been polite to me, but I haven't always accepted you especially as a silent witness. There is something about you that makes me want to confess all my sins, while others of my kind find you oddly attractive."

"Even though I work at a mortuary?"

Perry chuckled as the plates were brought. "You don't have to talk to us about death. That is what we are trying to avoid."

They fell into a comfortable silence as they devoured their meals. Perry was definitely a carnivore. Just as it was impolite to ask a blood member, or, as humans called them, vampire, how old they were and where they were staying, it was impolite to ask what kind of animal you became. Funny, although everyone knew that she wasn't totally human, no one had dared ask the question exactly what Anthea Black was. Even if they did, Thea wasn't sure how to explain it anyway.

Thea finished the last of her meal, Matt looking at her with furtive glances. He was shifting in his seat, clearly restless.

"He wants to know if you are still mad at him," Perry remarked casually.

"*Annoyed* is a better word for it. It was by accident that I met Arkin Kane, and everyone seems to think I'm his own personal secretary."

"He seems to trust you. That is a rare gift, considering you two did actually just meet. The Seven would like this evening if possible."

"All I can do is ask."

Perry cleared his throat, foot tapping on the floor in impatience.

"You want me to call and leave the message while I am sitting here with you? You trust me so little?"

"I don't want to get off on the wrong foot with you, but the others will ask, and this is the only way I can assure them that you followed through."

Thea gritted her teeth. He always knew how to rub her the wrong way. "I could be dialing for a pizza for all you know."

He shrugged.

Thea sighed as she brought up her purse, rifling through it to find her phone. She had already called him once. Thea hit redial and waited. A very firm female voice answered with just a *hello*.

"I would like to leave a message for Arkin Kane. This is Anthea Black. I can leave a message with you or in his voice mail. It's not private." Thea was looking at Perry, obviously annoyed. "Will you tell him that the Council of Seven—and if he isn't familiar with that term, it is a council of changelings in our city—would like to greet and meet with him this evening. As far as I am aware, the time is open to his convenience. He can call me back with an answer."

Thea waited a few seconds.

She sighed, closing her eyes and shaking her head.

"Yes, I would be agreeable to escort him if the need arises. Yes, I understand that he would ensure my safety and they understand he can bring an entourage for security. Yes, the standard number is four. I don't think I would have need of security. They know me. Yes, thank you."

Thea hung up, tossed her phone in her purse, and stood.

"Are we done here?"

"Yes, and thank you. You do very good phone."

She rolled her eyes, gesturing Matt out of his seat and to the door. She had had enough of Perry's company for now.

* * *

Em was standing behind the reception desk, eyes on his sister as she entered. He could tell she was more than mildly annoyed, and when her purse was tossed onto the table, he hesitated to ask. Matt guiltily headed for the back prep room. Em wondered what was up. It was unusual for her to leave for lunch; usually, they ate in.

"You look mad enough to eat someone," he stated, concerned.

"I would if I could. I want to go home this evening, Em. I mean to the country, away from everyone. I'm feeling put upon."

Em nodded. "That suits me. Polly can run around. You can rest…take to the woods if you like. The night sky is beautiful out there."

She sighed, leaning into him.

"What has your dander up?"

"The Seven want to meet Arkin Kane so they come to me? How stupid is that?"

"Actually, you are probably their only resource. Think about it. He killed three of his own kind, Edden only knows him through you, so sorry, but you are the go-to girl."

She stuck her tongue out at him.

"And you don't want to be."

"I don't want to be in the middle when all this explodes. I am supposed to be a witness, not a participant. I don't want anyone pissed at me."

"I don't know of anyone who can stay pissed at you. You have grace, Anthea. You have a bright and good soul."

"And what does that buy me?" she asked, seating herself as the phone rang.

"My love and admiration." He kissed the top of her head as she answered the phone, all sense of anger drained away.

* * *

It was seven thirty when the call came. Anthea was sitting on a bench outside in the commons. She had enjoyed watching the sun set, feeling the air cool around her, and she was just beginning to doze. It was Nirvana.

"Anthea Black," she answered, sounding sleepy.

"Anthea, it is Arkin Kane. I hope you are well." His voice sounded so soothing, and with her eyes closed, she could think of a multitude of possibilities with that voice and body.

She frowned, sitting upright, trying to throw such thoughts out of her mind. She had been hanging around Tasha too much, she decided.

"I am well, thank you. I'm sorry that I had to disturb you."

He chuckled. "You can call on me anytime. I consider you my only friend in this unknown town. And, my dear girl, you are just the messenger. I will meet with the Seven. Can you be ready in twenty minutes?"

"Yes. I can call them and let them know you have agreed, find out where we are to meet."

"Then I will swing by your home. Or would you prefer the mortuary? I have security. Rest assured, you will be safe with me."

It was Thea's turn to chuckle. "I'm not the one to worry about." Thea stretched as she hung up, dialing the Seven's business number. She figured that they would be waiting for the call.

It was Perry who answered.

"He has agreed. Twenty minutes for him to pick me up. Where do you want to meet?"

"He asked you to join him? I presume he doesn't trust us?"

Thea didn't comment.

"We are meeting at the square."

Of course. She should have thought about that. But you just didn't know if the Seven would want to let a possible enemy into their house.

"Thank you for making this meeting possible."

"As long as you don't hold me responsible for the outcome, we are okay," stated Thea.

A knot was slowly forming in her stomach. You just never knew what was going to happen when supernaturals got together.

Thea had twenty minutes, and she decided to put it to good use. She dashed across the commons and into the house, startling Polly, who was sleeping with her ball in between her paws. Thea raced upstairs, followed by the retriever. She tossed off her clothes, washed her face, brushed her hair, and pulled on comfortable clothes, a pair of dark-blue jeans, a white dress shirt with a flowered vest. If she was going to have to deal with all this crap, she was going to do it comfortably. She slipped on a pair of flats and glanced first at her reflection and then at her watch. She had seven minutes to spare.

Em caught her by the shoulders as she leaped down the stairs. "Where is the fire?" he asked, curious. By the looks of her clothing, he didn't think it was a date.

"I'm hoping there isn't one tonight, but if you see the square go up in flames, that's where I am, right in the middle of it."

"Arkin wanted you there?"

She nodded, patting Polly on the head and then ruffling Em's hair.

"You are popular among the boys."

"I lead such an exciting life. So many men, so little time."

Em chuckled, watching his sister dart out of the house, across the commons, and disappear into the mortuary. Polly stood next to Em, ball in her mouth, wanting to play.

"You have more energy than the two of us." He sighed.

* * *

There was something subtly sexy about Anthea Black. He had expected her to be dressed in a suit, but this evening, she had changed into casuals. And she looked hot, schoolgirl-crush hot. Arkin blinked back the thought as the dark-gray Cadillac smoothly pulled to the curb. She stood for a moment, looking over the caddie and follow-up car. It was Arkin, who opened the door for her. He gestured into the back seat of the Cadillac.

"Your chariot awaits, Ms. Black."

"Usually, I get dinner before I end up in the back seat," she commented jokingly as she climbed in, sitting next to Marta. She nodded to Marta, who smiled, glancing past her to Arkin. If he could blush, he would have at the comment.

"Forgive the tight fit," he commented as she pulled on the seat belt.

"I get it, you need security, and since you invited me, I have to have security as well. I appreciate it. And just so you know, I won't be the first to rush in, but I won't run away either. If push comes to shove, I can fight. I would prefer not to, though, since I am human and all."

Marta looked at Arkin, who could sense that there was something else lingering in that gene pool and they couldn't identify it. Odd, considering how long they had wandered the Earth, that they had not sensed this before. Though Marta, like many of Arkin's other children, could have had a city to herself, she preferred to stick close at home. You always needed someone you could absolutely trust. That was her.

"Can you give directions to Jackson?"

Thea nodded. "That's 2424 Birdsong Drive, parallel to the old town square. It has a clock tower and everything. The Seven find it quaint. The square is where most of the main paranormals have set up shop for meet-and-greet events. Those born of the blood own the historical Renard building across from the fountain and square. It's not occupied. Since it is a symbol of solidarity and they haven't yet decided on who should run the city, it has been left wanting."

Thea fell silent, thinking that those in the car had already decided it would be Arkin, if they had their way about it, that he would set up shop there. If he was better than Yardley, everyone would welcome him, and Thea thought just about anyone could be better than Yardley. Arkin sat very still, his body pressed against Thea's. There was something very comforting about her presence, a sort of serenity. Someone a long time ago had told him that every once in a while, you would find someone with the light, a soft glow in them that drew both human and nonhuman into it. He wondered if that was what he was sensing about Anthea. He frowned slightly, leaning back over the seat to glance at Marta, who met his gaze, voice soft in her mind. It wasn't often that they spoke this way; it was considered rude among their kind when the creator spoke to his or her child this way. It smacked of secrets.

Am I just imagining things since I am male and she is female? Arkin asked Marta's senses on alert.

No. There is a definite grace about her. Whether she realizes it or not, I'm not sure. I could see why they made her a witness, but for those who don't want to understand, it can be dangerous.

"Do you know anything about those you are going to meet?" Thea asked, curious.

Arkin's first wave had given him a pretty good dossier on everyone of import in the city. "I would be a poor guest, indeed, if I didn't study my hosts."

She smiled at him. Gosh, he was good-looking, she thought.

"I would, however, be interested in a one-sentence description from you about them, since I am sure you know them better than I do."

Thea snorted derisively. "They prefer not to know me at all. I am not of their blood, as Copper has put it rather often. I'm not sure how helpful my insights might be, but I can manage a sentence here or there. Lyle is a traditionalist. He doesn't like to upset things. Arabella likes men, any men. Perry likes to see their side with the advantage of power. He is a bit of a snob. Hilda, or Copper, as they call her, thinks the world owes her. She can be rather greedy. Hector and Li are the more practical of them. They would like this resolved, things moving back to better than normal. And Zara doesn't look all that scary, but she likes to dole out the punishments. These are snippets that no one would mention to you, things I have seen. I am sure they have tried to summon some information on you as well. No one likes to be left in the dark, especially with all the things that haunt it."

"Good luck with that," muttered Marta.

There was no way in hell they would be able to dig up anything on Arkin. He didn't really officially exist. Besides, they would learn way more than they wanted to if he did indeed decide to take this city to task.

"What they know of me is what has recently happened. That should speak volumes."

The car came to a stop in front of the building. The double doors were part glass, part polished wood. It had been a while since she was at the square, not since the blood had split into territories. Security exited first, followed by Arkin, and then Thea. She, like security, stopped for just a moment, her eyes scanning the light by the bubbling fountain. Trees swayed in the breeze, lights danced off the water, and she tried to look deeply into the shadows.

"Something wrong?" Arkin asked, voice almost a whisper, trying to follow her line of sight.

"No, just looking," she lied.

Something was out there, something different that she hadn't sensed before, but something she felt she should know as well. She shrugged off the feeling, passing through the open doors into the foyer. The floors were polished marble, and there were two winding staircases on either side of the hall, with double doors straight ahead. They were open and inviting.

"Through the double doors?"

Thea nodded as security preceded them. Arkin gently laid his hand on her arm. He didn't seem tense, just cautious. As they passed through the double doors, security looked left and right. All the action was in the center, a rather old-fashioned wooden round table with comfortable-looking leather chairs, pitchers of water, and the Seven. Out of everyone, there she was, dressed the least impressively. Arkin's people were in gray, which seemed to be his chosen color. The Seven, in business attire, looked more like a hostile boardroom. Then again, businessmen could be predators. The Seven certainly were. All eyes bypassed her and locked at Arkin, who stopped at the edge of the table and pulled out a chair for Thea. He didn't seem intimidated. Of course, he had probably gotten this look a thousand times. It probably took a lot to impress him.

"Good evening," he remarked, shattering the silence.

"Mr. Kane, thank you for seeing us on such short notice," Lyle remarked politely.

"You should thank Anthea for agreeing to set up this meeting. She is the only reason I returned the call or agreed to come."

"Should I introduce everyone?" Anthea asked brightly.

"If you like," Arkin remarked, but she was pretty damn sure he knew whom he was dealing with. Anthea went from oldest member to newest.

"Arkin Kane, may I introduce to you Lyle Wegman, Arabella Rogers, Perry McCoy, Hilda Witherspoon, though the council calls her Copper, Hector Romero, Li Feng, and Zara Amard. Ladies and gentlemen, Arkin Kane and escorts."

Anthea seated herself, stepping out of the way, letting Arkin make his own first impressions.

Lyle was tall. He looked like he was out of place in a suit and should be chopping down logs somewhere in denim and flannel. He had dark hair, beard, and moustache. Arabella Rogers was tall, lean, cool blue eyes, and highlighted blond hair. She was dressed in a deep-green suit with spiky heels. Perry was dressed as he had been at lunch. He nodded to her with a thankful expression on his face. Copper had flaming-red hair and gray eyes. She usually grabbed any man's attention, but Arkin didn't seem overly impressed by her, however. Nor did his gaze linger. Thea had to refrain from a smirk. Hector, Li, and Zara were all about the same size, under six feet, with creamy, warm skin, dark hair and eyes. Hector and Li were each wearing suits, Hector's brown, Li's deep brocade blue without a collar, more Nehru. Zara was wearing a bright-orange sari. Each shook hands with Arkin then stepped away to give him and his security a wide berth. The council's security stood at the back of their chairs, as if expecting something.

Thea already felt tired.

"Can I get you something to drink, either of you?"

Arkin glanced down at Thea, waiting for her to either agree or decline. If she agreed, he would as well.

"Hot tea, if you have it. If spiced, two sugars. If plain tea, two sugars and milk," she asked politely as they all began to take their seats.

"It would be impolite not to drink if my witness is drinking," added Arkin as he, too, seated himself, twisting sideways, with his legs crossed. He looked two damn comfortable, too relaxed for the situation he was in.

"Welcome to our city, such that it is," remarked Lyle. "I see you found our witness before you found anyone else."

Arkin chuckled. "That was just a coincidence. I don't think she wanted to be where we met. As it was, I am most grateful to the fates for having introduced us. Her help has been most welcome," he said. "Why don't we come down to the real reason for this meeting, your questions? What are my plans?"

"That would save time, if you were that direct," answered Zara politely.

"I am a traditionalist. I value respect, civility. I believe that brings power and prosperity," he said. "There were seven of my blood in this city, and not one could truly step up, take the reins, and now they are hiding in little fragmented territories. I prefer solving issues and problems by talking, having a rational discussion, rather than fighting, if possible."

"You tell that to Garrick and Cordelia," quipped Copper as the tea arrived.

Anthea huddled around the warmth and took a long, deep sip. Since she seemed to trust them, Arkin sipped his fresh, warm blood. They were good hosts, if nothing else. It wasn't everyone who opened a vein for their kind. He inclined his head in thanks.

"Garrick took exception to me killing Pick. He had, after all, tried to kill Ms. Black. As our law demands, I brought the body to him. He chose to attack me. He failed in that attempt. Cordelia sent several of her men after me. They were sidelined, and I thought it proper that she and I have a conversation as to her reason for the attack. She didn't want to talk at that time."

"And what of their ventures? What of their people?" Li asked, curious.

"Everything continues on as it did, but under a more watchful eye. There are rules to our lives, ladies and gentlemen, maybe more so than if we were just human. I intend to approach the others still with open arms. I hadn't planned on making my entrance into this city so awkwardly."

"You appear no worse for wear," Arabella remarked, a sly smile on her lips.

"Others tend to underestimate me," remarked Arkin as he noticed Thea seem to settle in more comfortably. But she looked weary.

"So you intend on staying? Did a council send you to clean up this mess? Or are you just a wandering gunslinger?" Hector asked.

"I intend on staying. I intend on putting our interests back into shape. This city is quite an embarrassment. Though many who are ensconced in this city are young, they should have a thorough understanding of what we will and won't allow."

Thea sat beside him, very quiet, eyes watching the proceedings with interest.

"How old are you, Arkin?" Zara asked, her eyes narrow. "You can't just throw that out there and not expect us to ask."

He smiled. Thea thought that Arkin's security looked narrowly at Zara, insulted by the question.

"I was told it was impolite to ask a woman how old she was as well as what kind of animal she might become. I would ask you that you grant me the same courtesy. Shall we say I am older than anyone in this city?"

Thea, like everyone else, was trying to do the math.

"So you want to clean up your kind's mess. And what do you expect from us?"

"Just patience. I don't intend to affect any of our businesses. I have made my point very clear to those remaining: stay and prosper or go. I don't want men and women who aren't serious about turning themselves around. They will learn."

There was a quiet moment, the council looking back and forth at one another. They wanted to believe him. And Thea did.

"Very well, then," Lyle remarked. "We appreciate your candor and your time this evening. You can understand our curiosity. Though we didn't particularly like Yardley, we worked with him to get things done in the city and maintain a positive atmosphere among the humans. While we can't, in good conscience, intervene, we hope for the best outcome possible."

Way to be vague, thought Thea. She set her teacup aside and shifted in the chair. Lyle turned his gaze on her.

"Now that we have spoken with Arkin, another matter has come to our attention."

Thea waited.

"Are you aware that Claire believes that something dark is on the way to the city to harm you?"

Thea drew a long breath and nodded. "She barged into my house before I was awake and told me of her so-called vision."

"Who is Claire?" Arkin asked pointedly.

"A woman who thinks she has the psychic gift but who has, in all her premonitions—shall we say, in the thousands—has only been right three times, and I attribute that to coincidence."

"Well, whether it is real or imagined, we must be on our guard," Li added warmly, his brown eyes on Thea. Arkin could sense more than an average interest.

"What, can't the poor little human defend herself against the big, bad dark?" Copper asked sarcastically.

"She won't have to," replied Arkin, rising. "It is our duty to ensure that she is safe so that our city can thrive. I don't know how she was chosen, but she seems to be respected and accomplished. Do you know how rare witnesses are? I can count the number of them I have met on one hand in my lifetime."

Thea stood up and met Copper's gaze. Her eyes were frosty.

"Copper, if you and I were to mix it up, you wouldn't even see me coming." There was a thread of truth that seemed to fill the room as Arkin gently placed his hand on her arm, drawing her away from the circular table.

"My thanks for this evening. It should be an interesting next few days. I am in hopes that the city can be cleaned up quickly and everything is back to better than normal," commented Arkin.

"Will you be occupying the space across the street?" Hector asked.

"Perhaps only when the need arises. There is much to do before I consider where I will hold court, as it were."

"You are pretty damn sure of yourself," Perry remarked cautiously.

Arkin smiled. "One has to be if one wants to be the victor."

Thea, sandwiched between Arkin and Marta, was hustled out of the chamber, into the foyer. Security closed the doors behind them. Arkin looked at her with an annoyed expression, almost as if she were a child. Marta could almost hear him fuming.

"You like to taunt wild things, Thea?"

"Only when they piss me off, Arkin," she added. "I'm tired, and I really don't want to get in the middle of things, but here I am. I did as they asked, and I brought you. I did as you asked and came with you. Can you do as I ask and escort me home? Long day."

Arkin's expression softened. He nodded. "Let's get you home. I'm sorry that I have relied on you so much these past few days. But I also don't like the fact that you have just dismissed this premonition."

"You could guess better by shaking a Magic 8-Ball," she answered tersely as she followed Marta into the car.

Marta was chuckling.

"This woman thinks she sees things?" Marta asked jovially.

"Yes, and everyone is nice to her because she was married to a man that everyone liked and respected. I like her, I really do, but I can't worry about something or someone that I'm not sure is even a threat."

Arkin glanced sideways at Marta.

We need to make sure she is safe. I would like a watch on her, he murmured in Marta's mind. She knew just whom he was thinking of, one of their detective teams. *I don't want her used against me.*

Does she mean that much to you? Marta asked, voice tinged with surprise.

I am as surprised as you are. Arkin, who had given up trying to feel for anyone for a long time, chuckled. Those you cared for could only be used against you, and sometimes the choices you made didn't have a happy ending.

Anthea wasn't asleep; she was just dozing, or so she thought, but it was Arkin's shoulder she was resting on when the car came to a stop. Arkin gently touched her face and hair, jarring her awake.

"I wasn't drooling, was I?" she asked, annoyed at herself.

"No. You don't snore either, at least not tonight," quipped Arkin as he opened the door to escort her out to the doorstep. He opened the small gate for her, and they walked down the stone path to the front porch. The light was soft, barely scattering the shadows among them.

"Thank you for this evening. I know you are tired."

She nodded. "Everyone is on edge. They don't know what is going to happen."

"Neither do I," confessed Arkin.

She looked at him with surprise in her eyes.

"And I don't even have a Magic 8-Ball to consult."

She chuckled lightly as she set her hand on the doorknob. Arkin impulsively tucked a stray strand of hair behind her ear, his fingers lingering lightly over her jawline, and then chin. He leaned forward so quickly and kissed Thea on the lips that she hadn't really had time to respond. His lips were warm, soft, his breath like cinnamon. One moment he had kissed her, and the next he was down the walk, frowning at himself, to Marta's puzzlement. He slipped into the car, not daring to glance back at Thea, who stood too stunned to reply or to move.

It was Em who opened the front door, frowning. His sister had the oddest expression on her pretty face. It almost looked like astonishment.

"I know you wanted to head to the country tonight, but it's late, and you look all done in. How about we go tomorrow night?" he asked.

She could only nod. It sounded like a plan.

"Something wrong?"

"Not quite sure," she remarked. She watched the car pull away from the curb.

* * *

"You okay, boss?" Jackson asked, curious.

He had known Arkin Kane for more than one hundred years. The nom de plume had only come recently with the need for him to tour cities where other blood-born resided. Arkin was much older than that. In fact, Marta was the only one who had been with him the longest, and he wasn't sure how long that was. She was the first he had trusted with his true name. Jackson knew that Arkin craved being anonymous, so in all their travels, he had never so much looked at a human woman the way he looked at Anthea Black.

Arkin was in deep thought. It was Marta's touch that jarred him out of his reverie.

"What is our next step with the city?" Marta asked, redirecting his thoughts away from Thea.

Arkin nodded his thanks. For some reason, he couldn't quite get Thea out of his thoughts. She was like a sliver under his skin.

"I don't care if everyone thinks this Claire is nuts. I want someone on Anthea day and night—casually, of course. Just until we secure our people in the city. I don't want her used as leverage."

"Could she be used as leverage?" Jackson asked from the driver's seat. He tried to keep emotion out of his voice.

"I don't want to have to make that decision. Have Chrisanne contact each of our blood, fragmented as they are. See if we can schedule a time to talk. I don't want anyone thinking firstly that we are weak and that any of our businesses are in jeopardy, nor do I want anyone thinking we are dangerous just yet."

"You could choose not to ask her to witness your discussions. You could let them call her in. But then again, you don't want to hurt her feelings," remarked Jackson, thinking out loud.

Marta cleared her throat.

"It's hard when dealing with humans. Sometimes I forget the nuances. You haven't." Jackson made a noise in the front seat that sounded like a cautionary cough.

"I don't remember you dancing with me before. You are usually blunt like an unsharpened knife," Arkin replied dryly.

"Yes, boss. I am only playing devil's advocate. I know you want to clean up the city, but do you want to stay and have a relationship with Anthea Black? And if you do, would she be open to it? Granted, there are perks to being with a human. They don't live as long as we do…"

Arkin frowned as he looked at Marta.

"You know what I mean. It doesn't have to be forever with a human, unless you would consider turning her," he said. "Chrisanne ran a brief check on her. She is very well respected in business and the community among both the humans and supernaturals. However, she doesn't seem to have a very long track record with men. Men flock to her, but some can't get past the fact that she works with the dead. If they get past that, she doesn't seem to work at the relationship. She works at work. I'm not saying that she isn't attractive. I felt some pull toward her myself, but there is something decidedly not human about her, and I don't know what the hell it is."

"Fey?" Marta offered casually. "Do you think she knows that she's different?"

"That doesn't trouble me, as much as her brother feels perfectly human to me," added Arkin. If they had the same parents, should they not feel the same? "Chrisanne might want to take a deeper look, not that I expect her to find anything. But if she is going to be in danger, I would like to understand motives. *Dark* isn't very informative."

"No, it isn't," sighed Marta. "But it does sound hazardous."

CHAPTER 6

Thea slept in until nine, which was unusual. It had been a blissful, deep sleep that seemed to help her recover and wake with a positive attitude. Since Carly was covering for her on the front desk, she could go in a bit late. Last night had tired all her senses.

Dressed conservatively in dark-gray pinstripes and lavender, she entered the office around ten. It never took her very long to dress, and she didn't use a lot of makeup, her hair usually the holdup. Both Caroline and Sarah had chided her on that account. What took her only a few minutes took them half an hour or more, but the results were usually spectacular. There were times when Thea thought it was false advertising.

Carly was sitting behind the reception desk in her wheelchair, blond hair curled about her shoulders, brown eyes hidden behind a pair of trendy glasses. She glanced up and smiled at Thea as she entered. There was a lot of talk buzzing about the paranormal groups lately, and Thea's name had come up more than once.

"Heard you had a long night last night, and I don't mind filling in at all. I love the extra hours," she remarked.

Thea set her purse aside, regarding the two new flower arrangements, one sitting on the desk, the other on a sideboard. She made a few adjustments to the flowers, inhaling their sweet fragrances.

"Yes, it was long, and is it Daniel who wants to know the details or you?"

Daniel was a very long-lost member of Carly's family, a vampire. With Arkin in town, information was probably at a premium, and you never knew who found what information to be of value. She had never been a gossip.

"Well, everyone is talking up a storm about this new man who seems to be in your life and who casually offed two more-experienced vampires, or should I say bloods." Carly drew a breath as the phone rang, answering it professionally. She placed the man on hold, turning to Thea.

"A gentleman for you. He would like to speak with you if you have the time."

"Put it through to my desk back in the prep room." Thea disappeared into the inner workings of the mortuary. It would afford some quiet and privacy. You never knew what you would end up discussing, and sometimes it was better not to do it in public. She put on her headset as she answered the phone.

"Anthea Black, how can I help you?"

"Ms. Black, my name is Tony Denard. How are you today?"

Thea didn't know a Tony Denard. "I'm quite well, Mr. Denard. I hope you are the same?"

"Better now that I have arrived in town," Mr. Denard responded. "We haven't met, but I believe we have something in common. In fact, we might be related."

Thea turned around in her chair, catching sight of Matthew, who had just passed through from the storeroom. She had to be very careful of her responses and guard any emotion that might seep into her voice. She had to play poker with this Tony Denard.

"Are you a friend of the Blacks?" she asked lightly.

"No. In fact, I haven't met any of them. I'm talking about your birth parents."

Thea drew a long, deep breath, crossing her legs as she considered the statement. Matt looked at her, the expression on her face extremely shielded.

"My parents are dead, Mr. Denard, and I know for a fact that they didn't have any family, or I would not have been put up for adoption," Thea answered politely but firmly. "Is there something specific you want to talk about or say, Tony?" she then asked, waiting impatiently for an answer. She wasn't in the mood for playing a game.

"I understand most people think you are human," he stated, voice holding a thread of anger.

"They would have to prove otherwise, and thus far, no one has cared to try. We all are a mixed bag of genes. It doesn't trouble me if it doesn't bother them. Did you have something of a business nature that you want to discuss? I don't chat about my personal life or my family to strangers."

Tony chuckled lightly. He wasn't getting shit from her, and now he knew it.

"I might be stranger than you know. So if I did want to chat with you about your family and you, what is the best way to go about it?"

"You can make an appointment with reception. Maybe we could do lunch. I'm not sure what you want to know, Tony. There isn't much to say."

"Oh, now I think you are being modest. Everyone has a story to tell. Yours and mine, I think, intersect somewhere."

She doubted it. "If you say so." She wasn't going to argue with him. "Is that all?" she asked coolly, annoyed.

"I'll make an appointment," he added, but she doubted that he would.

"You do that," Thea remarked as she hung up the phone and turned around, startled by Matt. She removed her headset and ran a hand through her hair to smooth it. Her face was flushed slightly.

"You okay? You sounded funny on the phone. You are usually much more put together than that, not that you weren't polite, but there was an undercurrent, for someone that knows you."

"Just someone who wanted to push some buttons. I had better get back to work. We have anyone coming in?"

"Yes, two. Carver should be pulling in with the bodies at any moment."

Thea stood, shrugging out of her jacket, and pulled on her lab coat. She nodded to Matt, heading out of the prep room into reception. She could hear voices in the display room. Carly had left reception, probably for her break, and Zander, dressed in his usual dark suit, sat politely by the phone. He glanced up, dark eyes on her. He had grown a rather nice moustache, which made him look years older; he had quite the baby face. He usually handled IT for them, for all their businesses, and worked in the back office at the florist shop. He was a very private person. She didn't ask, and he didn't tell. He also could keep quiet and wasn't a gossip.

"Can you do something for me, on the QT?"

"Just ask," he said, pen and paper in hand.

"I just got a call from a Tony Denard. Any info you can find on him would be helpful, even if you don't find something that might be helpful too. I am presuming his name is Anthony Denard." Thea spelled it for him using a best guess. "Em doesn't need to know, and you can email me the info."

Zander nodded as she gestured him to rise.

"You go. I'll sit the desk until Carly comes back."

"Only one question. Is he dangerous? I know I'm human, but I also know what you do on the side for those who are not. I also know what Claire has been spouting."

By now, probably everyone knew. Claire wasn't very circumspect; she always did like the attention, especially after her husband died.

"You mean about something dark coming my way? It is entirely possible, but I'm not going to worry about him until he shows up. I told him, if he wanted to talk, to make an appointment."

Zander smiled, nodding. She was assuming it was this Denard fellow. "I bet he won't."

She returned his smile, seating herself. "I bet you're right."

* * *

It should have been relatively simple to find Anthea Black. Cherise, one of Arkin's daytime secretaries, called the mortuary, the florist, and the chapel. She called their home and then the cell number, which forwarded her back to the mortuary. Finally, Arkin decided to give it the old college try himself and was able to find out that they had retreated to their real home, in the country. Carly was more than chatty with him. With Jackson driving, Marta and Lang for company, they headed out of town and into the country. With no streetlights, the road appeared very dark, and the houses distant from the road. Here and there you could spot just a speck of light in between the dark shadows and trees.

"I can see why they like it out here. Even with a half-moon, you can tell it's lovely," commented Marta, staring out the window absently. "Must be hard to work all day and then have to turn around in the evening and deal with paranormals."

"We can be big babies, can't we?" Lang quipped with his usual lopsided smile. "But she seems very gracious in agreeing to help. It might have been fate that delivered her into your hands, and to think we ribbed you about going to a speed-dating club, boss."

Arkin smiled slightly, eyes on the street ahead, Jackson pulling down a winding road.

"You can see greenhouses from the road. They must grow many of their own flowers out here. They have quite a business."

"I'm glad that our discord hasn't spilled over into their world yet," Arkin remarked. "I wanted to do this the easy way."

"They attacked you, boss," answered Jackson firmly. "You shouldn't bite the hand that might be feeding you."

Jackson pulled up in the circular drive and turned off the headlights. You could hear the wind whispering through the tall pines, and the insects buzzing about. Lights from the porch and window made the two-story house warm and inviting. Arkin stepped out of the car, glancing up at the porch, finding eyes on him. Emlyn Black stood at the door, brow furrowed, unasked question on his lips.

"My, this is a surprise. Fancy meeting you here," commented Em dryly. He nodded to the other vampires who stood aside Arkin, the darkness bathing them in shadows, their eyes glittering in the dark like a predator's. It could be easy to forget what they were.

"I am sorry to intrude. I have to say, it is lovely out here."

"We like it. If we didn't have to work, which we don't that often but do, you couldn't get us to leave here." Em blinked nervously. "Sorry, I'm rambling. How can I help you?"

"I came to see Anthea. Is she in?"

Em faltered slightly, looking back toward the kitchen. He frowned faintly. "She is here, but out back with Polly, in the forest, on the trail…I can give her a call and see if she is on her way back, if you would like to come in and wait for her?"

Arkin nodded, stepping across the threshold. Em left them at the door, walking straight back through into the kitchen, and then out the back door onto the patio. He normally wouldn't turn his back on a vampire or more than one, but Thea seemed to trust Arkin, and she had excellent sense. His voice lifted up into the night, calling to his sister.

Marta chuckled. "When he said *call her*, I thought he meant using a cell phone."

"He did it the old-fashioned way," added Lang. "Like a hollerin' contest."

"Your upbringing is showing," cautioned Jackson with a wink.

Em stood on the patio, looking into the forest that surrounded the house. There were smatterings of light from the various rooms in the house, and the back porch, that spilled onto the shadows. Moonlight glinted down around them as Arkin joined him, staring out into the dark. Odd to be jogging in the dark, though it was a lovely night to be out. There were safer times for a human to be running. Arkin could hear Polly barking in the distance and then saw her race forward with a stick in her mouth, tail wagging. Em caught her removing the stick and a feather that was stuck to her mouth. Em laid the feather on the nearby table, tossing the stick back into the night. He picked up the soft white towel that was lying over the railing as he saw his sister slowly move out of the ring of trees toward the house.

Arkin could see her clearly, though it was probably too dark for human eyes. She was wearing sneakers, loose black shorts, a small black-and-white polka-dotted halter top. Her hair was in tendrils around her face, having escaped a braid. He could see the perspiration on her face, see the fatigue, but she smelled as fresh as the night air, still alluring, looking as tired and worn as she was. What was this thing about her that intrigued him so? Em bounced down the steps and handed her the towel as she regarded Arkin and his security spread out on the porch. She reached down and patted Polly on the head.

"I am sorry to have disturbed you. Being able to withstand the light, isn't it dangerous to jog in the dark? I would think sunrise might be more appropriate."

"Let's just call me a creature of the dark," she responded. "How can I help you, Arkin?"

Em handed her a tall cold glass of what looked like lemonade. She downed it and made a face. "Needs more sugar," she remarked, face crinkled.

He laughed. "Not if I want to see that smooshy face," he added, accepting the glass back from her.

"Would you be so kind to show me around while we talk?"

Em refrained from a comment; he could see that his sister was at a loss by Arkin's attention.

"Not much to see—house, greenhouses—but we can sit in the gazebo, if you want privacy." She stepped back, gesturing for Arkin to join her.

Em glanced at the others. "You just are going to wait up here?"

"We'll spread out, if that is okay. Mind if we play with your dog?" Jackson asked.

"No. Tire her out, please," begged Em. "Do you know why he wants to see my sister? Is it business or pleasure?"

Marta arched an eyebrow, watching Jackson, Polly, and Lang dance across the lawn, eyes on the gazebo, where Thea and Arkin were slowly strolling toward.

"Is big brother prying?" Marta asked, curious.

Em leaned against the rail and folded his arm across his chest. He regarded Marta with cool interest. "The operative word is *big brother*. So what if I am a bit overly anxious regarding my sister? Lately, paranormals have been very interested in her, and I don't want to see her get hurt, either physically or her heart crushed because of some game."

"Arkin finds your sister very lovely and approachable. He tries not to play games, and he hasn't had a steady male-female relationship in more than, I believe, one hundred years. Why don't you let them decide how they best want to interact with each other? Your sister is a big girl as well."

"As long as I don't have to pick up the pieces. I have seen some pretty ugly breakups in my time."

"You and I both." Marta sighed, realizing it was the truth.

Meanwhile, Thea wiped her face with the towel, seating herself on the swinging bench. Arkin joined her, his arm on the back of the swing, close to her shoulders. He looked at her softly then brushed a few wet strands from her face. There always seemed to be this connection, this zing between them. He wondered if she felt it too.

"You had quite a workout."

"Yes. I love the forest for the privacy and the coolness. It seems at peace.... What do you need, Arkin?"

Cut to the chase. He liked that. "I was sorry to hear about your parents."

Thea gave him a blank look.

"The Sheridans, your birth parents."

She nodded. That wasn't unexpected. "Checking up on me, are you? It's not common knowledge. I have been with the Blacks as long as I can remember, and I think people forget or are too polite to ask."

"Em seems to love you very much."

Thea glanced back at the house. "Yes. I love him very much. Maybe you could call him my kryptonite, and maybe it wasn't smart of me to tell you that just now."

"But the fact that you did tell me means you trust me."

"I guess I do. You haven't so far done anything that is against the laws as we know them. You seem to treat your people well. They don't seem unhappy. I haven't heard any rumblings from those you have taken under your wing, though I know you have to clean house. Your people seem more than competent."

"I don't tolerate those who are not committed. I require an oath from them, and it is reciprocal," he responded and paused, albeit only slightly. "I have made appointments with the other blood members, and I would appreciate you acting as silent witness. I am hoping there will be discussions and no challenges."

"They will want to know what is in it for them," cautioned Thea as she shifted on the bench.

Arkin thought she moved closer. Maybe she was chilled. He shrugged out of his jacket and laid it across her shoulders.

"You shouldn't, I'm sweaty," she protested.

"I like the way you smell, Thea. It is enticing."

She looked at him with amusement. "Quite the charmer, aren't you?"

He chuckled, a lock of hair falling over his eyes. Wow, he was attractive, and it was a really bad idea to get involved with him, she thought. They had all the time in the world usually, and that meant they didn't always stay in one place. She didn't want to be a fling.

"I haven't actually tried to seduce anyone in one hundred or so odd years," he answered with a shrug.

"Out of practice, are you? Well, I can tell you that you don't seem rusty at all." She smiled. "So you want me to accompany you to all your meetings?"

"Yes, just to certify, should anyone ask, that it was civilized," he remarked casually.

"We don't know that yet."

"Well, I want them to be. If they aren't, whatever follows will be well within the law. I don't like to kill my fellow blood. We are small in number, though humans might disagree. So many of us were lost when we had to keep our existence a secret. But now here we are."

"And those in residence are most curious about you, I bet. I have been asked, and I have referred them to you. They seem reticent to approach you."

"I am always approachable. You can ask me anything, and I will try to tell you the truth if it won't harm you. I have an open-door policy."

"I don't think they believe your name is Arkin Kane."

"Well, you aren't really Thea Black. You were Anthea Sheridan."

"I was. That was a long time ago," she answered with a sigh.

"True. So maybe my true name was also a long time ago and isn't worth sharing."

Her eyes narrowed slightly as she pulled the jacket around her body. "I can't see anything about you being worthless."

"You are too kind," he answered, cherishing this discussion.

"Not usually. I abhor stupidity and lies, especially when my friends lied to me about going to that club."

He chuckled. "But then we would never have met. That would have been a shame, Anthea. I like you very much."

"As a person or as a witness?" she asked, curious.

"As a woman," he added softly, his fingertips drawing a line from her chin to her lips. He barely touched her lips, slowly leaning in, with a sudden urge to taste their softness, when Polly bounded up between them, stick in her mouth.

"Didn't know that Polly was a rescue dog, huh?"

There was amusement in his eyes as she watched him stand. "You mean she rescued you from me?" Arkin asked.

"Yes, and my passion. I haven't dated in a long time, Arkin—if you can call them even dates—and that was with human men. I can't imagine dating anyone as experienced and powerful as you. It frightens me a bit. After all, I have the feeling you can see right through me. But a girl has to have her secrets."

"Keep yours, Anthea. Only share them if you feel safe and if you must. I see Asao night after tomorrow. Should I pick you up at work?"

"That would be fine. He was a good starting place," she added, returning his jacket to him.

With Polly in tow, they headed back to the house, security closing around them both, Arkin taking a polite leave. Em stood beside his sister on the front porch, watching the car disappear into the night. She closed the door, leaning against it, towel in hand.

"Surprised he found you out here?" he asked. She shouldn't be.

"I didn't know he was looking."

"So what is it between you and fang boy?"

Thea frowned as she left the door and front foyer for the stairs.

"When you were twelve, your genes outed you. We vowed that there wouldn't be secrets between us. I have told you all sorts of things about Lucy and me, some I'm sure you didn't want to hear, but I'm just curious. I'm not judging."

Thea sat on the stairs, looking up into her brother's eyes. He knew her track record with boys and with men. She had had a few dates in high school, but the boys didn't stick with her for very long. Most wanted to be friends more than a boyfriend. As they grew older, both Sarah and Caroline seemed to take advantage of the boys who flocked around her but didn't dare invade her heart.

"I like him. He's attractive and dangerous to my heart. He has a good soul, and I know you won't argue with me on that account. Why is he interested? I'm something new, like a dog with a chew toy—he will pursue until he's tired and then move on."

"But a chew toy doesn't come to the dog. You interested?"

Thea sighed, folding her arms across her chest. "I guess I am, but right now, things are way too unsettled. I like the fact that he seems to be a good person. I think he could keep me safe, he has the underlying authority of power…but even with my feelings, how attractive he might find me, that doesn't mean we can overcome obstacles."

Em knew exactly what she meant. "You don't see him being a vampire as an obstacle?"

"You didn't seem to be bothered by Lucy being a wolf in girls' clothing."

Em chuckled. "True, but maybe I just think no one can live up to my expectation of you, of who and what you are."

"Thinking I might get struck down by a lightning bolt if I stray from some sort of true path?"

Em slid down to the floor and crossed his legs. "No. And I think you should live your life and screw the ideals. I mean, as far as we know, we only go around once, and I'm not even sure how long a life we have. If you can be happy and he can make you happy, I'll be happy for you."

She rolled her eyes. "I just told you I like him. He tried to kiss me—that's as far as we have gone so far. It's not like he proposed. I try to take it one day at a time. We always have."

Em nodded, leaning back against the wall.

"I have Zander working on something for me. I had a call from a Tony Denard. He seems to think we are related."

Em opened and then closed his mouth. Since they were sharing, she might as well go all the way.

"Does he even know what you are?"

She shrugged. "I told him to make an appointment to see me if he wanted to talk. And no, I don't think we are the same. It took me how many years just to figure out what I thought I might be, and even then, there was very little info on it."

"Do you think he is the dark that Claire spoke of?"

Thea stood, frowning. "Honestly, no. Denard doesn't scare me, but he isn't like me. Maybe he is the other side of the coin."

"How could he have found you?" he asked warily.

"If he is looking for something magical, he could purchase a spell to find it, I guess. But I'm not a witch, so I wouldn't be sure how to do that. He may have power, but he isn't like me." Thea was certain of it.

"You keep me in on the loop, all right?" Em stood, he kissed his sister on the forehead as she stood on the stairs. "You know, we would be perfect for each other if we truly didn't feel brotherly and sisterly toward each other."

"You flirt, Lucy would skin you alive talking like that! Besides, I'm not your type. I'm not naughty enough. I'm not the bad girl."

Em's eyes twinkled.

"But I could be if I tried."

Chapter 7

It was agreed that Thea would take the day off since she would be working as a silent witness that night. She needed quiet me-time. Em knew he was in trouble when she agreed without a fight. He left her sitting on the porch with a hot cup of tea, Polly at her feet. Their lives hadn't been as complicated as it was of late. The first thing he wanted to do was check with Zander to see what he found on this Tony Denard, but Thea beat him to it. Once he pulled his car out of the drive, she was inside and on her laptop. She checked her email and then dialed Zander's extension.

"Morning, boss lady. Hear you're taking the day. Good for you."

"Just trying to keep my sanity. Nothing important," she responded. "How did it go looking up Denard?"

Zander chucked. "Nothing earth-shattering. I can give you a quick synopsis if you like."

"I'd like very much." Thea leaned back on the couch and closed her eyes.

"He was born in San Leandro, California. He is thirty-two years old. His mother is dead, died soon after he was born. Father is a tax accountant. He went to school, four-year degree in philosophy and religion. Works at a conference retreat. He is about six one, with dark hair, dark eyes. Attractive, I guess, if you like that cocky type. He apparently runs through women as if they were tissue. His aunt is a certified witch."

Thea sighed, nodding to herself. "Is he human?"

"Nothing to say otherwise, but I get the feeling that he has an attitude. Nothing to suggest that he has gone to the dark side other than his attitude toward women. Also, nothing to suggest he is in town."

"He may call work to set up an appointment to see me. Put him through. If his intention was to pique my curiosity, he has done that."

"Is he going to be a problem, boss? Is Emlyn going to ask me about him?"

"He might. Tell him what you told me. Denard just came out of the woodwork and intimated that we may be related somehow, but I'm not sure in what way."

"Well, you are attractive. You do a good business, have certain power in the community. It is probably like winning the lottery. Then you have people coming out of the woodwork to be your friends. You know you have resources to keep you safe."

Thea smiled. "Thanks for the reminder, Zander. No one else needs to know about this until it becomes a problem."

Zander was quiet a moment.

"You told me yourself, nothing remarkable about him. I don't need to stir anyone up until I have more information."

"We worry about you."

Thea chuckled.

"Sometimes you are just too good for this world. Emlyn would agree."

"You know where I am if you need me."

"Hopefully, we won't need you." Zander signed off, leaving Thea to her thoughts.

Maybe she had overreacted with Denard, but you never knew what to expect, and his comments were cryptic. Granted, she had the ability to know what he was intimating even with their brief conversation. That was one of the reasons she wanted to meet Denard. There was no way in hell they were related by family blood. But power maybe? She closed her eyes, not wanting to think about it.

Just enjoy the day, she told herself. Worry would always be waiting around the corner.

* * *

Arkin entered the Blacks' reception area dressed in his signature color of gray, delivering a very attractive smile to Pearl, who was on the evening watch. Pearl was a witch in training but couldn't resist a slight sigh as she looked hard at the new arrival. Pearl was Jamaican, and although the job called for a subdued manner of dress, she still managed to bring color to her wardrobe, which suited her dark eyes and skin. Pearl realized that Carly was right; this Arkin was Hollywood handsome. Arkin's eyes riveted to Thea, who breezed out of the back hallway dressed in a maroon business suit with sparkling gray shell, her hair pulled back in a chignon. Pearl could almost feel the electricity in the air as their eyes locked. She resisted the urge to fan herself. Thea returned Arkin's smile as she picked up her purse.

"I hear you took a day off from work. I hope you were able to relax."

"And her brother didn't even have to argue with her, imagine that," interjected Pearl, smiling. "She does need some life in her life."

Thea rolled her eyes. "Now everyone is a critic," she said. "I am off for the evening. You can call Em if anything urgent happens."

"And you will call and do the same?" Pearl asked, an edge to her voice as she glanced at Arkin. She raised her finger at him. "You invited her, you keep her safe."

Thea had champions.

"My one goal in life: at the first sign of trouble, I shall throw myself on top of her," quipped Arkin.

"Just watch that knee to the groin," uttered Pearl as Thea promptly headed to the door. "She really does have a fun side. You just don't always see it when she is working."

"Then maybe I should ask her out on a date," Arkin remarked before stepping out into the night.

The sky was dark, clouds blotting out any twinkling stars. Thunder rumbled across the sky, lightning arcing in the distance.

Thea smiled, mind reflecting back to her conversation with Em about being struck by lightning by being with Arkin. Marta sat in the seat to her left as she climbed in. She smiled and offered Thea her hand; it never hurt to be nice to the boss's lady, and the way Arkin spoke about her, Marta wasn't at all sure that such an arrangement was so far off.

"Fancy meeting you again, and so soon. I feel we are fast becoming friends."

"I'm not the mani-pedi kind of girl, but I do like to shoot a good gun once in a while," quipped Marta.

"Who doesn't?" Thea grinned as Arkin slid in beside her. "Do you have directions?"

"We have an escort, the white Audi," commented Jackson, once again behind the wheel. Thea quickly understood that among Arkin's staff, he had his favorites.

"Asao lives in what they call the New Mod district. It isn't by any means historic. He is a gracious host and progressive in his thinking. He prefers not to fight if possible. He was a good choice to start with. He can help with the others if need be."

"Your insights are helpful," Arkin remarked with a nod.

She shook her head. "Was he always such a suck-up?" she asked Marta as Jackson and Lang snorted.

"Only to beautiful women," she commented dryly.

"Oh, then only to those born of the blood," added Thea. "They have far more in the looks department than I do."

"But you have the air of mystery about you, plus you have drinkable blood," remarked Lang.

"Oh, yes, your favorite food of choice. I prefer pizza myself, and, of course, a well-chosen chocolate dessert."

"Has anyone blooded you yet?" Arkin asked, trying to sound casual. It was getting harder and harder for him to sit so close to her and not feed this lust more for her body than her blood, but there was something more that existed between them. But damned if he knew what it was.

"No. I probably wouldn't volunteer unless it was an emergency," she answered, unsure what her blood might do to someone. She had a feeling it might be poisonous. "And I haven't dated any of the blood that reached that stage in a relationship. Most have other sources of fare." Thea stared out the window at the passing houses lit warmly in the night, hoping to quiet that subject. A few drops of rain splattered the windshield. "Not a night to be out," she muttered to herself.

"Or in the company of your enemies?" Marta asked, meeting her gaze pointedly.

"I don't consider anyone my enemy until I have no choice to do so. I have too many paranormal friends. They want peace and status quo. Prosperity is nice as well."

"Does Emlyn have a girlfriend?" Lang asked curiously, changing the subject.

"Lucy. They are on again and off again. She doesn't like his close relationship with me. She knows I'm adopted, but for some reason, she thinks Em and I are closer than we appear."

"Families all have their secrets. Maybe because Em won't share and she is jealous," remarked Arkin softly. That had explained why both brother and sister felt so different.

"Sometimes, no matter how much you care for someone or love them, it isn't enough because there is always that possibility that they hear what you say but can't accept it. Is it worth the risk? We each have to decide. Besides, all women have secrets. That is what makes men crazy, all men."

The gray SUV pulled past the gates and into the circular drive. If you expected the house to be Asian in nature, you thought wrong. It was Mediterranean, with tile roof, fountain in the center of the drive, wrought iron balconies, and farther down the back slope were other buildings, including a stable. Thea had been there once before for a meeting, but always it was for business. Just once she would love to have a tour of the house and grounds as a friend. Asao's security opened the double doors. Thunder rumbled overhead, and he knew it was just a matter of moments before the storm came. He stood with his back to the light, eyes on his company. Asao stood just a finger length higher than Thea. He had chocolate-colored eyes and dark straight hair that he had grown long. It was pulled back into a long ponytail that lay across his back. His slacks were black, his shirt more a jerkin in emerald green, emboldened with a black-and-gold dragon. He watched as Arkin exited the car with Thea in tow, their hands together. Arkin Kane—the name meant little to him, but somewhere in the recesses of his mind, he thought he should know this man, or at least who he was. He was tall, was very straight, and looked as if he had been a warrior at one point, attractive by any woman's standards, and having just met him, he could tell that he felt protective of Thea.

Thea darted forward into the light as the sky opened up and it began to rain.

"Asao, it is good to see you again. May I introduce Arkin Kane. Arkin, this is our host, Asao." Thea stepped back and let them shake hands and size each other up. It was going to be an interesting evening.

"Please come in out of the rain. Not an auspicious beginning, but I am hopeful. The gardens need the rain."

Arkin and Thea followed him along the tile floor and then turned right into a small salon or study. This was more an English traditional room with large overstuffed chairs, a fireplace, and books shelved against the wall.

"Would you care for your usual?" Asao asked.

Thea nodded politely as he gestured for her to sit in one of the tapestry chairs. He watched carefully as Arkin seated himself next to Thea. Interesting. Usually, the witness sat between them, not next to either side. They were supposed to be neutral. Security, of course, waited at the partially opened door. Asao seated himself, crossed his legs, and leaned back comfortably. He let silence fill the air between them.

"I want you to know that I don't hold any enmity toward you for Garrick's or Cordelia's deaths. They were unworthy of their position, and it was just a matter of time before they died. Talking should always be the first step. You can always fight later when you have a cause or no choice."

The door swung open, and a tray was brought over to the table between them, a cup of hot tea for Thea. She nodded her thanks, picked up the pretty china cup, and took a sip. It looked as if her entire body relaxed. Asao smiled.

"She does love her comforts. You will notice I included almond cookies."

"You are my kind of host, Asao. Thank you."

"Was Yardley worthy?" Arkin asked, curious.

"He was when we first arrived. He was driven to portray us well, for all of us to succeed, but as time lapsed, he fell into avarice, was rude, and abused those who served him. He did not depict us as well as he could have. Others had left, not wanting a confrontation, and prior to his death, I was looking to move our house out of the city, but then, of course, he was killed."

Arkin turned his gaze onto Thea. She raised a curious eyebrow, waiting for a question. "Did Yardley abuse you?"

Thea cleared her throat, glancing at Asao, not used to being included in a conversation.

"Answer honestly, Anthea," Asao cautioned.

"He never physically abused me, but he did verbally make comments that were upsetting. You just kind of work through it. Others needed me, and I didn't think he would let me go so easily if I declined assisting him."

It was an oddly grim expression on Arkin's face. He reached over and patted her leg.

"I am sorry that you had to endure that." Arkin turned to face Asao. "So after Yardley had fallen, did you not think to take up command?"

"You flatter me if you think I would be an appropriate leader," he responded. "After Yardley was killed, Raisa tried, then Morgan, and then finally Victoria. None of them succeeded in staying very long. Their own power base fell apart, and we ended up in a territorial kind of existence. I had considered stepping up, but in truth, I have had my fill of killing for power. I have executed my share of our kind, and I am tired of it. I do not fight unless there is a need. I was waiting to see which way the wind was blowing, and it blew you here."

Thea took another sip of tea, Asao stiffening slightly. His hand went to his ear, as if he was listening to someone. "It looks as if I am going to need to fight. We are under attack."

Arkin sprang to his feet, voices erupting around him. Asao leaped over the table and around the chair to the nearby bookcase. He hit a panel only he could see.

"You take care of Thea."

Before Thea could argue, Arkin had bodily picked her up and carried her into the very small space behind the wall. The bookcase closed, leaving both Arkin and Thea in close quarters; the only sliver of light was from the opposite wall, a small two-way mirror. Light spilled through it, fragmented in the shadows. She could barely see Arkin's face. Thea was pinned up against the wall, body straddling Arkin's thigh. Her hands were against his chest, his hands on either side of her head, and he was listening. His body was tense. She figured he probably wanted to be out where the action was, but since he had brought her to this dance, it was his responsibility to see that she survived it. Thea could hear voices, screams, what sounded like the clash of swords, and gunfire. Every new sound pushed Arkin's body closer, his attention fully riveted on the fight. All Thea could think about was how every movement of his body went straight to her groin. The junction of her thighs was grinding into his leg, the movement driving her closer and closer to orgasm. Her fingers fisted his shirt as she bit her lip, trying to control what little shred of self-control she possessed. She closed her eyes, body throbbing, so close to tumbling over that sweet edge. A noise just outside the bookcase door jarred Arkin. His leg jerked. The lusty orgasm that was coiled, ready to strike, enveloped Thea. Her back arched, body pushed into him, hands tugging on his shirt, eyes closed as she let the pleasure wash through her. She was trembling, too caught up in the orgasm to show embarrassment. It had been so long. Her eyes fluttered open, and Arkin stared at her, his expression one of amazed delight.

He leaned to her, whispering in her ear, "I wish I had done that on purpose."

Thea let her fingers uncurl from his shirt, face turned away from him, embarrassed.

"I hope my leg is wet with your sweet cream."

The slap that stung his face was considerably gentler than the push she gave him when the door opened, and Asao stood, waiting for them. The slap wasn't forceful, but the shove—that girl had some strength in her, he decided. Arkin stumbled back out the door, caught by Asao. There was an eerie silence around them.

"You both are well?" he asked, concerned.

"We should be asking you that, Asao," she remarked as she looked over his blood-spattered face and slightly torn shirt. She avoided looking up at Arkin as she stepped out of their hiding place, eyes drinking in the damage to the room. Table knocked over, her teacup in shattered fragments, two bodies lying dead. She drew a long, deep breath to try to maintain control. Firstly, the carnage, and then the lust she had displayed with Arkin. She needed to leave. Thea stepped around Asao, gingerly walking to the body. She made it past the first one who was missing his head, walking toward the second body that seemed to be cleaved in two. Thea took a careful step. Her foot hit the wet pool of blood, and down she went, hitting her backside and then cracking her head on the floor. Stars swam before her eyes. She groaned as she lay in a cooling pool of blood. Damn shoes. She was usually so much more graceful than this. A face danced before her eyes. Gratefully, she thought, it wasn't Arkin.

Marta held up her fingers. "How many?" she asked lamely.

"Two fingers and a thumb," she gurgled out as Marta chuckled. She had a scratch along her face and one near her neck, her clothing splattered with blood.

"You took quite a fall. Let me help you up, slowly, all right?"

Thea nodded really slow as Marta slid a hand under her back and helped her sit upright. To her relief, the bodies had been removed, although the blood still remained. Thea reeled back and forth, eyes on Asao and Arkin, who were standing out in the hall, talking in low voices.

"Your clothes are probably ruined. Yuki, one of Asao's people, is bringing you a robe you can wear. We will stop by your house and pick up some clothes. Since we were attacked this evening, the boss wants you with us, for safety reasons."

"Who attacked us?" Thea managed to ask, her eyes on the broken teacup, the scattered fragments of a table next to a broken lamp.

"They were a mixed group. Three fled from Garrick's group when we took them, two from Cordelia's, and the rest were from Ulrich. Whether he knows about the attempt or not, I can't say. They weren't all vampires. There were two shifters and a witch involved."

"How many casualties?"

Marta smiled, lending her a hand up. Her arms curled around Thea to keep her upright. "All on their side dead, three wounded on ours. We did good."

Thea raised her hand to her hair, and Marta shook her head.

"You're covered in blood, none of it yours. Let's get you out of the wet clothes and into the robe."

Thea could see a pretty brilliant-green-and-black-haired Asian, Yuki, standing just behind Arkin with a robe in her hands. The robe was black with a white heron or crane on it.

"There is a powder room just this way. You can go in and change. We will take care of your discarded clothing. The rain has stopped, so you should not get wet. You broke a heel, so you will need to go barefoot."

Thea nodded as she was ushered into the very tastefully decorated powder room. She avoided staring at herself in the mirror; instead, she peeled off her clothes down to her underwear. At least that had survived. She bent over and stuck her head in the sink to wash the blood out of her hair. She towel-dried what she could, leaving the clothes in the sink, wrapping the robe around her. She quickly pinned her hair out of her eyes and stepped out into the hallway. Everyone was quiet as they regarded her. She managed a weak smile.

"Sorry about having to borrow a robe."

"It is nothing, Anthea. You are well?"

"I am okay," she added, not wanting to meet Arkin's gaze. "Did Marta tell you that you would be staying with them this evening?"

"Yes, but I don't understand what happened."

"The witch wasn't with them, apparently," added Lang. His clothes were torn, and he was bloody, but he seemed in good spirits. "I understand from your staff, Master Asao, that you have an open-door policy, that anyone can come to speak with you. Knowing this, my guess is that he—that is, the witch—came to speak with Anthea this evening, knowing he would not be turned away. We found cigarette butts where he was waiting, and he got caught in the fight. His name was Theodore Worth. Do you know anyone by that name?"

"I don't work a lot with the witches. They handle their own problems. I haven't met Theodore, either in business or personally," answered Thea thoughtfully.

"My staff is on the phone to the various parties as we speak, but you don't need to know that. Take her back to wherever it is you are staying, Arkin. And I don't want to know."

"Once I get her to safety, we shall speak and decide on next steps."

Asao nodded as Jackson offered Thea a hand. She took it to steady her nerves as he walked her down the hall, avoiding various shards of glass, pools of blood, and out into the crisp night air. The rain had stopped and had formed puddles about the drive. The air was rife with moisture. She drew a deep breath as if to strengthen herself.

"Back to your place and then to our home?" Lang remarked. Arkin wanted her to have some of her things to make her feel comfortable in a strange place and among strange people.

"You mean your lair?" she asked as he swung her up into his arms, since she was barefoot. She gave a surprised yelp as he set her in the back seat of the car.

"I'll turn the heater on so she doesn't get cold," offered Jackson.

Thea was sandwiched between Marta and Arkin. She was staring at her hands lying on her lap, trying to get a grip on what happened. It was just supposed to be a simple discussion. Arkin hadn't made any moves against anyone, and yet they felt they had to fight. They had attacked him, not even on his own grounds, but involved Asao, and he was not happy. If the fight was unexpected for them, it must have freaked the poor witch out. Talk about being in the wrong place at the wrong time. They were going to be pissed at the vampires. There were going to be questions, like, Why was Worth waiting to see her? She hadn't a clue, unless… Denard's name flashed to mind. So far, he had just been a voice on the phone, but maybe he was the dark that Claire had foreseen. Thea mentally shook off the thoughts. She had one more thing to worry about, Arkin. The close quarters, the rush of adrenaline, and of course, the movement of his body against hers. It shouldn't have happened, but it was wonderful. She didn't dare look up to meet his gaze; just the feel of his body against hers made her leg burn. She was glad it was dark. Maybe he couldn't see her blush.

The car came to a halt outside the house. The porch light was on.

"Is Emlyn at home?" Arkin asked, voice clipped.

"He is out with Lucy this evening. I'll need to leave a note."

Arkin scooted out of the car, Thea following behind. As Lang had previously, he swung her up into his arms. She struggled briefly, but his grip was tight.

"Bare feet," he muttered in her ear.

She shivered as he put her down on the porch. She dug into her purse for her keys, opened the door, and entered. Polly must have been out back or at one of the businesses, because she hadn't come bounding up, tail wagging. She liked to be near someone most of the time, and she could find belly rubs just about anywhere.

"My go pack is in the front hall. I need to leave a note and pick up a pair of shoes."

"I don't want to stay much longer than we have to. If the attempt was more than just on us, they will want to ensure you are dead. You can't be dead if you turn up here."

He added as he stood in the hallway, leaning against a suitcase that was black with red hearts.

"Oh, no, no, no, not that suitcase. My go pack is the black duffel."

Arkin frowned as he looked down at the bag. "What is the difference?"

Thea bent over in the closet and pulled out the bag. She tore the other from his hands and shoved it back into the closet.

"That was a gift from Tasha. It is full of unmentionables."

Arkin frowned. "What is an unmentionable?" he asked, truly curious.

"Something you don't mention in mixed company," she remarked, exasperated. She stopped to look at him and that damnable smirk on his face. "Tasha likes her men and toys. She thought I might be interested in toys, and I don't mean Barbie."

"Oh," commented Arkin casually. "I understand."

"Good, 'cause I am just about ready to blow a gasket. I'm embarrassed enough." With duffel in hand, a pair of flip-flops on her feet, she moved to walk past Arkin.

Arkin gently grabbed Thea's arm. He turned and met her cool gaze as they stood in the front entry. Lang could see them from the road, and he wondered briefly what the deal was. He knew why the door was left open, for security reasons; he just wondered what the discussion involved.

"He's kind of stuck on her, isn't he?" Lang asked, curious. "It's a first, I have heard."

"In a very long time." Marta sighed. "Don't know whether it is a good or bad thing."

"Right now, it is just a thing," added Jackson. "I do like her, though."

"Are we going to talk about what happened at Asao's between you and me?" Arkin asked as she glanced down at his hand curled around her arm. She could feel the heat of him crawl up her body. He slowly released it, giving her free rein to move away or closer. She met his gaze, unabashed.

"Here is what I know, Arkin. It wasn't planned. It shouldn't have happened. Am I embarrassed? Yes! Will it happen again? I am hoping I have more control should a next time arise. And did I enjoy it? Yes. Does that answer your questions?"

Arkin's expression softened, a smirk appearing on his pouty lips. "That was exactly what I wanted to know."

Marta noticed that Arkin seemed rather full of himself as he sat in the car, body pressed up against Thea, who had laid the black duffel on her lap, eyes closed. He had that self-satisfied smirk that she didn't see very often. It was rare when he stopped worrying and relaxed or amused himself.

I can't read your expression, Marta remarked. *Not that I need to know, but you seem awfully pleased with yourself.*

Can we just say that I now have a fondness for tight places?

Marta rolled her eyes and turned away. *Only you could turn an attack into a positive event with the undertones of sex.*

How do I do it? he asked, chuckling to himself.

Thea felt the car turn a corner sharply. Her eyes flickered open as they passed through wrought iron gates. She stiffened slightly, eyes on the monster of a house ahead of them. It was a large stone house three stories high, with windows that looked like eyes, and on either side, two one-story rooms that always seemed to look like burly shoulders. Now, as an adult, she found the house had classic architecture.

"You're staying at the Carlyle residence?" she asked, voice sounding odd to everyone.

"Is there a problem?" Marta asked as Thea chuckled.

She shook her head. "Naw. Just that this was our town's haunted house when we were kids. It was the one we all dared everyone else to go and sneak a peek through the windows. My parents took a rather practical approach and explained that there were caretakers looking out for the house, though at times it didn't seem to look all that inviting. The owners of the house were away and there was nothing to be afraid of, and if I so desired, they would introduce me to the caretaker. Their feeling was that a house wouldn't kill you, live things might."

"How terribly true," quipped Lang.

Jackson pulled the car into the separate garage, lights scattering the shadows that lay across the covered walkway.

"If you don't mind? Marta will see you to your room, make sure you are comfortable. I am sure you want to wash up, considering that you ended up on your backside in a pool of blood."

"Thank you for not making some comment about that. I was trying to be careful."

"We are grateful you aren't hurt," Lang added with a curt nod, disappearing into the house.

With bag in hand, she followed Marta into the house. It was true that a house couldn't kill you but people in it could, and right now, she was surrounded by Arkin's men and women, a host of blood, shifters, and other magical beings. She shivered slightly as she followed Marta up the long flight of stairs.

"I bet you're tired," she commented.

"I'm sort of hungry as well," she added, glancing down the hallway.

"To your right and at the end, it is what we are calling the blue room." Marta swung open the door. It was blue, all right. "I'll make sure the bed is made. Go ahead and take your shower. I'll see what we have in the house. The carnivores might be ordering pizza."

Thea's eyes lit up as she entered the bedroom. It had a large sleigh bed, big enough for two and large double windows that looked over the front lawn. It had a decorative wood dresser and a makeup vanity. It was one of those rooms you dreamed of living in when you were a child.

"Okay?" Marta asked as Thea nodded quickly and headed to the bathroom. It was blue and white. It felt a bit cold until she turned on the water and drowned herself in hot steam. A small knock on the outer door let her know that Marta had returned with towels.

"I presume you have everything you need in your go pack?" she asked, curious.

"Yes. I don't use it that often, but the times I did, I made note of things that were missing and repacked so I am good to go." Thea turned off the water and wrapped her hair and then her body in the soft light-blue towels.

"I take it that Arkin doesn't own this house?"

"A friend of his lent it to him while he is here. I doubt it will be a final residence if he decides to stay."

Cagey, Thea thought as she stepped out wrapped in a towel. She thanked Marta with a smile as she wiped down the mirror.

"If you have everything you need, I'll leave you to it." Marta slipped out of the bathroom, out of the blue room, down the stairs, and into the study that Arkin was using as an office.

His face was a mixture of emotions. He and Asao had a lot to discuss. Arkin hung up the phone, eyes on Marta.

"Is she all set? Does she seem okay? She took quite a spill."

"She seems all right to me. Nice figure. She does have two marks on her back upper shoulders. Could be bruises, birthmarks, or scars. I don't think they are tattoos. Why are you thinking of going exploring? Just to caution you, she had curlers out of her bag and has some goop for her face. I hardly think that qualifies as attractive."

Arkin shrugged. "I guess that depends on what is under the goop."

"The nonblood want to order pizzas. You want to find out what she prefers on hers? She did say she was hungry." Marta tried and failed to hide her quirky smile. "Or is business keeping you from pleasure?"

"Asao's house was attacked. He is taking that very personally, so he is handling the next move, and I am with him on that. Tomorrow, perhaps. We will have to see."

"And how long are you keeping Thea?" Marta asked as she watched Arkin jog up the stairs. She failed to hear his whispered response.

Later, there was no sound of the shower as Arkin entered the blue room. He walked quietly up to the door and found Thea standing in front of the mirror, hair wrapped up in soft curlers, and she was just wiping something off her face.

"Do you really think that is going to stop me?" Thea frowned.

"Stop you from what?" she asked, uncertain what he meant.

Arkin closed the space between them. He took his left hand and cupped her chin, bringing her in for a very hot and delicious kiss, pulling her body closer to his. His right hand slipped up under the towel, dancing along her soft flesh upward toward her lush heat. She moaned into the kiss as he dared touch her. His thumb slowly rubbed in circles, causing her hips to push harder into him. Suddenly, he could feel her right hand caressing him through his trousers. He groaned, feeling an orgasm building, wishing that there wasn't the fabric between them. Their bodies worked at an unseen rhythm, Arkin thrusting two fingers gently into Thea, and he felt the explosion, how her body tightened around his fingers, clung to them, milking them with force. She was trembling in his arms, but her own passion hadn't stopped her from rubbing Arkin faster, bringing him over the precipice, making him come so sharply he pulled away from the kiss and drew in a surprised breath. Their eyes met, but no words had to be spoken until Marta's voice shattered the intimacy of the moment.

"I..." Arkin cleared his throat. "I was supposed to find out what you like on your pizza," he muttered to her, moving in to rub his face against hers.

"Pepperoni, extra cheese," she whispered as Arkin then shouted her preference to Marta.

"Great. Should be here in twenty." Arkin finally stepped away from Thea. "You are addictive, Anthea Black."

"I don't mean to be, and I guess you are right, curlers don't deter you."

"Nor does that lavender goop. I am after more than just your pretty face and luscious body."

Thea blushed, eyes turning away from Arkin as he glanced down, his trousers a mess.

"That hasn't happened to me in a very long time. You are a minx. I hope I am the first one you have ever done that to."

Thea's eyes narrowed, her lips in annoyance.

Arkin chuckled.

"Be ready for dinner in twenty. You will be allowed to go to work tomorrow, but one of my people will take you. I'll introduce you around tonight. This isn't settled until we see Ulrich."

"When do we see Ulrich?" she asked, curious.

"I already had an appointment to see Terence. Asao says that we should keep it, make no move against Ulrich, as if we didn't know that some of his people were involved, and then confront him. He wants our strength to be up in case we have to take him."

"And you trust Asao?" she asked pointedly.

"It was his home that was invaded. I came in peace with no agenda. He won't forgive that."

"And what does he gain? Does he become your second in the city?"

"Only if he earns it. You, my darling, have earned my admiration. You would be something in bed."

Thea opened her mouth to snipe back a comment, but Arkin was already leaving the bathroom. That shouldn't have happened, but it was wonderful.

The pizza arrived in twenty minutes. Thea congregated with the other humans over several boxes of hot pizza and soda. There were introductions, casual conversation, and it was decided that Shona would be her bodyguard tomorrow. Shona was a big girl with blond hair, bright blue eyes, and the physique of a Valkyrie. Both Marta and Lang watched Thea warily from a distance. She met their gazes with a smile, a nod, but ignored their curiosity. She was too tired to think right now. It had been a hell of a night. When the clock chimed two, she had decided to head back up to bed. With her flowered pajamas on, hair still up in soft curlers, she was ready to settle down for the night. If someone had told her she would be sleeping in the house she always thought was haunted, she would laugh. It was a nice place inside, all the comforts of home, but it didn't feel like Arkin Kane. It had been beyond daring to touch him the way she did, but it had felt good to have some control, to see him lose his. She had just crawled into bed, snuggled down in the sheets, when the bedroom opened.

"I came to say good night. I hope you sleep well, though I wouldn't mind having you at my side. I wouldn't want to color your reputation."

"I have a rather pristine reputation, but that wasn't created on purpose, it just happened. I'm not usually as bold as I was tonight."

"I enjoyed it. I haven't had a release like that in a long time. It was almost painful. You are very responsive to my touch. I rather like that."

"Don't embarrass me, Arkin. I'm not very good at playing the bad girl," Thea said. "I thought those of the blood slept during the day."

He chuckled.

"You know a bit about us, but not all there is to know. Maybe sometime we can discuss it, in bed." He crossed the room swiftly, planting a sweet kiss on her lips and forehead before leaving her to a blissful night's sleep.

CHAPTER 8

Shona was assigned to be her security. Anthea didn't know if the woman had volunteered or lost a bet, but it would be her job to drive her to work, then pick her up at the end of the day, and drive her back again. It was Adam, a human detective, who would be following her when she was out of their sight or away from Arkin's protection. He was good at what he did. A onetime police officer turned private eye with a team of his own had been instrumental in Arkin's fold and took his job very seriously. He wouldn't be needed today since Shona was acting as escort or bodyguard, but it never hurt to get the lay of the land, to see where Black worked, where she lived, and whom she agreed to meet with. He had helped Chrisanne and Cherise dig down deep and discover she was adopted, and he was certain there was more to Anthea Black than met the eye. He sensed it in his gut; you didn't argue with his gut. Adam Beckford was average in height, average in looks, so he blended in a crowd easily and was hard to remember or to pick out of a crowd. He liked average just fine, but he had an above-average intelligence. He would be Shona's backup just in case, because like Arkin, those of the blood also had their daytime allies.

It had been a quiet ride in, Shona preferring music to conversation, which suited Thea just fine. There wasn't a lot to say, and the car was more than comfortable. It was nice to be able to enjoy looking out the window and letting her mind wander. Thea wished it were as peaceful when she walked into work. Emlyn was waiting for her at the reception, concern plain on his face, gaze staring at Shona as she pulled away from the curb in front of the mortuary. He turned and regarded his sister, who met his gaze head-on, as if she was ready for the challenge. He realized she wasn't wearing her customary suit, but a very pretty color-block dress, showing very nice cleavage.

"You want to explain your note?" he asked, sounding surly.

She exhaled. "I thought it was pretty succinct. It said that Asao was attacked while we were with him and that I was forced to stay with Arkin. I am not going to argue with a vampire. What part of that didn't you understand?"

"Pert. What I wanted to know is if you are all right. Not a scratch on you?"

Thea turned around to let her brother look her over. "Just as good as I was when I left you, though there are others who can't say the same."

"And your pretty big chauffeur?"

Thea could hear the agitation in her brother's voice. "Think back to the note. We were attacked, and Arkin doesn't know why or whom they wanted to kill or disable. He has already scheduled a visit with Terence this evening, and as a witness, I have to be there. There are others who worry about me besides you, Em, and sometimes I'm too tired to argue. He knows the law as well as you do. He asked for me to be present, so it is his job to protect me. You know that as well as I do. You think I should fold and run when the you know what hits the fan?"

"Was he worried about you personally or the fact that you are a silent witness to the city?"

She shrugged, setting her purse down and ignoring Matt, who was sitting at the desk, trying to ignore them. He was having a hard time looking busy. So far, the phone had been silent.

"Both or either, it doesn't matter, as long as I am safe. Correct?"

Emlyn snorted and ran a hand through his hair, pacing before his sister. She refrained from a smile.

"Yes, of course, but…it doesn't matter." He turned and hugged her. She patted him warmly on the back.

"Are we okay? You didn't seem to have any qualms about this part of my job when Mom and Dad prepared me for this. I have been doing this a while, and I can tell you, that Yardley was a hell of a lot more mean to me than Arkin has been thus far."

"Yeah, but those days seemed less complicated," Em remarked.

"And they will be again." Thea smiled. "Arkin will clean up the city, and we will all go back to doing what we were doing," she added optimistically.

"And will you be doing what you do alone or with Arkin?"

Her eyes narrowed, and Emlyn realized he might have overstepped his bounds. They should not be discussing this either in front of Matt. This was the first time Em sounded like he was trying to be an older brother; it was damn annoying.

"Very cheeky. Do I make comments about you and Lucy or whomever you decide to date? Did I make any snide remarks when you had to be present for certain events of the Seven? I don't throw stones at love. It is too rare."

Emlyn took her arm and gently led her toward the sales floor, amid the silence of the coffins. His voice was low.

"You are an adult, and you know what you are getting into."

She nodded at him. "Yes, I am, and right now I just want to get into work." She was shutting this conversation down.

"Fine," Em answered with a sigh as he shook his head and left her standing alone among the silky satins and hard polished wood.

She smoothed back her hair, prepared to go back to work, when in through the front door walked Esther Caldwell, the local head of the coven of witches. That was all she needed. Thea put on her best professional smile and walked over to greet her. Esther was one of those women who liked to wear broomstick skirts and crystal pendants, going with the natural look, her hair a pile of dark curls messily piled atop her head. It totally put people at ease. People who met her—at least most humans, that is—didn't know that she was a really powerful witch. Thea had met her on two other occasions. They were acquaintances, but they were not friends.

"Good morning, Ms. Caldwell. How can I help you today?" she asked as professionally as she could.

"Is there somewhere we can speak in private?"

Thea thought a moment. "Would it offend you if we talked in the chapel?"

Esther laughed lightly, shaking her head. "Not at all. Lead the way."

Thea gestured past the front reception desk to the adjoining door. "My team will have finished with the flowers, so we won't have anyone in there until this afternoon. There is a wedding."

Esther followed Thea up the steps, through another door, and into an array of flowers by the altar. She gestured Esther into one of the cushioned pews. The chapel was empty, silent, colored light dancing through the arched windows on either side of the chapel, painting them in splendor. Thea seated herself and waited for Esther to speak.

"I'm here about Teddy Worth."

Thea nodded. She was not terribly surprised. "I am sorry about his death. I wish I knew why he wanted to see me, but as you know, I don't do much professional work with your coven."

"I know. That is why I am wondering why he came to you, or needed to see you. I understand that you are working as a silent witness with this Arkin Kane, a new blood in town."

"Yes. He wants to clean up the disorganization, but I am only doing what I normally do. Teddy was just a casualty of being somewhere at the wrong time."

Esther sighed, chin resting on her hand as she leaned against the pew. She was silent for a few moments. She had hoped for more information than that.

"What did Teddy do in the coven, if you don't mind me asking?"

"He was security. He, like the other paranormals in the city, watch for anything dangerous, or maybe a better word is *abnormal*." She watched as Thea smiled.

"That is a big area to watch," Thea commented.

"And normally we don't have any problems. We don't watch the blood. We don't watch the fey or the shifters. They monitor their own people. We watch for things that dangerously slip through the cracks."

Thea stiffened slightly, Esther noticing.

"You thought of something?"

Thea wished she had a better poker face; she wasn't sure if she wanted to trust Esther with this information, but then again, the more information they had, the better they could act. The more people they could keep safe.

"I had a call from a Tony Denard the other day. I don't know him, but he seemed to want to meet with me. He was cryptic."

Esther frowned.

"I haven't heard from him since, nor has he shown up here to speak with me."

Esther nodded.

"I had my people do a background check. There wasn't anything terribly unusual about him, and I don't even know if he is in the city."

"Do you think this might be connected with why Teddy came to see you? Why did this Denard call you? You think the call was business-oriented? Better yet, why do you think he would offer violence?"

Thea shook her head. They were a lot of good questions. "All very good questions, Esther, and I wish I had answers. All I can say is that his name just popped into my head when you asked why Teddy might have wanted to see me. That is the only unknown in my life right now. My father always said, 'Listen to your gut.' That was his sixth sense."

"We all know that while you appear human, there is something decidedly different about you, but I don't get an evil vibe from you. In fact, no one I have talked to wants to talk about what they sense or delve into it any deeper than what we think we know. You aren't totally human, there is enough of that about you, but nothing more."

Thea shrugged.

"If I asked you pointedly, would you tell me?"

"No, because it doesn't have a bearing on who I am or what I do. You have to trust me when I tell you I am not a threat. It is just blood." Her voice was firm.

"I will take your word for it now, but if it causes a problem later on, we may have words."

Thea nodded.

"Do you think this Tony is here for you? I heard Claire spouting some premonition about you, and while we like her, humor her, sometimes you don't know where the warnings will come from. This sounds like a warning."

"And don't you claim to be keepers of the light? Can't you find the darkness that might be coming this way?"

"I wish it worked like that, but magic is complicated," Esther remarked firmly.

"Isn't everything?" Thea asked. "I am sorry about Teddy. I wish I could have spoken with him. I wish he had survived the attack."

"Will your Arkin do something about that?" she asked, gaze narrow on Thea.

She didn't flinch from the stare and met Esther's gaze instead. "He isn't *my* Arkin, Esther. But yes, he will be confronting Ulrich."

"Good, because if he doesn't, I will." Esther promptly rose, smoothed her dark-brown skirt, and proceeded down the chapel, her sandaled feet quiet on the carpeted aisle.

Thea remained in the pew a while longer, enjoying the silence and the fragrant air. It was coming down to a revelation, and she feared she would be the one revealed.

* * *

Thea knew it was quitting time when Shona showed up in reception. She looked around, appraising the place and looking at Matt with curiously flirty eyes. Thea stepped from the prep room, surprised to see her so soon. She glanced at her watch. Where had the day gone?

"I thought we could get something to eat before we go meet the boss."

Thea, mildly interested, nodded. Boss—it made Arkin sound like some businessman, but it was better than the word *master*.

"All right, let me get my purse. Matt, this is Shona, a colleague of Arkin's. Shona, this is Matt, a changeling and employee."

They nodded, Shona extending a hand to him. Thea could almost feel the energy spark between them. She rolled her eyes as she entered the prep room, hand moving to the coatrack, where her purse hung. Em entered, with his girlfriend, Lucy, a step behind him. Odd that he would have allowed her back into the prep room; non-employees just didn't visit behind the scenes. But sometimes he didn't think with his head.

"You heading off now to another meeting?" he asked, holding Lucy's hand.

"This one I hope will be more courteous. Lucy."

Lucy was a tall lithe girl with golden-brown hair and tigerlike eyes. She was pretty, but not an alpha, so Thea didn't feel so obliged to be threatened by her jealousy. They were brother and sister; that would never change. There wasn't anything between them, save her secret, and one day the world would know it too.

"Thea," she remarked coolly. "You have been busy."

"Such is the life. We both are. See you when I see you," she added, ignoring the edge to Lucy's voice. Life was too short to play games.

"You look nice today. Dressing to impress?" Lucy asked. "Or to attract?"

Thea looked down at her dress. "Actually, this was in my go bag. It's a nonwrinkle, two-sided dress. It was handy." With purse over her shoulder, she darted out into reception, leaving her brother to deal with the attitude.

Matt and Shona were chatting casually. Thea hoped Emlyn wouldn't marry Lucy, because unless there was a turnaround in her attitude, Thea was never going to like the bitch.

Since Shona didn't know the area, Thea took her to Edden's. They had time for a leisurely meal before they had to be back at the house and Arkin was awake, at least chose to make an appearance. Adam had followed them to the pub/restaurant, but he wouldn't have to follow this evening; he knew where they were going. He would be there before they arrived, just another car wrapped in shadows. It never hurt to have another set of eyes on them this evening, especially after the unexpected attack. Adam knew enough about Arkin, that he was making Ulrich wait. The anticipation must be killing the vampire, because if he knew anything about the blood, it was that they didn't like to be kept waiting, especially if it might be bad news. Ulrich had two of the blood pissed at him, Arkin and Asao. Waiting would be torture. Adam smiled.

They all arrived to the party in separate vehicles. Asao waited for them at the curb, just outside the decorative wrought iron fencing of Terence's house. Arkin sat in the back of his SUV, turned to his side, and met Thea's gaze. They didn't speak for a few seconds.

"I was never much of a believer in fate, but I wonder now that I have met you."

She shook her head at such a romantic notion. "Don't be foolish," she hissed as he leaned down and kissed her right in the center of her breasts.

He drew a long breath of her scent. His gaze was heated as he raised his head and met her surprised expression. He flung open the door and stepped out into the night, the devil. Thea sputtered for a moment before following. She needed just a moment to regain her composure. She caught sight of Asao standing at the bricked pathway. Security had already opened for them the gates that led into a garden. The house seemed fairly hidden, but that was the way Terence liked it, hard to see anything from the road. As usual, there were, of course, eyes on them as they approached, Arkin's and Asao's security taking the lead, followed by Arkin, Thea, and Asao. There was a tenseness in the air, all eyes looking for a threat. The three of them stopped sharply as the door to the house, that resembled an English Tudor, opened to reveal Terence. Despite what anyone might think, Arkin and Terence had met many a century ago, and it was doubtful that Terence remembered. He remembered those that could do something for him and dismissed the rest. Thea had said that he was a shark; well, he would circle Arkin if he sensed a weakness. He was dressed to impress with an expensive suit, hair combed just so, gaze coolly detached, as if he didn't care about their visit. Oh, he cared, all right. And Thea thought that there might be a flicker of nervousness around his eyes. To her dismay, Tasha was standing at his side, dressed in ballet flats and a black corset dress, her hair in curls up around her head. Dressed not for success, but maybe seduction. She was playing the look-at-me-I'm-not-a-danger card, which Thea knew better about. Tasha stood next to Terence, eyeing Arkin with blatant, heated interest. She tugged on her curl slightly, a twitch of her lip as she smiled. It was one of those stand-offs, alphas each sizing the other up, so Thea pushed her way past the blood-born and took the initiative.

"Terence, may I present Arkin, and Asao. Arkin, may I introduce to you Terence, and Tasha, who is an unexpected guest this evening."

"I don't like to wait on handsome men," she quipped.

Terence extended his hand first to Arkin, and then to Asao. There was a shaking of hands. Arkin brought Tasha's hand to his lips. She giggled suggestively, but there didn't seem to be any heat in his gaze as he played her game. Yeah!

"Also, Jenner is Terence's second, and Kale is Tasha's. Now, can we go into the house and not stand on the doorstep like some lawn jockey?" Thea brushed past Tasha, entering the front hallway. The others followed.

Arkin had brought Marta, and Asao brought Yokayo. That rounded everyone out. Tasha looked down her eyes at Thea, who was the shortest in the room. Even Asao was taller. Yeah, she was vertically challenged.

"My, I have to say, that dress gives you a good cleavage. Hardly businesslike, however."

"I was under quarantine. I wear what I have in my go bag," added Thea, more than mildly annoyed, and if Kale didn't stop staring at her breasts, she was going to pop him one right in the snout.

"Have you brought Asao here as your second?" Terence asked as they stood in the archway that led to the salon. The room was very masculine and dark in nature, but Thea had been there before, so it wasn't a surprise that the house mirrored what Terence liked. She plopped down on her favorite brown brocade chaise.

"I came because if there is another fight, I want to be part of it. I gave my assurances to Arkin that he would be safe. It never occurred to me that Ulrich and others would violate that trust, or our law, so blatantly," Asao remarked, voice holding an edge to it.

"Times have changed," commented Terence dryly.

"Well, they will change back," retorted Arkin firmly as he looked into the room.

"I have to say that I am a bit surprised that you decided to keep this appointment. I would have thought Ulrich was at the top of the list to deserve a visit."

Arkin chuckled coolly, entering the room. He chose a rather overstuffed deep-gold wingback chair to sit in. He looked up, regarding Terence casually. Thea had to say that Arkin could command a room, even in someone else's home.

"One day gives him time to either clean house, apologize for the lapse, or prepare to die. Either is fine with me."

Tasha raised a curious eyebrow as she danced into the room, sitting on a small round ottoman as close to Arkin as she could, to get a good look at him. Kale lingered between his mistress and Thea.

"We should offer you something to drink, shouldn't we, Terence? Thea? Something virgin, perhaps?"

Thea sighed, looking up at Terence.

"I'll have a Maker's Mark, neat, no ice, no need to kill it with kindness." She could afford to drink. After all, liquor didn't affect her. More's the shame. She also didn't always like to be predictable. Plus, she didn't feel like tea.

"Fine, then we can do business," added Terence. "Tasha thought she would save you a trip. After all, you seemed to want to meet with each of us. You think you can clean up the city?"

"I think I can get it back on its feet again. We won't have territories, but we will be respected. We will be supportive of one another and prosperous. To have such factions invites usurpers and chaos. I am not fond of chaos."

"Isn't that what we could call you? You just happen to waltz in and try to clean up what you think is a mess?" Terence asked bluntly.

"Don't you think it is a mess? How can you do business when you can't trust your own blood? We are one race, we should behave as such," answered Arkin as a tray was brought, Thea served first.

Both Kale and Tasha were startled to see her down it in a few single gulps. She sighed and leaned back, waiting to listen to what Arkin and the others had to say. There were times when this job was boring, but other times, when, hell, it was very entertaining, all she needed was popcorn. This was a reality show at its best.

Terence took a sip of his blood, Asao doing the same. Arkin waited for the next comment.

"I see you met our silent witness rather quickly. Your meeting was luck, or it was calculation."

Arkin smiled, taking a sip of the blood. "It, perhaps, was both, but Anthea Black is not the issue here. Our standing in this city is. You are either part of the problem or part of the solution, to use a very old phrase. It matters not to me."

Terence eyed Arkin, sizing him up, and in truth, Arkin didn't look all that dangerous, and yet he had killed already three of his own kind. "You are very cavalier about all this," he commented, voice wavering slightly.

"Because you all should have taken care of this. We are all old souls. We have been through good times and dangerous times. You do not invite others to fix your problems for you, nor do you anger them and make them suspicious. You have laid open this city and your business concerns. It must be fixed quickly, and I have met with the Seven, as it were, and confirmed that I am to do just that."

"And what do you promise us?" Tasha asked, curious.

"That everything will stay as it is as far as your businesses are concerned, but there is a hierarchy here. There must be laws and controls put in place so something like this doesn't happen again."

"And you want to be our master?" Terence asked, voice just above a whisper. He was holding on to some tether of control.

"If you were up for the job, Terence, you would already be sitting in residence at Yardley's manse," added Asao. "Or were you waiting for others to weaken and slip right in?"

"If I had wanted to do that, it would not have been Ulrich's brood who attacked you. I would have been leading the charge. I want what is best for this city. Not all of us who are blood wanted to be made blood. Not all of us were suited to immortality and such power."

"Agreed. That is why we should be careful whom we bring in," added Tasha. "We are not the absolute power here."

"No, but we need to be a power. I have had my say. You can ask anyone who has worked with me, but I am fair, I listen, and I do not have inclination to rule the world," Arkin added.

"Just our sliver of it?" Terence asked, inquiring.

Thea could see that he was relaxing now; the tension seemed to have ebbed from his body slightly.

"And do you intend to take one of us as your second, or perhaps a mate?" Tasha asked, leaning forward to show her cleavage off to her advantage. She was breathtaking.

"I trust my people foremost, Tasha. Until I am shown that I can trust all of you, no one is my second. However, Asao shows great promise."

"You speak as if you have done this before and expect us to fall under your tutelage, call you our general," muttered Terence softly. "Yet I do not know your name."

Arkin shifted casually in the chair, setting his crystal wineglass aside.

"We have all moved through time under different guises and names. And you are right, I have done this a thousand times before, and no one ever said that they were sorry for following me. It is up to you. Stay or go. Your position can be filled by others wanting to prosper in peace."

"You think me so easily to displace?" he asked, jaw tense.

"No, I think right now you are in doubt. You don't want to trust me, or fear me, but you do. If you are waiting to see if Ulrich can displace me, you have a long wait. He will either fall into line or die. I will not have our people at the mercy of others. You know what that is like as well as I do. It is a different era. These are different times. We do not go to war with swords and armor. These days we do it politely, with lawyers, but there is something to say for a strong hand. Am I wrong?"

"No," answered Asao. "You are not wrong. You don't have to make a decision now, Terence, or Tasha. I am with Arkin just so you know."

"You have never wanted to fight. What has changed your mind now?" Terence asked, turning on Asao.

"I will fight to keep what is mine and to keep our peace. I have children that I do not want to see destroyed. I have trained them in the old ways, and even they don't like seeing the shift."

"And that is all you have come to say?" Tasha asked. She turned, looking at Thea. Thea met her gaze with a smile. "You seem to be very fond of our silent witness."

"Ms. Black has been a valuable resource. I can't tell you how many times we have tried to find a reliable witness. Sometimes we were lucky, other times we failed, and yet we have one who will sit in residence with any of us paranormals. Such a position deserves respect, for we can be a trial to anyone. I find I like her very much."

"And as master of this city, will you take what you find you like?" Kale asked pointedly.

Arkin slowly rose from the chair, eyes not leaving Kale's. You could feel the tension up slightly.

"I don't take what is not freely given. However, I will protect what is mine, and ours. She is under my protection. If no one else will man up, I do. The Seven will."

"And you believe you have commanded respect from the Seven already?" Kale asked gently, as if fearful of stirring Arkin's ire.

"They are waiting to see if I can hold true to my words. Once that happens, then I will have their respect," stated Arkin.

"And what of Ulrich?"

Arkin glanced at Asao, letting him answer Tasha's question.

"It was my residence that was violated. They were my people and a wayward witch. He has to pay, and if that is in blood, so be it."

There were a few moments of silence that followed Asao's statement, as if no one was quite sure how to continue the conversation. It was Arkin who motioned to Thea. She stood gracefully, smoothed her dress, and joined Arkin by his chair.

"I see you have already made up your mind," Tasha remarked tersely. Thea met her eyes, showing no fear, which startled Tasha. All this time, she seemed like a pliable young woman. Maybe Tasha was wrong to goad her.

"I would have liked to think that we were friends, Tasha, but maybe I was wrong. Perhaps I was more of a toy for you to play with and amuse yourself."

"And you have known me longer than Arkin, my girl. I would have thought that you knew better than to side with the unknown. I did consider us friends. I am disappointed."

"Is it that sliver of blood in you that isn't human that makes you so bold to taunt us so?" Terence asked, looking down at her.

She managed a soft smile. "I have always been bold, Terence, but no one noticed before. And my blood is mine, not yours for the taking. You shouldn't be so brave when you don't know what you are dealing with."

With that cryptic remark said, Thea stepped away from Arkin and Asao, walking to the archway door, where Marta was standing.

"I'll be in the car."

Voices drifted in the air. Thea could hear them very clearly. Asao thought the discussion went well, though it was off to a rocky start. He was pleased that Akin wasn't distracted by Tasha and her wiles, if you wanted to call them that. They stood on the sidewalk, speaking softly before parting company. Arkin climbed into the car and met her gaze. She already had her seat belt on and arms folded across her chest. He didn't know if she was angry or just cold.

"I presume you are ready to go home?" he asked dryly.

"Terence is an idiot. Just go ahead and poke the skunk," hissed Thea.

"Am I the skunk, or are you the skunk?" Arkin asked with a smile.

Marta snorted.

"I think we both are. So what happened after I left?" she asked, curious.

"Terence and Tasha both pledged to me. That only leaves Margaux and Ulrich."

"You may have to kill Ulrich," Thea remarked.

"I might at that, but killing him won't keep me awake, as you humans say."

"Won't keep me awake either," Thea replied honestly.

"I take it you think that you can go home safely tonight?" he asked.

"Ulrich is still out there, and I haven't heard your phone ringing for an apology. You think he might try to hurt me?"

"If he thought it might hurt me, yes."

Thea looked at him with fluttering eyelashes, amusement on his face. He cared.

"And we only just met. You are easy, aren't you, Arkin Kane?"

Arkin cleared his throat as his phone rang.

"Speak of the devil, maybe," muttered Marta as the car pulled away from the curb.

They watched as Arkin listened to the caller, revealing nothing, if not very little. It was strictly "Yes," "No," and "I understand."

"I hate it when he does that," remarked Marta as Arkin closed the call with a polite goodbye. "Talking but not really saying anything."

"Do you know where Ulrich lives?" he asked Thea.

She nodded. "Yes. Do you need directions?" she asked, anxious.

"Yes. There has been a coup. I am requested."

Thea drew a breath of surprise, almost on the edge of her seat if she weren't already belted in.

"Who couped whom?" Jackson asked from the driver's seat.

"Emily couped Ulrich."

The amazement on Thea's face was almost worth it. Her mouth opened, but nothing came out.

"I take it that was unexpected?" Arkin asked as Thea managed to nod. "Do you know Emily?"

"Yes, just in passing. She never seemed like the violent type. Maybe it is always the quiet ones."

"Well, necessity makes us that way. She took care of Ulrich, along with a few others. Now they want to pledge to me."

Thea sighed, leaning back in the seat, stunned. Wow, she hadn't seen that coming.

"I need directions," asked Jackson.

Thea gave Jackson directions. They weren't that far away from Ulrich's compound, as he called it. It was one of those large plantation-like houses with columns that you would expect to see along the Mississippi. Lights blazed in the darkness, and somewhere in the distance, a dog barked. The night was in turmoil.

Emily met Arkin at the door to the house, standing at the threshold splattered with blood. She stood tall, rather proud. If she had beaten Ulrich, then she deserved that look of triumph. Arkin stepped from the car, Thea ducking her head out, wondering if she should join him. He extended a hand to her. *Rats.* She had to take it to be polite. Thea joined him on the lower step, walking with him up toward where Emily was standing. Emily had been wearing a light-gray shirt and dress trousers. The shirt would never be able to be worn again; it was now decorated with blobs and sprays of blood in a surprisingly decorative pattern. Her long ash-blond hair hung about her face, stiff; the expression on her face was one of glory. Her eyes twinkled. There wasn't any other way to describe it. She had won.

"Arkin Kane, welcome. I am sorry to have called you on such short notice, but sometimes these things come as a surprise to all of us. It is as I have said: Ulrich is dead, and those who supported his tyranny have also passed. What stands before you and awaits your oath is loyal blood-born."

Thea watched as Arkin took her hand and placed it over his heart.

"You were brave, indeed, Emily. You have my thanks, and my thanks go out to those who assisted you."

Emily nodded as she turned and gestured him to follow her into the house. Thea followed behind him and beside Marta. Marta whistled slightly. The place looked like someone had spray-painted red across the walls. You could smell that copper in the air. It would make most humans ill, but Thea had seen worse but wouldn't dare speak about it.

"It will need to be cleaned, but I would like to stay here, if you will have me stand in Ulrich's stead."

Arkin looked down at the pile of dead. Ulrich was on the bottom, that much Thea could see. His hand, with his signature ruby ring, lay out from underneath another body. Thea counted at least six bodies. Emily had been busy.

"You are most welcome to stay. You have shown your worth and loyalty. It is unexpected."

"You should not have to clean up our mess. He should not have sent others into Asao's home and tried to kill you, let alone a silent witness."

Thea was certain that Emily had lost someone because of Ulrich's pride.

"I thought I would save you the trouble. We are honored that you have come to our city. I would not have thought it a possibility."

There was a subtle silence that fell about the room, and something unspoken passed between Emily and Arkin. Thea had the feeling that Emily knew or had guessed just how important Arkin might be. If she didn't know him personally, she suspected who he was or who he had been. Emily glanced at Marta and Jackson.

"I should like you to trust me. You do not need to fear for yourself or for Ms. Black. We are yours."

Arkin nodded, impressed.

"Margaux will not be difficult. If you like, I can speak to her prior to your visit. I will also let Asao know that he does not need to seek revenge."

"Very thoroughly taken care of, Emily. It is impressive," added Marta with a nod. "Congratulations on your promotion."

Emily laughed. "I didn't want to resort to the old way of doing things, but sometimes they just don't listen to reason."

"Yeah. Men, what are you going to do with them, kiss them or kill them?" Marta chuckled lightly. "Thanks for the invitation. Sorry we were late to the party."

Emily inclined her head, and Arkin surveyed the others that had gathered, peering out of doorways and rooms. It was a mixed bag of blood-born, humans, and a few shifters. Word would spread rapidly that the blood were falling into line. The city would be back to normal soon, or as normal as it could be.

"You have my thanks, Emily. When we arrive at a certain position, we must remember that we were put there for a reason and by our people. If we fail in their faith, they are likely to call us to account for it. I will send Sean, one of my people, to come discuss the ascension. You will have the rights to his businesses. We can help you sort out what needs to be done. See if anything needs to be fixed."

She nodded as Thea took a few steps back out of the room, drawing deep breaths. There would be no bodies come the rising of the sun. They would be deposited on the lawn and turn to ash. It was a fitting end. Thea felt as if a weight had been lifted off her shoulders. Her life would soon be her own again. After Margaux, Arkin would be on his own again. He wouldn't need her for business, unless he wanted her for something else. That thought made her shiver slightly. Arkin laid his jacket over her shoulders as he joined her on the front step, thinking she might be cold, or at least in slight shock over the pile of dead in such a well-kept house.

"I am sorry you had to see that."

She chuckled. "I work in a mortuary. I have seen the dead, just not walls painted in blood. It was a fight."

"Yes, one I didn't have to participate in. For that, I am grateful."

"I got the feeling that Emily did it for you, as if she knew something about you. Don't tell me that there wasn't something unseen that didn't pass between the two of you."

"You are very astute, but we all have to have our secrets. If you would like to share one with me, I will reciprocate."

Thea remained quiet, just fluttering her eyelashes at him.

"Does that work with your brother?"

It never had.

"It works on most men." She paused. "So I can go home now?" she asked, sounding tired.

"I think you are safe, at least from the blood, for the time being. I will need to let Asao know what has happened, and I will contact you when I need to see Margaux."

Thea nodded as he gestured her toward the car.

"I would have preferred that it ended another way, but sometimes you can't reason, or they can't see the sense."

"What did you think of Tasha? Emily seemed suitably impressed, if you wanted a lapdog."

Arkin cleared his throat as he climbed into the car beside her. He impulsively kissed her on the lips, a rather chaste kiss, but enough to grab her attention.

"Do I detect a hint of jealousy?"

Thea's eyes narrowed as she glowered at him. He chuckled.

"Tasha is much like many women I have met. That sort does not impress me. As for Emily, she was flushed from battle. I am her new liege, and you, my dear silent witness, have my interest."

Thea opened her mouth to reply, but Arkin kissed her again, this time more deeply, his tongue dancing with hers, until they heard Jackson cough, making enough noise to tell them that he was getting in the car and their privacy was at an end. Thea broke the kiss, flushed.

"Does that answer your question?" Arkin asked in a whisper.

"Yes and no," murmured Thea.

Jackson drove them back to where Arkin was staying temporarily. Thea imagined that he would be moving into Yardley's home soon; it would be more suitable for those born of the blood after they disposed of Yardley's taste in decor. Thea found her duffel where she had left it by the front door. She was surprised when she returned to the car to find that Arkin was waiting for her in the back seat with Jackson at the wheel.

"You don't have to come with me. Jackson knows where we are going."

"I owe you a debt, and I would not see you just drive off with another man. I will escort you home."

"This isn't a date," Thea remarked, trying to keep her eyes forward as the car pulled away from the house.

"No, but maybe one day we can have a date," Arkin remarked.

Thea turned to regard him with curious eyes. "Really? You find me that interesting, that appealing, and you don't mind mixing business with pleasure?"

Arkin chuckled. "And what sort of pleasures are you thinking of, Thea?"

Thea cleared her throat, flushed, as she turned away from him. She could feel her thigh pressed against hers, his arm brushing her shoulder, the flush warming her body. She was extremely happy when they arrived at the house. She almost bolted out the door, but it was Arkin's hand that stayed her escape. She turned to meet those lovely eyes.

"I'll call you."

She smiled at his remark. "Men always say that," she quipped.

"I'm not just any man," he added, and she knew he was right. But she just wasn't any girl.

Emlyn had heard the car door slam, so he opened the front door, holding Polly eagerly back by the collar. He smiled, happy to see that his sister was home for the evening, somewhere he could keep his eye on her. He watched his sister bound up the walk, an odd expression on her face. She bent over and kissed Polly on the head and then hugged him.

"I take it that he thinks you are safe for the evening?" Em closed the door as Thea tossed down her duffel in the front hall.

"Things are afoot, and do I have stuff to tell you."

He watched as she kicked off her shoes, entering the living room. She curled up in her favorite blue chair, eyes on Emlyn.

"Okay, something good or something bad?" he asked tentatively.

"Terence and Tasha have pledged an oath to Arkin, and Emily killed Ulrich."

Em's mouth fell open in amazement. He barely noted that he had seated himself on the ottoman. Polly sat down and pawed at him for some love. He absently stroked her head.

"Emily? Man, I had her wrong. I thought she was some sweet little obedient…so that is why you are back? Arkin thinks you are safe now?"

"For the moment. Once he sees Margaux, he will be able to call them all together and get his city and their businesses started. Then things should be back to normal. The Seven will be pleased. The witches will want to meet with him after he is crowned so-called master, yada, yada, yada."

"You sound sort of wistful," added Em, curious.

She sighed and shrugged. "I don't like drama, you know that, and I want everything to get back to what was at least normal for us."

"But are you worried you won't see Arkin again?"

She frowned at him."

Don't play, give me that innocent little stare, or flutter those eyelashes. I know you too well. Look, I don't claim to be any great, knowledgeable lover. Relationships come and go, but it is nice to see you are thinking of having one. There is more to life than work, and I would like to see you happy."

"Even if it is with a member of the blood?"

"Even if. I won't be around forever, you know that."

Thea looked down at the patterns on her dress.

"It would be nice to know that you have someone looking out for you."

"You don't think they are evil incarnate? Or that my interaction with them will blacken my eternal soul?"

Em smiled softly, patting her leg. "Even if he could try, he couldn't do it. You are a rare gem, Thea. I know that, even if it is only our little secret. But that is what scares you, isn't it? That someone other than me might figure it out."

She flicked her hand at him as if to say it didn't worry her. "The thought crossed my mind. It isn't such a terrible secret, but it is something inexplicable. You either live with it or you let it loose on the world."

He shrugged. "And you live with either consequence. Why don't you go to bed? No more thinking tonight. We have work tomorrow. It's a full day. Will we have the bodies from the coup?"

"I don't think anyone is going to want to save the ashes." She stood with a groan. "After all, we are talking about Ulrich. If he had wanted friends to look after him when he died, he should have made some."

"Sis, he didn't think he was going to die," added Em.

How true.

Chapter 9

Em had been right, of course, since he had studied the calendar. It was a busy day. They had two weddings in the chapel, three funerals, flowers requested galore, and the odd number of surprise corpses. By the time the end of the day rolled around, Thea was going to be ready for a hot bath, some curlers to do something with her hair, and a good movie to watch. Em begged off. Apparently, he had an appointment and she didn't ask. He hadn't called it a date, so maybe it was a business meeting. She hoped it wasn't Lucy. Thea had nothing against changelings and shifters, but Lucy had an attitude that didn't seem to be going away. Thea pushed back a stray strand of hair, shrugged out of her lab coat, and grabbed her purse. Carly was sitting at the desk, finishing up paperwork and looking over the orders for tomorrow.

"Busy day, huh?" she asked as Thea nodded. "I heard that Ulrich is doing the dance of the dead. Emily did him in."

Gossip ran like water in this town.

"You wouldn't be wrong in that assumption. I am guessing that everyone is happy about his demise?"

Carly nodded as she opened the side drawer and brought up a piece of chocolate.

"Everyone who knew what an ass he was, yeah. Emily, huh? Always the quiet ones that get you in the end. Night."

Thea nodded to Carly, not interested in rumor. After all, she was kind of there. Thea had her mind set on a relaxing evening, but she was going to soon see it wasn't meant be.

Even though Ulrich was just a pile of ash that danced away on the dawn breeze, that didn't deter Arkin from asking Adam to still stay on the case, and that case was Thea. Though danger seemed to be eliminated, there was still strange Claire's premonition that something dark was on the way straight for Thea. Everyone else might think that Claire was crazy, but you never knew, and part of what made Arkin so successful was the fact that he didn't take chances. No, he planned. So Adam sat in front of Thea and Emlyn's city house, eyes on lit rooms, wondering just how this evening was going to play out. He had done a hundred or so stakeouts, and most were busts, but he was used to the stillness, being alone in the car with just this thoughts. He had everything he would need in the car for a long evening, because with humans, just with paranormals, you never knew what was going to happen, and there was still one more blood to rein in, Margaux.

Adam glanced down at his phone as it vibrated in the seat beside him. He glanced at the caller ID: Arkin. Checking on him and, of course, Thea, no doubt. It wasn't that Adam knew anything more about Thea than Arkin did, but he had a detective's intuition, and something told Adam that she wasn't what she appeared to be. But she also wasn't the sort of evil you'd find skulking around in the dark. And while it was true that a blood-born could watch her in the evenings, they weren't trained for this sort of task, and some vampires thought they were above this type of menial work. In those rare instances, Arkin made sure that their attitude was adjusted. No, Adam was the best; he could get by on little sleep, and his reports were always well-written and factual. Arkin knew a gem when he found one.

He smiled to himself, answering his phone. "Evening, boss. I'm right where I'm supposed to be at the city house. It looks like she is in for the evening."

Adam was silent a moment as the front door of the house swung open and out stepped Anthea Black.

"Whoa, sorry, spoke too soon. She just stepped out. She's wearing worn blue jeans, old sneakers, a black halter top and is pulling curlers out of her hair. My bet is, she's pissed at having to go out… unexpected, maybe? If I were closer, I might hear her cursing. I'm going to follow her to see where she is headed. You can track me with my phone."

Adam watched as Anthea jumped into a small red Mini Cooper. "We are off and running."

* * *

Anthea was muttering to herself. This was not the kind of evening she had expected. No, she wanted a hot bath, she wanted to curl her hair, and she wanted some popcorn and an old movie. Em was supposed to be at an appointment. She hadn't known whether it was business or pleasure, and she hadn't wanted to pry. If it was business, he would be back before midnight. If it had been for pleasure, he wouldn't be back until after dawn. His call was unexpected and forced. How did she know he was being coerced? He used his distress word; he called her his angel. She shook her head, jaw tense as she jumped into her car. This was not good. Claire's words echoed in her mind: something dark was coming for her. Maybe it had gotten ahold of her brother first? She had pulled out her curlers, stuck a gun in the back of her waistband, and headed off to what was supposed to be a state-of-the-art building to find out just what trouble had found her brother.

She drove quickly, but within the confines of the law. She didn't need a cop or something worse following her, because depending on what she and Em were facing, they didn't need any prying eyes. Em was human; he was used to explaining the fact that her parents were dead and she was adopted. He had come up with all sorts of excuses for the sliver of otherworldliness that others saw in her. They believed him. He could be quite charming when he wanted to be and was not a bad liar, but Thea knew that time was going to run out eventually and then all hell would break loose. Explanations would be forthcoming, or she would have to flee. She wasn't ready to leave the city yet, and she didn't want to spend the rest of her life hiding.

Thea stopped her car next to the newly poured curb and looked in through the chain-link security gate that surrounded the "under construction" office building. The plans said it was supposed to have a restaurant on top with a startling view of the city. It had been one of Yardley's pet projects, but of course, with his death, the project had been shelved and it wasn't going to open in a month. She wasn't at all sure it would open, but with Yardley's demise, there was no security on the building. And Thea realized that she was alone. It was probably better this way. While she didn't want to hurt anyone, she also didn't want any witnesses. An abandoned building was a godsend. Thea didn't have time to wonder how Em had been caught or who had caught him; she just knew she had to save him.

Thea exited her car, jogging across the dirt by passing the dark construction trailer and dodging large machinery. The best case would be that Em was caught by a human; worst case was that it was something supernatural. But she couldn't imagine who might hold a grudge against her brother or who might want to piss them both off. If she were truly a friend of Arkin's, and he was an emerging power in the city, he might take offense and then they would be in trouble. The fleeting thought drifted across her mind that it might be Denard, but she hadn't seen or heard from the elusive fellow. It had been Thea who had piqued his curiosity, not her brother, Em.

Thea shook off the train of thoughts, touching the cool door handle of the nearby glass door. It was unlocked. No power, so no elevators. She would take the stairs up to the top floor, up twenty-odd flights. She had more stamina than the average human; she could do this and maybe come out surprising whoever it was who held her brother.

* * *

Adam pulled the car opposite the construction site, his gaze narrow as he watched Thea disappear into the partially completed building. He dialed Arkin and gave him a quick synopsis of what he had seen thus far. Adam was pretty sure he wouldn't be sitting there alone, waiting for long.

* * *

Em's eyes were locked on the stairwell door that opened into a hall. Although the top floor was built to be a restaurant, they hadn't installed the doors yet and not all the furniture had been moved up. The place was a hazard. Em glanced sideways toward the figure, the man that had kidnapped him, though the figure stood in brief shadow, a small LED lantern dispersed light over both hostage and kidnapper. Until he turned, Thea didn't know if she knew this man.

Tony Denard was waiting, staring at the various entryways, for his guest to arrive, and she would come. There was no doubt about this. Tied to a chair not far from where Tony waited, Em didn't want his sister to come to his rescue. There were so many other ways for this to go down, Em thought, and some not in their favor. Above all else, he wanted Thea to maintain her anonymity. That was what he wanted most for his sister. He didn't want a fight; he really didn't want her to face Denard. But they had no choice. It was the two of them against this man from nowhere. They would have to rely on themselves.

Em sighed, testing the ropes again; it wouldn't be very long before he was hopefully free and had his hands wrapped around Denard's neck. Denard should have used cable ties. Em would wait until his sister lulled Denard into a false sense of security, answer whatever questions he had, and then he would spring.

Denard turned quickly to his left, staring at Em, his dark eyes narrow, expression hard to read. Em would agree that Denard was slightly attractive, his body well-built, speed and reaction time faster than humans', strength stronger as well, because ordinarily, Em would not have been caught so easily. Denard paced back and forth, now uneasy, and as far as Em could tell, he didn't have a weapon in his hand, no gun. That told Em he was overconfident. He shouldn't be when facing his sister.

There was a slight click of the door as Em watched it open. Thea slipped into the hall as quietly as possible, not to disturb or jar anyone's attention. Denard stopped pacing, eyes riveted onto Thea, who strolled down the hallway casually, stepping across the threshold into what would eventually be a restaurant. She looked more than casual; she looked rough in old jeans, a black halter top, and sneakers. Her hair had been hastily tied up into a ponytail. He bet she had been wearing curlers.

Em opened his mouth to say something but fell silent as Thea pulled the gun from her waistband, raised it at Denard, and fired. Em was shocked by the attack. Denard hit the ground with a growl, left hand on his right shoulder. Thea had never been a terrific shot, but then again, maybe this was a test to figure out what kind of thing she was dealing with. Most supernaturals could forgive a shot, especially if it didn't kill them.

Denard rolled and got to his feet, teeth clenched as he looked at her standing with gun in hand.

"Anthea Black, I presume," he muttered, teeth clenched, blood staining his shirt. But the flow didn't last as long as it would have if Denard had been human.

"You had my brother call me. Who else would I be? I told you to make an appointment." Yeah, she had made the connection probably on voice alone.

"You're a hard woman to see. I thought this would get your attention. I have to commend you. How did you know that he was in trouble? The conversation seemed quite benign. You should have just come to meet him, not expecting trouble."

"Don't ask me stupid questions," she responded. "You okay, Em?"

"Been restrained before for fun. This isn't fun."

Thea nodded.

"Sorry about this. Wasn't thinking I was at risk."

"No, it's not fun," she responded then turned to Denard. "So you got me here. What do you want?"

Denard managed to regain his composure, his eyes never leaving Thea. But she didn't seem very impressed. "Denard, my name is Denard."

"That still doesn't tell me shit," Thea hissed.

"You're right, because we have never met before. We spoke once on the phone, as you intimated, but I found you by a spell."

Thea wondered absently what kind of magic and what he had been looking for. "Found me for what?"

Denard shook out his left hand and moved his shoulder. He tore off the fabric, revealing a wound that was slowly healing. Thea wasn't impressed; she had seen better and faster.

"So you patch up nice. What else do you do for an encore?"

Denard chuckled, coughing slightly. "You have an attitude. I don't like that in a woman."

"We aren't dating," Thea remarked, eyes turning to Em to see what lay behind those eyes.

"I found you to ask you one question, and I hoped you had an answer for me. I wanted to do this on more congenial terms."

Thea was quiet as she sized him up. He wasn't exactly human. He felt familiar, as if she should know what he was. She had felt that odd inkling before, when she had been with Arkin at the square. She and Denard weren't the same, but they weren't totally human either.

"You are not forest folk, you are not vampire, you are not shifter. We, the two of us, are different. Do you know what we are?"

"So you took Em to ask me a stupid question like that? Why didn't you just walk in and talk to me?"

"And have you deny, hide from me, because someone might hear us? We have utter and complete privacy here. I want to know. I'm different, I have greater endurance, speed, healing abilities, and yet…they know I'm not human. But I'm not sure what I am."

Em looked at Thea, cautioning her.

"Did it ever occur to you that I, too, looked for answers but finally gave up? Those who have information hoard it. They don't like to share their myths and legends, and I don't have the funds or words to make them help me."

Denard stood very still, staring at Thea, who had gradually walked forward, tucking the gun into the back of her belt.

"So you just came in guns blazing?" he asked, sounding bitter.

"If you were human, my problems would be solved. If you weren't, you would forgive me for being a simple human who thought she could fight your power. I took a shot, literally." She sighed. "I can try to put you in touch with someone who might know or might be able to answer your questions."

Denard shook his head, beginning to pace slightly. "You know the answers I seek. You are lying to me. I can't think that you wouldn't have given everything to know how you came to be and what you are. Your parents are dead. You are an orphan."

"Common knowledge," she responded. "Look, I hear a lot of things, most I can't give credit to. When you live around the supernaturals, you hear all sorts of gossip, whispers. True, I feel human to everyone, but they can't tell me what it is I feel like aside from that. Aren't we all just a wee slice of monster?"

Denard chuckled. "You should win an Emmy for your diatribe. You must really think me stupid."

"It's too soon to say that, Denard. I'll tell you what a psychic once told me. She told me that there are other creatures on earth other than what we see and know. She told me there is a heaven and a hell and creatures that occupy both. According to one source, they are allowed to inhabit this world for one year. Whether it is a reward or punishment, I do not know, but they have a vessel that appears human. Do they remember who they are? Do they know others of their kind? I can't be sure, but she wondered about and told me what she believed to be true."

Denard stood very still, eyes locked on Thea, whose face was a mask of seriousness. It was Em who broke free and lunged at him. Without thinking, Denard grabbed Em, spun him around, and tossed him toward the windows. Thea screamed as Em fell through the window and plummeted over the edge of the building. Thea was racing forward, Denard screaming at her as she ducked through the jagged glass. As her sneakered foot went over the edge and her body fell into the night, dove-colored wings jutted out of her back to catch the wind. Her eyes were locked on her brother, who was barely clinging to a partially installed flagpole.

"On three, let go!" she shouted as Em closed his eyes, counted to three, and let his hands slip.

Thea embraced him, her wings allowing her to glide down toward the earth, landing deftly on her feet, her arms letting her brother slip to solid ground. She spun on her heel as if to launch herself back into the sky, back toward the broken window. Em grabbed her ankle as they both gazed up toward the face of the building. You could barely see Denard staring out of the upper window, his shadow blocking the light.

"Leave him. We can deal with him later. Fold back your wings before someone sees you. You aren't going to fight him alone."

She turned, staring at her brother, who was lying on the dirt, his fingers wrapped around her ankle. He managed a small thankful smile. Her eyes were ablaze with emotion.

"I always said I was the wind beneath your wings. Don't ever make me do that again."

He slowly let her ankle go, assured that she would stay earthbound. He watched as she folded back her magnificent wings and they vanished from sight against her back. He sat up and retrieved a fallen feather. He held it tightly in his hand.

"He isn't like you, is he?" Em asked as she extended her hand to him. He took it and pulled himself upward. Her strength was truly inhuman.

"No. He is from the other side. You know, 333, only partially evil."

Em chuckled as he hugged her. "I hate to fly," he said, dusting himself off.

"Yeah, and I'm afraid of heights. I got over it real fast. Come on, you can tell me how you got caught. Nice distress word, by the way."

Em chuckled. "I know, right?" he said as they walked to the Mini.

* * *

Adam opened his mouth to say something, to say anything, but it was Arkin who raised his hand to silence him before he could begin. As Adam predicted, Arkin had been curious what Thea was up to and, with Marta in tow, arrived at the deserted construction site in their SUV. There was something about this woman that drove Arkin to distraction, and though he had let her go home thinking she was safe, he hadn't the faintest idea why she would go to a construction site alone at night. He had asked all sorts of questions upon their arrival, but Adam didn't have any answers, as they sat in the car. Until they saw what they saw. Now they had more questions than answers. They had been staring up into the night; they had seen something come out of a window, and then they saw Thea.

"Not a word. I need to process what I just saw," Arkin remarked as he sat shotgun, staring out of the windshield, eyes looking up and then down at the building. He had the oddest expression on his face. His mind was spinning.

"I think it is pretty obvious. Em went out of the building through a window, and not of his own accord, and his sister went after him. It just so happens that she has wings. Maybe she is a Valkyrie?"

Adam shook his head at Marta, realizing how calm her statement had been. "You have been around a long time, boss. I know you have seen a shitload of things. But have you ever seen anything like this?"

Arkin shook his head, mind awash with almost too many thoughts. "I thought she was coming out here on a silent-witness gig, maybe the Seven had summoned her, maybe to talk to the witches. This was totally unexpected."

"Mr. Understatement," cooed Marta, who leaned back in the seat, shaking her head. "She's an angel."

Both Adam and Arkin twisted around in their seats, staring at Marta, who shrugged.

"I mean, she doesn't feel fey, right? She has wings. What else has wings like that? From what I could see in the scattered light, they appeared white, gray-speckled. They were gorgeous, actually."

"An angel? How does one become an earthbound angel?" Adam asked, frowning.

"Maybe you have to be born one. But I think that answers the question about what that sliver of nonhumanness is about her," stated Marta. She looked at Arkin, who seemed to be too intent to enter the conversation. She gently touched him. "You were right to try to keep her safe, but although she likes you, I don't think she is totally ready to come clean about what she is with you, or others, for that matter."

"And how exactly do you have that kind of conversation?" Adam asked, shaking his head. Hard to imagine. "Darling, I have to tell you, I'm an angel, an honest-to-God angel."

"There would be dangers to such confessions," muttered Arkin. "The dark."

Marta nodded. "I'd say so. Humans don't usually go out of windows on purpose unless they are committing suicide. And Em doesn't seem the type. They were fighting something."

Adam started up his car. He needed to go back to the Black household and take up the watch. He figured Marta and the stunned Arkin would head back home in their SUV.

"Some detective I am. Sure, we found out she is adopted, but there is more to her than that. I take it you want us to look into the angel angle, right? I mean, find out more about angels?"

"That would be helpful, Adam, but don't explain to anyone why," added Arkin softly, still deeply in thought.

"So this is definitely confidential, right?' Adam asked, both Arkin and Marta staring at him, amazed he would ask such a stupid question. He shrugged. "Just confirming."

"Not a word until we can figure this out. It is business as usual," he said, voice sounding foreign to his own ears.

"Does it help to have an angel in your corner?" Marta asked, curious.

"Does a bell really ring when they get their wings?" Adam asked as Arkin shook his head and rubbed his eyes. This was more than he had bargained for, and though they both had secrets, Thea's was way more dangerous than his.

* * *

Thea had dropped Em off to pick up his car, and they headed home together. They had a lot to talk about. She was following him when her phone rang. She glanced at the caller ID. It was Arkin. She drew a breath to steady herself, regaining her composure.

"Evening, Arkin," she said brightly.

"Evening, Thea. I hope I didn't catch you in the middle of anything?" Arkin asked casually.

"Just curling my hair. What's up?" she asked, trying to sound lighthearted.

"I am to see Margaux tomorrow evening. Are you available?"

"Yes, for the last of these meetings, I will make myself available. Do you want me to meet you somewhere, or will you pick me up at work?"

"We will pick you up. Until then. I know you are eager to get these meetings over with. I fear I have monopolized your time."

"Oh, that is what a silence witness does. If we can get this city settled, it will be worth our time."

"Well, you have been an angel about it, really," remarked Arkin as he said goodbye, Marta looking at him with amazement as he sat in Adam's passenger seat, the car door open. Though Jackson and Lang wanted to accompany them, he had said no. He hadn't really thought there was any danger to Thea's evening jaunt. He was glad that the fewer who witnessed her winged descent, the better. He was smiling, amused at himself.

"You are bad," she stated, hitting him in the shoulder.

"Only slightly. She was lying to me," he stated as he stepped out of the car and into the night air.

"You both were lying to each other," added Adam. "I presume you still want me watching her?"

"Yes, more than before," he said adamantly.

"And if she finds out you know what she is, do you think she will kill to protect such a secret?"

"I would give her our word. That we would not reveal her secret to anyone, and I would kill to enforce it."

Marta knew he was a man of his word, but Thea might not believe him. "Would she believe you, boss?" Marta asked, concerned.

"I would make her believe us," he added, eager to go home, eager for the thoughtful silence.

* * *

Em peered into the kitchen and found his sister curled up in one of the cushioned chairs by the light of the stove, fingers wrapped around a mug of hot chocolate.

"I thought you would be asleep by now."

She shook her head quietly. Em seated himself across from her.

"I'm sorry I made the call to you. I should have said no, fought harder against him. I'm sorry he caught me so easily. Funny, I've never been Tasered before. Nor come to think of it, have I flown without the use of an airplane."

Thea met his gaze.

"It was pretty awesome."

"Don't be sorry. If you hadn't called me, I would have had to come looking for you, anyway. You are pretty predicable. That is one thing we are good at is communication. Too many dangerous things out there, waiting in the dark, and all we have is each other. You know, I knew when my wings first appeared that one day I might have to make a decision to reveal myself. Then it is my decision whether to stay here or leave everything behind. I'm not ready to leave everything. I feel like Clark Kent being exposed as Superman, not that I'm super. But you get the idea."

"Yes, the shadow of your anonymity. Right now, only Denard thinks he knows. And who would believe him? Who would trust him? We can kill him. We know where to bury the bodies."

That comment made Thea smile.

"You know that I am here for you. We have enough money that if you felt the need to disappear, you could. I would support that."

"I don't want people thinking I'm some sort of miracle worker, that I can heal, or…I have wings. That and a few other things make me different, but still I don't want to be."

"I bet you shocked the hell out of Denard when he saw you leap from the building after me. I would have paid good money to see his face."

Thea set the mug on the table.

"You two aren't the same. You are a good person, you have a soul of light…no one will think you are a monster, nor will they believe you are truly divine, though I am sure Arkin might think that, the way I have seen him look at you."

Thea rolled her eyes as Em patted her hand.

"Tell me what to say or what to do and I'll do it."

Thea thought a moment, seeing the sincerity in her brother's gaze. He was hurting.

"First, I have to stop this pity party. I have to stop worrying about what will happen. When it happens, I'll deal with it. I won't want to, but I will. We have to concern ourselves with Denard right now. I don't think he is only a threat to me. Call Rose Marie and see if she can locate Denard. While I wanted to wrench his spine from his body, it was a good thing that you stopped me. RM is one of the best detectives in the city."

Thea and her brother had been introduced to Rose Marie when her older brother got married in their chapel and her younger sister died, having the service at their mortuary. That was when she decided to leave the police force and open her own detective agency. They saw each other probably twice a month, if that. Thea always thought that RM, as she called herself, was a better fit for Emlyn as a girlfriend, but she wasn't one to meddle in anyone's love life. After all, she didn't want anyone messing in hers.

"Sounds like a plan," he answered with a nod.

"I'm going to see Esther and let her know that there may be problems in the offing, though I'm not sure what type of problems. He isn't a witch, but he may have had some training since he said he found me by a spell. I wonder what kind of spell it was. I am afraid if he wants to find his roots, he would have to go looking in the dark."

"Demon dark?"

She nodded sadly.

"That can't be good."

CHAPTER 10

Esther was a bit surprised to find Anthea Black leaning against her car, with coffee in one hand and hot chocolate in the other. It was the only car in her parking lot. She frowned slightly, walking toward her, sizing up the woman's mood. Esther had to admit that although they didn't use her services very often as a silent witness, everyone thought she was a good person, had good work ethic, and was trustworthy. Thea smiled, raising a cup toward Esther.

"Black, one sugar," said Thea proudly.

"Good memory. You gotta have an appointment at the spa, or are you here to see me?"

"Although I could probably use a good spa day, I'm here to see you."

Esther leaned against the car, taking a dark, deep sip. She sighed, enjoying the warmth of a rising sun. "So what's up?"

"You remember when you asked me about Teddy Worth?"

"Yes, and you told me about Tony Denard."

Thea nodded. "Yes, and I just wanted to caution you. He isn't a witch, but he might have had some training, and he may be thinking about doing something very dark and very stupid. I ran into him last night, and let's say the meeting didn't end well."

"So you think he might be dabbling in our art form?"

Thea nodded. "I know that you don't deal in what humans call black magic. All magic is power. It is what you do with it that makes it good or bad. In fact, I'm not really sure that many of those texts are still out there, but just in case, all right? He would need information and supplies. Your coven might be the first hit."

"I appreciate the warning. You got a picture of the fellow?"

Thea frowned. "He has a Facebook page. I don't want the police to get involved since he hasn't done anything yet. But he is certainly suspicious."

Esther laughed. "I'll take that under advisement. Any other info you can give me that you think might help? You really think that Worth found out something about Denard?"

"I think Denard asked Worth to do something against his morals and that was why he came to see me. I wish he had gotten to me. This is just my initial gut feeling."

"I'll trust your gut. Why did Teddy contact you and not me, as head of his coven?"

Thea shrugged. There was no way to expand on this conversation without giving herself away. "I don't know. Since he's dead, he can't answer for himself. He was also a guy."

Esther regarded Thea with narrow eyes. "You don't really want to get into the middle of things, do you? But you end up in them anyway."

"Yeah. I'm a magnet for trouble," quipped Thea.

"Well, I have heard you might be a magnet for our newest vampire leader."

Thea rolled her eyes, stepping away from her car to open the door. Not her too? "You heard wrong."

"My mistake," added Esther as she watched Thea back out of the parking lot and drive away, thinking Thea protested too much.

* * *

If Thea had her choice of girlfriends for her brother, it would be Rose Marie Kanarvan. She was a pretty little thing with blond curls, warm brown eyes, and a hell of a right hook, or so her old partner had said. Everyone underestimated her, and that gave her an edge in the business. Plus, it helped that she had been a respected cop. As usual, RM, as she called herself, arrived at the mortuary on time, nine thirty on the dot. Em had been waiting for her, on edge about the situation. They shook hands, and he led her back to his office, where they could talk in private. RM was human, though she seemed to have good intuition. She was wearing a well-fitted pantsuit in brown and at least two guns, but she wore them well. If you didn't know her, you would never suspect.

RM seated herself across from Em, who had moved his chair out from behind his desk. To anyone else, it would look like a casual meeting, but to Em, this was serious.

"Thanks for coming so quickly."

"Part of my job to be responsive. What can I do for you?" She was all business.

"We are looking for someone, Tony Denard. He has a Facebook page with picture. He is in the city, but I'm not sure where."

RM nodded, taking copious notes on her e-tablet. "What sort of trouble is he in or am I getting into? Is it blackmail, defacing corpses?"

Em smiled, shaking his head. "No, just mischief. He took me by force the other night. Thea was able to get me free, but he has some delusions of grandeur. I think he is thinking of bringing his family into the mix, and believe me, you don't want to meet them." Cryptic.

"Connected?" she asked, thinking in human terms.

"Darkly. He may be trying to cast a spell, so Thea has gone to warn Esther. We think one of her witches might have tried to warn Thea that Denard was trouble."

"Why is Denard interested in Thea?" RM asked, and Em answered rather quickly; he must have thought she might ask this question.

"He thinks they have a connection," added Em. "He might even find her intriguing." The stalker angle would do.

"Doesn't everyone? You're being mysterious."

"I am, and I was hoping that I wasn't being that obvious." Em glanced up as Thea entered the room, her face brightened.

"How is this city's most famous detective?" Thea drew RM into a hug.

"I can't complain, and you have given me a job. I hear you got a nasty who is giving you some problem. Just to clarify, you want to know where he is and maybe what he is doing, is that correct? Does he know you might be looking for him?" Thea glanced at Em as she leaned against the desk. She folded her arms thoughtfully.

"I'm not sure he has that much common sense, but I would consider him dangerous. He is human, but there is an element that is unaccounted for. It makes him faster and stronger."

RM considered Thea's remark. "I'll keep that in mind. Is he faster than a bullet, you think?"

Thea chuckled. "Not a chance, but you better make it more than one."

"Good." RM stood up and shook hands with both Em and Thea, finding her own way out.

Em glanced at his sister.

"I like her," Thea stated. "I feel confident she can get the job done."

"I know you do, and seeing her again makes me want to ask her out. Get to know her a bit better," Em remarked, Thea's eyes widening. She would like that.

"Lucy might skin you alive."

"I carry silver with me that might deter her for a bit," he responded. "What did Esther say?"

"She thanked me for the warning. I was as vague as I could be, but she will be careful. If he is going to try to summon family, as it were, or at least half of his family, he will need a place to do it, instructions, and ingredients."

"Do you think he will try to corral a witch?" Em asked as his sister stood, setting her purse aside and swinging on her lab coat.

"I think he already tried." She sighed. It had cost Teddy his life.

* * *

Arkin Kane was still trying to process what he, Marta, and Adam had seen last night. He remembered it as surely as if it were happening right before his eyes now. Adam said that Thea went into the building through the front door. She had to have climbed up to the twentieth floor and then followed her brother out of the window, suddenly sprouting wings. He never would have guessed that she had wings; there was no evidence on her or by looking at her. Though Marta remembered the marks on her back. In all the time he had lived, he had never come across a creature, such a beautiful creature like her. It had been difficult to remain in the car, not to race over to her, touch those feathered wings, and tell her that he understood, that there was no reason to fear. The three of them had sworn one another to secrecy and hadn't brought up the subject as they headed home. It was obvious from the brief conversation with Thea that she didn't want to confide, and in truth, he had no clue what sort of difficulty they might be in.

This evening, however, Marta and Arkin were ready to get in the car and ride out to pick Thea up, and they needed a plan. Marta stood just outside of the garage portico, eyes looking up at the stars, as Arkin joined her. She wondered briefly what it would be like to be up in the stars, and then the thought occurred to her, that evening they had visited Thea out in the woods. A perfect place to hide a flight at night when no one was looking and where there were no neighbors.

"We didn't talk about what we saw," he whispered.

"I didn't know what to say," added Marta. "I have heard stories, thought they were myth and legend. But those were real wings, and not the barbecue kind."

"I'm not sure what to do. And to think I was being overtly…"

Marta chuckled. "Nothing has changed, Arkin. She is still the same person, you are still attracted to her, but there is the secondary element. She is either an angel or part angel. I also didn't see her turn down your advances. Just act normal or as normal as you can. There may come a time when you have to tell her you know, but not right now. She is dealing with something just as we are."

"I feel unworthy of her, and I know that sounds totally stupid."

"Arkin, you are probably the only person who is worthy of her. The only thing I know for sure is that she deserves protection."

"Agreed," he added firmly.

* * *

Thea was a bit dismayed when she was relegated to the back seat of the car in between Marta and Lang. Arkin sat passenger side, with Jackson the chauffeur for the evening. He turned around and smiled warmly at her. She frowned slightly.

"So how was your day?" he asked casually.

Marta closed her eyes. This wasn't going to go well. This was not Arkin acting naturally.

"Fine. Just like every other day. People marry, people get buried, they order flowers…so this is your last stop?"

"We see Margaux tonight. Once we have established that I am staying in the city, we will move into our permanent residence and gather everyone together for a state of the union."

"So housecleaning has been going well?" Thea asked tritely.

"Yes. There aren't that many who oppose us now. I presume they will wait and see if I do something that dissatisfies them, then they may take action."

"Will you be taking over Yardley's home?" she asked, glancing at Marta, who managed a smile back, a rather odd smile back, if you asked Thea.

"Yes. I have had my people working to get it habitable. It was built for our safety. I have sent for my personal things. It will do, and there is suitable land around it. Have you seen it?"

"Once, although I don't remember it very well. Other things were happening at that time…Tasha, men, women, a grotto, sex orgy…you know, the unusual."

Arkin opened and then closed his mouth. He cleared his throat, turning around to face the road.

"You're joking, right?" Lang asked, curious.

Thea shook her head. "Tasha enjoys her extracurricular activities just as Kale likes to hit on me. It always makes for an interesting business visit. Yardley didn't always make everyone tow the line. He liked to see people squirm."

"Why don't you make Emlyn go to places like that, especially if it is your other business?" Marta asked, curious.

"Because she won't talk to him and she does do a good deal of business with us. You are going to have your hands full. It is like working with children, Arkin. You shall have to be a patient parent. You will find that Margaux is rather aloof. She likes to think she is the oldest member of your race in the city, that everyone should come to her for advice and she be the grand dame."

"In other words, she can be an annoying bitch," added Jackson.

"She's no angel, that's for sure," added Thea as silence fell around the car, no one daring to look at her.

Arkin opened the door for Thea and offered his arm politely. His manner to Thea seemed standoffish, almost formal, but it was forgotten when Margaux's second opened one of the double doors. Krist was tall, big, foreboding; he looked as if he could be a bouncer for a bar. He was physically imposing, but he didn't have that scary-blood vibe that Arkin had. It was Jackson and Lang who preceded Arkin for introductions and to get Krist out of the way.

Arkin slipped from Thea's grasp, stepping forward. Their eyes met, power flared, and Krist was outmatched. A rather preemptory voice resounded over the house and lilted out into the night.

Margaux had arrived.

She was one of those women lost in time and liked to wear clothing from the 1900s. Always the lady, never trousers, never anything so uncouth. She always looked like a Jane Austen sort of character. Her business was antiques, a tea shop, and tasteful retail, as Tasha liked to call it. She also had a wineshop. Her hair was almost white-blond, piled atop her head, and for dramatic effect, she stood at the top of the stairs with handkerchief in hand.

Arkin met her gaze and sighed. There were so many of their kind who liked the affectations of appearing to be lost in time. Just one look at Arkin, and Margaux knew she wasn't the oldest creature in the room. Her expression faltered as she descended the stairs.

"Good eve to you, Arkin Kane. Welcome to my home."

"Margaux, it is a pleasure to meet you. You have a lovely home."

"Thank you. I try to express my love for the past with my need for a peaceful future. Are you that future, Arkin?"

Arkin took her hand and allowed her to lead him into the salon, a room filled with ruffles, in pink, in white gold. It made most men cringe. Yardley had hated it; he was usually the one who squirmed in that room. As always, she ignored Thea, who didn't take it personally. She took her usual chair in the corner, away from the discussion and the action. It was a very uncomfortable bustle chair. Arkin glanced at Thea, an odd expression on his face as he realized she was sitting beneath hanging cherubs and an angel painting. He cleared his throat to gather his thoughts.

"I want you to know, Margaux, that I didn't come here for your approval. I came because this city needs to be run well, and I intend to do it. This is a courtesy call. If you wish to stay and abide by the rules and laws we have established as a race and I intend to enforce, I welcome you here. If not, then you may leave, but your business concerns will stay."

Margaux's hand went straight to her chest, as if Arkin had stabbed her. "Have I given you any reason to doubt that I will serve this city well for you?" Her voice was slightly high-pitched and betrayed her nervousness.

"No, but I understand you were closer to Cordelia. It was nothing personal, you understand. She attacked me. I do not follow the three-strike rule, to use a sports metaphor. I will be taking over Yardley's manse since it seems to fit my needs. We will be meeting in a few days to discuss those issues that are most urgent, that perhaps Yardley didn't tend to. I want everyone in the city to realize that we are no longer divided."

"And you brought enough of your people to enforce your rules?" she asked coyly as Arkin shrugged.

"Most people are glad to have direction, not having the buck stop at their desk."

"And you have been doing this for a long time?" she asked, curious.

"Long enough to know how it is done. If you do not object and challenge me, then we can get together, iron out our differences."

"Emily took Ulrich, I understand. Bold of her."

"Maybe fortune favors the bold," added Arkin.

"Like you walking in here and trying to take the city?"

"I am taking the city back from a mess you all could not consolidate. I have met my critics so far, and they have fallen by the wayside, dead. I am prepared to meet others with words, not weapons."

"Then I agree. You must understand, one of the stumbling blocks to our kind is the age at which we transformed. People think us young and inexperienced. Unfortunately, we tend to think the same way ourselves. You look lost in your twenties."

"I was younger than that when I died," Arkin responded honestly.

"Yet I bet you are the oldest of us in the city."

Arkin didn't disagree.

"I will give my oath to you now and after our formal meeting. I will ensure that my people also abide by your rules."

"They are our race's rules. Some have fallen by the wayside but should be enforced. Others are no longer needed in this world of technology, but our city will prosper."

"And what do the Seven think of your arrival?" she asked, curious.

"Cautiously optimistic," he answered with a chuckle.

Thea sat listening to the conversation. It had gone better than she had hoped. Probably, killing off those who stood against him started a trend. See how he did, and if he was successful, accept him. Arkin wasn't a fool; however, his coolness toward her confused Thea. She sat patiently throughout the discussion, taking note of words and attitude. She was grateful when they were done and preparing to leave. Arkin barely met her gaze as he escorted her out, hand behind her back, but not daring to touch her. She drew a breath to calm her ire. It was a rather quiet ride back to the house, Thea staring at Arkin, wondering what might have happened between them.

"You must be pleased. It seems that everyone else has fallen into line."

"Thus far. They always try to test, see how you side and if you have favorites," he answered.

"Do you already have a second?" she asked, trying to fill the awkward silence between them.

"I have had more than several. My current second is currently running a separate city for me. I will take Asao. He is more in line with my beliefs, and I think he can be formidable."

"You mean scary? It's that Asian inscrutability."

Arkin smiled and nodded.

The car pulled up along the curb in front of her house.

"Will you walk me to the door, Arkin?" she asked, extending her arm to Marta and Lang, signaling them both to stay in their seats. Of course, Jackson was driving. Arkin climbed out of the car, opened the door, and gestured for Thea to join him on the walkway. They sauntered up to the porch, where Thea turned and met his gaze. She stepped forward slightly, and he stepped back into the hardness of the wall.

"Can I ask you a question?" she asked pointedly.

"Anything," he murmured softly.

"You went from flirty to formal. Can I ask what happened between us?"

Arkin managed a soft smile. "I realized that I had secured your talents for business and I was being unprofessional. It is my fault, and I apologize."

Thea was silent as she regarded him. "So just to clarify, you don't want any of…"

Thea stood up on her tiptoes, ran her hands through his hair, and laid a series of kisses on his lips. Arkin's hands itched to embrace her. Thea's hands slid down the front of his shirt, slipping in to caress the flesh of his chest. Arkin was strung so tightly he fisted his hands and stood very still, as if he thought if he went very still, Thea would ignore him. She pressed closer so that her body was up against him. He closed his eyes for a heartbeat.

"No," he muttered.

She removed her hands and stepped back away from him. "Okay, just checking," she added as she spun on her heels and entered the house.

Arkin was trembling as he slowly stepped away from the wall and walked back toward the car. Lang and Jackson were trying to ignore him, but Marta's curious gaze settled on him. She was not going to let this lie; they were going to have more than one word on the Thea subject.

"You are letting her go."

He managed a nod as he crawled into the car. "It is what's best for her," he answered flatly.

"What is best for her is safety and protection should someone uncover her secret."

"I can do that without being intimate with her. I will always be here for her."

"Is that what your head is saying to your heart? How long have we known each other? How many times have you felt this connection with anyone? Don't deny you feel it."

"I'm not denying anything, and maybe when things settle down, Marta, maybe."

He was lying to himself.

"How many centuries and decades does it take for us to settle down?" Marta shook her head and crossed her arms, disappointed. He was making a mistake. He needed to seize the moment now, or when he was ready, she would not be there for him.

"You think I'm wrong?" he asked.

"Damn right," she hissed.

* * *

Adam, with his partner, Cecelia, or Cece, as she liked to call herself, sat in their dark-gray Camry just down the street from Thea and Em's city house. Cece had been with his division of Arkin's collective for about two years. She was a big girl and former Marine. She was dressed just as casually as Adam but looked better-rested. She had tried to get him to let her take over this duty, but for some reason, he was slightly obsessed with Thea Black. It had only been ten minutes since Arkin and his team had left, so Adam figured that she was probably going to settle in for the evening. He lay back, closed his eyes, and tried to reconcile himself to the fact that he was actually watching, guarding a possible angel. So far, initial searches on the subject yielded nothing, if little.

A nudge to the ribs brought his eyes open. He glanced at Cece and then over toward the house.

"I know you thought our girl was in for the evening, but apparently not. She looks dressed to kill."

Adam frowned as he looked across the street at Thea Black. She was dressed in a white dress with turquoise flowers around the hem, waist, and neck. It was demure, but for some reason, she made it look sexy. She had high heels on that matched the blue in the dress, and her hair was up in a mass of curls. He watched as she walked down the street with a flounce in her step. She didn't have a purse with her.

"Third pocket." Cece remarked, tapping her cleavage. "Looks like she is heading to Edden's place. Do we need to call the boss?"

Adam sighed. He nodded, hitting speed dial on the phone, waiting to hear Arkin's voice in his ear. He wasn't sure how Arkin was going to take the news that his little angel had flown her coop.

* * *

Edden glanced up from the bar and did a double take. This evening, Thea looked the opposite of how she always looked, businesslike. She had an uncertain smile on her face, but with that dress, those eyes, and that hair, no one would be looking at her smile. Edden whistled in appreciation.

"Hey, there, beautiful."

She chuckled lightly as she walked over to the bar. She leaned on the wood and hopped up on a nearby barstool.

"Do you think your boss would let you have the evening off to take a friend out dancing?" she asked coyly. He was the boss.

"Well, now, where did you have in mind on going, and in that dress? Does your brother know you are out trolling for a date?"

Thea tugged on Edden's collar. "What he doesn't know is none of his business," she remarked with a wink. "You up for it?"

Edden met her expectant gaze. Something was going on, and he had better be the one to figure it out. This was unlike Thea. "I know just the place for good drinks, appetizers for you, and all the dancing you can handle."

She shivered as he stepped out from behind the bar.

"But if you ride on my hog, you have to wear a helmet and a Kevlar jacket. You are too precious to waste in a collision. Give me a moment to get things together, and I'll meet you out front."

Thea touched his cheek, sliding off the stool to step back out into the growing darkness. Neon lights danced over her features as she waited for Edden.

* * *

"She just came back out of the bar, boss. Wait, there is Edden, and he has a helmet and jacket with him, one of those safety jackets, I bet. Looks like they are heading somewhere. Yeah, we will follow."

Adam glanced at Cece as they pulled away from the curb. Arkin was perturbed and a bit mystified at Thea's behavior. You didn't have to be a girl to know that Arkin had, in a way, dumped her, and Thea had to be hurt. Adam knew from Jackson, Lang, and Marta's talk that their boss was highly interested in the girl, more so than any other woman he had met. And then she turned out to maybe be an angel. Was that a deal killer?

Cece was on her laptop.

"According to this, she and Edden are old friends. Sort of grew up together, if that makes sense. I emailed one of our sources in the city. There has never seen any sort of romantic intentions between the two."

Adam nodded as they sighted Spectrum. He slowed the car and touched the Bluetooth.

"They are at Spectrum. It's an upscale dance place in now Emily's territory. You can country line dance, waltz, or disco. It is frequented by all races and is in a good part of town. You want Cece and me to go in?"

Cece was listening intently. Adam shook his head at her.

"He is sending Jocelyn and Moody to keep an eye on them. We are to wait here." Adam signed off, sighing. He leaned back as Cece regarded him. She was a woman, so she was curious.

"I take it that he is unhappy with this development?" She was probing.

"For reasons I won't go into, he blew Thea off but didn't really want to do it. It's a long story. No time. Anyway, I think she's hurt."

"I would be if I thought someone was interested in me and then dumped me with no reason given. He shouldn't have shown any interest in her to begin with, though she is hot."

"Yeah, and the more you know about her, the hotter she is." Adam sighed. "He is a big boy. He will either have to deal with her dating others or he will have to give in and make his move."

"He would be happier if he made his move."

"We all would be," added Adam, knowing the truth of his words.

It wasn't difficult to get into the club. Edden, with Thea in tow, crossed the waiting line and waded in through the crowd. What got them in was Edden's fame as tavern owner and friend of Emily's and the fact that he was with their silent witness. Often, payment was returned to Thea in terms of things rather than money. This was her first time here, and she stopped suddenly. Edden pulled back practically in her embrace. Her eyes were wide in amazement. The place was a network of glass, colors, light, and music. To her right was a bar and dining area, straight ahead was the disco room, and to her right was country music and the old-fashioned music that ranged from the waltz to the boogie-woogie. She looked up into Edden's gaze. He smiled.

"You brought me. Where would you like to dance?" she asked with a grin.

"If you ever breathe a word of this, I choose disco." Edden pulled Thea along behind him and through the glass doors, music rolling over her as if it were water. He swung her into his arms and began to move to the beat. He figured that if he tired her out, maybe she would sit down and talk a bit. This was very much unlike Anthea Black.

Edden knew that Thea needed a break. Her face was flushed, she was sweating slightly and panting, but she felt good in his arms. And boy, could she keep up! There were a few curious gazes from those who knew she doubled as a silent witness. Never did you see her out having fun. Edden made sure to make it known that she was with him. He wrapped her in his arms and drew her out of the dance area and over toward the bar and dining room. It sat on several levels, with neon rails of light separating them. Thea plopped down in the chair and kicked off her shoes. Now, this was the Thea he knew. Edden signaled for a drink for him and something cool for her, a virgin daiquiri in strawberry. It was one of her favorite flavors.

"You are hot on the dance floor. How come we haven't done this before?" she asked, fanning herself.

"Because we are friends and you don't usually do this sort of thing. You want to tell me why you are doing it now?"

Thea refrained from comment as her drink was brought. She raised it toward Edden just as Moody and Jos arrived. They easily caught sight of her and took a table right above hers to the left. It was easy to hear the conversation. Jos ordered two drinks, Moody surveying the area and then Thea with curiosity. So this was the famous woman who had their boss tied in knots. Very nice, but as far as he was aware, nothing overly special. Arkin had ordered them over to Spectrum as fast as they could make it, and they weren't particularly dressed for a dance club. Moody was tall, was broad, and looked as if he could carry a sword easily. He had blond hair and dark eyes. Women always stole glances at him. Jos was like a little sister to him, his complete opposite, dark skin and eyes, short, with a fierce expression to the women who liked to try to linger around her partner. She placed her phone on the floor near her feet, by the edge of where their table sat. Thea took long, hard drinks, eyes scanning the people at the club.

"Do you think I would look better blond, like a white blond?" she asked politely.

"No," Edden remarked emphatically.

"What about if I had a better tan? I'm kind of pale, but I could probably try sitting out or going for one of those spray tans."

"I like you pale. You are perfect just the way you are. Why do you want to change?"

She exhaled, leaning across the table. Her expression was wistful. "Because the way I am doesn't seem very attractive to men. I'm not sure whether it is my looks, my job, or my attitude."

Edden understood now. For some reason, Arkin had cooled his relationship with her. He had noticed, heard inklings of how much he seemed to care for her, and now something had gone sideways.

Edden took a sip of warm blood. "What makes you think it's you and not them? You are all together. Sure, you're not model perfect, a thin waif with a trowel of makeup on your face, but who wants that? It's not real. You have a respected position in the community, you have money, you have a sense of humor, you can dress up or down and still be attractive. Fuck them if they don't like what you do. Someone has to do it, and you provide an important service. And don't even get me started about what Caroline and Sarah did. You don't deserve to be ambushed that way."

"I'm tired of always being the good girl. You have time on your side. I'm not so sure about the time I have."

"You're not sick, are you?" Edden asked, concerned.

"No, just of being alone, and if you weren't so concerned about fucking up our friendship, we might be good together."

Edden rolled his eyes.

"So if I can't date you, humans don't like my job, whom do you think I should date? I have tried to be very businesslike with changelings. I didn't want there ever to be a misunderstanding. And some of them have hinted more might be interesting."

"Well, right off the bat, do not date Kale. He is too fast for you. He would have you on your knees twice for different reasons."

Thea opened and then closed her mouth, blushing. "Edden, what you said…," she remarked, face flushed, embarrassed.

"Don't tell me that I'm wrong about that. He isn't the stick-around kind of guy. Fun, if that is all you want, but I know you want something more. Look, if you are tired of dealing with the same old people, why don't you find someone in Arkin's crowd? They are new to the city, and that might be the fresh start that you need."

It wasn't a moment later that Moody's phone rang, Arkin on the other end of the line. Moody couldn't keep from grinning as Arkin asked him to show Thea a good time. He had heard their conversation, and it hadn't occurred to him that she would be so hurt by his distancing himself from her. It was really the best thing to do; they were just too different and she was too good for him. His heart was already in knots for making that decision.

Thea glanced up to see a really handsome blood standing next to the table. He knelt down, gave her a winning smile, and asked her to dance. Her face brightened as she stood. Edden stood also.

"Just so you know, she came with me and she leaves with me."

Moody winked at Edden as Jos seated herself in Thea's warm seat. Edden glared at Jos, his eyes narrow.

"Rein it back in, Edden. We are part of Arkin's crew, and she is safe with my partner."

Edden sagged slightly, taking a long sip of blood. "What is going on?"

Jos shrugged. "There are several things going on. First, he, meaning Arkin, wants to make sure that any asset is safe. Thea is an asset, being a silent witness. There have been some dangerous things going on, and we are around to make sure she survives them."

"I thought all the introductions were out of the way."

"They are, but Arkin is careful, and you don't get to be that old without being careful."

Edden's gaze drifted over to where Thea was dancing with Moody. It was a waltz.

"The second thing is that Arkin is attracted to her, but I think that he thinks she is too good for him. The fire is there and burning just as bright, but he denies stepping into the heat. He extricated himself politely but, in the process, hurt her feelings. His personal business isn't my business, as long as he isn't in danger and she doesn't endanger us. They are going to have to work it out."

"I saw them together, they are a match, and maybe he thinks someone in the enclave will be pissed. Maybe he is waiting for something," offered Edden.

She shrugged. "Don't know, and not my business. He heard your conversation. Sorry about the eavesdropping, but he slightly freaked out thinking she might take a walk to Tasha's wild side. He definitely doesn't want her near Tasha. This was a nice place to take her. Clever thinking."

Edden shrugged. "First time she has come out and wanted to run wild. It's not like her. She is normally reserved with strangers and more comfortable with friends. If she makes it known to changelings that she is ready to date, there will be a few who will take her up on her offer. They have been waiting, I think, for something to break. There might even be two witches interested," he said. "Arkin will need to make up his mind soon. She deserves to be happy, and if he can do that for her, I'm glad. I don't want her making a mistake, and the way she is feeling now, she might just run before she walks."

"None of us want to force her into something she isn't ready for." Jos stood up, leaving the table as Moody escorted a flushed Thea back to their table.

"Moody, this is Edden, my very best male friend. Edden, this is Moody, a new male friend."

Edden refrained from a smile as they shook hands. Thea collapsed in the chair. She beamed.

"Feel free to give me a call anytime. I really enjoyed dancing with you."

"I'm old-fashioned, but I like to know who and where my date is," Moody remarked with a chuckle. He bent down and kissed her lightly on the forehead, like you would a child. Most people would find that annoying, but many born of the blood were so much older than those around them it was a habit. Thea watched as Moody waved his goodbye, disappearing into the crowd. She sighed.

"Had a good time?" Edden asked cautiously.

"For once, I did. He was very nice, not grabby at all."

"Well, you are too nice to grab," Edden responded. "Let's get you home. I think you could use the sleep."

"I mislead you, Edden."

Edden frowned, knowing that Jos was sitting very close to them, probably eavesdropping on their discussion.

"What, you didn't want a night out with your very best guy friend?"

"No, I did. I wanted to be with someone I trust, but I wasn't honest with you why I felt this way. My parents used to say that you would know the one when you saw him or her. That is why I know Lucy isn't the one for Emlyn, but I believe RM is. Though I wouldn't push him toward making any sort of decision based on just my intuition."

"Em once said that he thought you could read souls. Knew if a person was good or bad."

"Now you make me sound like Santa, naughty or nice. You just kind of know. And when I met Arkin…you'll think I'm stupidly romantic, but something clicked. My parents didn't care if I loved a changeling, a human, a witch, or a born blood, as long as I was happy. But you see, Arkin has seen my kind come and go. He may be tired of being bereft. He may think of me as some silly child, and to him, I am young. I thought that we seemed compatible at first, but he was so formal in the way he dismissed me…you know, I might make a very good nun."

Edden chuckled as he stood. He extended her a hand. "Let's take you home and put you to bed. Tomorrow the world will look different to you."

Thea chuckled, and she hugged him. "You know, you are a light in a sometimes-dismal world," she muttered in his ear. "You are dear to me. I want you to be careful."

Edden curled his arm around her waist, walking her to the door. He cast a backward glance at Jos.

"Do you think I am in danger? It's Claire who said that the dark was coming for you, Thea."

"True, but I think it might make things darker for me if someone took away my light."

CHAPTER 11

It wasn't even seven thirty in the morning when the doorbell chimed. Polly barked, jarring Thea out of bed. This morning, she resembled death warmed over in a microwave, only better dressed. With her robe wrapped around her, Polly nipping at her heels, she pulled open the front door, finding RM standing on her doorstep, looking pretty and fresh.

Em peered over his sister's shoulder, a quirky smile on his lips.

"I thought I would come over and report. Then I am heading home for a shower and bed."

"You want company?" Em asked, cheeky.

RM met him in the eyes and smiled. "Sure, if you shower, brush your teeth, and dress in something that is easy to get off."

Em stood for just a second, considering RM's reply, and then bolted for the stairs. RM chuckled. "He is such an idiot, and slow to boot. Don't know why it was his job to look out for his little sister."

Thea was the one that wasn't human; it was her job to look out after him, find someone to grow old with. "Come on in and sit down. You want something hot to drink?"

RM patted Polly on the snout and shook her head. "No, I'm good." She seated herself in the chair, watching Thea make hot chocolate. "You aren't all that scary in the morning."

Thea managed a weak smile, running a quick hand through her tangled hair. "Thanks," she said. "So Denard."

"He's not in any hotel, lodge, motel, or B&B. That leaves renting a house, staying with a friend, or hiding in a foreclosed property. We are still looking."

Thea leaned against the cabinet in thoughtful silence. The landline rang, and Thea glanced at the caller ID. It was Esther. Thea held up her finger, gesturing for RM to wait.

"How does everyone know I'm up?" Thea asked as she put Esther on speakerphone.

"The library was broken into last night." So much for hello.

"Which library?" Thea asked, knowing there were several.

"The one that would be very bad to have something missing from," Esther added, sounding exasperated. "There is a section in our coven house dedicated to protecting books that cannot or should not be used. They eventually get destroyed. We go to great lengths to secure them. Each coven makes it their mission to destroy that which might destroy us. I know they say magic isn't good or evil, it's what you do with it, but that's bullshit. Doreen is taking inventory. I'll let you know what's missing."

Thea glanced at RM. This wasn't good news. "Wouldn't the coven house be spelled against that sort of thing?" Thea asked, sipping on her hot chocolate.

"Bingo! So how did the son of a bitch get through the wards? I didn't think there was anything that should be able to get past them without alarming us."

Thea wondered if it was spelled against demons; they were, after all, considered to be inhabitants of hell. You just didn't see them walking down main street. The wards might not be protection against angels either.

"Thanks, Esther, for the update, and I'm sorry that was the news you had to tell me. Let me know what is missing."

"You let me know how you think this Denard got into a warded room. I can't think that one of my people helped him, especially not after Ted's death." Esther hung up, the room very quiet.

RM met Thea's gaze. "There is something you aren't telling us about this Denard. If he isn't totally human, what is the part that isn't?"

Thea was very quiet, the tension ratcheting up as she considered how best to respond. She liked RM. She walked over to the table and sunk down into a chair. Her hands huddled around her mug as if the warmth could take away the chill that crawled up her spine.

"Your word?" she asked, her voice sounding soft, almost conspiratorial.

"You're my client, you damn well have my word. As long as I can kill him, with the weapons I have, I won't be worried."

"I don't know for sure, but I think he might be half-demon."

RM's eyes narrowed as she considered Thea's response. She leaned back in the chair and regarded Thea with a wrinkled brow. Thea could see RM's mind working.

"How does one get to be half-demon? I mean, I have known some girlfriends who were like that once a month, but…really?"

Thea shrugged.

"I see why you didn't tell Esther. Too early, huh?"

Em appeared freshly washed and dressed, calling RM's bluff, but it wasn't a bluff. Their eyes locked, and she stood. That was the end of the conversation.

"My car's unlocked. Get your pert little ass out there."

Thea smiled as RM winked at her. She watched them exit the house into the morning sunshine. She glanced down at Polly and sighed. Everyone seemed happy. Why couldn't she be?

* * *

Em sauntered into the office just after lunch, a grin on his face, as Thea sat at reception. Their eyes met, and she could tell he was happy. He seemed relaxed, almost as if he had made a momentous decision. He wasn't one to sleep around. He had dated quite a bit, but usually after one or two dates, he could tell that they weren't meant to be as a couple. Thea believed that he was not only thinking of himself, but of her as well, always trying to be the keeper of her flame. He had been slow with Lucy, letting her go, but everyone had their weak spots.

He met his sister's eyes. "Damn it if you aren't always right."

It was a soft smile he gave Thea, and she returned a grin. RM would never be jealous of her, never try to separate that bond, and she would keep the secret, should she marry Em, that her sister-in-law was an angel.

"I told you she was more your type than Lucy. It's not really magic or anything like that, it's just a girl thing. But remember, Lucy has claws. She isn't some human to be tossed aside easily without a fight. She won't go after RM, she will go after you."

Em chuckled as he walked around the desk, bent over, and kissed his sister's head.

"No, I'll go after you," added Lucy as she plowed into the mortuary, eyes ablaze and claws out.

Lucy's claws slashed through the air to intimidate both Em and Thea. She knew better than to actually use her claws in a fight with humans. Em bent over to punch in the code to open the bottom drawer. There was more than one gun available in the office, but he wouldn't need it. Although Lucy went for Em, Thea intervened and took a hit to the face. To Lucy's utter surprise, Thea remained standing. Lucy's eyes were wide with astonishment as Thea leaped around the desk with supernatural speed, grabbed her by her shirt collar, and threw her out the front window into the street. By the time she hit the asphalt among shards of glass, Em had his gun out. Adam had also leaped out of his car and crossed the street to enter the fray. Matt was out the front door, trying to restrain and talk some sense into Lucy. He had the strength to handle her. He also had the knowledge to try to get her to adhere to their law.

Thea pulled a tissue from the box on the desk and spit blood into it as Em winced. He knew why she had stepped in; she could take more damage than he could since he was totally human, but it wasn't something he wanted her to do. It was his job as her big brother to protect her. The left side of her cheek was black-and-blue. He reached out to touch it, but she turned away as Adam surveyed the scene.

"Do I need to call the police?" he asked, concerned.

Thea shook her head. She figured Matt would have one of the Seven's security out here fast enough to take care of the wayward bitch.

"No, but thank you for your concern," she replied softly.

"You need to get something cold on that," he added, brow furrowed, wanting to help but, at the same time, not wanting to give himself away, that Arkin had asked him to look out for his newfound angel.

"How about Lucy's heart?" muttered Em through gritted teeth.

As expected, Matt, who was glowering at Lucy and trying to keep her calm, called security. In this instance, it was Luther, who usually turned into a very large wolf, who appeared with backup. They promptly took Lucy off the scene. He eyed the gun that Em had pulled; it now rested unused on the desk. His gaze flitted to Thea, who was still standing, the bruise obvious on her face. He was amazed that she was still upright and coherent after being hit by a changeling. He shivered slightly.

"What happened?" he asked as he dug into a satchel and brought up a cold pack.

Thea nodded thanks and put it on her chin.

"Lucy and I aren't exclusive. I'm seeing someone else, and she didn't like it," added Em.

"So she took a swing at your sister? How come you're still standing?" he asked bluntly.

"I was bitten by a radioactive spider when I was on a field trip," quipped Thea as Luther raised an annoyed eyebrow.

Adam stood by one of the pretty flowering plants, very still, as if he feared to be noticed. He listened intently.

"Would you believe I am from the Amazon and I parked my invisible plane out back?"

"You are just too funny. Don't give up your day or night job. Thank you for not shooting her. I presume silver?"

"Always," added Em as he watched Thea walk to the window.

She stared out into the afternoon sunshine. Luther's team was already sweeping up the glass, and they would have repairs made probably before the evening. Adam didn't follow; he knew Cece was out there, watching. He had to be careful. Thea wasn't stupid. As if in a trance, hearing Luther still discussing that situation with Em, she wandered out the door. Cece saw Thea leave the mortuary, and instead of turning toward Edden's tavern, one of her favorite places, she turned to the left and casually walked down the street. Cece hopped out of the car and nonchalantly followed. To Cece's surprise, Thea wandered into an ice cream shop and ordered almond-butter ice cream in a sugar cone. She proceeded to take one of the café chairs beneath an umbrella that sat along the sidewalk. It wasn't long before her brother found her, taking the seat across from her. He was very quiet, eyes looking over passersby. He watched her sister devour the ice cream. The coolness felt good to her mouth.

"You didn't have to take the hit for me," he muttered.

"If she had hit you, she would have broken your jaw or your neck," Thea remarked softly.

"You threw her through the front window," he added.

"That was the least that I wanted to do to her. I thought I showed some restraint. After this Denard thing is over, I want to go somewhere alone. I need to think through some stuff. It's not that I want to hide forever, but maybe just for a while longer."

"Luther doesn't have any answers, and I think he wants some," commented Em.

"We all want something." She paused, as if thinking. "Maybe one day, but not today," answered Thea with a sigh.

Em's phone rang with a soft classical tone. It was RM. He put her on speaker.

Cece sat a seat away, casually sipping on her milkshake, trying to listen into the conversation.

"We found where he was staying. It was a rental home, but he has since moved. It looks as if he is planning on creating something. The place was a mess. I'm not a paranormal, but I know something is happening."

"I appreciate all your efforts," Thea remarked with a nod to her brother.

"We aren't done yet. He is going to need privacy for whatever he is planning, so we have expanded our search to abandoned commercial buildings. No messages, nothing left at the scene but a mess."

"Thanks, RM. I'll see you for dinner," offered Em as he hung up, a riot of emotions crossing his handsome face.

His phone rang again. It was Zander. Esther had called into the office to speak to Thea. Em thanked Zander and quickly dialed Esther's number. There were no amenities. No polite conversations.

"A man fitting Denard's description was in Misty's store. She didn't have everything that he needed, but he is up to something. Chester's store was broken into last night, and he was assaulted."

Thea shook her head, rubbing her face, feeling tired.

"You were asking after the book that went missing. It's small, about the size of your two hands put together. It is a treatise on heaven and hell. I can't see where it would benefit anyone. There didn't seem to be any spells. Most of it was readable, but there were other passages that no one could read. It was in some language I had never seen before."

Thea glanced at her brother, wondering if that would make a difference to a half-breed.

"That might not stop Denard," muttered Thea. "Thanks for the update. I have RM looking for him as well. Between all of us, we should corner him before he does any significant damage."

"Then you truly believe he can use this book to do something?" Esther asked expectantly.

"I think he thinks he can, and that makes him more than just dangerous," answered Thea, voice tight.

"If we catch him, what do you suggest?"

Thea glanced at Em, who shrugged. "This isn't a matter for the police. If you can give me a call, we can make the decision then. He was the one who contacted me first. I might be able to better deal with him, but I don't think there is a way to reason with him."

"Is he capable of killing someone?" Esther asked.

Thea met her brother's eyes. "Yes, quite capable." She was quite certain.

* * *

The front window of the mortuary was repaired with lightning speed, and the day continued as it did, without any more excitement. Lucy had been taken away by security, and Thea figured that Lucy was going to get quite a lecture. One didn't lose your cool in public, nor did you strike a human. The chances of killing them were very likely. With claws and a possible wound, there was a risk of infecting the victim as well. Adam, the well-meaning bystander, had left, offering whatever service he could supply as a witness. He found his partner, Cece, in their car, and she updated him on the conversation between brother and sister. Adam didn't know who Denard was, but apparently, he wasn't good news for the siblings.

It was Thea who had delved back into her work. There was an evening wedding, a large flower order, and three corpses that had to be prepared. She ignored the pain in her jaw, knowing that the bruise would soon fade. It had been instinctive to protect Em; she knew that she could take the abuse much better than her brother could have. It was and wasn't a mistake. It wasn't a mistake to protect him, but it was a mistake to do so in front of witnesses. She had a keen awareness that her time hiding was running short. It was Matt, however, that was creeping around the prep room, stealing gazes at her, with unasked questions in his eyes. Thea ignored him. If he was so damn curious, he could ask. It just didn't mean that she would answer.

It seemed like a long few days to Adam. It wasn't that he didn't enjoy his work; it was the pressure of keeping a secret that he felt was explosive. It was hard for him not to tell his small team what was up, but in truth, he wasn't sure what was up himself. He and Cece had followed Thea home, where it appeared she was staying that evening. He noted that she didn't seem too thrilled to see Perry, one of the Seven, show up at her door unannounced. She had him stand on the front porch as they talked. She was dressed in pajamas and a robe, her hair pulled back in a ponytail. Her arms were folded across her chest, and Adam knew she was more than annoyed just by her stance. They didn't talk long, and soon it was Em who broke up the conversation, asking Perry to leave. Adam knew what Perry wanted to know: How had Thea remained standing after Lucy, a changeling, had hit her? How had she not had a broken jaw or neck? Adam knew the answer; he was also pretty sure that both Em and Thea didn't want anyone else to know the answer. Adam was worried for her. It was going to come to pass that her secret might be revealed, and she was going to need strong allies. It annoyed him that Arkin had backed away from her just when it seemed she needed the support.

With his second team, Fran and Kyle, watching the house, it was his turn to report. He felt a tinge of guilt as he drove away. It was like a twisted reality show and he had a hard time not watching. Adam arrived at the house they had been using. It was slowly being dismantled. They were leaving their temporary quarters for the house that Yardley had built and lived in, Arkin's team having gotten it livable. Since Arkin had been recognized as their new leader, hopefully drawing the factions together and erasing the territories that had been created, they could move into the city and stake their claim.

Adam arrived at the house and pulled open the fridge, finding the remains of a pizza. He warmed it in the microwave, his stomach growling in anticipation. With pizza in hand, sitting on a paper towel, he plopped down in a chair by the window in the study. He devoured it with a satisfied burp, pleased with the chair and room he had chosen. It would be a private-enough area to talk, and he was quite sure they would do some talking. Adam leaned back and closed his eyes, waiting for Arkin. He didn't have long to wait.

Arkin, with Marta at his side, stood over Adam, watching him sleep.

"At least he is not drooling," she commented casually.

Adam's right eyelid eased up. He stifled a yawn and stretched, paper towel still clutched in his hand. "Sorry, long day, and it's damn hard to keep a secret as wild as this one."

Marta seated herself on the empty desktop, Arkin regarding him with interest. "Why was it a long day?" he asked, hungry for news about Anthea. Although his head was telling him that it was the right thing to do to stay away from her, his heart, body denied it. He wasn't sure how long he could hold out.

"You know that we had the whole Edden-and-Moody issue where you dumped her and she is feeling hurt."

Arkin glowered at him.

"Just saying, that's what it looks like to her. Apparently, her brother is seeing RM Kanarvan. She's an ex-cop who has a detective agency, and they just recently hired her to find someone called Denard. He appears to be heavily on their minds, and I'm thinking he might be what drew her to that abandoned building, but I have no proof, just gut instinct. Anyway, a changeling came into the mortuary and there was a fight."

Arkin stiffened.

"Before you ask, she has quite a shiner along her chin, but she didn't go down. That may be the problem. I got in there to see what had happened, especially when the changeling flew out the window."

Marta opened and then closed her mouth.

"The girl's name was Lucy. Apparently, she was dating Em and took exception to a breakup. They didn't call the police, but Matt, an employee of theirs, called for changeling security, and this Lucy person was escorted out. Luther, changeling security, asked Thea very pressing questions, but she didn't answer them straight. In fact, she was downright sarcastic. I say, good for her."

"How can she take that risk?" Arkin sighed.

"She left the office and got an ice cream. I figured she needed time to think and consider next steps. She saved her brother from severe injury, because that changeling wasn't pulling her punches. Cece followed her and listened as best as she could to the conversation. They are actively looking for this Denard fellow. There have been a few thefts, a book, and some spell-binding materials. It sounds like, when whatever this is over, Thea might be disappearing for a while." Adam let Arkin stew in silence. The expression on his face was mixed. Marta had never seen him so torn.

"Look, this is none of my business, but you are king of the city now. Shouldn't you be looking after her as one of your subjects, so to speak? I know she isn't a member of the blood. In fact, she isn't a member of any race I currently know, but that makes her unique. I know you have us watching out for her, but I'm not sure that is all she needs right now. I don't think you could further endanger her, but I think you could do a hell of a lot to pick up her spirits. Unless, of course, you want just Moody to entertain her to keep her away from others as you bide your time. Then when he pulls away, you can hurt her all over again. But that just seems cruel, and I know you aren't like that."

Arkin's eyes narrowed. Marta could feel the tension elevate in the room.

"You know, I have liked you for your brutal honesty, Adam, but sometimes you are just too brutal," Arkin responded. "I came to this city to clean it up. So far, I have everyone on board, but you know that can change in a heartbeat. I didn't come here to fall in love or put someone innocent in danger. I'm not innocent anymore, Adam."

"No one can stay innocent forever, Arkin. You know that. When all her innocence is stripped and she comes out into the world, she is going to need some support system and strong friends. You need to be that one, you need to be there for her."

"When things are settled, when I am sure that she won't be used against me, maybe."

"That *when*, Arkin, could pass you by." Adam rose from the chair. "Just saying." He paused. "I have to get some zees. I'm taking over in the morning. I'll listen to see if I hear any more about this Denard fellow. He means trouble, I'm sure, for her, and I think the city."

"I'll ask Esther about it. We have a conference call scheduled for this evening. She just wants to verify that there won't be a violent outbreak of blood and that the city is being mended."

"Don't be surprised if she is not forthcoming. I'm not sure she knows you well enough to trust you with her secrets. I know you have scheduled a meeting of the blood. You are going to choose Asao as your second, I think. Then you have to schedule a meeting with the other leaders in the city. It is then, I think, the trust will build."

"That is the plan. We seem to be of like mind."

Adam nodded, stepping past Arkin. "I'll keep you informed. If it comes down to some sort of fight or something, I'll let you know. If it looks as if she is going to fall off the innocent wagon, I'll let you know that as well. You do deserve her, Arkin. You just have to believe in your heart that it is true. Everyone who saw you together believed it, but maybe you are afraid to speak it. It has been a long time coming to find a soul mate."

Arkin remained quiet as he watched Adam leave the study. He closed the door behind him. Arkin glanced at his watch. He had time.

"So you want to berate me as well?" he asked Marta, meeting her gaze.

"I'm with you on settling the city, but I'm not with you abandoning Thea. I like her. I think you two fit together, but you have been around longer than I have. Maybe I'm colored by romantic, girly-girl feelings."

Arkin rolled his eyes. He could still feel the pressure of her body next to him, feel the tickle of hair on his neck as she sighed leaning against him, and the tremble of her body as she came undone in his arms. It was a heady power she had over him.

"Fine. After the city is settled, after everyone has acknowledged me, I'll speak with Thea."

Marta smiled, inclining her head. "A wise decision." Marta hoped it wasn't too late.

Arkin always had an open-door policy, but sometimes he wished they were a bit more scared to open that door. He appreciated the comments of those closest to him, and usually, they were of a like mind, but in this case, they weren't. Arkin had closed the door to the study after Marta had left. This would be the last night that they would remain in this house. It had served their purpose, but it wasn't as viable for them as Yardley's mansion. He leaned back in his chair as he glanced at his watch. And then the phone rang. Esther was right on time.

"Good evening, Esther. I'm so glad that we could speak this evening."

"I'm rather glad you decided to come to the city, Arkin. We don't like disruption or infighting. I am hoping you can corral that. I understand you lost a few in your ascension."

"It happens, and it was not my choice, but sometimes a choice isn't given us. We are meeting tomorrow to discuss next steps."

"And what are your next steps?" she asked boldly.

"To take care of those things that haven't been taken care of, outstanding items regarding people, business…they have autonomy as long as they show they can use it well."

"Have you chosen your second yet, or did you bring someone in with you?"

"A good question, and no, I didn't bring someone. My second is in another city. I will be choosing someone from here." It was the way that Arkin worked; he had more seconds than he could count on his hands, and always, when he felt they were ready, the city would be theirs. Esther was quiet. "You're not even going to guess. I would think a woman's curiosity would get the better of her."

"I think I already know, and if I did guess, you might not feel free to tell me. You will have your hands full with two of your women, as it stands. I know Yardley did at times. Glad to see you are getting your use out of Anthea Black. Although we don't work with her very often, she can be trusted. She has a good reputation. In a situation when changes occur, it can often cause ripples that affect others. I want to be prepared for any ripples."

"I will be reviewing all our interests in the city. If one is not profitable, it will be dismantled or reinvented."

"That sounds rather ruthless."

Arkin chuckled. "Compared to the centuries I have lived, it is very tame," he responded. "Something of interest did come across my desk, so to speak. A name that I don't have any association with. Tony Denard?"

Esther was silent a moment. She knew Arkin was fishing. She also knew via the grapevine that he was maybe more than overly fond of Thea.

"We believe that he is behind a rash of thefts," he said. "One of our stores was broken into. Anthea Black ran across him briefly, and he had delusions of being a witch, though he isn't one. She cautioned us and is looking into his whereabouts. We are all looking for him before he does something stupid or dangerous. As a silent witness, you know that she has the quality where people want to tell her things. Sometimes you can keep those things to yourself. Other times, you have to do what is the greater good and let everyone know that there might be an idiot out there."

"Ah, thank you for that. A friend of Thea's, is he?"

Esther shrugged, collating her thoughts. "Not to my knowledge. But you know that she had that inopportune moment of speed dating. Maybe they met there," she said. "I thank you for your time and belaying any troubling thoughts. We would like to know whom to get into business with without having to look over our shoulders. This should make it easier. You have our thanks."

"We will keep you informed should anything come up pertaining to your business interests." The phone call ended. Arkin sat in silence, phone still in hand. Esther shrugged off the connection.

* * *

Thea had received Arkin's check. She had a moment where she wanted to rip it to shreds but then thought better of it. If she decided to disappear for a while, the extra funds would be appreciated. She was trying desperately not to dwell on Arkin's rejection; she had more important, worldlier things to consider. Denard was at the top of the list.

She was just heading out the door when Parkerton appeared on the front porch. Parkerton worked for Asao; he was a tall angular-looking man who wore black, gray, and red, with a Mandarin-style collar and had a dark, neatly trimmed moustache and goatee. He smiled warmly to Thea as he bowed. He handed her a white envelope with gold writing. An invitation. Knowing how important it was to Asao, she opened it and read the invite. Arkin was gathering the leaders of the territories together. Asao wanted her there as a silent witness. She cursed to herself as Parkerton stood politely, waiting for her answer. He didn't have a clue regarding her feelings for Arkin, but she wondered if Asao did.

"Tell Asao I would be glad to attend at his request. Is that tomorrow evening?"

"Yes. It is a gathering of the bloods."

Thea sighed, nodding. Parkerton turned and gestured back to the black town car that was waiting at the curb. A young woman scampered across the walkway and presented her with a garment bag. "Since it is short notice, Asao would present you with something suitable to wear. He believes it will be most fitting."

Yeah, Asao knew how she felt about Arkin, the little meddler.

"Tell him thank you. I will expect you at what time?" she asked politely.

"Seven thirty."

Thea nodded, stepping back into the house to hang up the garment bag on the coatrack. She unzipped it slightly. Then she whistled. The material was lovely, and probably pretty expensive. It was a gown of brocade in white, with silver and gold threads. A small bag lay over the hanger and contained what she used to call chopsticks, but they were slender golden skewers, or hairpins, that would hold her curls at bay.

Em walked up behind her, silently startling her. She jumped slightly.

"Where did you get the threads?"

She turned and frowned at her brother. "Where did you just come from, the eighties? Asao brought them for me. He wants me at a meeting tomorrow night and has supplied me with clothing."

"That is more than just clothing, that is wow!"

She sighed, taking the dress, laying it over her arm.

"You seem a bit quiet. What's on your mind?"

"What isn't on my mind, really? Denard, Arkin, possibility of discovery…what else? Maybe I should be brave and bold and not give a shit if everyone finds out what I am. After all, the blood-born, the changelings all had to take the risk and step out into the light of discovery."

"True, but they aren't one of a kind. As far as I know, you are the only earthbound angel that we know of. If you want my opinion, and I know you didn't ask for it, after the meeting is over, step back and let Arkin handle the city. Let the witches find Denard. After all, he is pissing in their pool. And get your mind together. Go somewhere, go anywhere."

She sneered at him, shaking her head. "You are so elegant in the use of your language."

"My job as your big brother is to watch out for you, not watch out for my diction."

"We watch out for each other. Didn't I tell you that you would be better off dating anyone but whom you were dating?"

Em held up his hand, nodding. "I know you did. You were right, I was wrong. Is that what you wanted to hear?"

"No, it's not. We all want to find happiness. We all want to find that one person who clicks with us, just to be near them makes you happy. I think RM can do that for you. I thought maybe Arkin, despite him being a blood-born, might be the one for me, but lately, I'm not sure. I thought we were thinking along the same lines, dating, but not now. I made a mistake and misunderstood the situation and him."

"He has a lot on his mind, sis. Let him get his city in order, and then maybe he will come back around for other things."

She hit him lightly in the shoulder.

"If he does come around for other things, you are going to have to confide in him. Don't be surprised if it scares the hell out of him, or maybe he will feel that you are more than he can handle, above him in status."

She snorted. "I'm no angel. Well, literally, I am, but you know what I mean."

"Yeah, I do, and I think you are wrong about that."

CHAPTER 12

The day started with grumble of thunder. A bit of lightning flashed brightly across the sky, and a light drizzle of rain coated the streets. It was a gray kind of day that extended to Thea's wardrobe and reminded her of Arkin looking so slick in his gray suits, a color that resembled a world that was neither black nor white. Although work was usually a soothing balm, keeping her mind focused today seemed unusually slow. There were no burials this day. A Christening was scheduled in the chapel around noon; she could double-check the arrangements. The floral staff were busy with a number of table ornaments, and because of the rain, people weren't just dropping in, nor had any appointments been made, so she decided to help with the floral arrangements, adding a few touches here and there. It wasn't until noon that trouble walked in literally in the form of Esther. The witch's expression was grim as she entered reception, gesturing for Thea with a tilt to her head to find someplace quiet to talk. Anthea gestured to the coffin display room. Most people didn't find that room very comforting, and few stayed to chat for long, but Esther was made of sterner stuff.

Esther walked to the front window, staring out into the rain through the soft white curtains. She turned, arms folded across her chest. She looked cold, though she was wearing a light raincoat dotted with droplets.

"Can I get you something warm to drink? You look cold," offered Anthea.

"One of our witches was murdered early this morning. He was hacked up, body barely recognizable. I am thinking that Denard did it, because certain ingredients were taken from the shop."

A moment of silence filled their conversation, thunder shattering it for them.

"Ingredients that, by themselves, aren't dangerous, but together, might be."

Esther nodded, pleased that Anthea was quickly putting the pieces together.

"I hope you understand that I had to give Denard's name to the police, though I don't have any proof. They needed to know that he might be trouble. There isn't anyone else I can point a finger to."

It was rare for a witch to be caught, let alone killed.

"You did the right thing. I don't have any proof either. I just know he is trouble. I am sorry, but if he is guilty, he will get a better deal from the police than he will from me. If he is in my sights, he is dead."

Esther met Thea's gaze. There was an unspoken silence between them.

"You promise that?" she asked in a hushed question.

"I already made the promise to myself."

There was a momentary lull in the conversation.

"If he has the books and ingredients to, let's say, work black magic, how long does something like that take, to create a spell?"

"I can't tell you if he got everything he needed at Wilson's. If he did, then maybe a day or so. It takes a lot of focus and energy. If he didn't, he will be on the prowl for what remains. I have already alerted everyone that I know. We are watching, we are trying to find him. What else can you tell me about him? If he is human, he shouldn't have been able to kill Wilson, but he did."

"I think he is only half-human. The other half is not from something we would often find in this realm."

Esther frowned a moment, head tilting to her left as she considered Thea's remark. Thea remained as stoic as she could.

"There are only three other realms that we consider to exist in this world: the fey, which sort of move in and out of this reality; heaven; and hell, or so the clerics believe."

Thea remained silent. There was no way in hell she was going to expound on Esther's supposition.

"You may want to kill Denard, but I don't think you should face him alone," Esther stated, serious.

"I don't want to face him at all, but somehow I think he and I will be meeting up again. I will be better prepared this time."

"Watch your back, watch everything, and if you need backup, call me. Although I am sure that Arkin would be delighted to assist you."

Thea's lip twitched in annoyance. Esther managed a weak smile.

"He likes you. I can tell. But right now, he has other things on his mind and that he has to deal with, but in time, he may come back around."

"Trying to play matchmaker?" Thea asked. "Give it up. Better women and men than you have tried and failed. I like Arkin, but fate may have dealt us different cards. Sometimes when you face your friends or enemies, you are never sure of how that confrontation will go or end. Both can surprise you."

"I hate it when people talk mystic crap, and I'm a witch."

Thea chuckled as she impulsively hugged Esther. "I am sorry for your loss."

They had never been close, never were friends, but for some reason, Thea felt close to Esther now.

"When Claire said darkness was coming for you, I thought we all might be spared. That was naive of me. I don't like making that mistake," Esther remarked. Interesting to think that darkness would enter a city and come for one person.

"Nor do I like that fact that she might have been right this one time." Thea sighed.

Esther talked for a few more moments. With Wilson having been a coven member with no family, she would ask the Blacks for help with the arrangements and funeral. This was a first with the coven. Although Thea was glad to see that they were beginning to build a trust between them, she was sad that it had to take a death to do so.

* * *

Em stood in reception for five minutes, staring at his sister, who sat behind the desk but also seemed to be staring into space, deep in thought. He wondered what she was thinking. Thea was thinking of Wilson. She didn't know him personally, but his shop was cute, situated on a busy corner, white-and-green-striped awning. It had fragrances, candles, and behind the counter, other things that humans wouldn't find interesting or need. Em waved his hand in front of her face, but his sister didn't stir. Finally, he touched her arm, smiling his apology as she looked at him.

"You need to leave if you are going to be dressed and ready for Asao. You always told me how anal he is about time."

"Right," she replied. It was a riveting reply. Thea stood.

Em still stood aside the desk; he wanted to know what she was thinking but didn't want to ask. Thea gave him a kiss on the cheek, as if to say it was okay. It wasn't. But maybe Em wouldn't ask.

"Knock them dead in that dress. You will be lucky if he can concentrate at this meeting."

Thea knew who the *he* was. Em was daring not to name Arkin. She rolled her eyes at her brother's comment, leaving her desk, Polly following alongside her out of the mortuary, across a wet commons, toward their house. The air was moist. The rain had subsided enough not to need an umbrella. It appeared Polly had found every possible puddle. She needed a good rubdown with a towel by the time that they arrived home.

Thea took a quick shower and changed into the gown that Asao had provided. It was perfection. She had drawn up her curls around the crown of her brow, added a few touches of makeup, and stood staring at her reflection in the mirror. She almost didn't recognize herself, and then again, every time she unfurled her wings, she didn't recognize Anthea Black either.

Asao's chauffer, Billings, pulled up to the curb of the Black residence, glancing in the rear mirror at Asao, who sat in the back seat. He was taking a chance interfering in the relationship between the silent witness and the new master of the city, but he liked both Arkin and Thea together. This was an easy way to show Arkin what he was missing should he give up on Thea.

There were surprised gasps as Thea stepped out of the house wearing that gown. She stopped for just a moment before carefully walking toward the car. Asao stepped out of the car, offering her his hand.

"The gown is lovely. You are very generous."

His eyes ran up and down her form, and he nodded. Men might argue that women of the blood were the most beautiful, but there was always something about Anthea Black that was more ethereal. The more you looked at her closely, the more you were drawn and the prettier she seemed.

"It would not do anyone else justice, Ms. Black. It is yours to keep."

She chuckled as she climbed carefully into the car. Such a flirt, she decided.

"I have been Anthea or Thea for a very long time, Asao. You don't have to stand on formality with me. I am not sure how I can help you this evening, but I will do my best. Once Arkin has settled in, I hope that my job as a silent witness will no longer be needed."

"You have been most patient with us," Asao remarked as they pulled away from the curb. "There is much that has to be done, and you were with us when we were torn into fragments. You must witness our rally as we surpass our failures."

She smiled warmly.

"I could sit in the dark and just listen to you talk sometimes, Asao."

He chuckled at the compliment.

* * *

Marta wasn't at all surprised that Anthea Black was accompanying Asao this evening, because Asao had contacted her team, notifying them that she would be attending as a silent witness. It was only polite to make those arrangements, and the one who brought her was responsible for her comfort and safety. If the gathering was going to be long, as they were supposed to be, Thea would need a break and sustenance. As far as Marta knew, she was the only nonblood who would be sitting in on the actual meeting, though there would be others about. She had expected a lot, but what Marta hadn't expected was the way Asao had dressed her. The gown was stunning, and she tried hard not to smirk, realizing how Arkin was mesmerized when he caught sight of Asao entering through the back double doors with their silent witness in tow. She was glorious in the gown that Asao had given her, and fairly glowed in the dim lighting of the conference room. If he hadn't known that she was truly an angel, he would have called her one.

Arkin stood teenage-boy-struck, staring, his mouth almost hanging open as he gazed at her across the room. Asao struggled not to smile at him as he gently laid a hand on her back, motioning for her to be seated in his section. He was playing with fire, but part of his job as Arkin's new second was his health, and he knew that there was more to their relationship than just business. A fire was smoldering.

Anthea never looked up or greeted anyone in the room. She kept her eyes downcast. She had been groomed by her adoptive parents to be a silent witness. She had an eidetic memory; she never forgot. She had a strong sense of work ethic, so she was perfect for the job, but Thea figured she had done her part for city and paranormals. It was about time she looked after herself. She would be resigning shortly. It was just too difficult to be working with someone she thought might be worth the risk of a relationship. Secrets caused rifts, but Arkin had been different—at least she thought so. Something had changed his mind about a relationship with her, and right now, she was just too damn tired to figure it out.

Asao seated her to his left so that Arkin could glance at her with ease. Thea sat in the chair, eyes looking down at her hands, which lay gently on her lap. Arkin could feel roiling emotions beginning to churn inside him. He wanted her. He wanted to ease the ache that he knew they both had to be feeling. What had possessed Asao? Arkin looked at him with narrow eyes, but Asao was unaffected as he politely greeted the others around the room. They hadn't had a great deal of time to redecorate or change the seating arrangements, so Arkin was stuck at the head of the table. But at least he had found a rather normal-looking chair. Some of the curtain affectations were down as well. It might be a nice room once it was updated.

Thea quickly took a side glance at Arkin. He looked highly edible this evening, she thought. He looked chic in the dark-gray suit, plum-colored tie, his hair neatly combed, face shaved. She drew a breath to steady her heartbeat, concentrating on her job and not the man she had been falling in love with. She surveyed those in attendance. Emily, the only new power in attendance, looked deadly serious this evening. She met Thea's gaze with a curt nod.

The murmurs had settled down as Arkin cleared his throat. She didn't look up but closed her eyes and listened. She knew who was in attendance.

"Good evening and thank you for coming. Tonight we are beginning anew, a city reborn. We shall be discussing our city and her needs. As always, transitions can be difficult, and I lament the deaths of our brethren, but tradition demands that we follow our laws, lest chaos takes us back to a time when, although we were one race, we were divided. I know that the world believes that we are many, but we are not, so we must fight to keep ahold of what we do have. With the death of Yardley, you divided into territories that will not stand. We must help one another's business, buoy new ideas, and make the city safe for all who dwell here. Before we begin discussions in earnest, you will note that I came into the city with allies and colleagues, but not a second-in-command. Over my lifetime, I have had more than a few, and I always leave them with a city to rule. So I have chosen from you one who echoes my beliefs, and Asao will be acting as my second for duties within the city."

Marta looked over those gathered, seeing flickers of agreement and a few narrow gazes of discontent. This was the way Arkin had done things for as long as she remembered; a city was nothing to the overall infrastructure of his empire, and one day, they would realize that Arkin Kane was just a facade and that they served someone far greater. But there would be a time when he revealed who he was, or had been.

Asao stood to deliver a deep bow to Arkin and glance at his brethren.

"You have lived in this city with me, but you do not know my beginnings or how I longed for peace to come for us. I will fight to protect it, and I believe Arkin can bind us together to be a force not just for this city but beyond. I have pledged myself to him and his aspirations." Asao reseated himself.

"I have a brief sense of your businesses, but I would like to expand on that this evening. I am sure, with Yardley's death, there were things left pending. My team has already combed through Garrick's and Cordelia's portfolios. We will be dividing those interests among you." There was a brief murmur of delight. "I also want to know how we can help invigorate what has already been established and discuss future endeavors."

"I'll need a bathroom break," muttered Thea with a sigh under her breath to Asao, who cleared his throat, amused.

"Shall we go around the room? Be prepared to offer up any supporting materials should the need arise within the next few days. We will be working with each and every one of you. I have a team of accountants, decorators, IT…anything you think you might need for your business revamp."

Arkin knew whom he was dealing with and their interests. Tasha preferred the sex industries, which included hotels, drinking establishments for both men and women, and lingerie. Terence dealt in security, IT, the white-collar industries. Margaux liked clothing, the beauty of women, spas. Emily, restaurants and retail furniture and decor, while Asao had real estate interests, accounting and financial interests. There might be some overlap, and that was what Arkin wanted to make seamless. He wanted each business to complement one another and intermingle so that there was strength. Tasha wanted her area to be more upscale, tasteful. While she might understand sex, she didn't quite understand decorating, so conversations erupted on how they could help one another. It was a start.

Two and a half hours later, it was Asao who asked for a break. Thea was extremely grateful. Although she wasn't the only so-called human in the building, she was the only one held captive. She slowly rose from the chair, feeling stiff. She stretched lightly, ignoring Arkin as he approached Asao. She politely stepped away, walking toward where the restrooms were, Asao's security not far behind her. She managed to freshen up and was ready for something to drink. Although she knew there wouldn't be any alcohol, it didn't matter, since it didn't have an effect on her.

There was Enrico. She brightened as she approached the bar, and right beside it was what she would call the food station. Enrico was tall, Spanish by birth, and one of the best chefs in the city. Odd, considering he hadn't tasted food in ages.

"Yoyo, there you are, girl. I have something wonderful for you to eat. First, what do you want to drink? I have something very thirst-quenching."

Thea seated herself at the bar, smile on her face.

"And wait until you try this." Enrico gestured for her to open her mouth, and in slid chocolate. But it wasn't just chocolate; it was a food orgasm waiting to happen. Her eyes widened.

"Oh, Enrico, what you can do with food, women would pay for in bed, if only."

He chuckled, sliding a plate before her. "Eat up. I think you are far too thin, and men like a bit of meat on their women's bones, Yoyo."

"Do you have to call me that?" she asked with a slight frown.

"All right, Cherub, would you prefer that?"

She rolled her eyes as she sipped at the drink. It was an icy-cold fruit punch. She sighed.

Arkin stood beside Asao, hands behind his back, trying to act casual, eyeing Thea from across the room.

"Yoyo?" Arkin asked, curious.

"The Blacks have been in this city a long time. It was news when they adopted Anthea, but she wasn't the best eater as a child.

When they first brought her home, they were worried about her. Enrico has been cooking since he was human and managed to make her a menu that she adored. When she was little, before she learned to walk, she would stand up and then sit down repeatedly, and so he called her Yoyo, but her nickname among the family was Cherub. He thinks of her as a little sister. He was under Garrick's thumb. Now you have freed him."

"Have you known her that long?" Arkin asked, eyes locked on Thea as she ate at the insistence of Enrico.

"About that long. She was a pretty child and improved as she aged. You don't have to worry about Enrico."

Arkin frowned. "Why would I worry about him?" he asked, sounding incensed.

"Kale, however, does not have such pure intentions. Tasha has been pushing the two of them together since she was a teenager. She likes the idea of having the silent witness in her court, and Kale is very handsome."

"But way too worldly," added Arkin as Asao politely nodded.

"I won't argue with you there. So far, she has ignored his pursuit."

Arkin's jaw was tight, and Asao pretended not to notice.

"Then there is Charm. Well, he isn't actually charming. He is our resident scientist, technology guru. He works with Terence. He has had a crush on Thea for a while but can't bring himself to act on it."

Arkin glanced across the room, gaze falling on Charm. He knew this blood-born, a long time ago, but of course that was by another name. Arkin had another name then. Their eyes met across the room. There was a slight nod of acknowledgment.

"He is quite brilliant, but socially inept."

Arkin watched as Marta slid in beside Thea.

"I see you found something to innervate you," she remarked lightly.

"Never underestimate the effect that dessert has on a woman. I could make some other dirty comment, but you get what I mean."

"Erotic chocolates. You know, I always forget you can do lots of things with food. I should talk to Tasha," quipped Enrico. "Eat what you can and take a walk to stretch your legs. You don't know how much longer you will be held captive."

"I'll walk the portrait gallery," said Thea as Marta regarded the dress.

"You look fabulous this evening."

"Asao supplied the gown," Thea remarked. It was expensive.

"But you supplied what filled it. Nicely done, by the way." She chuckled as she watched Thea with gusto finish her drink and clean her plate.

"She always eats what I give her. Isn't the right, Yoyo."

"You made eating fun. You are an array of noises and impressions." She winked at Marta as she stood.

She smoothed her gown and hair, ignoring Asao and Arkin. With a slight sway to her step, she retreated up toward the stairs and the portrait gallery. With her small purse in hand, she turned on her iPod and music to take her mind off the evening. She had always liked the gallery. The blood-born had filled the walls with silhouettes, small and large portraits from times long forgotten. There was a Halloween party picture, times when the world seemed simpler. The main, or largest portrait, was gone. Yardley's picture had been torn down. All that remained was a hole in the wall and a piece of wire.

A hand touched her arm, and she jumped, uttering a slight expletive, finding Arkin standing beside her. She pulled out her earbuds and turned off her iPod.

"You guys are just too damn sneaky. We should put a bell around you," she uttered, annoyed.

Arkin refrained from a smile. He had seen her retreat up to the gallery, security hanging back at Asao's orders, hoping to give them some privacy. No one would be disturbing them. Marta would not have thought him a matchmaker type, but she would not intervene, just watch. Marta thought Asao was justified.

"I apologize if I startled you." Arkin gazed over the wall of pictures. Some were photos, others painted portraits. His fingers played with the wire sticking out of the wall. "I take it that this was where Yardley's portrait fell?"

"He liked to be extravagant. I don't know what decade or century he was born in, but he had the habit of overdoing. He also liked to show off his supposed attributes and fancied himself a celebrity. He should have lived in Hollywood. He thought he was quite the ladies' man, but I found little attractive about him. Maybe that was why he could be cruel. You can understand why some of your race might have been hesitant to accept someone new after the way he behaved and treated them."

"There is that saying 'Better the devil you know,'" commented Arkin.

"Yes, and I knew eventually someone would come around and kick him to the curb. I'm not saying that those residing here didn't have the strength. Maybe they just are tired of the fighting. I am grateful that you came to our city. Although I don't know you all that well and we are of a different race, you seem to be of a kinder nature. I think you will do all right by us."

"That is one of the nicest compliments I have heard in a long time, and you are being generous. I have never been called kind. You know I will try to bring peace and cooperation to this city. On another front, I have tried to be a gentleman with you, but I seem to be failing rapidly. You're like a damn addiction. You are under my skin and in my blood."

Thea opened her mouth, unable to respond.

"Is that lipstick the kind that smudges?"

"No," she remarked as he pulled her to him, tangled his hand in her hair, and kissed her hard as if he were gasping for air or drowning. They stumbled back against the wall, their bodies melting together. They fit so damn perfectly together. A moan escaped her lips as her hands tangled in his hair, wanting more, daring him to go deeper, to be less the gentleman.

"If I didn't have to go back to the fucking meeting, I'd lay you on that table and have my way with you," he murmured in her ear, teeth tugging on her earlobe.

"Keep talking like that and you are going to end up on Santa's naughty list," she whispered right back at him.

He chuckled. "Do you prefer naughty or nice?" he asked, hand snaking up past her belly to her luscious breasts. Angel or not, she was his.

"I think I would like a bit of both, please," she quipped.

"You are mine. Say that you are mine," he remarked, insistent, voice dangerously low.

"You are mine," she repeated, smiling at him, her words meaning the same as his. They were each other's.

They remained locked in that embrace until they both had the strength to part, both slightly mussed. She brushed down his hair, and he adjusted her curls, until they looked appropriate again. They stood staring at each other, a silent understanding between them. He took her hand, leading her back toward the stairs, and Thea tried to keep that smile off her face. But she was failing miserably. It was stupid to risk her so, make her a target for anyone who wanted to hurt him. It was stupid to try to destroy the innocence of a true earthbound angel, but he was never one to ignore fate or destiny. And in this case, something was driving him toward her. Their hands drifted apart as they descended the stairs, Asao waiting politely as Thea passed him and entered the room beyond. It was Arkin who stopped in front of his second.

"She is mine. If anyone else touches her, I'll rend them limb from limb," Arkin stated bluntly.

"Quite understood, Arkin. I'll make sure it is known throughout the city," he added with a bow.

Arkin's lip twitched as he regarded his second. "You do that, little matchmaker."

Asao opened and then closed his mouth.

"Don't even try to deny it."

"I wasn't going to even try," he added with a wink.

The burning passion that she had just let engulf her answered all of Thea's unasked questions. He had wanted her, he did like her, and it felt as if a weight had been lifted off her heart. He did return her feelings for him; he had just been trying to fight it.

The evening drifted by, words and deeds blending into a pleasant haze, Thea stealing gazes toward Arkin. She had wished to stay behind when the meeting had broken up, when the blood had come to an understanding that their businesses would be visited, reviewed, and revamped if necessary, but Asao had brought her and he was a traditionalist. She would leave with him as well. So with a final farewell where Arkin delicately kissed the palm of her hand, his warm tongue creating circles and heat, thoughts of them both being alone together and his tongue going other places, she had to say goodbye. She didn't look back as they exited the building.

"So I hope the evening wasn't too tedious for you," Asao remarked casually, trying to keep a smirk off his lips.

"No, I think quite a bit was accomplished this evening. Thank you for the invitation."

"If I am a good judge of character, I would say that you were not very keen on the invitation at first."

"A girl has the right to change her mind, Asao. Always remember that."

CHAPTER 13

Em had agreed that since his sister had been up late doing the witness gig, she should just stay at home and rest the following day. He wasn't about to get an argument from Thea. Lounging around in her pj's all day wasn't a hardship; in fact, it felt kind of decadent.

Thea had been dozing slightly on the couch when her phone rang. It had been one of those great naps that seemed to take the edge off the day, relax her body, and let her mind rest without dream or worry. She hated to let it go. Thea sat up and reached for her cell. She glanced at the caller ID; it was from Caroline. That was unexpected.

"Caroline," she stated, but it wasn't Caroline's voice that followed.

"She isn't able to answer the phone right now, Ms. Black, but I am sure she would like to see you. We need to meet."

Denard.

Thea closed her eyes, feeling her heart thump hard in her chest. She sat up and cleared her throat, gathering her thoughts. "Where would you like to meet?" she asked.

"This evening at Tristimon Park. We have some things to discuss, you and I. I believe the park will be suitably empty at that time of night."

"I'm not sure that we have anything to discuss," answered Thea honestly.

"I thought you and I were of the same blood, but we are not. You are more than I expected, but does that make you better than I am?"

"It does if I don't steal and murder."

Denard chuckled lightly. "So you think the true nature of my half other self is coming to light? I am part demon, you appear to be an angel. I do not believe that they are friends. I would say that they are enemies."

"So that makes you my enemy? We live in this world, not any other. We don't have to do this."

"All I want to do is chat. Come and see your friend Caroline. Eight."

Thea opened her mouth to reply, but he had hung up. She sat very still, jaw tight, mind racing as Polly climbed up into the couch beside her. She laid her head on Thea's leg. Thea absently stroked her ears and snout.

"I need an alibi, Polly. You know Em is going to ask what's up for this evening, and I can't tell him that I am seeing Denard. He would want to come, and I don't want him hurt. I can't tell him I am seeing Caroline because he thinks she is a waste of my time, and he knows we are on the outs. I can't just tell him I am going out, because he worries. He won't believe I am working at the office, and if I say I'm staying home, he will call to check up on me. Damn, troublesome having a brother who cares. It is doubtful he will believe that I have a date."

Thea considered her options as Polly pushed against her for more attention.

"I could tell him it is a different kind of work, that the bloodborn need me. He wouldn't check up on me. Not Tasha, Asao maybe. Or Marta. We are sort of friends, she and I."

Thea glanced at the clock. It was six o'clock.

"I can leave a message with her. She's a girl, she'll understand."

Thea sat, letting her thoughts run rampant. Arkin's number would put her in touch with his people, and she could leave a message for Marta. And that was just what she did. She made it sound matter-of-fact that Em wouldn't approve, but she needed to see her girlfriends. It was plausible.

* * *

It wasn't one of the first things Marta did when she woke, but now, with the tech age upon them, it was something she had to remember to do. Marta always checked her voice mail and email before making plans for the evening. Marta listened to the message from Thea. In fact, she listened twice. But she was listening between what was being said and what her friend really meant. Something was up, and Marta didn't like it. She left her quarters to find Arkin.

It was legend and myth that the older the blood-born was, the less he had to sleep during the day, and the more power he commanded. As far as Marta knew, it was true with Arkin. He could choose when and if he slept. She knocked once on the door and heard his voice, so she entered. She found him as she usually did, sitting in a nest of covers on the bed, with his laptop and other reading material close at hand. He was dressed usually in his pajamas, but this sunset, he was looking more dignified in a smoking jacket. He glanced up at Marta, who was wearing a silky short robe, standing at the threshold of his room. She had an odd expression on her face.

"Something is up," she declared.

"With whom, where, and when?" he asked, curious.

"Well, with Thea, and that is all I know. She left me a message and asked me to be an alibi for her. Apparently, she is going to see one of her girlfriends that she is on the outs with and Em doesn't approve of their continued relationship. She wanted me to cover and say we were together if he called."

Arkin frowned slightly. "And you don't believe her?"

Marta shook her head. "Not a chance. I'm a girl, I get the girl-code thing. Sometimes you are on the outs with a bitchy girl and your family says leave her, you are better off without her, but Thea isn't that good of a liar or convincer. You need to call Adam and Cece and see if there is anything going on with her, or better yet, we need to follow her."

Arkin was silent. He had become accustomed to Marta's intuition, and though she could have been his second, take a city, she preferred to be his right hand and travel with him wherever she was needed. Marta had never let him down.

Arkin was out of bed and on his feet. "Check with Adam. I am supposed to see Asao this evening. In fact, he is either on his way here or already waiting upstairs."

Marta stepped into the room and picked up Arkin's phone. She quickly speed-dialed Adam. He answered quickly.

"Adam says she has left the house and appears to be on the move toward what he thinks is Tristimon Park."

Arkin was silent for a moment, his mind a tumult of thoughts. "Tell him we are on our way."

Marta opened and then closed her mouth. "I didn't want to stir up everyone. I mean, there is a chance I could be wrong."

Arkin shook his head at Marta. "You are rarely wrong. That is why you are valuable to me. Considering what we saw a few nights ago, she may need help. And this Denard…something is going on and she is afraid to let in anyone to help her."

"You think there are things out there that an angel can't handle?" Marta asked, concerned.

"Yes. For every good light in the world, there is the shadowy dark. I don't want to leave her alone in the dark."

Marta nodded, darting back down the hall toward her quarters. She could hear Arkin's distant footsteps disappearing up the stairs. When he topped the last stair, he threw open the door into the main hall, where Asao stood, waiting politely.

"Change of plans, Asao. We need to stop our silent witness from possibly doing something stupid."

Asao opened and then closed his mouth; he could only nod as Arkin decided he had to trust his second with one of the most important secrets in the city.

* * *

As expected, the park was eerily empty this evening as Thea pulled into the parking lot. She was in her Mini and had entered the area with her lights and engine off, coasting in to be as quiet as possible. She got out of the car, dressed in dark jeans, sneakers, a halter top, with jean jacket over her shoulders. The jacket helped hide the gun that was tucked in her waistband. Her hair was pulled up into a tight braid out of her eyes as she stood by her car, scanning the shadows. There was a hint of light over the small hill away from the slide and swings. It wasn't like the flickering light of a fire, but more like the blush of dawn on the horizon, just a hint of a glow. She broke into a light jog, topping the small hill, and froze. It was not what she expected. In fact, she wasn't sure what she was seeing. There was a pattern in the grass burned in blood and fire. Off to the left was a crumpled, fallen body, Caroline, by the looks of the clothing and hair. Though Thea couldn't see her face or eyes, she knew enough that her throat had been slit. It had to have been a mortal wound, with the amount of blood spilled.

A pit of sadness formed in her chest as she thought of her friend lured there to die. If Denard was charming enough, he could have gotten Caroline to follow him anywhere. This one time, however, her lust for men was deadly.

To the right lay what looked to be the crumpled body of Denard. It was what stood in the center of the ornate pattern that chilled her blood, but its gaze jarred her into moving forward. The form inside the sigil resembled a well-tanned man with dark eyes, blondish hair, wearing jeans and a collared shirt. He looked human, but Thea knew that he wasn't.

He raised his hand and spoke as she approached.

"Peace, daughter of heaven. I mean you no harm. I am not your enemy."

Thea slowed her jog, hand reaching around behind her back to grasp the gun in her waistband. It might not kill him, but it might distract him enough to give her a chance.

"I know you look human, but you are a demon, a full demon."

He managed a gentle smile and nodded. "You are correct. I am a demon, but not the one you should be hunting. I am not the one who did this."

Thea was weary as she stopped just outside the sigil. She barely glanced at Caroline and then turned her gaze quickly to Denard. She needed to keep an eye on the demon before her. Caroline was past helping, and if Denard wasn't dead, he would be shortly. She'd hurry the bastard along.

"I am an archdemon. I was summoned here when one of the forbidden laws was broken. This Demonkin," he said as he kicked Denard none to gently in the stomach, "secured a summoning spell. He brought forth a full demon, Akazhreil. He over powered the Demonkin and fled. I arrived as soon as I could and managed to bind the demon to the city so that he cannot leave. Akazhreil needs to be returned to my realm as soon as possible."

The archdemon looked down at the bloody body of Caroline. There was a glimmer of emotion that crossed his face. Thea was thankful for that. If he had feelings or showed emotion, he could be bargained with and talked to.

"I am sorry about the woman."

"Her name was Caroline. She was a friend. I have known her since we were children, and though we might not always see eye to eye, we usually had each other's backs. Denard used her to get to me. He knew this would twist me up. Denard, Demonkin or half-demon, did this because of some hate. Maybe his need for answers, which he thought I was hiding."

"I would agree. You know that our kind as well as yours are allowed a year's sabbatical in his world. My kind tries to remove any of the harmful books, any knowledge that could cause just such a mishap."

"Mishap…"

Thea drew a breath, trying to reach a level of calm so she could think. Her eyes were filled with unshed tears. She cleared the thickness from her throat, regaining some of her composure. She needed to concentrate not on the dead but on the loose demon.

"You said Denard brought forth a full demon who has escaped. How does one go about returning a demon to your realm? Will angel fire do it?"

The demon looked puzzled as he regarded Thea. She wasn't sure what her ability was, but once you saw it, there was no other name for the power.

"What is *angel fire*? Will you show it to me?"

Thea nodded as she shrugged out of her jacket, tossing it onto the ground. She extended her arms outward to her side, wings spreading out into the darkness. The demon smiled. His eyes glimmered in the dark as he regarded the beauty of her.

"I didn't know any of your kind existed earthbound."

Thea reached behind her, touching the area behind her shoulder blades. She brought up a small poniard rift with flame. It lit up the night as she brought it forth toward the demon. He regarded it with suitable regard.

"Ah, while this is powerful and can kill anything in this world, it will not return our missing demon to his realm."

Thea cursed under her breath as she replaced the blade, the light of the fire dying as it touched the area between her shoulder blade and wings. She had to try.

"You will need a spell to find him. I will supply you with that when I believe you are ready for it."

"It's Denard's mess, but now it falls on me to fix it because of what I am. Do you have any suggestions on how to return a demon?"

The demon nodded solemnly. "Talk to your people."

Her people. Thea blinked once, considering his answer. How odd. She had always considered the Blacks her people. She didn't even have any idea how to contact her people. Thea chuckled, shaking her head as she turned to regard the fallen Denard. The situation was just too weird. She gritted her teeth.

"Is he dead?"

"Only the human half. The demon half will return with me for punishment. I wish I had been quicker, but this was unexpected. Rarely would one want to genuinely summon a demon, and he will pay the price for it."

"I hope he burns for it, because others have paid the price of his stupidity. Thank you."

The demon nodded. "It is a wonder you were not afraid of me."

She shrugged, and he seemed amused. "I'm getting used to the unusual. After all, I am one of them, aren't I? I didn't think there was anything much left in this world to surprise me, but I was sadly wrong."

"Thank you for not calling me a monster." The demon gently leaned forward, his voice low as he spoke. "As a gift to you, I will tell you that we are not alone."

Thea froze for a moment, then whirled around to her left and then right, eyes struggling to see into the shadows. To their left was a row of bushes that gently rustled in the breeze. Her eyes darted back to the demon, who took a step farther back into the pattern Denard had wrought with Caroline's blood, delivered a flawless bow, and vanished in a puff of fiery smoke, taking whatever was left of Denard with him. A soul perhaps. She turned and regarded the bushes again to find Arkin rising out of the shadows. She closed her eyes, ready to shed those tears. Of all the people who might have discovered her secret, he was the last one that she had wanted.

"Thea." He spoke as she stepped back away from him.

She turned to her right and braced her legs slightly, taking a leap, wings catching the air. A lone feather wafted down from the dark stars above as she vanished into the night, only the sound of her wings giving her away. Arkin sighed, bending to pick up the feather, her jacket, and the keys that had fallen out of her pocket. He turned to regard Asao, whom he had to keep silent by covering his mouth when it was revealed Thea was an angel. He had just about given their hiding place away.

"I have lived a long life, my friend, but never did I expect to see an earthbound angel. She is truly, in the entire world, unique."

Arkin could only nod, his face filled with sadness. "I think I know where she is going. I'll return her car and speak with her, though I am not sure she wants to see me. If you will, see to the body of her friend for me. I would appreciate it. Denard's body is here, but I take it his soul is elsewhere occupied. Explain that he killed

Caroline, as Thea called her. The authorities can take it from there. There should be no further investigation."

For Arkin to drive, it was serious indeed. He was more a horse-and-buggy kind of guy. Asao knew that there was so much that needed to be said, so many questions, but time wasn't their ally and he knew that Arkin needed to comfort Thea.

"And what about this other demon?" Adam asked as he knelt down, looking over Denard's body.

"We will worry about that when we need to. First, we have to get the angel back on our side."

"It was her secret to keep. I am sure there was a time when she thought it would be better to tell you or anyone for that matter," Asao remarked thoughtfully.

"You're right. She was probably waiting for the perfect time to tell me, though I can't think of a perfect time. I think she thinks that it might change the way I feel about her, but nothing could. I am in love with her. I have come to realize that now."

There, he had just laid out his feelings to those around him, his intentions clear. It might be only to his companions and the night, but he had said it; he needed now to say it to Thea.

"You need to tell her that," Adam remarked as he turned over Denard's bloody body. It was a fitting death, though Adam wanted to do more.

"I intend to," commented Arkin, a sadness in his voice.

Chapter 14

It wasn't hard to determine where she might have flown to. Even saying it made Arkin shake his head, *flown*. He knew she wouldn't go to the city, but the home in the country—that was the perfect place for her to hide. She had been hiding there since she was a child, he guessed.

He pulled the car up into the drive. There weren't any lights in the front windows, but he knew, felt that she was here. Arkin walked around to the back of the house, where the soft glow of light scattered the shadows of the back porch. Anthea Black sat on the back stair, wings folded neatly behind her back, her face streaked with tears. She was crying for the loss of her friend Caroline. She was crying for the loss of a secret that had been so much a part of her life. And she was crying in fear that she might lose the one man that she was growing to love. Nothing would tear him away from her, and she needed to know that.

Thea glanced up, meeting his gaze, and blinked back a stream of tears as he managed a warm, sweet smile.

"I returned your car. Your keys fell out of your pocket as you took flight. I thought you might not want them discovered when the police come to the crime scene. We will take care of the bodies and any questions asked by the police."

She nodded, snuffling. "That was thoughtful of you, but I'm not sure why you were there. Em always said that I suck at lying, but

I keep trying to hone my craft," she remarked dully. "Who was with you?"

"No one who would dare betray this secret. You have my word on that."

She sniffled again, vaguely nodding. It really didn't matter now. "Why couldn't you let me keep my secret just for a bit longer?"

"You are a silent witness. I wanted you safe for the benefit of the city and my rule, but also because I have fallen in love with you."

She met his gaze as he slowly approached her. His eyes lingered on her face and eyes, not her wings, and for that, she was grateful.

"We all have secrets, Arkin. That is the one small part that we save for ourselves and decide when and if to share it, should our heart deem one worthy." She wiped her eyes with her hand.

"Please don't cry. Especially don't cry because I discovered you are an angel."

She stiffened at his term as he pulled out a handkerchief from his pocket. Of course, he was from an era where men carried such things for ladies in distress. She was in distress.

"I am sorry about your friend Caroline."

Thea wiped her eyes thoughtfully. "We might have had our differences, but Denard knew it would hurt me if he used her. He used her blood for that spell, but in the end, what he summoned killed him. Since you were in attendance, you know that there is a demon loose in the city."

Arkin nodded as he dared another step forward until he could sit on the bottom step, her right wing just a touch away. "And there will be time to deal with him since he is sealed in the city." He made it sound so simple, as if they had all the time in the world. She knew that they didn't. A demon loose in their city wasn't good news; she had no idea what it might have planned.

"Arkin, what am I to do?" she asked earnestly.

Arkin reached up to tuck a stray strand of hair behind her ear. "You can start by calling me by my true name, Benedict."

She frowned slightly as she met his gaze.

"That is my secret. The name won't mean anything to you, but among my people, it is a name to be feared. I believe, among my people, reports of my death are more bountiful than my exploits."

Thea shifted on the hard surface as she plopped down one step closer to him. He extended his hand to her, and she took it, pleased.

"My mother was my father's second wife. He had two sons before he had me. They met and married very quickly. He said that he loved her the moment he saw her and had to be with her, but she only lived one year, dying soon after my birth. My father never married again and left me in the care of his two sisters. One was a widow, and the other was a spinster. You can guess who was the more caring of the two. I was raised just as my half-brothers were, but it was clear that I was cleverer, more determined, and my father's favorite. I never bragged, never brawled with them. I was a good person, thinking us family. That was where I thought wrong. As it became clear that I would be given over the duties by our father, that he wanted me to carry on instead of them, they decided it was time to rid themselves of family."

"I am sorry," she murmured.

"The story has an oddly happy ending, though, Anthea," Arkin said. "My brothers had heard of a man who could be hired for coin to kill. They went to him, told him their tale, and would pay him to kill me. He wanted to meet me first, see what kind of person I was, maybe get to know his prey, so to speak. They were oddly naive to trust him, but that was what saved me. I met Osric one evening in the city. We had never met before, but he greeted me and asked me to sup with him. He told me exactly what my brothers had planned, and I was smart enough to believe him. Although they had never physically abused me, they were not kind. Words sting more than blows, and I knew that there was a rift that might never be mended. Osric said it was my time to go. He offered me a way out of the city, a way to make my fortune if I served him. My brothers would think me gone, I would be safe…it was a kind offer."

"Did you know what he was?" she asked with innocent eyes.

"I knew he was powerful. There was an air about him that bespoke truth, power, worldliness. He was old."

"How old were you then?" Thea asked, curious.

"How old would you say I look now? I was just barely twenty-one. That is the problem with being a blood-born, people forget how old you are and just look at how old you appear. I agreed to go with him, but my brothers were impatient and, two days later, took matters into their own hands. They tried to kill me, but like everything else in their lives, they messed that up to my benefit. Osric saved me. It was not the way he would have had me initiated into the blood, but it saved my life. He was just in time."

"Did you kill your brothers?" she asked softly.

Benedict gently brought her hand up to his lips. "No. I did worse. I ruined them and their businesses once I had recovered. Osric, though he was old, had never chosen another blood-born. I was his first and only. He taught me everything that I knew, and I adhere to the old ways, to his rules and our laws. I was not always popular. There have been times in the past when we were set upon."

"But you always prevailed."

He nodded. "At each attempt, I returned, stronger and more determined, but sometimes if your own kind haven't seen you for a while, it can be safer to let them think you are somewhere when you are not."

"So you used another name."

Benedict nodded. "I have moved through time trying to build a blood-born empire, trying to get us to be one race, stronger…and it was not easy to come out, step out into the world, and let humans see us after hiding for so long."

"Who among your kind knows who you are?" she asked boldly.

"All my seconds, Marta, those who have oathed to me, and soon, everyone here will know as well. I can't say that they will be happy or unhappy about it, but they will know I am not some upstart. Who knows what you are?"

"Emlyn," she answered in a whisper, as if she thought the night could hear.

"Not even your parents?" he asked as she took his hand and gently let him caress her wing. They were soft, ticked his flesh, but he knew they were strong.

"They can withstand a bullet," she commented to his surprise. It was gratifying to see. "When I turned twelve, I got my period and my wings. In those days, you could be schooled at home and only go in for certain days to meet with your teachers, to participate in physical education. That morning, after I got out of bed, they appeared, sprang from my back, and knocked over a dozen or so things in my room. I told my mom I wasn't feeling well. I felt ill and spent the next twenty-four or so hours trying to get my wings to vanish, disappear. It wasn't that easy."

"You must have been shocked," he added, voice filled with emotion.

"I guess I was, but I didn't have time to worry about it. I just wanted to appear normal as quickly as possible. I spent the next year trying to determine what I was, where I was from, about my birth family, the Sheridans. I can tell you there isn't very much out there about angels and nothing about them being stuck on earth."

"What did you learn about the Sheridans?" he asked, his attention riveted on her.

"I believe that both of my parents were angels. They are allowed a year on this earth, whether for punishment or reward, I can't say, but that is what I believe. Whether I was an accident or planned, I don't know."

"How did Em find out about you?" Benedict asked as he leaned in and kissed her cheek, tasting the salt from her tears on her skin.

"Since I couldn't find out much about what I was or where I came from, I was determined to know how to use this gift, curse…I would come out here from the city, ride my bike, and learn to fly. I landed on him by accident one summer's day. Needless to say, we had quite a conversation." She laughed lightly. It was good to hear.

"And he has known all this time. And although we know you aren't quite human, has no one asked bluntly just what you are?"

"No. They just think that they know."

Benedict kissed her cheek and then angled for her mouth. She moaned softly as he kissed her, his hand gripping her braid. There was a slight rush of wind as her wings disappeared against her body and she tumbled into his embrace.

"I love you, Anthea Black, all of who you are and what you are."

"Ah, Benedict, you fall for the first angel that you see. You are too easily impressed. I am not the only creature from a realm far from earth. We have a demon on the loose."

"Yes, and you will not be the only one facing it. I told you once before that you are mine, but I am also master of this city and no one will be put into harm's way without assistance."

Thea pulled away, reseating herself on the top step. She looked at him with caution. "You take too much for granted. You love me, you want me safe. That doesn't mean that everyone will volunteer to help me. You can make the blood do so because you command them, but the others…I am not ready to come out and reveal myself, not yet."

"I won't make you do anything you aren't ready for, Anthea. The demon said that in order to conquer this creature of hell, you need to speak to your people."

She snorted, shaking her head.

"If you were going to talk to your people, where would you go?"

Thea got to her feet, leaning against the rail, eyes lost in the darkness of the surrounding forest. Her people—it sounded ridiculous.

"You make it sound so simple, like I can invite what you call my people to lunch. I went to church every Sunday of my early life and no one spoke to me out of the ether. It is a good question, one I'm not sure I have an answer for."

"Maybe this one time they will speak to you. Go with your gut. Trust yourself. Think about it."

She clenched her jaw in anger, and Benedict came up alongside her, his body hugging hers, trying to take the rage, take the fear, away from her.

"St. Mark's, I guess, is the most pious place in the city, run by monks. They have a shelter, vocational school…I would only need a few moments in the chapel alone."

"You think they would let you in for a suitable donation?"

She sighed, feeling bone-weary. However, the sadness seemed to ebb as he held her. "Benedict," she stated.

"Look, I may have done a lot of things in my past, but most of the time, it was for the right reasons, for the good of all. Having a demon running loose in the city isn't a good thing, regardless of what he can promise. Oh, and he will promise, and there might be some willing to take him up on his offer, but what does the loss of a soul cost you now? Nothing, because it is unseen, but later you would come to regret it. We will speak to them and see if the monks will allow you privacy at the altar."

"That isn't the hard part. I need to know what to say to a choir of angels, how to convince them to give a damn about me or about a city. I'm not the most devout person in this city."

"But you were born from their world. If nothing else, they have to acknowledge it."

Thea was quiet.

"You are naive," she said as she touched his cheek.

She had gotten what she had wanted, his declaration of love, and strangely enough, he hadn't enticed her to return his words. It was enough for him to tell her that he loved her. Her heart soared, but she wished it had been under more romantic circumstances. There was still much to come, and love didn't always survive.

"There are only so many assurances you can give me, Benedict. You say you love me now, but we are just two people whispering in the dark. We haven't faced the city, we haven't faced a demon yet. Can love survive all that?"

"I have waited a long time to find someone that I truly felt a link to, and I have looked, Thea. I have looked, lived, and yes, tried to love, but there was always something lacking. You are that piece of my soul that was missing. It is filled now because I have found you."

Thea chuckled. "You are damn romantic, Benedict."

"I love it when you say my true name."

"Then know this as well, Benedict. I know we can't face a demon, just the two of us. Others will have to be drawn into this duel, but I am not ready to reveal myself. I cannot work miracles, I just have wings, and it took me a long time to know how to use them."

"I came into this city to save it. I am determined to do so. I love a challenge, and I love you. Can we just take it one day at a time?"

"I have more than one day at a time. I seem to have stopped aging when I hit twenty-five, and I think that was one of the things that Em worried about. When he was gone, whom would I be with? Who would take care of me and keep my secret?"

"You have me now," he said proudly. "No, we have each other. And I give you my word, that I will find a word of endearment for you that will not involve the word *angel*."

She smiled. "I would appreciate that."

He kissed her gently, smoothed back her hair. "You have had a tough night. As much as I want to drive this battle forward, you need to rest. You need to grieve."

"Do you honestly think that I should use the time that I have so unwisely? I need to know if my people, as you call them, will help, because if not, we need a backup plan."

"Do you think they would abandon you?" he asked, concerned.

"I'm not even sure they know I exist or care. Can we do this tonight? It would ease my mind if I knew what to expect."

Benedict met her gaze, saw the need, and nodded, agreeing. It would help if they knew what their next step had to be; it should be acquiring a weapon.

"All right. You and I at St. Mark's, but you will need to drive. I brought your car back, and my people…"

Her hand tensed on his. "Who were your people?" she asked boldly.

He patted her hand as if to calm her. "Asao, Marta, and Adam," he answered honestly.

"Who is Adam?" she asked, brow furrowed, searching her memory for a face.

"A very fine private detective I had watching you to make sure you were safe. There was a time when I thought you were human and you needed me. I wanted to make sure you were safe," he responded. "Marta was the one who didn't believe your cleverly crafted story. It will be okay. I'll kill anyone who prematurely reveals what you are, but in reality, there may be few who would believe it. I barely believe it myself. Please trust me."

"I trust you, but there are others I doubt."

Chapter 15

It was out in the open. He had declared his love to her, and he knew without her even saying that she loved him, too. That she did. He could feel it in his heart, in his very soul. He knew they were a match, and it was a good thing that they were, because they were going to face some impossible moments and trials ahead.

Thea took a moment to freshen up, Benedict deciding to call Marta to see how things stood. He needed to know before they left the house. She answered the phone, and you could hear the concern in her voice.

"Is she okay?" she asked, worried.

"She is now. She will be, I promise you. What is the sit rep?" he asked, sounding like some movie character. It made her laugh.

"The police have taken Caroline's and Denard's bodies away. We gave our report. Asao was very believable, if not slightly shaken. I think that sold it to both the humans and sups. We are on our way back to the house. What do you need?"

"I need you to meet me at St. Mark's. I need at least two humans with us. Adam and Cece will do." He could almost hear her frowning.

"St. Mark's? You're going to a church?" she asked, stunned.

"Yes. The operative word is *going to*, not *in*. Thea will be doing that."

"And she is all right?"

"I told her I love her, I told her my real name and story, and I told her that her secret is safe. It is a start."

Marta sighed. She knew that was a great start to trust her as much as she had to trust him. "And this having to face a demon? That doesn't put a crimp in your love life?"

"Marta, it puts a crimp into everyone's life."

* * *

Thea stood on the top stair of St. Mark's, her jacket wrapped around her, eyes on the pools of light that dotted the street. She paced back and forth, not any great distance, just enough to burn the anxiety that was setting her on fire. They had arrived alone, glancing up at the beautiful facade lit by streetlight and candlelight. This was their first hope. It wasn't long before Marta, Adam, and Cece had arrived, Asao blissfully absent. Although they had not been introduced before, now was the time. Benedict explained that Marta and Adam knew her secret, but not Cece. Marta hugged her, and Thea could almost feel Marta asking for forgiveness from her in the embrace. She patted her on the back as if to say it was all right. Actually, she wasn't at all sure it was. Adam shook her hand, giving her a curt nod, eyes full of unasked questions. Thea recognized him now. Yes, she had seen Adam before. Cece just nodded, eyes on the night more than on Thea. They were to wait on the stair as Adam and Benedict negotiated for whatever time they could manage.

"How is Asao?" Thea asked very softly to Marta as they stood slightly apart from Cece.

Marta smiled and shrugged.

"I understand he was with you."

"Stunned, gratified, and his faith has been buoyed. I am sorry that I got you into this mess."

"It is my mess, and I have to work on being a better liar."

Marta chuckled. "But it will turn out okay," she remarked, sounding as if she truly believed it.

"You want to sign a document to that effect?" she asked as she saw Benedict and Adam turn the corner and walk to the stairs. He had a smile on his face. He hopped up the steps and gestured toward the door.

"I bought you thirty minutes alone in the chapel. I will be here at the front entry, Marta at the back door, with Cece inside with Adam. He will follow you into the entry, but not the main chapel. It is just in case you need some help."

"How much did you have to spend for that thirty minutes in the middle of the night?" she asked softly.

"It was negligible. I offered a suitable donation, $1,000."

Thea opened and then closed her mouth as Benedict gave her that look. He would have spent more if they asked for it. He turned her around as Adam opened the church door and nudged her forward. She stepped over the threshold, drawing a deep breath to give her strength.

"I can't guarantee anything," she murmured to anyone listening.

"In life, no one can," added Adam.

Thea stood inside the door of the church at the end of the aisle. To either side of her sat the pews. You could smell wood polish, incense. See light dance through the stained glass windows from streetlights outside. It was eerily quiet. Thea shrugged out of her jacket, laying it on her left arm. She closed her eyes and stretched her neck before her wings appeared. There was a rush of air as they stretched out to either side of her, candles flickering off to the side of the altar. Thea folded them neatly behind her as she started down the aisle, her footsteps muffled by the dark-green carpet. She slowly walked down the aisle, eyes on the stained glass at the end of the chapel. Angels in flight, doves winging their way around the windows. She drew a steadying breath as she laid her jacket down and knelt. She tucked her wings against her back, their tips brushing the floor. She bowed her head but didn't close her eyes. She spoke out loud, shattering the peace.

"I am Anthea Black, but I am sure you already know that, and maybe even why I have come. A demon told me that Akazhreil has to be removed from this realm, and I don't think I have the power to do it. My heart is willing to serve. Allow me to be your servant. Can you help me?"

Thea knelt very still, not knowing what she expected. Would there be a voice? Would there be a presence? She just didn't know. She raised her chin, looking up into the candles, past the pretty greenery that her florist shop provided. She had to admit, it was a long shot, but still she waited. But how long should she wait? Finally, Thea drew a long, deep breath and stood. She concentrated, her wings vanishing from sight. She picked up her jacket, turned around, and just about stumbled forward over a hand's length gold object that lay at her feet. She stumbled, grabbing a nearby pew, eyes on the hand-beaten gold. A small smile crept across her lips as she bent down and gingerly touched the object. It looked like a golden pen, but the moment her fingers touched it, she could feel the connection, a warmth traveling through her. The object that had been the length of her hand sprang forth, a cross piece like a hilt, and then a blade. It wasn't dagger or sword length, but like a poniard, like her blade without the tendrils of fire. No, there was light, eye-watering light. Thea turned the cross piece backward and the light died, the object becoming just simple gleaming gold. She secreted it in her jacket. No need for everyone to want to touch and see it. She had a feeling it could kill the unwary. She drew on her jacket, turned back around to the altar, and spoke.

"Thank you. I'll return it as soon as I can."

Thea glanced at her watch. Her thirty minutes were up, and she could now hear voices at the side door. She ignored them, walking back toward the front entry, where Adam stood waiting just beyond the doors. She smiled to herself, thinking that Benedict thought she needed a guardian. It was kind of him to try to protect her, but what was coming down would even surpass his power. She nudged open the door with her shoulder, Adam meeting her gaze. He had hope in his eyes.

"How did it go? Did you have any luck?" he asked, hopeful.

"Remember when I thought I didn't have a prayer? Well, apparently, my prayer was good enough."

It was good news, and at the time of the suggestion, no one wanted to voice their doubt that perhaps they would be left to fend for themselves. Apparently, heaven had a heart. Someone had listened to Anthea's plea, an uncertain plea, and supplied her with a weapon. It was the start of a demon's downfall.

As she stepped out of the double doors of the church, no one asked to see what she was carrying, no one asked her to repeat what was said or even maybe promised, because they had all been in similar situations and they knew that she was hanging on by a thread this night. Marta figured it was probably one of the worst nights of her young life. She wished she could convince Anthea that this would be the worst of it, but she was never one to give false hope.

"We are running out of night," commented Marta as she stared starward, standing on the steps of the church. She wasn't nervous. No, it was just a statement of fact. "There is still much to be done, but you need rest, Anthea."

"If you use my name like that, you make it sound like you're my parents and not my friend."

"Maybe I am a little bit of both," she answered, hugging her. Marta thought she felt cold.

"She is right," added Benedict. "Let's take you home so you can get some sleep. Forgo working, because tomorrow night we will face unbelievers and we will need more than just my people to take on this demon."

She looked at him with curious eyes. "You must be one hell of a man if you can convince your people and others that something they have never seen exists and you want them to face it with me, someone untried in battle."

His eyes twinkled at her suggesting that he was one hell of a man.

"How do you broach such a delicate subject? Hi, guys and gals! There's a demon in the city, and we have to send it back to hell."

He smiled as he embraced her with one arm. "Sometimes you have to be blunt. No sense in lying or sugarcoating the situation. If their lives are at stake, they need to know it."

Thea snorted. "And you don't think they will ask more questions than you care to answer?"

"I can answer the ones I think are most important. Go to sleep, love. Let me take care of the rest of the burden. You just carry the weapon."

Thea laid her head on his shoulder, reluctant to leave his embrace as they began to walk down the stairs toward the car.

"All right, just this once, I'll let you handle the details."

"I would handle everything if I could." He kissed her chastely on the lips.

"And when do you think we can do more than just talk?" she whispered in his ear.

He grinned, surprised that she was thinking about such a thing at this time, but maybe it was something that was keeping her going, made her look forward to the future. He wasn't going to take that away from her, and he did want her. "If we survive this, my darling girl, you and I are going to take a long time to discuss how we feel about each other and what we like to feel and…"

She blushed, pushing away from him. As much as she wanted to linger in his arms, dream of the time they could spend together, she knew she needed her rest. The world seemed to be spinning faster than she could compensate.

By the time Thea had reached the bottom step of St. Mark's, she started shivering so violently that even Benedict's strong arms around her made it difficult to hold her in place. He and Adam got her settled in the car, piled what jackets they had around her, and turned up the heat as they drove her home. She leaned her head against his shoulder as he gently caressed her hair. Thea wasn't sure why she was shaking. Was it the shock of Caroline's death? She had seen people die before. She knew that eventually, all her friends would come to their mortuary. This was unexpected. It was sad. Was it the fact that she had walked into St. Mark's, asked and received the answer of a weapon they needed? Her people—the demon had said *her people*. Emlyn had always been her people. He had been enough for her. Now she had unzipped her fly and spoken to others in that realm. Was that a good or bad thing? Right now, she just didn't know. Or was it the fact that she had spoken quietly to a demon about how to kill another of his brethren? Then the miracle on this horrible night occurred. Arkin had shared his secret with her and the fact that he loved her. All of it was a lot to take in. It was times like this when she wished drink affected her. She would take a long gulp of whiskey, or maybe several.

"I want you to stay with me this evening. You are in no shape to be alone. You have had one hell of an evening."

She chuckled, burying her head in his chest. She felt so safe next to him. It was ridiculous, but she couldn't help what she was feeling. He glanced at Marta, who sat beside him, Adam and Cece in the front seat. Cece, although she had no idea what was going on, knew better to ask. Adam would tell her if he needed her to know.

"I know you feel you need to protect me, and I think that is sweet. You are a handsome, loving, sweet man, and you are mine," she whispered in his ear.

The only one who might have heard her soft words was Marta, and she was trying hard not to pay attention to the intimate moment.

"As much as I would enjoy your company, I would like time alone to think. You will agree that I have a lot to think about, don't you?"

He kissed the top of her head as they arrived at her house. A small light in the front window added warmth to what looked like an empty house. No one had ever called him sweet before; he knew he had this stupid grin on his face. Marta glanced at her watch. It was 3:30 a.m.

"Are you sure you want to stay here by yourself? Adam, or Cece, could stay."

Thea glanced at Adam, who turned in his seat. He nodded to her, more than willing, and it was more than Benedict making it an order. He seemed to genuinely care. She had no idea who he really was, but he was part of Benedict's circle. If Benedict trusted Adam, she would as well, because soon it wouldn't matter. Things were unraveling, and Thea wasn't fast enough to grab at the threads.

"It is part of the job as a detective, a very private and confidential detective. I crash on couches really easily."

Thea could see that Benedict was worried about her—she could feel the tension in the air. It seemed they really thought she might fold under what she had witnessed this evening. Of course she had always known that there was a heaven and hell; she just counted on never meeting either. She had been strong before all this, but sometimes you had to lean on the strength of others.

"If you are so inclined," she added as she twisted in her seat, unbuckled the seat belt, thrust off the coats, and opened the car door. The night air brought back the chill to her, but she wasn't shivering as badly. Benedict was right behind her as they walked up the pathway. There was a silence in the air, as if even the creatures of the night didn't want to shatter the moment or her thoughts.

"We have a plan, Thea. Marta has already contacted my team. Plans are in motion for the meeting, if not later today, this evening, then tomorrow. I don't think it is prudent to let the humans know, because there is nothing they can do about it and they can't survive as much damage as we can during a confrontation. As it stands, you are the only one who can send the demon back, but you need our support. We want to give you support."

"I appreciate that, but I can't see where anyone is going to be happy about this. I thought about this demon, and if I were him, I would want to prove myself worthy to stay. I would want to be invaluable to those who might hold the key to returning me. Power is an easy aphrodisiac, though it might not sway me easily. There are others whose inclination to destroy him could be colored."

"We stand firm for what is the right thing to do. Sending him back is the right thing to do. I am with the archdemon on that decision." She leaned in and kissed him, ignoring Adam, who was standing at the end of the walkway, giving them some privacy. He averted his eyes casually, humming to himself.

"Agreed. Then I will have time to deal with everything else," she muttered.

"Am I everything else?" he asked with a saucy pout.

"You are the best part of everything else," she added as she opened the door, Adam jogging up to join her.

He met Benedict's gaze, nodding. Benedict knew that he would watch out for her. Sometimes you had to watch over the angels when they had no one to look out for them.

Adam closed the door behind them, standing with his back to the door, waiting to be ushered in. She turned and met his gaze. He didn't flinch.

"How long have you been following me?" she asked as she absently petted Polly, who had crawled out of her bed in the kitchen and came to see the company.

"You want me to tell you honestly, or do you prefer not to deal with this information now?"

She sighed, shaking her head. "On second thought, I don't want to know. We have a downstairs guest room, off to your right, end of the hall. It has its own bath."

"I'm only here to make sure you are okay. You look pretty together, but I have seen stronger men than you collapse. I don't want to see it happen, but if you feel you are sliding, I'm a good listener."

"How long have you worked for Arkin?" she asked, using his current name. She wasn't sure what Adam knew, and when in doubt, be cautious.

"More than ten years. He and you can trust me."

"You don't look that old or experienced."

Adam smiled. "Perhaps that is one of my secrets."

Adam found his way down the hall to his bedroom. It was a comfortable, neutral-colored room that would do just fine for this short visit. Thea found her way to the cognac; it might not help her forget, but she could pretend. She stood with the tumbler in hand, at the back French doors, eyes staring out into the commons area at the light of the failing moon. She wasn't sure where she should begin as far as collating her thoughts. She could feel the weight of the weapon in her pocket, and she knew it wasn't a long-ranged weapon. No, she would have to get up close and personal with the demon. She knew if that happened, she wondered how long before everyone watching discovered what she was. Thea wasn't naive; she knew the day would come. But she wanted to have a choice when she revealed to the world what she was. Lately it seemed she had no viable choice. Would Benedict still be hers when the world found out that an angel existed on earth? A voice from behind her jarred her thoughts. Emlyn stood in his robe not far from the foot of the stairs.

"Hey, I thought I heard someone. Polly didn't bark, so I figured it was you. My evening was awesome. I worked with RM in trying to find Denard, find out more information about the thefts…how was yours?"

Thea stood very still, taking another sip of cognac. There was tenseness in the air as Adam stepped out and introduced himself.

"You must be Emlyn Black. I'm Adam Beckford. Your sister was kind enough to offer me shelter this evening. I work for Arkin Kane. It has been one hell of a day for her. You might not want to ask her any questions just now."

Em frowned at Adam, who nodded insistently, trying to convince Em to let the subject go.

"If I were you, Em, I would listen to Adam," Thea muttered, the crystal tumbler leaning against her shoulder, her gaze still distant in the growing light that slowly seeped over the commons. Dawn wasn't very far away.

Em walked over toward his sister, the robe billowing out behind him as if it were a cape. He stood by her side, following her line of sight. She wasn't looking at anything. No, she was just in deep thought.

"Anything I can do?"

Thea turned to him and laughed. At first, it was just a chuckle, but then it became a laugh that she couldn't stop, and when she did manage to catch a breath, she began to cry. Thea crumpled to the floor, cradling the tumbler to her chest, body folded up almost into a ball. Em turned, glancing at Adam, who rushed toward Thea, kneeling down next to her.

"Get a cold cloth and a blanket. Once she cries herself out, we can take her up to bed. She won't be working today."

Em stood still for a moment, almost too stunned to act, but RM had made her way down the stairs and was already wetting a cold cloth. Adam had pulled the quilt from the back of the couch and wrapped Thea in it as if she were a child. RM handed the wet cloth to Em, who thrust it at Adam. Adam gently began wiping her face, her neck, as if the cold could settle her down, bring her under greater control.

"I haven't ever seen her like this."

"Do you need anything else?" RM asked, concerned.

"Turn down her bed. We'll take off her shoes. Like I said, she had a rough night." Adam carefully took the tumbler from Thea's trembling hands then slid his arms under her, trying to get her into his arms so he could carry her. "We can put her to bed like this."

"Then will you tell me what the hell happened?" Em asked as he pulled off his sister's shoes.

"Not my place to tell you, but suffice it to say, it was bad."

RM had volunteered to sit with Thea once they had gotten her to bed. Polly crawled up to snuggle against her, adding warmth to her body. Thea seemed content for the moment. Em led Adam out of the bedroom and down the hall. His face was a mask of mixed emotions. His voice was barely a whisper when he spoke.

"I get it, Arkin was worried about my sister so he asked you to sit with her. But I'm her brother, I have a right to know what happened. She was standing there, looking so lost. For the first time, I wasn't sure what I could do for her."

"Em, I'm not sure either. Frankly, I had expected her to break down before this, but that question you asked her, it was just too…"

Adam grabbed Em's arm, pulling him down the stairs and into the living room. He pulled out his phone and dialed.

"If Arkin says I can tell you, I'll give you the entire scoop, all right?"

Em frowned. "What does he have to do with this? She is my sister," he asked, sounding bitter. "He isn't family."

"Well, I think he is about to be," added Adam with a confirming nod.

* * *

Benedict hadn't wanted to leave Thea. As he drove away, he could feel the pain wrack his body. But he understood. She needed time to sort through what had happened this evening. Benedict had decades like that, so many unexpected things to consider even he was having trouble trying to concentrate. It hadn't been the most romantic time to tell her how he felt, but it was necessary and it was straight honesty from his heart. If it had startled her, it had astounded him. After all, he had lived centuries. To find his soul mate like this and to find out she was an angel as well, it was just too preposterous. An angel in trouble, for the dark had come as Claire had predicted. No one who knew Claire actually believed her. More was the pity. He wished she had been wrong this time. Asao, Adam, and Cece had assured him that they had taken care of Caroline's body, the subsequent police activity, and their rendition of what had happened was a simple explanation one to be believed. Human police had no trouble believing in the evil of man and magic. The parateam who dealt with such activity daily took it all in stride. They didn't ask any of the really hard questions. They would know eventually since they themselves were paranormal beings.

Benedict had spoken with Asao, who was only slightly freaking out, realizing he had known Thea all her life and never knew that she was an angel. Who would have known that they really existed? It kind of threw him for a loop. It had cracked his rather-stoic Asian facade. Benedict told him to join the club; it wasn't one of those average days. His orders to his team were simple. Schedule the meeting with everyone they could get ahold of, witch, blood, changeling, even fey, if possible, for the darkness had arrived and wanted to live on their doorstep. Also the city's teams, regardless of who or what they were, should report anything out of the ordinary. How did one quantify a demon that looked like a human or what was out of the ordinary in a city filled with paranormal beings? He would have to rely on their experience and hope that Thea was right and that this demon would have some sense of tradition or law. Benedict didn't want to think about it; in fact, this one evening, he didn't plan on working. No, this time he needed the rest.

Dawn was just lightening the horizon when he settled into bed. His phone rang, and the ID said Adam. Fear clutched at him for a moment.

"Is she all right?" The first words out of his mouth before even Adam could reply. Thea meant a lot to Benedict. It didn't take a detective to see that.

"I had to put her to bed. She had a bad moment or two when her brother asked her how her evening had been and if he could help with anything."

Benedict nodded to himself, wishing he were there. "Understandable. Emlyn wants to know what's happened, doesn't he?"

"Yes, and I wanted to check with you first before I said anything. Thea is down for the count. I can't rely on her to be coherent enough to respond to questions. What do you want me to do?"

Benedict was silent and thoughtful. Emlyn deserved to know. "Tell him what you know, but he's not to do anything stupid like go look for the demon."

"You have my team casually making inquiries, right?" Adam asked, curious.

"I have all our teams taking a look at the city as circumspectly as possible. It was said that we would get a spell, I presume, to find it or him. Thank you for checking with me first. I don't want Thea mad, but at the same time, she wouldn't want her brother to worry. Once this unforeseen event is over, she and I can hash out our relationship issues and our borders as it were."

Adam chuckled. "Sorry, it just sounds all so human, you having relationship problems. But you haven't done this in a while, have you?" Adam asked pointedly. Was it as easy as facing a demon? Adam wondered.

"I haven't found someone like Thea before, so yes, I guess you could say that. Good night, Adam."

Chapter 16

Em was pacing back and forth in front of the cold hearth, the first rays of sunlight glinting through the window. He pulled the curtains too, not eager for the start of a new day. He turned to face Adam.

"He said it was all right. Have a seat. It's a kind of long story." Adam could see that Em wasn't happy, but it wasn't his job to make him happy; it was his job to do just that, his job.

"You take your oath of loyalty seriously. What affects my sister affects me, and I'm not sure how Arkin Kane figures into this story. I know my sister is sweet on him…," Em remarked, plopping down on the couch, whining like a child.

Adam shook his head, annoyed. "Arkin is a good man. He is more than just impressive. He and your sister have an understanding between them as of this evening, and I wouldn't get in the way of that, by hurting her or doing something that might be against her best interest. I mean it, Em. You don't want to get on Arkin's bad side. He is in love with your sister. In fact, I am pretty damn sure that was declared this evening, one good thing out of a lot of bad."

Em leveled his gaze at Adam. "Tell me what was bad."

Adam nodded. "Since Arkin has taken an interest in your sister and she is our silent witness, I was ordered to follow her, my team of six. We are detectives, just like your RM, only we work for Arkin. We can go places and do things as humans that others might not be able to, but don't think I'm weak or not experienced. I may not be as long-lived as blood-born, but I am just as tough. I started out as a cop and had to work my way up to detective and then into the fold. From what I understand, it all started when she called Marta and asked her for an alibi. Her excuse was that she was going to see a friend of hers and you wouldn't understand, so if you were looking for her, she was to say they were together. Someone less experienced might have believed her. Marta didn't."

"And that was a lie?" Em asked softly.

"Well, in the end, she did see her friend." Adam sighed. This was not going to be easy.

As soon as Em heard the name Denard, he went off, softly, but still leaped to his feet and began a rant that Adam had to stop with a harsh word and cold glance.

"Do you want to hear the story or not?"

Em's eyes narrowed, his face flushed from anger.

"I'm not here for you."

"Go on," he hissed.

"So Denard called her on Caroline's phone. He wanted to meet with Thea alone. With Marta's concern and when I saw that she was leaving the house, I called Arkin and we followed."

Adam saw Em stiffen slightly. Adam knew what he was thinking, and he was right.

"Denard, with the help from Caroline's blood, raised a demon. The summoning killed him, but still, by the time your sister had arrived, Caroline was dead and a pissed archdemon stood in its place."

Em opened and then closed his mouth, uncertain how to respond. "An archdemon?" Em asked, eyes a bit wide.

"I know. Who knew, right? He explained the situation to your sister, that a demon was loose and trapped in our city."

Em whistled, amazed.

"He also apologized for Caroline's death and said that he would take Denard's soul for punishment. He left what remained of his body at the crime scene. In order to defeat the demon, send it back to hell or wherever they reside, he explained that we would need a weapon from a different source." Adam was silent as he leaned back in the chair, waiting for Em to ask the inevitable question. Em met Adam's gaze, leaning back in the softness of the couch.

"She didn't know you were there witnessing this, did she?"

"No, and when she asked if another weapon might be appropriate, she revealed herself to the demon. He told her we were there watching, out of courtesy, I guess."

There was a stillness in the room, Em frozen, as if he thought he could make the situation go away.

"Who was there?" Em asked gently, hoping RM was indeed upstairs with his sister.

"Arkin, Asao, myself, and Marta."

Em closed his eyes, shook his head, feeling weary.

"When she found out that her secret was revealed to us, she flew to your house in the country and Arkin followed her via her car to speak with her. We helped explain the crime scene to the authorities and clean up the mess as best we could."

Em sat on the couch, blinked a few times, and considered what Adam had said. "You said flew," muttered Em.

"Yes, I did, and I know you understand the reason for me saying it. We are truly amazed and humbled by your sister. She has no reason to fear from us or to worry. We have given our word."

"And how long do you think that will last?" Em asked with a heavy sigh.

Adam shrugged. "Until we face the demon, I presume. Arkin spoke privately with her. What was said, I can only guess, but they have come to an understanding. They love each other. You can see it in their faces, hear it in their voices. Arkin won't let anyone hurt your sister."

Em nodded. "I knew that she was growing more and more fond of him. It was always so obvious, but I think she was scared to get to close. I mean, how do you explain what you are to someone who has no concept that such a thing exists? I didn't believe it when I saw it with my own eyes, and she was my own sister. It changes your theology, and now with demons popping up…"

"It is a sight to behold. However, the secret cannot last. Deep down in our hearts, we know that. We met Arkin and Thea at St.

Mark's, where your sister asked, prayed for, and received a weapon to dispatch the demon. If you see something you haven't seen before, I would not touch it if I were you. It is in her jacket pocket. Arkin wanted her to return with him this evening so that he could care for her, but she had much to think about."

"So when I asked her what I could do, literally there is nothing."

Adam shook his head. "Except be there for her. Her friend Caroline is dead, she has to face a demon, her secret will no doubt be exposed, and she had fallen in love. Though she might have rivals at first for Arkin's attention, it won't last once they see what she is."

Em picked up what remained of the cognac in his sister's tumbler and took the last few drams.

"Thank you."

Adam shrugged.

"It's more than what you were charged with doing."

"Hey, that is the nature of my job. You know how it is."

Em smiled. "I do now."

Adam had tried to maintain a quiet household for Thea's sake. RM and Em had left around nine in the morning, Em having explained to RM that Denard was no longer an issue. As far as she was concerned, her job was done. She had questions but was polite enough to wait until they were out of the house. Em would answer her as best as he could with an edited version of what he knew; he didn't want to lie to her, but at the same time, he needed to be cognizant that RM was sharp. She could put pieces of a puzzle together. Polly came in and out as she saw fit, sitting with Adam through breakfast and then lunch. It was almost dinnertime when Thea ambled down the stairs still dressed in her clothes from yesterday, hair a nest of tangles. She sauntered into the kitchen and took a deep breath.

"Something smells good," she commented, drawing a deep breath.

"Chili. You had all the ingredients. Hope you don't mind."

She shook her head, sinking into the chair, eyes turning to stare out the window and the failing light.

"Before you ask, the meeting will be tomorrow. They couldn't pull it together for tonight."

She nodded absently.

"Someone sent you flowers, no card."

She nodded again, looking at the pretty arrangement.

"That's our florist. If they do a new arrangement, they usually send one over for me to review." Her fingers absently touched the lilacs. The air smelled brightly fragrant; it brought hope to her heart.

"Cool," Adam remarked. "Your brother is at work."

"I take it you explained my breakdown?" she asked dryly.

"After I consulted with Arkin, I did, yes. Emlyn had no idea what you had been through and feels like shit that he sparked your slight meltdown. I left any explanation he wanted to ply to RM up to him."

"Funny, I feel the same way." She smiled at Adam. "I just realized you know more about me than I do about you."

Adam slid the bowl over to her with a spoon and crackers. "Not much to tell. Come from a family of cops, married my high school sweetheart, had two kids, moved from cop to detective, worked with the paranormals, so when my wife wanted something safer for me to do, I jumped at the chance. I was working in Alexander's city then. My wife died of cancer, my daughter is a cop, and my son works with me in my team as my IT tech guy."

She nodded, taking a spoonful of chili. Her eyes brightened. "You forgot to mention you can cook."

There was a gentle silence between them while they devoured the meal. Adam thought it was soothing to her, almost normal, until the doorbell rang and a voice that Thea recognized penetrated their contentment. She closed her eyes and drew a deep breath as she rose from the table.

"Let me get it," Adam suggested as he stood, leaving the kitchen for the front door. The voice was shrill, to say the least.

Thea heard the door open. Sarah's voice was thick with emotions, and a few sniffles.

"Who are you?" she asked tersely.

"I'm Adam. I'm a friend of the Black family. And you are…?"

"Thea's friend." Sarah pushed past Adam and stalked into the kitchen.

Although Thea could tell that she had been crying, Sarah was dressed nicely and had managed her makeup. Thea wasn't that put together. Sarah had been known to be a drama queen, but the three of them had been close, and Caroline would probably not be dead if she hadn't been Thea's friend. It was a hard burden to bear.

"Caroline is dead. Mal called me."

Mal was Caroline's third husband and the executor of her will.

"She was murdered by some crazy last night. Your brother picked up her body. I went to the police, but they said you had it."

Adam let Thea take this one; he had a few choice words that he wanted to say to this woman, and it might make the situation worse.

"Sarah, take a deep breath and have a seat. You know Caroline prepaid her funeral expenses after husband number 4, Rick, right? She wanted to be cremated, put in the vault with her parents and her poodle, Bootsie."

Sarah wiped her face with a handkerchief; her mascara must have been waterproof.

"Mal is a very good lawyer. He will take care of what remains, and we will take care of her body, all right? I want you to calm down before we have to take you to the doctor."

"Is that why you aren't here working on her?"

Thea's jaw twitched. "We all grieve in our own ways, Sarah. I'm sorry you're so upset. She didn't want a big funeral. She loved attention when she was alive, but she wanted to pass away quietly. We have to honor that."

"Do you think she went with him willingly, or do you think he grabbed her?"

Thea shrugged. Denard was good-looking; it was hard to say.

"Do you think Mal would let me have her collection of purses?"

Adam frowned, glancing down at Thea, amazed at the transition in Sarah. One minute she was in the middle of mourning, and the next thinking what she could get out of the death that was some friend.

"You would have to ask him. I don't know what the will said."

Sarah looked hard at Thea, eyes crinkled in thought. "You look worse than you usually do. Did you sleep in your clothes?"

Thea nodded, taking a sip of the soda Adam had poured for her.

Sarah looked sideways at Adam. "He spent the night here too?" she asked, brow arched in disdain.

"Em knows Adam is here. It's nothing personal, Sarah, and you should be more concerned about yourself. You get sick easily." Yes, turn the situation and attention back to her. It would work perfectly.

"I do, don't I?" she remarked, standing. She sighed, gripping her purse. "Tell me it will be okay, Thea."

Thea stood, and Adam watched the woman he knew to be an angel, but you could only stretch goodwill so far.

"I wish I could tell you that, Sarah, and almost any other time I would say yes, but this one time, I can't even be sure."

Sarah sniffled, turned, and left Thea standing by her chair, a quietness falling over the house. Thea heard the door slam. Adam whistled.

"Okay, that was weird."

Thea chuckled.

"Well, considering she is human, yeah, that is weird."

"I would say 'Welcome to my world,' but you are already here." Thea drained what was left of her soda, walking her dishes over to the sink. "I really lost it, didn't I?"

"Well, considering the circumstances, I was surprised you didn't do it earlier. Your brother walked into it. While he was out with RM, you were dealing with all sorts of shit."

"You are being nice," she remarked.

"Don't ever accuse me of that. I have a reputation to uphold as a hard-ass. I know we aren't having the meeting this evening, but did you want me to take you over to Arkin? I know he would love to see you. He was concerned."

"You know, he can make all the promises he wants, but in the end, I have to reveal myself and deal with the consequences. He may want to try to make it right for me, and I'll love him for that, but I also have to handle things my way."

"He can only respect you for that. How about you clean up? I'll let him know we are coming to see him. You haven't seen the new residence, have you?"

She shook her head as Polly followed her out of the kitchen.

"I think you will be impressed."

"I'm more impressed by their owner," commented Thea. "Do you think the blood-born in this city truly respect him?"

"Sometimes, if you can't go for the respect, you have to go for the fear. He doesn't like it, but maybe you don't have a choice. After tomorrow's meeting, things will change. They will know that he truly means to make this city his own and make it profitable."

"In other words, they don't know who Arkin Kane is?" she asked, standing on the bottom stair step.

"My understanding is that they go through name changes on occasion, sometimes to save themselves, sometimes to avoid bad memories. When you come into his fold, he tells you who he is. I presume he told you?"

"We exchanged secrets."

Adam nodded.

"I still use the name he uses here so that there won't be a slip until such time as it is made widely known. Benedict has a city in every state pretty much operated by his seconds, and he has had a slew of them. You don't get a city until you are ready, and he hasn't, wouldn't make an HQ until he found the right place. This might be the right place because of you."

Thea blushed slightly as she started up the stairs.

"Hard-ass, my eye."

CHAPTER 17

Benedict was as nervous as a teenager on prom night. Adam had called to update him on the situation, mainly Thea's mood. It was imperative that she remain positive, especially as she faced the darkness of the demon. Benedict had no doubt that she would triumph but was concerned that during this so-called battle, she would reveal herself and secret. He had experienced many things in his long and unnatural life, but never could he have dreamed to meet an angel or how the world would take her appearance.

Benedict stood on the front porch as Adam pulled into the circular drive. Cece was riding shotgun, Thea in the back seat. She smiled through the window at him as she saw him, and his heart lightened. He jogged down the array of steps and held open the door for her. She stepped out, wearing his signature gray-color pants, with a pretty pink top and sweater. Her hair was a pile of curls. He leaned in and kissed her on the cheek.

"Can you tell that I'm carrying the weapon?"

Benedict's eyes widened slightly as he stepped back and regarded her with interest. If she was carrying it, where was it? He watched as she primped her curls.

"I tucked it in as a hair accessory. You know that the demon will be suspicious."

"You are amazing," he remarked as he curled his arm around her waist and walked her up the steps.

She took a moment to survey the outside of the house. "It looks more approachable. You cleaned the brick, landscaped. I like what you have done with the place."

"Good, I'm glad. I may not have a head for decorating, but I know what I like, and so do my people."

"Well, good taste is timeless," she added as they stepped into the foyer, surrounded by dark wood.

"Would you like something to eat or drink?" he asked, concerned for her.

"Hot tea would be great. Did you have anything in mind for this evening?"

He shrugged. "I was leaving that up to you. How about we just talk about what will happen? I want to make sure you are okay, that if you have any outstanding questions, they are answered. My main concern is you."

She brightened. She stood on tiptoe and kissed him chastely on the lips. She turned, as she felt a nuzzling on her hand, to find a large Irish wolfhound and a pretty German shepherd staring at her with curious eyes.

"And a dog man at that. Wow, why hasn't anyone snagged you before me?"

"Because I was waiting for you," he added. "I am a great believer in dogs. The wolfhound is Dane, and the shepherd is Katie."

Thea leaned over and rubbed their ears, their snouts, and of course, their backsides, where they danced ecstatically. "You have made friends for life. Sometime, we should bring Polly over for a play date."

Thea laughed as Benedict ushered her into the front living room. There were still some boxes lying around, but the furnishings had changed and there was a small portrait over the fireplace of Benedict. Thea walked closer to admire it. It had to have been painted in the late 1700s, or so she thought.

"I didn't commission that. One of my staff decided I needed a portrait. How he managed, because I rarely sit still, amazes me."

"I think he captured not only your outer beauty but your soul as well."

He looked at her, mildly skeptical. "You are too kind, Thea, far too kind for the likes of me."

"Do you doubt an angel, that she would not know a kind soul?" Thea asked as she seated herself on a divan, looking very natural among his things.

"Who am I to quarrel with such a divine creature?"

She laughed as tea was brought on a tray for her by Chrisanne. Chrisanne was a tall bespectacled girl with her brunette hair pulled into a very businesslike chignon. She was wearing a gray suit casually and politely nodded to Thea. Everyone knew who she was. She was the talk of the compound, that Benedict had fallen in love with what everyone believed was a human. That thought would be changing shortly. She hadn't been introduced to his staff yet. There would be time for that. Benedict waited until they were alone, watching her fix her tea. He was waiting for her to break the silence, to talk about what concerned her the most. But if she didn't speak, he could sit there all evening and just enjoy looking at her.

"So what exactly happens tomorrow at the meeting?" she asked, taking a long sip of tea. Her body seemed to unwind. Benedict sat at the end of the divan, his hand resting gently on her feet.

"Once everyone arrives, I am going to reveal who I am."

Thea opened her mouth to ask, but he held up his hand to silent her protests. "It is important for them to know whom they are dealing with. They don't know Arkin Kane, but they will know of Benedict. It will settle any future rivalries and also make them decide on how they want to move forward, especially in this particular case. As far as facing the demon, I will be with you, as well as Asao. This is not open for negotiation. I assume Esther will want to be there, with someone she can trust but who is expendable, if you will pardon the bluntness. Her second will be off-site, safe. Beyond that, I can't guess who will want to accompany us. We can, of course, swear them to secrecy if you believe—"

Thea held up her hand. "The weapon I was given is not long-range. It has to be delivered up close and personal. I wouldn't even try to throw it. That means I have to be as close to the demon as possible to ensure success. What do you think my odds are of not being discovered?"

Benedict was silent; he had a hard time answering her question.

"See? That is what I thought. My chance of coming out of this as I walked in, looking human, appears to be slim. That means I have to deal with the fallout and questions after this skirmish."

"No, *we* will deal with it. I am at your side regardless of what happens. You will have me, and you will have my people at your service. Whether you are demon or angel, I love you."

She gently caressed his face in thanks. It was more than she could have hoped for.

"We were supposed to have a spell delivered, I presume, to assist us in finding him, but I have a feeling we might not have to wait for it to arrive. I can't see him waiting around for me to find him."

"You think he will call for a meeting?"

She shrugged. "I am the only one he thinks can define his fate. I am hoping he doesn't know about the weapon. I want to appear as innocent and neutral as possible."

Benedict nodded. "You will let me know if he calls you, right?"

She rolled her eyes at him. "Oh, I'm not going out there alone. I learned my lesson."

She was silent for a moment.

"So let's say that everything goes awry and I am discovered to be an angel. Does that affect what you and I have? I know, in some instances, the blood want the head of their city, those in power, to be with another member of their own kind. I also wonder if others aside of the blood might question an angel with…I want you, whatever happens. I need you to know that. I mean, this isn't the city of angels, but there is an angel in the city."

Benedict leaned forward and kissed her, their eyes level. "I don't want you to worry about things that you don't need to worry about. I have pledged myself to you. My staff has already made it known that I am courting you, as it were. We are formally an item. I needed my seconds elsewhere to know that you exist. Should something happen to me, you won't be bereft of help. I don't believe there will be an objection, and there won't be once my kind in this city knows who I am."

"And everyone else in the city?" she asked, curious.

"You just worry about the demon. If they haven't taken an interest in your life thus far, they have no control over your private life now. I want you to feel safe and protected. I don't want anything to change for you."

"That is pretty naive," she quipped.

"Let me have my delusions. We are a mixed city, anyway. Why not just add an angel to the mix? Just another unique entity in our realm."

She nodded, draining her tea.

"Would you like a tour of the house and grounds? We have tried to make it less like a brothel or palace and more like a home. There is enough room for one more should you desire to stay with me."

Thea flushed slightly, standing. He took her hand and guided her out of the room; it would be a memorable moment, a feeling of safety and normality before having to face darkness.

Thea stood with Benedict's hand in hers as they sauntered out of the front salon. She looked around, noting that most of the wallpaper had been removed, the air smelled of fresh paint, and there was a beautiful vase of fresh flowers in the front foyer. She smiled lightly, knowing that they came from her florist. Even the wood seemed to gleam under fresh polish.

"I saw the front of the house. It was impressive what you did with it. It looks like just another normal house on the street, and the landscaping is very pretty. I would not know it was the same house if I hadn't seen it before. I am sure the neighbors are pleased."

Benedict nodded this thanks. "Yardley had a lot of fenced-in land. We will make good use of the outbuildings. What you see here is just a small fraction of those I command."

"Impressive," she added with a nod.

"They do so because they like to do so. No one serves me who doesn't respect me or whom we don't mutually need. The house, when we first looked at it, resembled a fortress. I thought that was ill-advised. The lawn and facade work covered the new security measures. I doubt anyone can see what was added. It helps to keep us all safe. I will work from here, but if we are to have any large conferences, I will do so in the city at the Renard building. That is the next project, to get the main gathering area to look more professional. We will need fresh flowers."

She chuckled as she looked past the salon into the next room, one of the sliding wood doors open.

"I will keep the salon and a room for a study. I will keep the kitchen, the family room where those who live in this house will dine, I think the decorator called it. I didn't need to keep the large dining room."

"Whom did you hire? Though I am sure you have a fine sense of style and color yourself."

Benedict shook his head. "Is this a rib at me for wearing gray? Collette Rousse, I was told she was one of the best in the city."

Thea looked at him, meeting his blue-gray eyes. "That was who helped me with our house and the mortuary."

Benedict knew that the moment he decided to make this house his home; he knew he wanted it to reflect her tastes as well, just in case it should come to pass that they decided to reside together.

"We did make a few changes. We added a communications and office area, a room for security, and an armory."

Thea nodded, not surprised.

"This house has three levels. We have gotten rid of most of the wallpaper. With fresh paint, it looks brighter, lighter of spirit."

"Maybe it likes its new owners."

Benedict walked her toward the back of the house and the kitchen. She was enamored with the blue-yellow-and-green kitchen; it was something she found very warm, very familiar. Benedict watched pleasure wash over her face.

"We have rooms upstairs, and of course, the basement is where I reside, but it is less like a dungeon."

"I am glad to hear it. I know that Tasha likes to sleep in a coffin. Do you?"

"No, I don't find them as comfortable, though I am sure the kind that you sell would be all right."

She nudged him in the ribs as she left his side to walk around the family room.

"It lacked a woman's touch. Of course, there is always room for another in this house and my life."

She turned around and met his gaze. "That was very smooth."

"You like that? I didn't really even have to think about it when I said it," he quipped. "We kept the pool. Anytime you or Polly would like a swim, it is open for you. I want you to consider this house yours away from home, or if you want it to be your home."

"You are too generous with this stranger who flew into your life," she remarked, closing the space between them. She kissed him lightly on the lips.

There was a slight cough behind them, and Benedict turned to find Cyr. The man was tall, well-built, dressed in black jeans and a gray turtleneck. He was wearing a pair of wire-rimmed glasses that gave him that Clark Kent kind of look.

"Thea, this is Cyr. His last name is St. Cyr, but we just call him Cyr. He is my donor."

It was a nice way to say *blood partner*, and she was surprised to find that it was a man. Then again, she would have been jealous if it was a woman. She knew in her heart she would.

"Ms. Black, it is a pleasure to meet you." He extended his hand to her. They shook hands. "I didn't want to disturb you. As you can see, we are very busy around here, still settling in, but I wanted to meet you and introduce myself. Though Ben has many friends and employees, he needs someone to hold his heart and keep his soul."

"Did I mention that Cyr is a romantic?" he commented wryly.

"There is nothing wrong with that. I have a romantic streak myself. I hate to say it, but I am glad, Cyr, that you are a man. I think I might have taken offense at a woman."

Cyr smiled at Benedict. He had guessed right.

"He only needs one woman in his life, and I would say that he found her. I hope I will be seeing more of you. Welcome to our home."

Impulsively she hugged him, and Cyr met Benedict's gaze and he winked. Between the two of them, they might just convince her that they truly needed her for herself and not for the power an angel might bring to his rule. Cyr, with a slight bow, left them alone, and Thea turned to regard Benedict.

"He called you Ben," she said, sounding slightly amused.

"I will answer to anything you can to call me, snookie wookums, cutie pie, or even hot stuff."

Thea winced. "I'll try to think of something not so embarrassing. Can I see the basement? I think you have made huge strides up here. I think it is taking on your personality."

"Even if it is gray?" he asked, amused.

"I'm not entirely without observation, Benedict. You have said that you have security, yet I don't see any obvious signs. Why advertise when those who live here know who they are and the job they do? Gray pants, or shirt, even a jacket, you can lay claim to them as an employee. I take it, for special occasions, you may even have a uniform of sorts."

"Beautiful and clever. I never thought it wise to let your enemy know whom they are facing. Everyone knows their job, and we know everyone. It works well that way. I have an eclectic group here, blood, humans, changelings, and witches."

"Were you going to add angel to that group?" she asked in a whisper as Benedict led her to where she thought the stairs were. She opened the door to find an odd closet. She turned to face him.

"I moved the door to the basement. It is hidden in this alcove, where the flowers are. Although you can make it down the stairs, you can't make it in without security seeing you or without the passcode. I have already given you the key to my heart. I will make sure you have the passcode as well."

"You trust me very much, Benedict, and it makes me nervous. How do you know that I am even worthy of—"

Benedict laid his finger on her lips. "Do not denigrate or doubt yourself in front of me. I was the one who pulled away, thinking I was unworthy. We are what we are, Thea, but together we are more."

"But you know that you may never be able to have my blood."

He nodded. "I realized that as soon as I discovered you were a being of light, but I only need your love, nothing more, Anthea Black."

The room that he had chosen for his bedroom was a suite, really, with a smaller room off to the right. It would be the perfect ladies' sitting room for books or whatever someone might desire. Benedict had heard that when she was a child, she had wanted a Victorian dollhouse. He had a fine network of operatives, and they could find out just about anything that they needed to, except, of course, that she was an angel, but then again, who knew? The colors were dark and rich, golds, greens, crimson, navy. It made Thea want to bounce on the bed and curl up to sleep.

She turned to look at Benedict. "Now this seems to be you. Are all these antiques yours?"

He ran his hand along his wooden valet and smiled. "I never really thought of them as antiques, but if you have had them more than one lifetime, I guess they are. The bed is big enough for two."

"Yes, actually, maybe four, if you had dogs curled up with you." She sighed as she seated herself on the end of the soft bed.

"I want so much for all this to be over. I'm eager to get on with my life. I have something to look forward to now, my time with you. Tell me no one can take that away from me or us."

"No one can, regardless of the outcome, regardless of who knows what. We still belong to each other. Though I am sure many will fault me for keeping an angel to myself, I can't let you go now that I have found you."

"You have made me feel so much better. You almost make facing a demon seem trivial, like just any other day before you and I can be together."

"I wish I had that power. I wish I could do that for you. I would try if you asked."

"I know Emlyn would as well, but I have had to face hard decisions. I have been in some interesting situations before. This is just another. But I won't be alone in the end. I'll have someone to talk to and someone to put me back together should I fall apart."

"You don't intend on falling apart, do you?"

She shrugged as he extended his hand to her, pulling her into his embrace. "I'll try not to, even if I have to be your date to your welcome-to-the-city gathering."

Benedict groaned.

"You didn't think that all this would make everyone forget that they have to welcome you and turn the city over to you officially, did you?"

"I was hoping everyone would forget." He sighed.

"Not if this group has anything to say about it. I am sure Emily and Tasha are working overtime on some grand scheme."

"I know that it is customary," he remarked. How many other cities had he been welcomed to?

"Oh, yes, it is, and I am sure you will be most impressed with their hard work."

"You're laughing at me," he said with a frown.

"Just a little. You calling this meeting has probably derailed their plans slightly. The dark coming for me—who knew that Claire might be right this time? I wish she had been wrong. What was Denard thinking?"

"Maybe he was thinking that he could speak with family. After all, you did at St. Mark's."

"Yeah, and I bet mine are just as dangerous as his."

Both Benedict and Thea wanted to linger, to stay longer in each other's company, but it was enough to leave the house this one evening and try for a bit of normalcy, because things would not be very normal after the meeting. She felt safe in his arms; he wanted her safe by his side, but it was time for her to go. It was time for her to ready herself for what lay ahead, for like it or not, she was the crux of this fight. With a longingly searing kiss, he let her go with Adam, to disappear into the night out of his sight. He felt as if a part of his heart was being pulled away from him as he stood on the step, staring out into the night, a few stars twinkling overhead. It was Jackson who came up beside him, laying a hand on his shoulder.

"I thought it went well this evening," he said hopefully.

"Oh, you did, didn't you? I thought so as well."

"You know we are getting questions about the meeting tomorrow," Jackson added.

"Did you tell them that I didn't have any answers?" Benedict asked with a chuckle.

"No, but when we mentioned the dark, they took the call for the meeting very seriously. You will have a captive audience for whatever you want to say."

"I hope soon to have a captive demon, Jackson."

Chapter 18

Emily and Tasha were more than a bit surprised, but were the only ones to show it, to find that not only had all the blood-born been summoned to this meeting but also witches, Esther, and her second, Gunnar, but two of the Seven, Li and Zara specifically. There were curious gazes at one another as they entered and made their way into the grand conference room at the Renard building. They wished it had been in better repair; it wasn't really fit for anyone outside the blood to see. There were soft murmurs as everyone tried to guess why the summons and what had Arkin meant by *the dark*. As they entered the conference room, Benedict was in evidence at the head of the table, as was Anthea Black at his side. Emlyn stood off to her right, and RM, a human whose reputation was known to the paranormal world.

Thea surveyed those funneling into the room. She was a bit disappointed that the Seven only sent two of their number, but at least these two usually listened more carefully and could make decisions faster than others. She hadn't wanted to deal with Copper this evening.

Slowly people took seats, heading off to where they felt more comfortable, among their own. There was tenseness in the air. Eyes darted about, curious, unasked questions on individuals' lips as Benedict stood to try to quiet the murmurs. All eyes turned to him, waiting.

"I want to thank you all for coming this evening and on such short notice. Although I wish more had deemed to attend, you shall be enough for what has to be done and said. Firstly, before I get into the very important matter as to why we are here, I think that you need to know whom it is you are placing your trust in. I walked into this city as Arkin Kane. No one among you knew who I was or where I had come from. I am sure you weren't even clear on my purpose, and I appreciate the trust and oaths you have given me." He looked at the blood-born. "What I am going to ask of you this evening suspends anything you may have been asked to do before, and it is only right that I have your complete trust. Although you know me as Arkin Kane, that is not the name that the majority of my race knows me by. As you know, we all take liberties, sometimes because we grow bored with who we were or because we have enemies. This name has served me well and allowed me into places quietly and without much circumstance. I took the liberty so that I could walk among us, making certain our laws and traditions were adhered to, that I could be first listened to, understood before being feared."

Thea was holding her breath as she sat beside him, her eyes looking out among the blood-born. He truly had their attention. Terence, Margaux riveted.

"The time has come to tell you that I am known to you historically as Benedict."

The room was silent, all eyes on him.

"Though that name may mean nothing to our guests who are not blood, I know that it has some meaning to my race, and I hope it carries with it enough power for you to trust me and believe when I say I want what is best for us."

"Well, that answers a question," commented Tasha dryly. "Commendable Benedict, your reputation precedes you. You have more than my loyalty. You have my admiration."

Benedict inclined his head, thankful for the compliment.

"But you are not the dark of which you spoke, are you?" Esther asked softly. "Giving us your name is not the reason for this meeting, is it?"

"No, I am not the dark, and there is more to this meeting than just my name or reputation."

"Is someone coming to try to take the city from you?" Zara asked, curious.

"No one would dare try to take anything from Benedict," added Emily smartly.

"Thank you, Emily, for your support. No, this threat is to everyone in the city, and it is unfortunately contained to the city. I gathered you, the most powerful, because of the strange situation we find ourselves in. Although this threat is to humans as well, they will not be able to deal with it on the level that we can. Emlyn and RM are here for Anthea, our silent witness, and will do what they can to assist."

"It sounds ominous," Li remarked, leaning back in his chair, eyes on Benedict. He knew that name but never would have thought that such a legend would walk into their city. This was excellent indeed.

"It is. We have been informed that there is a demon loose in the city, and it has been sealed here, so it cannot leave."

Voices erupted. Thea tensed as she looked on. Benedict raised his hand to try to quiet the discussion. Esther looked at Thea and believed it.

"A demon? I thought they were legend. Then again, a legend stands before us," commented Terence. "How does a demon come to be in our city?"

"Who told you there was a demon here?" Margaux asked, doubt in her voice.

"An archdemon who wanted to prevent a summoning told us. He arrived too late to stop the demon from entering our realm. Esther can tell you that a book and other items were stolen for a black art summoning. The person who did the summoning is dead, but what rose escaped and is on the loose. All the archdemon could do was warn us."

"What do you think the demon's intent is?" Asao asked as Benedict shrugged.

He had known that Arkin was more than he appeared, but now that he had his name, Asao was more than just proud to be called his second.

"I would assume to create a power base, to negotiate with us against sending him back to his realm. He may think he can keep this city safe for us, and all he might ask in return is to remain unfettered. That, however, is not negotiable. We have been given a weapon to send him back to where he belongs, and we will be given a spell so that we can locate him."

The room was very quiet. Thea could feel doubt linger in the air. He was deadly serious.

"So let us get this straight. Someone decided to raise a demon?" Zara asked, trying to wrap her mind around Benedict's statements.

"Yes, a man named Denard. He has since been taken to hell for punishment."

There were a few more murmurs.

"And you were there or witnessed this summons or the remains thereof?" Li asked.

"I was, among others. Anthea Black was there as well," Benedict responded firmly. A few eyes turned toward hers, Esther's for one.

"So when the demon was raised, the summoner was killed but also brought around an archdemon who, out of the kindness of its… whatever passes for a heart, decided to help you?" Terence asked, voice filled with disbelief.

"Yes, to keep it simple, that is what happened," Benedict stated, unsure whether anyone truly believed him and if you could call that simple.

Esther and Gunnar looked very grim, Emily and Tasha thoughtful, but regardless, they would have to help. At least the blood-born would.

"And this demon has provided you with a weapon and a spell?" Zara asked.

"No, the spell…"

Benedict fell silent as a piece of parchment wafted down, appearing from out of nowhere, hitting the table in front of Esther. She looked at the beautifully inscribed parchment.

"The spell has just arrived, and if the coven will assist us, we will locate the demon. As far as the weapon is concerned, that was provided for us by a demon's enemy."

There were a few looks around at one another, frowns, as they wondered just who was an enemy of a demon besides themselves. There was an air of fear growing around the room.

"I don't even want to know who is an enemy of a demon. That isn't our expertise. We maybe monsters to humans, but this is far removed from us. What is it you want us to do?" Li asked bluntly.

"Well asked. We are here so you could impart this information to us, but you haven't told us what we must do, or what you will do," Tasha said, voice trembling.

"I need you to contain the demon so that the weapon can be used against it," Benedict stated firmly.

Esther nodded to herself. She understood well as she dared to pick up the parchment. Yes, the spell could be done. It wasn't something she had ever seen before, but she could do it. She would find this demon and witness it, though it was an odd chance of a lifetime. She glanced at Gunnar; if she didn't come back, he would be a good choice to run the coven. She would have to find someone else to accompany her to the actual event.

"I have reviewed the parchment. I can do this. I and another of my witches will stand with you."

Thea glanced at Esther and nodded her thanks.

"And who wields this weapon?" Zara asked, her brow furrowed, mind deep in thought.

"Anthea Black will take the weapon to the demon once we locate it."

Voices were muttered around the table, eyes turning to her. Em laid a hand on his sister's shoulder, RM at his side. There was no other way to do this, and in the end, those who dared face the demon might get a look at an angel.

"I like Thea as much as the next silent witness. I have known her a long time. She is a good person, but not a fighter. She works with the dead, has a good sense of humor, but I have never known her to take a kill shot," stated Tasha bluntly. She nodded to Thea apologetically.

Thea stood, smoothing the suit that she was wearing. She needed to look businesslike this evening; she needed to look serious. Gazes turned toward her, and she could see dismissive stares from Li and Zara.

"I understand what you mean, Tasha. You all think, because you are blood-born or a changeling, that you have more ability and power. Perhaps you are right, but not in this circumstance. You don't have to worry about me taking the shot, and I don't think you can argue with me carrying the weapon. I'm the only virgin at the table, so there isn't room for discussion. This weapon is special and would not allow just anyone to carry it. I am the only choice that you have, and I'm not any happier about the circumstances than you are. This is not our mess, but it is our city, and we have to protect those who can't protect themselves. That is the oath you have always given, correct? You may let others think of you as monsters, but you aren't. You are just another arm of humanity, and now is your time to prove it."

Thea and Benedict had not discussed the reason for her to enter the fray; it never occurred to him that they would think her unfit. After all, they were not going to have to do it themselves. You would think they would be relieved. Benedict cleared his throat and tried not to look at her. It was as good an excuse as any.

"If you find it, I will kill it. All I need you to do is form a cordon to keep him in his place. The rest will be up to me."

Esther stood with Gunnar at her side. "I'll start on the spell. It will take me a few hours and most of the power of my coven. I can have it ready by tomorrow night if all goes well. I take it you will want to be there, Benedict?"

"It is my job as the master of this city. Asao also wishes to be in on the kill. Choose among you who will accompany us and know that what occurs at this fight, between the demon and Anthea Black, shall be confidential. What we see, we keep and do not share. There is no need to cause anyone panic or converse about what has happened. Decide."

"And if we don't?" Terence asked, standing.

"Then you forfeit your right to rule as a blood. I won't kill you, but you will be shunned from the city, exiled. You will not be allowed in any of my cities. I think you know that I have a few under my power."

That was an understatement, Marta thought. He was the most powerful blood ruling in the world as they knew it. Here he stood, right before them, with only a fraction of his people, and still he was dangerous.

"I will choose from my ranks the best fighters," added Emily, standing. "The others don't have to if they feel they are not up to the challenge."

Benedict glanced at Li and Zara.

"You will have some of our people as well, but not any of the Seven," Li remarked.

"I would prefer it that way. I want the fire in their hearts, the blood of true fighters, not someone who wants to know what is in it for them. Have them assemble here. My teams will take care of outfitting them, ensuring communications..."

Margaux chuckled as the sentence trailed off.

"You have done this before," she murmured.

"On all the continents pretty much in the world," Benedict added with a sigh.

It hadn't started out all the promising. It was hard to get them to believe, but Benedict's name had solidified the honesty and the danger even if they didn't truly believe in demons. RM and Em stood back and watched from the corner of the room as voices erupted, struggling to determine the next best course of action. Esther and Gunnar had reviewed the parchment and asked to take their leave. They would keep Benedict's people informed of their progress. So far, they had Benedict, Asao, Esther, and one more of her coven. Emily had suggested Edden and Enrico because they were good fighters, but they also liked Thea very much. They would fight to keep her safe even if they didn't care for Benedict. Benedict could respect that. Li agreed to Matt and a few others of their kind but didn't commit names. It was a start.

It was Tasha who walked up to Thea and regarded her with interest. "You have come up in the world," she stated, sounding none too pleased about it.

"I was always here in your world, Tasha," she answered.

"It would seem you have chosen a very staunch ally in Benedict. He is myth among us. You aspire to great heights."

"I just want to live to kill the demon," answered Thea coolly.

"You know I would have helped you rid yourself of that pesky virginity if you asked." Thea chuckled.

"But look how it has come in handy. Don't sweat yourself over this, Tasha. I know you are all cat and claws, but you aren't a fighter truly. I'm not really either, but I want to survive. As you said, I have much to live for now that Benedict and I are an item."

Tasha nodded to both Thea and Benedict, turning to leave them in thought.

"Well, Em, you certainly know how to show a girl an interesting evening. I wouldn't miss this fight for anything. I have guns, bows… never met a demon before. That was on my bucket list." Em hugged RM, slightly shaking his head. "You don't think they would go out and look for the demon, do you?" RM asked, curious.

"How does one find one in the city if they don't have a spell?" Asao asked as a small trilling noise sounded.

Thea excused herself, walking away from the main table, over into an alternate corner filled with fluttering shadows. The caller ID didn't say anything, but that wasn't uncommon; there were many a paranormal who didn't want their name bandied around.

"Anthea Black," she said quietly.

"Ah, Ms. Black, I have heard a great deal about you. I am sure you are learning about me."

"I don't know. Who are you?" she asked, a flutter forming in her stomach. Of course, the demon would have her phone number. Why not?

"I am sure you can guess. I am a new arrival to your city, and unfortunately, I will have to be staying."

Thea stood very still, her eyes looking for Benedict in the gathering. She waved her hand at her brother, trying to motion for him to get someone. Marta happened to catch a glimpse and pushed her way to Thea's side.

"And you have me at a disadvantage. Your name or the name you would like to be called?"

"I rather like Alexander. It has a ring of authority about it, don't you think? A name of power perhaps, and I am not without. You do know that, don't you? Denard had quite a few things to say about you, but he was rather garbled as he died. However, what I gleaned is that you are the only thing in this city that might be able to stop me. If you were so inclined to do so. But I am sure we could reach some sort of agreement. Give me a few days to get my life in order. As I mentioned, I am new, and much must be done."

"I wouldn't get too comfortable. I don't think you will be staying," Thea remarked.

"Ah, this puppy has teeth. So you want to play the hard line and believe you can take me? You are a child. I am sure it wouldn't surprise you to learn that I am old."

"Yeah, well, old dog, no new tricks. What do you want?"

"To live and let live. This city could be a mecca for the world, not for just you, but everyone else. The blood, the changelings, the fey, and lastly, humans, they all want the same thing. They want power, they want safety. We could be a hell of a team."

"Operative word being *hell*?" she asked, wondering just what he would want for his help. Maybe souls. What did a demon lust for?

"I can see that I can't convince you with my words. Well, until we meet in person. I take it you will be looking for me? Good luck finding me."

"We don't need luck, we have right on our side."

Alexander laughed. "It is pleasant for you to think so. Your kind always think they are right, pure, moral…"

"It wasn't my kind who wants to send you back. It was an archdemon." She hung up, jaw tight.

"You are popular," commented Marta, hand on her arm. There were flashes of anger in this girl's eyes. "You okay?"

Thea drew a long breath to settle herself. She struggled to stop the trembling that her body craved. "I'm okay, but he isn't going down without a fight, and neither am I," she muttered.

Everyone else might have been shocked that the demon would make the first move and call her, but honestly, Thea wasn't. Here was a demon sealed into a city, and he had so far no allies of his own kind. But he did have humans to coerce. He had to either hide, living his life in fear that she would catch up to him and fight or he had to make the first move and impress her with his power, make her an offer she might not want to refuse. In any other lifetime, she might have found his voice sexy. She was sure that his visage was more than just pleasing to a woman. But this was her lifetime, and she had Benedict. He was her mate, and she was certain of it, regardless of what they were and when they were born. He would be the one sure thing in her life besides Emlyn. She had worried about her brother because she had known that she had stopped aging at twenty-five, probably one of the reasons that Sarah and Caroline had gotten bitchy with her.

Thea was jarred from her thoughts as she realized RM and Emlyn were staring at her. They had arrived at home, and the car was stopped. She had been sitting in the back seat, silent, eyes not drinking in the passing scenery, the city embraced in night and a demon prowling the streets. Though Benedict feared she might be faced with the demon coming after her personally, he also realized that she needed some time alone. When Esther finally finished the spell, then they would spend the time together. She met their gazes and raised an eyebrow, coaxing them to ask.

"What?" she asked tersely.

"We're home. You ready for a good night's sleep? Do you think you can sleep?" Em asked as she shrugged.

She pulled open the door to the car and stepped out into the night air. She turned around, surveying the shadows. Alexander knew who she was and could easily find out where she lived. She was not so lucky to know little about him. He was a demon. He was old, and he had to be sent back. That, for right now, was enough.

"I'm a little wound. I'll see. You staying the night, RM?"

RM glanced at Em. "First, I want you to know that I love your brother and I'll take care of him as best as I can. I know that you both aren't siblings by blood. I know that there is a secret between the two of you, and I won't ask. I also know that you have a habit of trying to save others from having to deal with something you don't think they can handle."

Thea put up her hand to stop her. "I'm not going after Alexander," she confirmed.

"Oh, great. Give it a name so it sounds less dangerous," retorted Em.

"It is the name he gave himself," added Thea as she walked up to the door. She could hear Polly whining and her tail hitting the wall as she unlocked the door. "We are in a situation where you have to back me up, Em, and I know you will do it to the best of your ability. There isn't anything you can do but that. As for thinking I might jump the gun, meet him for drinks, not likely. I'll wait until we hear from Esther, then we form up and ash the son of a bitch."

RM chuckled. "I like that sound of that," she remarked as she followed Thea into the house. "So what does one wear to a demon killing?"

"Something one doesn't care if it gets ruined," added Thea as the doorbell chimed. Em and RM stopped and stared at the closed door as if it were a dangerous animal. Thea looked at them, amused.

"He isn't going to come up to the door and ring the bell," she remarked, but she still looked through the peephole, not too surprised to find it was Li and Zara. The blood had to do what Benedict asked them to do or they would face the consequences. The changelings, however, they had a bit of wiggle room.

Thea opened the door, leaning against it for strength. She was too tired for this bullshit. "Fancy meeting you here. Come to doubt me in person?"

Zara cleared her throat, flushing slightly.

"You are too obvious. You didn't want to piss Benedict off, doubting that I can do it. How about I present you with the weapon and you decide who is best to hold it?" Thea reached into her jacket pocket and brought out the small golden object. She let it lie in her palm, and it glittered in the dim light, untouched by shadows. "If you do decide to take it from my hand, I suggest that the other one stand aside. I'm not sure how it will destroy you."

Li and Zara looked at it as it sat looking very unimpressive in her palm. She pushed it toward them.

"I know you don't think very much of me. I don't really care. But this one time, you have to suspend your previous opinions and know I will do this. Give me this and I won't ask anything else of you."

Zara had looked as if she might reach out for the glittering gold short staff but held back, though Thea was sure that her fingers twitched. If it were Copper, she would have tried.

"Very well, but know that words don't sway as well as deeds."

"Well, duh, Li," muttered Thea, shaking her head. "You two just love to poke the skunk, don't you? This city has a chance to be great. You all have a chance to be a better council than anywhere else in this state, but this one time, you can't sit by the sidelines and see how it comes out. You have to get your hands dirty, or Benedict won't assist you."

"And how did you manage to turn him so easily to your side?" Li asked softly.

Thea chuckled. "So you doubt that I am fair enough to capture a man, that I seem to have no redeeming qualities for a man of power. My, you do think highly of your kind and little of us humans."

"You are not entirely human, that much we know."

Thea smiled, pocketing the weapon. "True, but shouldn't that scare you just a wee bit?" she said. "Night to you. I'll see your people when we are ready to take the demon. I am sure they will distinguish themselves."

Thea closed the door, mumbling to herself, disgusted.

"They think they are so self-important," muttered RM.

"Well, we will see how important they are when others find out that Benedict has taken the city. Others will want to come to take the council and distinguish themselves in his eyes. They are in for a rude awakening."

RM nodded as Thea glanced at Em. Em seemed to understand what she was silently asking. He shrugged.

"You know, RM, I trust you in so much as you do love my brother and will try to keep him not only safe but happy as well. If you want, I'll tell you the secret that we harbor."

RM shook her head as she started up the stairs toward Em's bedroom.

"I'm sure that I'll find out eventually, and I do love to be surprised. Keep it, Thea. But thanks all the same."

CHAPTER 19

Sleep came grudgingly. It was easier for her to sit with Polly and try to doze for small snippets of time than to try to lie down and force herself to go to sleep. She had curled up in her pajamas and let her mind wonder about her future, considered the past, and she came to the conclusion that she was good. Regardless of what happened, she would take it one day at a time. She had Benedict and the blood backing her. Tasha's opinion of her had changed, but her thoughts of people were fleeting anyway. The changelings, Matt would be a good choice for a fighter. She wondered who else they might choose. Though Em had said he was going to work at around seven, peeking into her room, she decided she wanted to check on Esther and the progress of the spell. If Em was going to work, RM was going to stick with her, not that she needed a bodyguard. But she could always use an extra pair of eyes and maybe her guns.

Thea showered, changed into some comfortable casual clothes, and found RM in the kitchen. She had made some frozen waffles, poured some juice, and fed Polly. Thea smiled her thanks at her new-found friend.

"Em told me that you always thought we were made for each other. Is that a gift, you being a matchmaker?"

"No. I just know that my brother isn't the best judge of what is best for him. He can be blinded by the initial attraction and doesn't look beyond."

"I always thought he was hot, but professionally, I sort of kept my distance. I figured, if it was meant to be, it would happen. Thanks for making it happen," RM said. "I have to say, Benedict is yummy."

Thea chuckled, draining her juice.

"Is it true what you said at the gathering last night that you are a virgin?"

With a mouthful of waffle, all Thea could do was nod.

"Is that part of the secret you keep, that it is better to be alone and virginal than with someone and maybe they find something out that they shouldn't?"

Wow, RM the detective was working overtime.

"You are very perceptive. To be honest, it hadn't occurred to me before that it might come in handy. It was sort of an excuse. My secret is actually the reason I can carry the weapon."

"I take it you are worried about being found out?" RM asked, concerned.

"Yes. It's not something bad, just unique."

RM nodded, as if she understood, and Thea could see her mind chewing on the puzzle.

"So what are you going to do today?"

"Well, I want to stop in and see how Esther is doing. If she thinks she has a timetable for when the spell will be ready."

RM nodded.

"I guess I have to see to Caroline's body. It should be cremated today. There will be a small gathering at the cemetery."

"Does it make you uneasy to know that the demon knows more about you than you know about it?"

Thea smiled and winked at RM. She stood, taking her dishes to the sink. "He knows some, but not all. Come on, I think I have a chauffeur waiting for me."

RM glanced out of the kitchen window. She nodded, seeing Adam's car at the curb. "He must have gotten some sleep last night. He is taking today's shift. I know of his reputation. He is good."

"And he really shouldn't be wasted on me, but what can you do?"

With RM in tow, Thea left the house and walked to the curb. Adam looked well rested, shaved, and armed. He and RM nodded to each other; they might not know each other personally, by reputation probably, but they knew that each other was armed.

"I don't know if you can kill a demon with a gun, but I am willing to give it a shot. Benedict thought you might want some company today. I am here for whatever you need."

"I would like to go to Esther's. Do you know where she is working?"

"She let us know last night. We have security out there to supplement her coven. We wanted to be sure she was safe while she was conjuring."

RM climbed into the back seat beside Thea. Adam introduced Nikki to them; she was riding shotgun. She was a tall tattooed woman with spiky hair and a pretty smile. She nodded to them as they pulled away from the curb and headed into the city.

"I have to go to Caroline's interment this afternoon."

Adam nodded as he concentrated on the road and traffic.

"Anything new? You seem kind of quiet."

"Nothing specific, but there were two reports of missing humans, one man and one woman. Don't know if it is related to the demon or not."

"Wouldn't he need someone on his side, someone to walk among us? What would a demon do with humans?" RM asked, curious.

"Devour their souls?" Nikki asked softly. No one wanted to think about that.

"Have you heard who will be there for the final showdown?" Thea asked, curious.

"The blood haven't submitted their final count yet. I am sure they are weighing their options, though Emily has already committed. Both Edden and Enrico were pleased to serve. They will be outfitted with anything that they might need. I heard that the changelings have given over four of their people, two wolves and two cats. I don't know of their skill, maybe you do. Matt, Craigory, Lanie, and Davis."

Thea thought a moment. She only knew of Matt and Lanie; they were personable, but she hadn't the faintest idea if they could fight.

"Well, I guess we will find out," she muttered to no one in particular as Adam pulled up to a warehouse-looking building not far from the park where Caroline died. Thea could already see security checking their vehicle. They weren't there for looks, and they were armed. She wondered if humans would even ask or if they just would rather not know.

RM and Thea climbed out of the car, nodded to the black-dressed, well-armed, and suspicious security team. They, of course, knew Adam and her, so they were ushered inside without challenge. The air smelled of fragrant herbs and incense. Though the entry looked like a standard reception area with a few plants, desk, laptop, it was what lay behind the door that betrayed the coven's inner workings. It was a cavernous warehouse that doubled as not only a meeting place but also a workshop cordoned off according to what needed to be done. And the coven was working today. She wondered absently how many of them had called in sick to their regular jobs to handle this spell. They were silent as they entered, not wanting to disturb anyone. It was Gunnar who tapped Esther on the hand to get her attention. She turned and looked at them with tired eyes and a tentative smile.

"How goes it?" Thea asked, extending her hand to the witch.

"I wish I could say that I didn't love a challenge, but to be honest, this is awesome. I may sleep for a week after this is over, but it is a chance of a lifetime to try to weave something like this."

"How is it exactly going to work?" RM asked, curious.

"Good question. We have been trying to decide how best it should be deployed. There are numerous ways, and I'm not sure what would work best. Do we go live with it and let it take us to this demon, literally lead us there? Or do we have it show us on a map?"

"Don't you think that once you put in the last element, it might decide for itself?" Thea asked, curious.

Esther pushed stray strands of hair from her eyes. "I had that thought as well. We may not get a choice. It is almost totally put together. All we have to do is add the last few ingredients and then utter the final chant. It will be ready for this evening, if you want to do it so soon. Do you know if the teams are put together?"

All eyes turned toward Adam.

"They will be at the compound by this evening, then it is up to us when we want to deploy. We could do it this evening if you are ready."

"I hate to leave a demon loose. I don't know much about them, but I do know they are a danger. I also know everyone wants this over with. I don't know what kind of weapon you have, but you have to know that if you have to get up close and personal with it, it will want to search you."

"That's all right. I plan to be as little dressed as possible. I was thinking a bikini that leaves little to the imagination. That should lull it into thinking that I'm harmless."

Esther snorted. "Really?" she asked as Thea shrugged.

"I don't want to have to strip in front of strangers, so I figured I would go prepared. I know it sounds stupid, but if we find it, Alexander has to know we are up to no good."

"And you get to get up close and personal with it. I don't envy you." She paused. "Give me a few more hours. Once we have put together the spell, we are going to get some sleep. We can do the final chant tonight when everyone gets here." Esther gently put her arm on Thea's. "Now, are you sure there is nothing that it can offer you to sway you to its side?"

RM sucked air, surprised by the question.

"I am just saying it out loud where others might be afraid to voice their fear."

"I already have everything I need, Esther. There isn't anything that it can give me."

"And if it threatens Benedict? Or Em maybe? What if you have to make a choice?"

Thea hugged Esther impulsively. "Trust me, only one of us is leaving there, and it will be me." Thea sounded so confident it managed to lay Esther's fears to rest.

They lingered an hour longer, getting her coven food, drink, and running any errands that might be needed, but with a glance at her watch, Thea knew she had to be at the cemetery. She took her leave of Esther with promising thumbs-up that she didn't quite feel and headed for the mortuary. She always had extra mourning clothes available. After all, you never knew when someone might die, and you needed to be dressed appropriately. RM said she would be at the mortuary with Em, and Adam said he would accompany her, so she breezed into the mortuary, waved to reception, and headed for the back office.

Em glanced up from his worktable, and she grabbed the suit bag and headed for the restroom. There were so many questions that Em wanted to ask his sister, but they froze on his tongue.

"Did you stop by and see Esther?" he asked, trying to get his voice to sound hopeful.

"It will be tonight, if everyone can get together. We will meet her at the warehouse and follow wherever the spell takes us."

"I have my bow, guns, and prayers, whatever you think it might take."

She popped out of the restroom dressed in black, with a white ruffled shirt. She kissed Em on the cheek as she tried to pull on her shoes. "Thanks for taking care of Caroline. I hadn't the heart." It was the least that he could do, and even then he felt he hadn't done enough for his sister.

"You had more important things to handle. I'm sure she understands that."

Em watched as his sister struggled with her hair. He took a long look at her, knowing as others might not that she had indeed stopped aging. He had known that two years ago, and it had frightened him thinking of her maybe alone as he aged and eventually died. In his heart he was relieved that she would have Benedict to rely on.

"Look presentable?" she asked, breathless.

"Beautiful," he added as she grabbed her purse and headed back the way she came in, passing RM. RM nodded to her.

"I'll see you tonight. I'll meet you at the warehouse. I'll be armed and ready."

"So will I."

Adam opened the door for her as she came out of the mortuary. She looked lovely, very professional, not at all dangerous enough to face a demon. But that was the rub.

"Thanks, you know the—"

Adam held up his hand. "Trust me, I know where every cemetery in the city is. Which one do you need to go to?"

"Memorial Pines, on Asher."

He nodded as she buckled up in the back seat and he slipped into the driver's seat. They pulled away from the mortuary and into traffic. They sat for a moment in silence, sunshine filtering in warmly through the windows.

"You have faith in those people who are backing you up, don't you?" Adam asked. "We aren't walking in there expecting tea and crumpets, you know. We have attended this type of party before."

She chuckled. "I don't know exactly how old Benedict is, but I don't think this is his first battle. Demon, maybe, but not his first fight. It's not so much the weapons, it is the ability to use them. The demon might convince a lesser person of his power to give them all they desire. I don't want one of our people turning on us."

"All we can do is keep an eye on one another. We will be there surrounding Alexander. You will be the one waltzing up to dance with him. I hope you dance well."

"I have never let my partner down yet."

There was a small retinue already waiting aside the marble mausoleums as Thea wove her way through the granite stones. This cemetery was older. It had all sorts of headstones that jutted up from the well-manicured earth. It was the smaller gathering that Caroline would have hoped for, then again, she hadn't been best friends with many people, and she could be catty. Women didn't forget those slights. Mal stood with the urn in hand next to Sarah, who looked very dramatic in a black hat and veil. Her arm was resting on Mal's, and Thea thought it looked a bit too friendly. She always secretly wondered if Sarah hadn't had a thing for Mal. Mal turned and smiled warmly as Thea approached with Adam at her side. There was a slight breeze, and you could smell the flowers that their florist shop had provided. They were lovely. It was just what Caroline would have wanted, except perhaps with more mourners. Mal leaned in and kissed Thea on the cheek. Sarah didn't seem too pleased by that show of affection. Then again, they had all been friends once. That hot stare didn't give Thea a second thought.

"The urn is lovely and expensive. I think it is more than she originally paid."

"She was a friend, Mal. I would have thought that there might be others to attend."

Mal sighed and shrugged the light breeze ruffling his blond hair.

"I put her obit in like she wanted. It was rather lengthy, then she wasn't always known for her brevity when she talked about herself. I'm not sure that there is much else to say. I wish she hadn't died that way, but it is the way of the world. Danger does lie in cities beautiful."

Sarah sniffled slightly as Mal leaned up against the cool marble and slid the urn inward.

"She would have liked being with Bootsie. I hated that damn poodle."

Thea chuckled lightly.

"I know that you had your differences with her, Thea, but you were a good friend. You put up with a lot of her shit."

"That is sort of what friends are for, Mal. I don't have anything to add either. I just wanted to be here and show support. Where is her current…fiancé? What was his name? Jake?"

"Out of town, traveling. The police let him know, but he couldn't be back in time, and if you ask me, I'm not sure he wanted to be. Caroline confided in me that she wasn't sure they were meant for each other, and for once, I agreed. She was searching for something, and I am sorry that I wasn't enough. I hear she was searching for you as well."

Thea nodded softly. "I think she would be pleased that I found someone finally. Might not like the fact that I found him without her, but in the end, I will be happy. I guess that is all we can ask."

"She left you a few things, mostly pictures of the two of you. I'll have them sent over. She also left you a trinket or two. You know, in the last few years, she began collecting things."

"No, I knew she liked to shop. She said it always took the blues away. What did she start collecting?" Thea asked, curious.

"Figurines," added Mal. "Angel figurines."

Figures.

Adam lent Thea a hand; it was time to go.

Adam offered her an arm as they turned away from the mourners, and he allowed Thea to steer their course. They stopped at the small marker for the Sheridans', her so-called birth parents. They were laid to rest not too far away from the Black mausoleum. Adam let Thea stand there and stare at the inscriptions for as long as she wanted, the wind ruffling her curls, her eyes distant in thought.

"If something happens to me, and it might—though I have stopped aging, I'm not all that sure that I can't be killed—Em knows where my will is. I left everything to him, all the businesses, but make sure that Benedict understands that he has my love, my heart, and what passes for a soul in us angels."

"Do you really think he would let anything happen to you?"

She turned and gently touched Adam's cheek. "You aren't that naive. My blood family gave me a weapon with no strings attached. How do I know for the asking that I'm not going to have to pay a price for their kindness? It has occurred to me. I could initiate it and both Alexander and I leave this earthly plane. I truly have no idea, but we are going to find out."

Adam fell silent as he followed her back to the car. It hadn't occurred to him. Had anyone thought of the price she might have to pay to destroy or send back this demon? If they had, they might have thought twice about this fight.

Adam escorted her back to their house. He wouldn't be at the final fight, but he was going to take her to the warehouse for the prep. He knew that Benedict had wanted to escort her himself, but his presence was needed to shore up the troops. He needed to give the orders to the blood and make sure that the changelings delivered as they promised. It was going to be a tense moment when the spell was released and they trailed the demon to his lair. For Thea's sake, he fervently hoped she remained in her human form. She shouldn't have to deal with a fight and then with the shock of her revelation.

He wasn't a praying man, but he found himself taking a few minutes out of every day to ask for this one grace. So he sat in the kitchen. He could hear RM and Em as they prepped for the fight. There was banter about weapons, clothing, and as they exited into the hall by the front door, they looked as if they worked for SWAT. They were dressed in all black, armed to the teeth, and with vests on, they were deadly serious. Adam nodded to them.

"I would like to make some comment about the kind of date that you go on, Em, but you two look ready to face hell."

"Well, at least one of its minions," added RM. "You delivering the weapon to the warehouse?"

It took Adam a moment to realize she meant Thea. "Yes. I know that Benedict would have liked to come himself, but we humans can handle this one task. I won't be the only one. You may not see them when you step out into the night, but they are there."

"Fair enough. We will see you on the other side. I hope we can dance at Benedict's welcome festivities."

"I'll save you a dance, RM." He stood, extending a hand to her.

Em nodded sharply as they stepped out of the house, leaving Adam in silence. He patted Polly absently. He was human, and though most craved not to know what happened in the supernatural world, it was the wrong way to live. You had to help your fellow humans, or so he always thought.

A noise at the door to the kitchen jarred his thoughts. He looked up, and there stood Anthea Black, barefoot, wearing an old trench coat that had seen better days. It looked as if it had come out of the great Detective Colombo's closet. Her hair was piled up in a mass of curls, some few strands trailing over her shoulder. She looked natural, until she opened the trench coat and revealed a smoking-hot red bikini.

If RM or Esther thought she had been joking, they thought wrong. Thea knew that Alexander would be suspicious of anyone within an arm's reach of him; he would suspect something. She would if she were him. He would be looking for a weapon, and he would be looking straight at her. It was better for her to walk in expecting to be searched than to assume that he would consider her innocent.

She also didn't want his hands on her. She had no idea what Denard had told him, but then again, it didn't matter. They were meeting as two unique individuals in a world that had not seen their kind ever before. The only thing she could think of that was less revealing was her underwear. A bikini seemed a better answer. She had several and had chosen a daring red two-piece. It gave Alexander a good look. Really, where could she hide a weapon in that? And it gave her ability to, if necessary, bring her wings to bear. She didn't want to face the fact that she might have to reveal herself to anyone, but she would if it meant saving someone's life. She had found her old trench coat. It had seen better days, but it would cover.

"What do you think?"

Adam cleared his throat, flushing slightly as she closed the trench coat. She waited patiently, serious in her question.

"Distracting."

She snorted. "Good, that was the look I was going for. You ready to go?"

"My chariot awaits. RM and Em already left. They looked like a SWAT team."

"I'm sure that everyone will. Are you sorry to not be in on the fight?"

Adam opened the door to the night, knowing his team and others were scattered around, ready to escort the weapon to the awaiting small army.

"I'm not stupid enough to enter into a fight that I can't win, but I wish I had the power to protect my people, humans as it were."

"Not to speak ill of your race, but they just ask silly questions. It's better this way. What they don't know can't coerce them."

Adam followed her to the car. He helped her in and watched her buckle up. It was going to look like a convoy, but it was well armed, and come hell or a demon, they were going to get her to the warehouse where the spell was to be deployed. It was going to be something to see, something he only hoped to see this one time.

CHAPTER 20

There was an air of anticipation about the warehouse. Benedict, Asao, Edden, and Enrico were dressed much as RM and Em were, only they were in dark gray, Benedict's signet color. They were working on setting up their communications. They weren't the only blood on-site, but they were the four going in. It was a hub of activity, Marta ordering everyone about nervously. Esther was with a witch named Kylie, both of them dressed in their robes, dark purple with hints of inscrolled silver and gold, looking just as dangerous. The spell sat before them on a table. When they were ready, it would be overturned and let loose into the air. They would be mounted up in vehicles to follow wherever the spell led them. The changelings had arrived. There was Matt, leading the so-called pack. She trusted his skill and intentions. Benedict at least knew him, as did Em. Craigory and Davis, both strong-looking men. Lanie, slightly more petite, but with predator-like eyes. She looked as if she enjoyed a good fight. They were all wearing comfortable sweat clothes.

It was Em who arrived shortly after them, and he had the guts to corner Matt to ask him the pertinent questions. After all, it was his sister on the line. He wanted to know if these changelings were fighters. He and Lanie were cats, Craigory and Davis were wolves, and they would change once they arrived on-site. They were good with guns or claws, Matt assured them. With that confirmation, all eyes turned toward the far opened door and waited for Adam to arrive with Thea.

They didn't have to wait long; the semiarmored SUV arrived along with their backups in the parking lot. Thea was impressed with the number of blood and humans who had been following them. She had not realized how many were involved in the escort until she exited the car. She turned to look over those who held allegiance to Benedict. It was a sobering sight. She nodded her thanks to them silently for their presence in this fight. They might not be facing the demon, but they were a part of the prep. That was just as important.

Thea turned to face those waiting for her in the harsh lights of the warehouse. Benedict. He stood in the center, looking like a Viking, a knight, or her king dressed in his uniform of sorts, ready to fight for her hand and life. He looked dangerous, if not well armed. She had seen plenty of fights in her life as a silent witness, but rarely had she been at the fight's center. These were the supernatural badasses, and they were at her command. She smiled gently, walking forward, barefoot, toward him. The floor was cold on her feet.

"I don't know what I expected, but I thought you might be a little better attired," commented Kale dryly.

He had been in one of the backup cars. Thea turned, pulling open the trench coat, giving everyone a good look at her form and the bikini. Lust spiked in Benedict's soul. If he were human, he would have blushed. Need coiled within him. He wanted her badly.

"I am suitably attired to kill. I didn't want his hands on me. This way, he doesn't have to search me to see that I am unarmed."

"Where is the weapon?" asked Lanie softly, her voice echoing over the warehouse.

"Wouldn't you like to know?" she remarked with a wink. She closed the coat, tied it in place, and turned to Esther.

"We ready to roll?" she asked bluntly.

Esther gestured to the cauldron on the table. "You want to do the honors?" she asked as Thea raised her foot and kicked over the table. There was a flash of blue and then red light, flames leaping into the air, and then the power coalesced into a ball that hovered for a moment then darted off, leaving a glowing trail behind it.

"Mount up," called Benedict. "You are with me, Anthea."

"Always, Benedict," she remarked as she heard Esther comment.

"Damn, I'm good."

Anthea had a rather absurd thought as they followed the bouncing ball through the city. It reminded her of a child's song when you didn't know the words but wanted to sing along. She shook her head, trying to clear any thoughts not pertinent to the situation at hand. She had to be sharp, she had to be alert, and she had to be deadly. Thea glanced out the window at the passing buildings. The spell was leading them toward the old Kenely Airport. Benedict gently patted her leg, as if telling her it was all right. It wasn't, of course, but it was a sweet gesture. Thea had to admit that it was a hell of a spell, and as they slowed their approach, they turned off their lights and eyed the old hangar. The area was slightly overgrown; it had gone into receivership and was to be turned around into a private airport for the blood, but with Yardley's death, that renovation had been put on hold. There were some small aircraft on the runway, covered with tarps, but it was the open hangar that caught her attention as she climbed out of the car. She kept her eyes on the lone light that tried to scatter the onslaught of shadows. Someone was in there, and the spell told her it was Alexander.

The hangar was open at both ends, with vague, dirty windows on either side. She didn't listen as Benedict issued the orders. She didn't stare as the changelings shed their clothes and formed into beasts that melted into the surrounding wildlife. No, she just willed herself forward over the cool, paved earth. There was nothing to say, nothing to do but continue, and she knew without turning around that there were people at her back. Thea walked as quietly as she could toward the closest open end. A figure crossed the light for a moment, and then a secondary light source flared up. The airport didn't have electricity, nor could she hear a generator, so there might have been lanterns. Thea stopped at the threshold of the hangar and stared inward. There were three people in the empty, cavernous bay. There was a man, tall, average-looking, dressed in jeans and a T-shirt. His eyes were glazed over, as if he hadn't a care in the world. The human woman was blond, wore a short skirt, heels, and a little top all in black. She, too, appeared to be under some sort of spell.

Then there was Alexander.

He turned, as if sensing her, surprise alight in his eyes. He was tall, just slightly taller than herself. He had dark hair, blue eyes, his body slightly tanned from the sun. He was wearing boots, faded blue jeans, and a dark-blue shirt. He brushed the hair out of his eyes and smiled. He had chosen a very handsome body, or he had fashioned it himself. She would have been impressed if she hadn't fallen for Benedict.

"Well, now, fancy meeting you here," he remarked, sounding unfazed by her sudden appearance. He stretched his arms wide, as if to say all she saw before him was his. "You arrived sooner than I thought. You must have had help."

Thea crossed the threshold. He held up his hand to stop her. It was then she shed the coat, letting Alexander get a long look at her. He whistled appreciatively, his eyes glittering in the fluttering light. Thea cast the coat aside. It landed on the floor of the hangar as she slowly walked forward. He looked at her with lust in his eyes and shook his head. He sighed.

"Aw, no fair. I was so looking forward to searching you."

She spun around to show her body off to its best advantage.

"I like very much. Your parents did good work."

Thea kept closing the space between them.

"My, you are a brave little soul. Aren't you afraid of the big bad demon?" He glanced slightly past her and then turned in a circle, checking out her backup.

"Oh, you didn't come alone. That isn't very fair you know."

She shrugged. "You know what humans say. All's fair in love and dispatching a demon."

He snorted. "You really think you can, little engine? You know I didn't ask to be here."

"Oh, boo-hoo, no one asked to be here or to be born. Stuff a stock in the whining."

He shook his head slightly and chuckled. "My, you aren't what you are advertised to be."

"Buyer beware," she muttered. "So is this your little demon lair?"

He shrugged, gesturing to the hangar. "It was a start. I didn't exactly have a master plan for arriving in this world. Denard truly was an idiot. He used a spell because he wanted to talk to his so-called demon family. I mean, really, who wants to do something like that? He had a few choice things to say about you, but they were a bit garbled, and then of course he died." Alexander stretched, wings like that of a bat arching out of his shirt, tearing the fabric.

She wasn't impressed. "And the two humans?"

Alexander turned to regard them. "Contrary to popular belief, I don't eat souls. I do corrupt them, but I don't eat them. I'm a 'seven sins' demon. I like the classics. I can feed off their lust or greed, whatever takes my fancy." He chuckled. "With that outfit on, I could feed off the lust of some of your backup. My, you are a nice piece of ass."

"Thanks for noticing. You said that over the phone you couldn't really get your point across. Now you have a captive audience. Why don't you wow me?" With each sentence, she sashayed her way closer and her backup closer behind her.

"You want my pitch?" he asked, sounding slightly astonished.

"You want to give it, or do you prefer to just go ahead and die?" she asked, curious.

He laughed, head back, the noise echoing across the hangar. He really was overconfident.

"You really think you can dispatch me? At most, I would call it a draw, your fire against mine. We are a match made in this world, I in hell, you in heaven. The last time I was in this world was when the Roman Empire was falling. Good times, that, by the way. Now, this is truly a different world, and it wasn't my time to come back. In truth, they weren't going to let me come back, but here I am, and I would like to make the best of it. All I want is a loyal entourage, much like you have here."

"Loyal down to their very soul?" she asked, just about within an arm's reach of the demon. It was a good thing that Benedict didn't have to breathe; he would have been holding his breath.

"You live in a city of possibilities, yet you fear for the future. We could all live here and be safe. I could ensure that no one waltzes in and tries to take what is ours. I would just be another member of your so-called council. We would be a power to be reckoned with. We could be one of the richest cities in the world." Alexander reached out and grabbed Thea's arm, dragging her closely into his body. She didn't stumble into him, but glided, expecting him to manhandle her.

"I didn't kill your friend. Denard did. So far, I haven't done anything to make you want to kill me or send me back. Are you so afraid of the unknown that you won't even hear it out? Odd, coming from the likes of you," he hissed as he drew a long, deep breath. "You smell sweetly pure."

"The night is young yet," she answered softly.

"I could do a lot for all of you," he muttered, taking his eyes off Thea as he held her left arm tightly in his grip, looking out into the dark. "Don't tell me that you aren't aware of those people who deserve a bit of comeback karma? I could be your delivery boy. I'm just another one of you in this world wanting to make my way. You can't blame a guy for trying. But you…" Alexander looked at Thea, met her deep gaze. "You want to try."

"Not really. I just want to succeed," she arched her body into him, drawing his attention downward toward her breasts. Her right hand snaked up into her curls, and she clutched at the weapon. That was when the flames of hell and perdition broke loose.

She knew, at the first sign of distraction, it would be her cue to strike. Though she looked unarmed and he looked alone, looks were deceiving. Though it appeared that he was alone, with only two humans, he might also be stalling; he might have backup somewhere. She needed to make this quick and as painless for her as possible. With the weapon held tightly in her hand, his eyes boring into hers, it was a shout from behind them that jarred Alexander's attention. It was one of the changelings, Davis, if she remembered the name correctly. He was in human form, running toward them.

"You have no right to speak for all of us."

With the weapon firmly in hand, she brought it to bear up under Alexander's chest cavity, holding onto it for dear life. The angelic blade sunk easily into his body. He struggled to dislodge both Thea and the blade before he was ash. His eyes riveted toward her, wide and startled as he felt flames beginning to lick at his feet and dissolve away his body. Thea hung on to the weapon and the urge to shift vibrating through her. She could feel his power rippling over her body urging her. Alexander's eyes were cold and deadly as he pressed what remained of his power onto her, but she held fast, still gripping the weapon. The air was filled with flames, smoke, and the acrid smell of a demon returning to hell. His voice was rising in screams that echoed around the hangar. Davis, not in wolf form, but in human form, was racing across the hangar, shouting at Thea to stop. Em knew he wasn't going in to help his sister, but the demon. He put two very nice silver-tipped arrows in his body. Davis crumpled to the ground with a thud. Thea hadn't noticed. It was the flames that tore at his body. Thea held tightly in the maelstrom, still gripping the weapon, a death grip.

Her voice shouted at everyone to stay back until finally there was nothing left to hold the weapon, and she fell back, hitting the ground with a thud. She twisted on the cold floor, yelling at them to wait, and in truth, only wisps of smoke curled up into the night, the heat of the blaze having subsided sufficiently for Esther, Benedict, and the medic that they had brought, Dr. Robbins, to dare launch themselves forward. They were the first to crouch next to her, the air acrid with what little remained of Alexander. No one dared touch the weapon still clutched in her right fist, but they certainly began scattering Alexander's remains with their booted feet. Robbins was a short middle-aged man with a no-nonsense attitude, serious expression, and cool blue eyes. He did a cursory exam that told him that she had first-degree burns on the left side of her face, second along her left arm and leg, some third-degree burns possibility. In truth, her skin was a mess. Some of her hair had been burned away, those lovely curls gone. She was going to need something for the pain, and Benedict was leaving it up to the doctor to help her.

Thea leaned against Benedict's body, away from the cold of the floor. She kept her right hand away from everyone, laying it out with the weapon now no longer a blade. She managed a tentative smile on her lips.

"I held on," she muttered, wincing, a groan escaping her lips.

Robbins slipped something into her mouth and then held up cool water for her to drink.

"Yes, you did. Don't fight the doc, he is here to help," muttered Benedict, holding her tightly against his body, trying not to touch her wounds. "I love you," he whispered to her as Robbins continued the treatment. He was mumbling to himself as she glanced up to see her brother closing in on the circle. She could see concern in his eyes, but also relief that she still appeared human to all those at this battle.

"I'll do what I can for her, but she isn't going to be very comfortable."

"She will be with me. I'm taking her back to our house. Asao, you take care of Davis. The Seven need to know he was going to intervene, whether they knew about it or not…that cannot stand. We told them what the outcome would be. We asked for their help."

Asao nodded.

"Do what you can so we can move her. She doesn't need to be out here in the night."

Robbins nodded as Kylie came up beside him. She knelt down, fingers gently caressing what was left of the hair on the left side of Thea's face.

"I know this sounds stupid, but I can even that up for her if you like. She shouldn't have to see herself like that. Do you mind?"

Benedict glanced at Esther, who was busy taking care of the two fallen humans.

"I know it isn't important, but it's a girl thing."

"Please, anything you can do to make her feel better," he remarked as she laid hands on Thea's head. There was a slight flare of light that danced around the strands, and Thea arched into Robbins's body. The smell of burnt hair drifted away on a circular breeze that filtered into the hangar.

Benedict looked at Thea. Though the curls were gone, she would always be beautiful, but right now, at least she looked presentable. It was silly, but to be honest, women worried about things like that. Kylie had managed to keep Thea's hair up to her shoulders now. Bangs brushed her eyelids, her face seeming almost serene. Edden laid a blanket over the right side of her body, the part that

Robbins wasn't working on. More light filled the hangar as a gunshot sounded. Everyone tensed, eyes searching for the cause of the shot. It was Kylie who nudged Benedict to join the fight.

"Go. You are more of a fighter than I am. I'll hold on to her."

Benedict didn't want to leave Thea as the team scattered to hold the hangar; they would find out later that Alexander had a few more humans in a corrupted thrall, but they would not live to know that their demon master was dead. He had ordered them to enter the fight. Now he had to prove that he could join them. Benedict nodded curtly to the witch before darting up and toward the onslaught of misguided humans.

"I have her stable right now. We can take her back home. Is that acceptable, Emlyn Black?" Robbins asked as Em knelt down next to his sister. He gently touched her cheek.

"You will be with her?"

"I'll be within arm's reach," Robbins remarked. "I might not be as young as other doctors, but I take my oath seriously, and I have experience in these sort of supernatural events. Trust me and trust Benedict."

Em turned around, staring at RM, who was shoulder to shoulder with Edden and Benedict, trying hard not to kill the humans, but at least disable them.

"I'll leave her in your hands. Keep me informed." Em gently took her right hand and brought it up to her chest, laying the blanket over her. She was still clinging to the slender piece of gold. He stood just as Benedict arrived at his side. There wasn't a mark on him, his hair slightly mussed and a spatter of blood marring his right cheek.

"I give her over into your care," said Em as Benedict nodded. He had so many questions he couldn't ask with Robbins close by. How quickly did she heal? Could she take any sort of medicine? He just didn't know what to expect, and he figured that Em didn't as well. It would be learning experience for all of them.

"Are we secure?" he called, voice filling the air.

It was Enrico who answered. He called from across the hangar. "Yes, you can move Yoyo now."

There was a soft, sputtering laugh that bubbled from Thea's mouth as Robbins carefully wrapped her up. "The weapon, I need to return it. I gave them my word."

"There will be time for that," he muttered softly into the shell of her ear.

"Let someone else carry her," offered Edden. "I'll be right beside you, promise."

Benedict nodded as he let Edden slip in, wrap his body around Thea, and stand. Robbins adjusted her in the vampire's arms and then gestured for them to walk to the car. Benedict turned to review the scene. Kylie was in conversation with Esther.

"You have my thanks for the spell. You did well for us."

Esther flushed, slightly nodding.

"You handled command easily. Your team scattered when we might be under attack. I am glad you were here. Though I could kill if I have to, I didn't want to make today the first time. Thea did well for us. You should be proud," Kylie remarked.

"Yes, she did, and yes, I am."

Edden managed to slide into the car with Thea in his arms, Robbins at his side, Benedict joining them in the SUV.

"She is mumbling about taking the weapon back. We can't do that for her, can we?"

"No. Signal RM and Em to follow. They can take her into the church with Robbins as a backup. There may be a reason she has to do it now. I won't gainsay her."

Thea could feel the rocking of the car. Her eyes fluttered open and then closed, voices around her. Soft lips touched her forehead, Benedict whispering in her ear. "Do we have to take it back now?" he asked softly.

"Please."

So instead of heading for the warm safety of the house, they drove for St. Mark's Church. Em, RM, and Robbins would have to handle Thea; it made him nervous, but he agreed. He also couldn't vouch for her privacy or any questions that might be asked. They stopped in front of the stone church, Edden stepping out of the car,

Thea squirming in his grasp. He swung her around so that she could stand, blanket still wrapped around her.

"I'm not sure you can even walk," Em commented as RM tried to steady her on her feet. She sort of tottered back and forth.

"Let me try," she muttered, pushing Em back.

With the blanket around her, Robbins on her right side, they helped her up the steps and through the door. A few monks were at service when they entered the church and started down the aisle. There were curious eyes on the four, two people dressed to kill, one dressed in a suit with a medical satchel over his shoulder, and a woman holding a blanket around her bikinied body. RM ran interference from up the aisle, ushering them back away from the altar as Thea took slow, deliberate steps toward the end of the chapel. She brought her hand out of the folds of the blanket, trying to ignore the throbbing pain that assaulted her body. She didn't dare try to kneel; she would fall over. So instead, she leaned forward and gently laid its golden length on the marble. She sighed, as if a great weight had been lifted.

"I always try to keep my promises." She sighed, turning away from the altar. Em rushed in to support her. She twisted in his arms to speak to the few monks assembled there. "If you are wise, don't touch what I just laid there, unless you want to die."

Murmurs chased them to the door until a voice from behind them spoke, shattering the silence. RM turned around to face the puzzled gazes of the monks. You had to admit, they were an odd group indeed.

"Is it true that there is as demon in the city?" asked a voice from behind Robbins.

RM wondered how they, as humans, had discovered its arrival. Then again, they were in a church, and there were probably portents.

"Not anymore," RM added with a brisk nod.

CHAPTER 21

It was a small murmur that indicated to Benedict that Thea was stirring. He glanced down at her as she lay aside him, body warmly covered by blankets. Her left arm was gently bandaged, and the left side of her face was shiny with antiseptic medicine. They had left the church for the house, and Robbins continued to treat her. He had also dressed her into something comfortable. It took a lot of trust on Em's part to allow Benedict to take care of his sister when she was so hurt. Benedict would not fail either of them. Thea's eyes fluttered open and then closed. Her right hand reached up to touch his chest lightly.

"I don't know where I am," she whispered, voice sounding light.

Benedict smiled gently, adjusting the blanket. "You are safe, Anthea. You are with me."

She managed a light nod, eyes fluttering, her body feeling heavy. She was trying to get her thoughts together, trying to remember, and it was a fleeting attempt.

"What time is it?" she asked.

"Two in the afternoon. You can go back to sleep if you want. There is no work for you to do. There is nothing else you have to do but heal."

Two in the afternoon, and Benedict was still awake. How odd life could be, considering just a few hours earlier, she had dispatched a demon. She had felt Alexander's regret, his anger, and at that moment, she wondered if she should even be on this earth.

"I don't feel as sore as I did. I feel a bit blissful," she mumbled.

"I'm glad. I want you to be comfortable. I was worried about you."

"You're sweet." She sighed, eyes closed once again.

"Do you remember what happened?"

She frowned slightly. "I was so close to him I had to take the opportunity. I couldn't wait. You were depending on me. There was fire when I stabbed him. I thought I was going to lose myself in it. I didn't," she answered proudly.

"I'm proud of you. After he caught fire, you fell back and were burned. Dr. Robbins treated you at the scene. We weren't sure how long it would take for you to heal, so we treated you as if you were human slow."

"Was someone yelling at me?" she asked, voice sounding small.

"Davis, one of the changelings. He rushed at you, but Emlyn caught him with two silver-tipped arrows. He saw a greater glory siding with the demon. His idea or the Seven's idea, doesn't matter. We gave you medicine for the pain. Kylie, Esther's witch, managed your hair. It got charred on the left side, but you still look as pretty as ever. Do you remember anything else?"

Thea thought a moment, her eyes closed. It had been that constant whispering in her ear that told her to return the weapon. She had tried to oblige.

"The church, St. Mark's. I remember that vaguely."

"You insisted on taking back the weapon that evening. I wanted you to rest, but you were adamant. RM, Robbins, and Em took you inside. I take it that your people will recover it at their leisure?"

"Why am I with you?" she asked, snuggling down into the bed.

"You are mine, and because I said so."

She sighed. "That sounds nice," she commented with a long sigh. "I'm glad."

"Are you hungry?"

Thea reached up and touched his chest, feeling something under his shirt. She looked at him with hazy eyes. He smiled as he brought out one of her feathers, which he had put on a gold chain.

"For luck," he whispered as he kissed her cheek and she fell back asleep.

* * *

Thea was sleeping, and Dr. Robbins wasn't sure that was a bad thing, but he knew there was more to his patient than what anyone was saying. She had been doctored up as best as she could, put to bed, and more than that, Benedict wanted to know how she was doing. She was healing, faster than Robbins suspected, but he wasn't sharing that with anyone but family, Emlyn directly, and of course those staff that Benedict okayed. Emlyn wanted her home, but Benedict could care for her better and had enlisted Enrico to cook for her. If past history was any proof, there was no way that Thea would turn down anything that was made for her by him. It was a good start to get her strength back and buoy her spirit. It wasn't just that her body was burned, but she had held fast against all coercion not to change, not to reveal herself. Both Emlyn and Benedict were proud of her, and it was inevitable that Em and Benedict would have a talk.

Emlyn knew that Benedict had his sister's best interest at heart. He wasn't going to gainsay him; he wasn't ready to face a very old master of the blood, after all. But as soon as he figured that Benedict was up and around, he was on their doorstep. It was Lang who let him in, managed the common courtesies that were expected, and ushered him into the front living area. Em had no idea just where his sister was but knew she was safe, but still, they were going to need an understanding between them since they both cared so much for her.

Em glanced at his watch. It was eight thirty by the time Benedict joined him. He looked refreshed in trousers, with a matching smoking jacket in gray brocade. It looked good on him, even if it did make him look like he was from another era. You would never know that half a day ago, he was geared up to take on a demon.

"Good evening, Emlyn. Please have a seat. Can I get you something to eat or drink?"

"No. I just had dinner with RM," he remarked.

"You and she seem to be getting along famously." It was just an observation.

"It had been my sister's idea last year. She thought we were suited for each other. She has that ability, you know, to sort of look at souls. I know there aren't real blood ties between us, but, Benedict, she is my sister."

"And I can respect that. I know she cares very deeply for you. I believe she would even reveal her true nature if necessary to save you. You have to know that I love her, that I will do anything to protect her and make her happy. I was attracted to her before I knew what she was and is."

"She held on and didn't turn," Em said proudly. "I wasn't at all sure how this would all play out."

"I apologize for being late to greet you. I was making sure she ate something. She has been resting mostly, and Robbins is pleased to see her healing. He doesn't know why, just that she is. I would like to keep her here for another day, and then she can go home. I think she can be stubborn and contrary."

"Well, then, you know my sister." Em chuckled. "It seems that we have the same goal in mind."

"I would like her to stay here, move in with me if she's willing. Since you and RM are hitting it off so well, it would afford you privacy and give us time together. It would also keep her safe. She has come this far. I wouldn't want anything to happen that she doesn't want to happen."

"Agreed." Emlyn was silent a moment, his gaze on his hands on his lap. "I know that she has stopped aging."

Benedict nodded. "I wondered if that was so."

"I noticed it a couple of years back. I wasn't at all sure. She is the only angel I know."

Benedict laughed. "And you would have thought I might have run into one before now, but no. They are a rare jewel indeed. Are we in agreement, you and I?"

"As much as she will let us be. Can I see her this evening? I can pick her up tomorrow evening, if that is agreeable, and take her home."

"That sounds fine. I am reluctant to let her out of my sight, but I understand she has to go home sometime. If you will follow me?"

It was a rare honor to be trusted into the quarters where the blood slept. This was the first and only time that Emlyn had been allowed. Even the whimsical Tasha wouldn't let Thea see where she slept. As he suspected, the chambers were in the basement of the house, but this was no extra room. This room luxurious, and Em wasn't about to ask if it was for his sister alone. He had a feeling that it was Benedict's room. His sister was a big girl; she could take care of herself. But he was glad to see someone else wanted to try. Em stood at the threshold, eyes on his sister, who was nestled in the bed, propped up by tapestry pillows, with a tray set on her lap. And bless his heart, Enrico sat at her side, prompting her to finish whatever it was on her plate. He looked hard at her and realized she had not been untouched by the battle. There were circles under her eyes, her skin seemed pale, and what had been one of her crowning glories had been shorn. He had to admit, with what Kylie had to work with, it was attractive framing her face; it just didn't look like his sister. She looked suddenly angelic. It startled him.

She looked up, her eyes meeting his gaze. She flushed slightly, as if embarrassed to be caught wearing a simple white cotton nightgown with eyelet around the neck.

"You look better today than you did yesterday, so any improvement is good," he remarked, walking forward. Em leaned over to kiss her on the forehead. "Benedict tells me you are making good progress."

"Both of them are making me eat. With you I can fight and be my stubborn self, but I am a guest here, so I have had to be polite."

Enrico nodded to her, taking her plate and cup. "That's a good girl."

"You didn't make any of the sound effects like you used to when I was a child," she muttered with a pout.

"To make you eat, I would have done just about anything. I'll come back with your snack a bit later. Good food will help you heal, and everyone here wants you well." Enrico nodded to both Benedict and Em. There had been rumors about both Benedict and Thea, some thinking that the announcement was just good politics. It wasn't. He clearly could see that Benedict loved Anthea Black. It was serious. They had better watch their comments and steps where it regarded her.

"Your brother and I were having a good discussion. He would like to take you back home tomorrow, and I am in agreement, if that is all right with you. Robbins says sometimes when you are home, you heal faster in comfortable surroundings."

"Benedict, my surroundings were never this comfortable. It's great, but I understand. You worried about me?"

"I have been worrying about you since my parents brought you home. It is a job that I will gladly give up to Benedict if you want me to."

Her gaze shifted to Benedict. She blushed slightly, looking down to adjust the bedcovers. "I would like that, Em. You have someone else in your life to look after, and though it isn't a competition, I want you to be happy as well."

"Why can't we both be happy? You have been looking a long time, and I think you found someone worthy of you."

Benedict stiffened slightly.

"He put himself on the line for you, and so far, your secret is very safe. And if you trust him with your heart, I do as well."

"You honor me," he remarked, laying a hand on Em's shoulder. "When you arrive tomorrow, I will hand her over to you, but you will have to make sure she is dressed and ready to come to our welcoming party. She isn't getting out of it that easily."

"Can't I play the invalid card?" she asked sweetly, fluttering her eyes at him.

Benedict rolled his eyes, amazed at how easily she could play his heart. "Robbins says you are making good progress. Your skin is renewing itself. Though he doesn't have an answer for it, he is grateful."

"Do you know or have you heard if the weapon was recovered from St. Mark's?" she asked, curious.

"I heard that after you had left that night, a bright light filled the chapel and then it was gone. Someone or something came and got it," Em remarked. "Needless to say, the monks are full of questions."

"I would say so, as long as they don't ask them of me. What happened with the changeling?"

Em glanced at Benedict. "You mean the one I put two arrows in? Apparently, he was speaking for two of the Seven. They were interested in negotiating with the demon. They left it up to him to see if he would be interested, but he couldn't stop you."

"And what happens to them?" she asked, mildly curious. Sometimes bad people got away with things.

"Their people will take care of them. I made it clear that they needed to do something, or I would."

Thea nodded, stifling a yawn.

"You need to go back to sleep, and I should clean up the house a bit, change your bed, get it ready for you. Polly will be happy to see you."

"Is work going all right?" she asked, trying to slip back into normal.

"All is well, at least for the moment." Em sighed. Benedict looked at him with puzzlement. "I am waiting for the other shoe to drop."

"What do you mean?" Benedict asked, looking at Thea.

"He means that I didn't reveal myself then, but it is just a matter of time before something happens. You know it, and I know it." There was a tender silence between them. "I wonder if I should pick the instance and not be forced into the revelation."

"You don't have to make any fast decisions, Anthea. Give it a while for you to heal, for us to settle in, and then I am with you in whatever decision you wish to make."

"Fair enough." She yawned again.

Em winked at his sister. "I'm off. I'll see you tomorrow evening."

"Are you and RM all right?" she asked.

"Always prying, aren't you? She was impressed that you were able to stick with it. She doesn't exactly understand what happened, but she accepts it. Oh, and Mal dropped by some things that he wanted you to have of Caroline's. I'm not sure you are going to like it."

She frowned.

"Angel figurines."

"Shit," she muttered.

* * *

It had been a very long time since Benedict had awakened with anyone in his bed, and this evening, he woke up with Thea pressed up against his left side, her arm thrown across his chest, and leg close to his groin. He curled his arm around her, gently kissing her on the top of the head. She made a sweet sigh of contentment, slowly turning over on her back, eyes flickering open.

"Em will be here soon, if he isn't already waiting to escort you home."

She pouted and sighed as he flung back the covers and twisted around, his eyes running up and down her body. He had felt the lust envelop him when she had stood facing Alexander, wearing nothing but a bikini. Even now, in the soft cotton, she fueled his passion. He wanted to rip off the frail fabric, kiss her into submission, and make her cry his name in ecstasy. Instead, he arranged the nightgown around her legs and scooped her up into his arms. He inhaled her scent, trying to memorize her body next to his, her warmth. Everything about her that made her Thea.

"I can assure you that after the festivities, we will be vehemently discussing where you will be sleeping and living, for that matter. Things will get back to normal. No more demons for anyone." With Thea in his arms, Benedict walked to the door. It slowly opened, revealing Jackson on the other side. He nodded to Thea, who lay in his arms, head against his chest.

"I was just going to tell you that Emlyn is here with RM. They have come to take this little girl home. Do you think you will be up to the festivities tomorrow?"

"Shush, Jackson. I am enjoying playing the part of invalid." Thea shifted in Benedict's arms, and he let her swing down, feet touching the floor.

"You look better today."

"Thank you kindly, and thank whoever gave up their nightgown for me."

"It was a spare," commented Marta from the bottom of the stairs. "Em and RM are waiting for you upstairs. They want to take you home. I'm sure Polly will be glad to see you."

Thea took a wobbly step forward, both Jackson and Benedict offering arms to see if she needed assistance, but she managed to the bottom of the steps with Marta. She offered a hand up, and they ascended to the top.

"I want to thank everyone who backed me. It could have gone a hundred different ways."

"Kudos to you for sticking with it. That fire looked hot, and he didn't look happy," Marta added as RM stood at the top of the stairs with a robe and a pair of slippers. "I'd hug you, but you still might be a bit sore. You are hell on wheels when someone gives you a magical weapon."

She chuckled lightly, leaning on Benedict, letting RM slip her feet into a pair of slippers. Jackson held the purple robe for her.

"We will pick you up tomorrow night," he confirmed.

"Where did they decide to have the party?" she asked absently.

"At the arboretum," Marta remarked. "Luckily, we have good weather for it, though I doubt anyone would want to disappoint Tasha. I have a feeling you would never hear the end of it. It should be nice."

"You sound jaded. Been to so many parties this is just another?"

Marta shrugged. "Nothing interesting ever happens at these sorts of things."

Benedict kissed Thea on the lips chastely.

"I hope not," murmured Em.

* * *

It was a quiet ride on the way home, Thea in the back seat, wrapped in her robe and slippers, thoughts and gaze distant. Em looked at the rearview mirror, wondering what was on her mind.

"A penny for your thoughts? Though I am sure they are worth more than that."

She chuckled lightly. "A lot has happened in the last few days, and much of it was out of my control."

"Life is like that," offered RM. "If you can get control of your life, let me know how you managed it."

"Are there rumors about?" she asked, uncertain if she should ask the question.

"You mean among the humans? Only those of an ecclesiastical nature. They somehow knew something dark was in the city. They are still trying to figure out what walked or arrived in St. Mark's to bring the light and take the small staff of gold. As far as the blood is concerned, you are Benedict's. No one seems to contest that, though some of the women in the city were disappointed that they didn't have a shot at their new lord and master."

Thea nodded.

"As for the changelings, there are problems in the ranks. The Seven aren't as cohesive as we thought, nor will they be for long. I have a feeling once word gets out that Benedict has taken the city, those who want stability and power will come in and vie for a place here. They may be more in line with what Benedict wants to do. Our Seven have been rather stagnant. I wouldn't mind seeing them tilted on their butts."

"You have a cruel sense of irony, but I understand," answered Thea as they pulled up to the house.

RM was out of the front seat and at her door. It was Polly who darted out of the front door, where Edden stood waiting, a smile on his face. She stood rather stiffly and adjusted her robe.

"Well, now, don't we look a sight! Ready for bed, are we?"

"Everyone wants to put me to bed, but no one wants to join me," she tartly replied.

She walked to the steps, Edden putting out a hand to help her up and into the house as Polly danced around her. She ruffled the fur on her head and played with her ears.

"You look good."

"I look like I danced with a demon. Well, hell, I did, and managed to come through it more unscathed than I thought. So what brings you to Casa Black?"

"I am delivering a gift for you. Emily and Tasha figured that you may not have time to shop for the festivities tomorrow, and they wanted to give you a gown to wear."

She looked suspiciously at the box that sat in the living room.

"You are surprised at their kindness?"

"Not so much Emily, but I wonder at Tasha. There is always a price for her kindness, but then again, to suck up to me might not be a bad thing for her. I do have the ear of Benedict."

Edden cleared his throat. "I bet you want more than his ear."

She elbowed him in the stomach as he laughed. Yeah, she was on the mend. It had been a frightening thing to see her stand up to a demon. She seemed too fragile to do it, yet Benedict had faith.

Thea caressed the box. "It came from Ruby's. That is rather an expensive place to shop," she commented.

"Well, you can't wear your usual suit," added Em as he gestured for her to open the box.

She pulled the bow, opened the lid, and drew out a golden gown. It was truly a gown fit for an angel. It was a formfitting, golden-beaded gown, and strangely, it was light as a feather. RM whistled, fingering the fabric.

"Wow, that is gorgeous!" she commented, impressed.

"Yeah, in the box. I'm not so sure it will meet expectations on me."

"You don't give yourself a lot of credit," added Edden. "I saw you in the bikini."

She met his twinkling eyes. He leaned in and kissed her.

"Save me a dance tomorrow, all right?"

"For you, sure."

Edden said his goodbyes and left.

"Let's go hang this up and get you to bed so you can rest. Some of the best makeup is sleep." RM headed up the stairs as Em came up beside his sister and gingerly hugged her.

"So far, so good," he whispered.

"I wasn't all that sure that I can hang on."

"And Benedict understands. And you trust him, right? That he wants you and not the possible power you can bring?"

She met her brother's gaze and nodded. "Yes. He is sincere, and he wanted me before he knew I was an angel. When I sent Alexander back to hell, I wondered if I, too, needed to be away from other mortals. He wasn't here to do good works, and I wonder if I am any better."

"Don't doubt yourself. You are pure of heart. You were able to hold that weapon through the fires of hell. That archdemon owes you one."

She laughed. "Yeah, like I could really collect."

CHAPTER 22

Anthea Black stood in the gown that Emily and Tasha had chosen. Strangely enough, it was backless, a halter gown. That fact alone made her laugh. It was golden like a sunrise, with beads and sequins clinging to her breasts and rib cage, flaring out at her hips. It had been expensive. She knew that because she didn't shop at Ruby's—no one who counted coins did. Though her hair lacked length, it was now shoulder-length, but she had curled it the best she could, adding a few combs in the forms of leaves in her tresses. She viewed herself in the full-length mirror, the burns she had sustained healing beneath the bandages that Robbins had secured. She had slipped on a pair of gold heels, managed a bit of makeup to add color to her face, and was ready to go.

There was a gasp at the door as she turned, finding Em in his tux, eyes wide.

"Wow! No, *wow* doesn't cover it. You are awesome!"

She shook her head slightly at the compliment as she picked up her clutch purse.

"Yeah, well, you are biased," she remarked, slipping past him. She walked slowly and carefully in her heels down the stairs and into the living room.

"The limo just pulled up," added RM. She was dressed in a deep blue, and that complimented her, and this one time, Thea wondered if she was armed.

"To answer your question, no, not this evening." As if reading her mind, she added with a chuckle, "Had a time of it with my hair, but your brother says I am gorgeous."

"You are," confirmed Thea.

"Not compared to you. You look like you don't belong among mortals," she added softly as the doorbell chimed.

Polly stood at the door and barked expectantly. Em opened the door to a tuxedoed Benedict. His tux was a smoky gray, his eyes only for Thea as she stood at the end of the hall. He didn't acknowledge anyone else, just stepped forward as if in a dream. He reached for her hand and kissed it lightly.

"I don't have words," he murmured to her as she flushed.

"That is maybe the sweetest thing you could say. Are you ready to go?"

Her words shook him out of his reverie, and he offered her a hand and they proceeded to the door. "There is enough room for all of us," offered Benedict.

RM and Em declined.

"You two enjoy the privacy."

Benedict was privately pleased with their decision, because as she slid into the car, there were flowers everywhere, even a bottle of iced champagne. Her eyes were wide, her joy contiguous.

"You didn't have to do all this for me."

"I would have done more," he added as Lang pulled the limo away from the curb. "I want to do more."

She patted his hand gently. "You are too sweet and generous to me," murmured Thea.

"Actually, I am a cad."

She raised a curious eyebrow at the old-fashioned word. "Oh, and how are you a cad, Benedict?" she asked, puzzled.

"I told you that you were mine, I have made it known that you are mine, but I have not made it official in any matter or means."

Thea opened and then closed her mouth as he brought out a small velvet ring box. She shook her head. "You don't have to do this."

"Do what?" he asked innocently as he laid it on her lap. "At least look at it, Anthea."

With trembling hands, she took the ring box and opened it. There was a lovely marquis diamond surrounded by a spray of stones. It was more dazzling than a sunrise to a man who had been blind all his life. It was set in platinum—she was sure of it. She looked up to meet his earnest gaze.

"A gift to you from me. It is my fervent wish that you allow me to be your knight, your partner in all things. If you want to consider this a marriage proposal, please do. Though many of us don't marry in the human sense, I want you to be mine."

"I already told you that you were mine and that I am yours, Benedict. I don't need a token."

"I want to give it to you." He took the ring out of the box and gently slid it on her ring finger. It was cool to the touch and a tad heavy.

"I don't have anything to give you, Benedict."

He laughed as he took her chin into his hand and kissed her impulsively on the lips. "You gave me the miracle of knowing and loving an angel. Just when I think there is nothing else to discover in this life, you bring me love and something I never knew could exist. I have wandered from city to city, and maybe I was looking for something other than rule, other than just my race. I was looking for you."

She blushed as she kissed him, their tongues mating. She groaned pleasantly in his mouth, his arm curling around hers, careful not to hurt her.

"I hate to interrupt this back seat make-out session, but we are here."

Benedict glared at Lang with narrow eyes.

"My lady and my gentleman, people are waiting for the guest of honor."

It was Asao who opened the door to the limo. He wasn't at all taken aback that there were flowers in the limo or petals on Thea's dress. He did catch the glimmer of a diamond on her ring finger as they exited the limo. He smiled to himself. Benedict had done the right thing. He had found love and a way to protect a most precious item.

There were best wishes, handshakes, and introductions as they made their way through the entry of the arboretum and into a fairy land that Emily and Tasha had created. Lights danced like stars in the trees. Soft music lilted over the fragrant air. This was a night to remember, and everyone was dressed to kill, all the blood, witches, changelings, and even a smattering of trusted humans. There were bold gazes, both men and women looking up and down at Anthea Black as if they had never seen her before. In truth, they hadn't, not like this. There were murmurs that ran through the crowd as Benedict and she took the first dance, a turn on the floor. It was true that she was his; was it true that he had given her a gift of his heart, a ring worth more than everything she owned? Was it true that she was to move in with him? How had she fought a demon, where had the weapon come from, and was she still a virgin? Em had heard this gossip and tried to ignore it. There was no sense in upsetting his sister, but those inciting the rumors just had better not let Benedict hear the talk. Marta and Adam were listening, as were Asao and Emily. No one would gainsay Benedict. Most figured she was just a passing fancy. After all, she was human, right? She lived for just a blink of an eye in a blood's time. There was no sense in getting upset. There were cool stares from some of the changelings, Copper for one. Asao and Terence had headed off any sort of discord. They were not going to spoil the evening by bringing up business. It was supposed to be a magical night, one that everyone would remember. And it would be.

The night air was cool, the stars so bright you could almost reach out and touch them as Thea stood at the rail of the patio. The landscape was dotted with flowering bushes, plants, and you could smell them in the air mingled with brief snippets of cologne. The music was soft and classical, not so loud that you couldn't have a conversation. It was all very tasteful and traditional, she thought. This was the perfect setting. A Greek gazebo stood in the distance, draped with lush velvets. There was a lovely, adorned sundial surrounded by cushioned benches should someone wish to sit. Shadowy corners should someone wish an assignation or perhaps a taste of their donor. It was all very romantic.

Tasha and Emily had outdone themselves on the party to welcome Benedict to their city. It became more when they realized that Arkin was indeed Benedict, something that was a myth to them, that they had been truly rewarded with someone who would let them prosper.

The night was dreamy, men and women gowned and jeweled, music, food, and blood. A city no longer divided, it seemed. There had been amazed eyes on her this evening. She had pretended not to see them staring. She had been in their city all this time, sitting in their chairs, witnessing their discussions and the growth of their businesses, and they had all just taken her for granted. Now things had changed, and they had to be wary of this little slip of a girl who had caught the eye of their new master of the city. She held power now through Benedict, and anyone looking at him knew he was smitten.

Thea drew a deep breath, feeling a chill run up her spine suddenly. She felt the tremor of goose bumps on her arms as she turned to look over the crowd at her back. Her eyes surveyed her brother and RM, who stood speaking with Matt and Adam. There was Benedict with Asao at his side, speaking to Copper, Terence, Esther, and Gunnar. She could see the glimmer of light dancing off their crystal goblets. There were no enemies here this evening; even Kale had kept his eyes to himself, talking in the corner with Emily. So what had caused her chill? What had caused her to be wary? She turned around, looking down across the verdant green, past the sundial, toward the bubbling fountain in the distance. She walked down the two steps and slipped off her heels to leave the stability of the stones for the cool green grass. She set down her champagne glass and made her way through the shadows as if she didn't want anyone to see her leave the party. The smell of roses was strong. Voices grew slightly distant and less coherent as she carefully walked down a slight incline and turned her gaze heavenward.

There was something small but bright overhead that caught her attention. She stared hard at what she thought was a star, watching it grow brighter and arc close. She shivered as she realized it wasn't a star she was looking at and it was coming perilously close to the earth. To her, actually. If she had been human, she would have had to turn away from the stunningly bright flare that filled the night and scattered the shadows, but instead, she looked at what had just arrived. The ground trembled under her feet as the earth shook, accepting the weight of what had just landed. As the white smoke drifted off on the night breeze, Thea could see who, rather what, stood before her. It was an angel, and against her will, her body recognized him as kin and her wings blossomed across her back. She arched, feeling them spread out from her flesh, curling toward his, and the feathers touched as if in welcome. She was startled by this and took a step back, eyeing him, not in fear, but in wonder. She had never met another of her kind. He stood bare-chested before her, his wings darker shades of gray. They were outstretched their full length. He was taller than she was, his blond hair tussled and clothing simple. He wore what looked like loose white linen trousers. His feet were bare, and the only ounce of jewelry or metal around him was a white torque or collar at his throat. That, too, seemed to continue to smoke as if it reacted to the air around him.

"Daughter of angels, Anthea Sheridan. It is time we meet." His voice was very soft, like a summer breeze across her body, but there was an edge to those blue eyes that captured hers. The spell was broken. Thea eyes were narrow as she regarded him, unable to turn away. She drew a breath to strengthen herself. It was done. This night was to be the night that she was revealed to the world, and it hadn't been her choice. No, it had been another angel's. They would be standing in the light of this being. No one, regardless of their race, could have missed his arrival. Nor could they have missed the appearance of her wings. She just hoped that Emlyn and Benedict were close.

"That would be Anthea Black," she corrected. "You have me at a disadvantage. You know my name, but I do not know yours."

"It is more a human concept than ours. I am unimportant. You, however, are unique."

"So I have been told. That doesn't make us best friends. Why are you here? And what do you want?"

He seemed dismayed by her brusqueness. "Admirable curiosity, but did it ever occur to you that while you were born here, you were not meant to remain? Are you not curious as to the realms beyond?"

By now, though, Thea could not see Emlyn or Benedict behind her. She knew that they were close by, ready to assist, listening. By now they knew there was no way to hide her.

"There were better times for you to come to me. Why appear now? Why wait until now?"

The angel chuckled, his smile beguiling. Thea wasn't buying it. She wasn't drinking his Kool-Aid. Something wasn't right.

"I returned the weapon. There isn't any need to contact me this way, unless you want something that I might not be willing to give."

"Sis, on your nine," muttered Emlyn from her left.

She turned to her left, taking a step back, feeling the strength of Benedict behind her as dark crimson smoke curled up from the ground. Within that wall of smoke formed something solid in the form of the archdemon, dressed similar to the angel, but in the colors of shadow. Webbed wings flared out into the night as the demon smiled politely at her, inclining his head in greeting. He held out his hand to Thea, trying to keep her where she stood.

"Stay where you stand, Anthea. Do not be soothed by his words."

"I hadn't planned on going anywhere," she retorted tartly. She glanced at the angel to see his reaction; he wasn't happy.

"Casren, come to destroy a child of your own host, within your own choir?" the demon asked.

"Liar, Galed. That is what demons do, they lie. This is none of your concern," replied the angel.

"Oh, but, Casren, it is. This child did us a favor, and it would be unforgivable not to repay my debt to her, though this hardly qualifies. She is here for a reason, Casren. I would not gainsay it, nor would I overstay your welcome."

Casren looked puzzled, until he glanced up, seeing another ball of light heading toward earth. He staggered back away, and Thea thought there might be fear in his handsome face.

"Ah, now, you face the wrath of an angry father."

Thea froze as the fireball landed to her right, sparkling white power drifting skyward into the dark night like fireflies. The figure formed, taller than Casren, wings vanilla in color, with Thea's blue eyes. It was Galed, the archdemon, who chuckled.

"She has your eyes, my friend."

Those blue eyes turned to look at and through Thea. She could feel herself flush, a power, a friendly power washing over her, painting symbols on her wings. In all the years that he had known his sister, Emlyn had not seen this. It was captivating.

"I was just holding Casren for you. I presume he is absent without leave?"

"Yes, Galed. You have my thanks." This new angel didn't tear his eyes away from Thea, a small smile forming on his lips. "By God, I think you are right, though she looks mostly like her mother."

"A rare beauty. She did well for us. I thought it prudent to intervene. Though she is an adult by human standards, she is a child to our realms. I am sure you can deal with Casren."

"I can, Galed. Again, thank you."

The demon folded his wings, bowed to everyone with a smug smile on his lips, and vanished into what seemed to be the earth. There was a series of gasps distantly behind Thea.

"Nylan, I came to see this child, who was granted permission to bear one of our most important weapons. How is it I have not heard of her before?"

Nylan ignored Casren, his gaze soft upon his daughter. His gaze flickered to the right and then the left, stopping on both Emlyn and Benedict. He turned swiftly, eyes narrow and gaze cool.

"Because it is not any of your business and you are stretching the limits of your grace. You are not supposed to be here. You have not been given leave to stand upon this earth. Did you have designs to steal her heart or to kill her?"

Casren stiffened.

"For Galed to come above, he must have thought she was in danger indeed."

Casren's jaw twitched and tightened. Thea opened her mouth to shout a warning, but Casren plowed into Nylan and they vanished in a cloud of sparkles and a few feathers. Thea, although she stood still, was trembling, staring at the empty earth. She closed her eyes and drew in a long, deep breath. She glanced at the sky hesitantly, as if she expected another arrival. What else could happen? All seemed quiet. That was a plus. She fluffed her wings and folded them as a hand touched her shoulder.

"Is everyone staring at me?" she asked whomever would answer her. She didn't want to turn around. She wasn't ready to see their faces.

"Not everyone," Em said, trying to sound cheerful.

With a long, deep breath, she turned to face pretty much everyone who had been invited to the festivities. The air was silent, save for the normal sounds of night. She managed a smile and met Benedict's concerned face.

"I could use a drink," she muttered as he squeezed her hand and walked her away from the scene of the so-called incident. It would be a party to remember.

It was Esther's voice that shattered the silence as she lifted her fluted goblet in Thea's direction.

"Well, that explains a lot."

Chapter 23

Benedict allowed his hand to slip from hers as Thea tried to casually leave the center of attention for one of the more-sheltered pavilions. He let her go alone, away from him as a surge of people formed around him and Emlyn. Voices were all heard at once, and it was a sharp whistle from Adam that reeled them in. They had questions. Didn't everyone?

Thea leaned against one of the white marble columns, wishing that drink would at least get her drunk for one night. It was a hell of a party. She had clung to Alexander, used all her energy to try to save herself, save her humanity, and then out of nowhere, angels came a-calling. She started to laugh, covering her mouth with her hand so it didn't sound so much like a crazy cackle. Tears formed at the corner of her eyes as she sniffled back her deep well of emotion. Well, it was done. That burden of when and where had been lifted off her shoulders. So now all she had to deal with were the questions and fallout. She closed her eyes, realizing that she didn't have to deal with this alone. She had friends. They might not be like Sarah, human, but they were more than that to her.

It was a gentle touch on her arm that broke her out of her reverie. Naheed, one of the Seven's wolves, was standing at her side. He had dark hair, caramel-colored skin, and deep-brown eyes that regarded her with a kind of awe. She looked at him and waited.

"Is it true, Ms. Black, you are an angel?" he asked, almost apologetically.

"Naheed, I am sure that there are those out there who would disagree with you on that, but yes. Why?"

"Because I have need of a miracle."

That was the last thing that Thea heard before the Taser promptly put her to sleep.

* * *

It was a gentle hand that shook her awake, another that pressed water to her lips.

"I'm so sorry, so, so sorry, Ms. Black."

Thea's eyes fluttered open, fixing on Naheed, who bent over her with an apologetic smile. She accepted the water, letting it cool her throat. She shifted, realizing she was on a very puffy pink-and-purple chair, and she was barefoot.

"I was desperate."

Thea gently rubbed her eyes, trying to regain her composure. It sucked getting Tasered. "Desperate about what, Naheed?" she asked softly, unsure.

"My little sister, she is sick, and I thought maybe you could help her. She is human. It might really cheer her up if you could, if she could see you as you truly are."

Thea sighed, feeling tired. This had been one of her fears, that people would think she might be able to grace them with miracles. That was not one of her abilities. She casually patted his shoulder, shoved the water at him, and stood. She grabbed the wall to steady herself. She glanced over Naheed's shoulder and found herself in a little girl's room. It had to be, because it was pink and purple, very princess-like. In the bed, surrounded by stuffed animals and a mountain of pillows, was a dark-haired little girl around eight, with big brown eyes and a curious smile on her face. Though she was naturally tan like her brother, you could tell that she was ill. She was looking at Thea hopefully as she hugged a stuffed pony. Thea pushed Naheed gently away from her, standing on her own two bare feet. The carpet was soft and furry, in the shape of a big purple footprint. Barney, maybe? She shook off her thoughts, turning to Naheed. He had such hope in his gaze, but she would fail him in the end. She didn't have the power that people might perceive, but it didn't hurt to try.

"I don't have any power to heal. The best I can do for her is pray with her."

He nodded, face grim. "Then, if you would do that, I would appreciate it. If she has to die, I didn't want her to be scared."

Thea nodded, though she didn't like being kidnapped. Naheed had seen his chance and had taken it. She might have said no if he had asked, but she knew she would have said yes. She just hoped he didn't get too badly punished for this indiscretion. You didn't just kidnap an angel from the master of the city who loved her. It was a dangerous decision. Then again, for family, you often did dangerous things.

Thea managed a soft smile as she walked to the bed.

"Her name is Reisa," Naheed whispered.

"Hi, Reisa. I'm Anthea."

"My brother told me. While you were sleeping, he told me that you were an angel and that he kidnapped you."

Thea seated herself on the bed, tucking a stray strand of hair behind her ears. "I am an angel, and Naheed took me from a party. A lot of people are going to be looking for me, and they might be very angry if all they find are my purse and shoes."

"If you're an angel, where are your wings and halo?"

Thea laughed lightly. "I don't have a halo, but I do have wings, but I wouldn't want to break anything in this pretty room of yours."

She brightened, looking eager. "Can I see them?"

Thea looked left and then right, hoping she didn't topple anything over and make a mess. With a slight cock of her head, her wings unfolded and stretched out prettily behind her. Reisa gasped in awe.

"I think that is the nicest reaction I have had to them," she murmured, bringing them slightly forward so that Reisa could touch them.

"They are so soft," she remarked, stroking them. "You are so lucky."

"We will see. Everyone just found out what I am today. So far, I don't know how they will receive me."

"How could they not love you?" Reisa asked, wide-eyed. "Naheed said that he thought you could heal me."

"Oh, Reisa, I don't have that kind of power. But I can pray with you if you would like. I am a firm believer in the power of prayer."

"I never thought much about heaven or hell," she muttered, lying back on the pillows, though it appeared that Thea had friends in both places. "Are there lots of angels like you up there? Why are you here and not up there?"

"I was born here. I'm an earthbound angel." Thea picked up one of the feathers that had fallen to the floor. She laid it gently on Reisa's chest. "So you remember me."

Reisa laughed. "Like, how could I forget you?" she said. "So you want to pray with me?"

"She hasn't seen anyone in a while. Her friends find it hard to come and see her like this," Naheed interjected.

"I understand. Some people aren't as strong as your sister." Thea took Reisa's hands in hers, her voice steady and soft. "Oh, heavenly Father, we ask that you bless us with your grace as we speak to you this evening. I ask that you grant Reisa your healing power and make her well so that she can continue a life that will honor you and her faith. There is much that she can contribute to your world and your children. Please allow her to heal and be well, for only you have that power. Give her the strength to fight and win against this illness. We ask that if you cannot honor this plea, you grant her family peace at her passing, that you allow her to join you without pain, without tears, and in joy. In your name do we pray. Amen."

Thea heard Naheed sniffle slightly behind her. She leaned over and kissed Reisa on the forehead.

"I can't promise that it will be okay or be perfect, but we can always try. I want your brother to keep me up on your progress and your will to fight this."

"I'll do my best." she squeezed Thea's hand and sighed. Thea turned to Naheed, who was wiping tears from his eyes.

"You have my gratitude. I'll take you back to the party."

Thea shook her head. "No, I don't I want to go back there. I need to go somewhere I can think, somewhere I can decide on what to do next. I didn't just step out of the closet, I was kicked out. There isn't a way to recover from this surprise. Everyone is going to talk, to try to solve the problem for me, but this is something I have to do myself. Call Benedict or whomever. Tell him what happened. Tell him I'm not mad and to be easy on you. Tell him I just need to think. I won't be long."

Naheed opened his mouth as he followed her from the bedroom, down the hall, and into the family room. She walked past the TV and kitchen, opening the sliding glass doors that led to the backyard. The grass needed to be mowed, but the stars looked bright and close now that she knew the skies might be filled with angels. The air was brisk, and the night quiet.

"Can I drive you somewhere?"

She turned and smiled, with a light chuckle.

"I'd rather fly."

With three decisive hops and a spread of her wings, she was gone. Naheed collapsed into the patio chair. It was an odd evening.

* * *

There was a pair of shoes, there was her purse, there was even a single earring on the ground, but there wasn't Anthea Black. Benedict stood next to the column, hearing those assembled search for her, hearing Emlyn call his sister's name, and they wondered if Casren had returned and if she had been stolen by an angel. They wondered, until Copper showed up with cell phone in hand.

"I think you can relax. An angel didn't take Thea. One of our wolves, Naheed, did. His half-sister is very ill, and he thought she could heal her. They prayed together and then Thea left."

Benedict's gaze was cool as he was handed the phone.

"Naheed, where did Anthea Black go?"

Benedict's voice was very steady, very nonemotional. Em stood next to RM, tense, as if trying to listen to the conversation. Although the party had been for Benedict, to welcome him into the city, it had become a coming-out party for his sister, where all eyes beheld angels and demons up close for the very first time. And for some, it was indeed very personal. She might have downed a drink and sought solace in the pavilion, but that didn't stop the questions, the amazement, and the incredulity of the situation. There were questions. Hell, they always knew there would be. But Thea had wanted time to prepare.

Em shook himself out of his thoughts, realizing that Benedict had ended the call. He looked perplexed and worried.

"Naheed said that she left, flew away from his house. She said that she needed to go somewhere to think and that she wouldn't be long." Benedict turned his stare on Emlyn. His voice was quite controlled when he spoke. "Where would that be, Emlyn?"

Emlyn's eyes widened as he shrugged. He opened and then closed his mouth. He had no answer.

"Normally, I would say she went home or to a hotel, but she wouldn't find any peace there unless it was in a human part of town. But rumor will have spoiled all that for her, I am sure by now." He frowned, eyes turning down to his feet, concentrating.

Would she go back to the house, our house? Marta asked in Benedict's mind, using the power between them to speak silently.

Doubtful, he added secretly.

"I went away to school for a while, Benedict. I wasn't always here for her, so I don't know if she has somewhere she likes to go. I'm sorry that I can't answer this question."

"You have all that land," Matt chimed in from somewhere back behind RM. "Could it be just as simple as that? We could find out tomorrow. Let us sniff out the property. If she is there, we can find her."

"And then what?" Esther asked, pushing herself forward toward Benedict. "I have to say that you can keep a secret, Benedict. How long have you known that Anthea Black was an angel?"

"Not long. Only when she faced the archdemon. She was revealed to me, and I pledged my silence. It was going to be up to her when she would reveal herself."

"Among all of us here, she is unique, and I doubt anyone would dare call her a monster. She was lovely, and those wings...people have questions."

"They always do, Esther," added RM. "That doesn't mean there will be answers. Do you imagine finding this out yourself and not having anyone to answer your questions? Sure, she had Em, but he is human. What can he tell her about her birth, parents, or what role she should play on this earth? Nothing has really changed. She is still Anthea Black. She still has her friends, her work. The only difference now, she has wings. She hid herself away because she feared the questions, the murmurs, the stares. You all should be more adult than that. I mean, you aren't humans, you all have lived longer than average lives. This is just another one of those amazing things you have seen in your lifetime."

"And he has stolen her for himself," added Tasha, who came around one of the back columns, fanning herself prettily with a lace fan. Her expression was hard to read. RM would have said it was envy.

"I knew the moment I saw her that I liked her. I had no way of knowing what she was. I didn't even know she was a silent witness until she told me. I won't be damned for falling in love. I have pledged myself to her in whatever capacity she is comfortable with, but I'm not concerned about what is going to happen. I am concerned about now. I think Matt's plan is solid."

"I agree," added Copper pointedly. "We can take a look at the forest circumspectly and let you know what we find, then you or someone can go in and convince her to come out. That is going to be the hard part."

"Oh, and you are all friendly with her now, are you?" a voice asked from behind. Copper smiled, shaking her head.

"She just confirmed my belief that truly there is a heaven and hell. I know where I want to go, where I should aspire to go, and I hadn't been on that road until now. Love is hard enough to find. Why should we care if it happens between a blood and an angel? She is ours, isn't she? She is in our city?"

"True," added Emily. "We should respect that she is just one more person who lives with us, who makes us and our city special."

There was a murmur of assent from the crowd.

"We still have questions," called out a voice from a distance.

"Write them down and she can address when she can." Em sighed. "I'm pissed that Naheed took her, but relieved it wasn't Casren. I hope you find her in the forest tomorrow. You are better equipped to find her than I am."

RM hugged him. "Sad but true."

* * *

It was a partly cloudy morning, though the forecasters didn't say it would rain. Clouds darted in and out of the warm shafts of sunshine, the breeze making the pines whisper as Em, Naheed, Matt, and strangely enough, Copper stood at the back gate to their property. Em had no idea whom the Seven would choose to try to track his sister. He figured Matt would volunteer since he worked for them. He seemed eager to help. Naheed was a complete surprise. Although Naheed had taken Thea last evening from the festivities, Benedict understood his reason, though no one was really sure how much help Thea could be. Naheed hadn't told them that his half-sister seemed to be doing very well, much better than he had hoped, by just holding the feather in her hands and praying with Thea. He owed her. He had stolen her from the party that was to greet the man she loved. He hadn't even asked, he hadn't calmed anyone's fears, and he had been bold. He would pay this debt to Thea by serving her the best way he could.

As for Copper, Em didn't ask; he assumed she had some reason. She had never been kind to Thea. In fact, there were plenty of times that Thea wondered if it would come to blows. Threats had flown like birds between them. Now here was Copper, standing out on a dirt road, feet bare, wearing a sundress that he imagined would be easily removed. Odd how such revelations changed the people.

Em realized that everyone thought he should know where his sister had gone. If truth be told, he had a couple of ideas, but if he could buy her some time, he would. Em knew she was trying to determine the next best steps in her life, maybe even to formulate responses to all the questions that would be asked. He knew that Benedict was anxious, but Thea deserved time. This was an event she had been preparing for her entire life, and now it had come to pass. Even as her brother, he had no clue what she was thinking. Benedict had just met her, and though he loved her, he, too, didn't know what thoughts an angel could have.

Em had laid out a map of their acreage, all three of the changelings reviewing it and deciding who would take which section. This was the only place that made sense. This had always been her haven. When she was found, he imagined Benedict would go in and talk her into coming out of the forest. Em had always taken such responsibilities to heart, but now it only seemed fair that the man she loved did it for her. He might have better luck.

Em could hear them whispering among themselves.

"What if she isn't here?" Matt asked softly.

"Then we deal with that when it happens. No pessimists, Matt," ordered Copper. She reached up and untied her hair and then pulled the dress up over her body.

Em politely turned away. He always considered it impolite to watch them strip and shift, as his sister put it. There was a slight howl that told him he could turn around.

"I'll be here when you get back. I'll have drinks and lunch," Em said, trying to sound optimistic as he watched the changelings disappear into the forest, nose either to the wind or to the ground. He figured, if anyone could find her, they could.

CHAPTER 24

The forest was cool, littered with leaves and all sorts of smells. Naheed loped along the ground at a pretty good speed, weaving back and forth, hoping to find that tangible scent that Thea was nearby. Cats could take to the trees, search higher for their angel. They wondered how long it would take and if she really wanted to be found. It was two hours later when Copper slowed her run through a rather thorny bush, peering out at the muddy shore of a lake. She could hear splashing, and just to her right was Anthea Black, bathing in the sunshine-glinted water. Her wings ruffled in the breeze, a feather slowly skimming the top of the water, heading toward shore. Copper lay down on the cool forest floor and regarded the angel before her. So far, Thea didn't seem aware of anyone, and Copper watched as she dived back under the water and then surfaced. Water took to the air like sparkling diamonds. Thea waded to shore, her feet sinking into the mud just to the left of the swaying cattails. She shook out her hair and wings before they were folded away against her back, invisible to the naked eye.

Copper watched as she pulled on a small white shift that looked as if it was made to go over a bathing suit. Copper could hear that Thea was humming to herself as she followed an unseen path through the forest, away from the lake. Copper didn't follow right away; instead, she walked to the shore and pawed at the feather in the water until it grounded itself. She picked it up in her mouth and then trotted after Thea. With anyone else, Copper would have assumed that she was camping, had some sort of comfortable campsite, but she was wrong. Copper stopped, eyes staring up at an amazing tree house. If she weren't carrying the feather, she might have opened her mouth in awe. It was more than a kid's tree house. No, this was a sanctuary away from home. It had windows, it had electricity, and she bet it had water. Somewhere along the line, she had created a home away from home that even Em wasn't aware of. Smart girl.

Copper shook her head slightly and tried to concentrate. She needed to know exactly where this was so that she could tell Em, so that she could give precise instructions to Benedict. Despite what the Seven said in private, she was glad that they had a strong hand in the city, and she truly believed that there would be others coming to challenge them. It never hurt to have the backing of Benedict or his consort. Copper was pretty sure that they were more than just a fleeting item; he was not going to let her get away. Copper sat on her haunches, taking note of the surroundings. With landmarks firmly in mind and feather in her mouth, she started back the way she came, catching sight of Naheed in the distance. He loped over to her direction, noting the feather in her mouth. Copper gestured with her head back the way she had come. Naheed pawed at the ground and gestured back that way. She knew what he wanted. He wanted to stay near her until Benedict or whoever came for her. Copper nodded, darting off into the brush. She caught up with Matt just as they were breaking out of the forest and hit the hard dirt road.

Em sat in the back of the truck with the cooler, eyeing their approach. He caught sight of the feather, hopped off the truck bed, and approached Copper. She spit the feather out at his feet.

"I see you found her." Em turned around as Matt hopped up into the truck and lapped at the cool water. Copper stretched, groaned, and shifted. Em tossed her back her dress, not daring to catch a glimpse of her slim naked body.

"Let me see the map." She and Em walked around to the front of the truck and regarded the map. She put a sharpened nail on the spot. "Right there. She had a pretty fancy tree house."

Em frowned and then chuckled. "She always said she wanted to live in the trees. I thought it was just a whim. She must have had it built when I left for school."

"Naheed wants to stay with her. I say we have lunch, get cleaned up, and head over to Benedict's."

"He would be asleep."

Copper chuckled. "Don't you believe it. He is old, and even I don't know how old for sure. You can bet he is awake and wants an update."

Em nodded. "And you want to be the one to tell him?"

Copper flashed a predatory smile at Em as she gestured to the back of the truck. She was hungry and thirsty. Matt was already digging into the roast beef that he had brought.

"Look, prior to him moving here, the chances that we would be challenged for a seat in our own city was unthinkable. Things were stable. Yardley wasn't the easiest to get along with, so we were content. Now we find we have a premier blood with ties all over the world. Don't you think others will want to move in here now? They won't be able to supplant him, but us…we haven't been what we should be, and to be honest, a few of the Seven I would throw over in a moment if given the chance. We will be challenged, and it helps to have the strength of someone scary behind you."

It made sense to Em. How like Copper to seize the opportunity.

"You haven't always been kind to my sister," he stated bluntly.

"No, and it was wrong of me. That sliver of inhumanity that we couldn't identify put me on edge. I always expected the other shoe to drop, and it did. Now that I know what I am dealing with, I am happier, more content. I don't like secrets."

"She doesn't have one anymore," Em added with a grim sigh.

* * *

It was security who allowed them on the grounds, Adam and Chrisanne who opened the door to them, but Adam was still armed. He looked at them with narrow eyes, and Copper couldn't blame him. After all, they were visiting during the day, when normally the host wasn't available. But everyone knew how critical this was and how eager Benedict was to find Thea. If Adam was surprised that it was an odd three of them, Em, Copper, and Matt, who patted along as a leopard, he didn't show it. Instead, he opened the door and invited them into the living room. That was as far as they were going to proceed, the rest of the house secure, and Copper was certain security was watching.

"Good afternoon. I take it you were successful?" he asked, holstering his weapon. There was enough firepower to take them out without his little weapon, though it wasn't obvious.

"Thank you for seeing us unannounced," Em remarked. "I wasn't at all sure we should come until this evening, but Copper sort of insisted."

"I know he has to be awake. If he has any age on him, and I know he does, he is waiting for word."

"Then what is the word?" Chrisanne asked coolly from the threshold of the room.

"She is in the forest. Apparently, she built a very nice, though small, tree house. I have the spot marked on the map. Benedict shouldn't have any problem finding it. Naheed is still there, circling. I think he wants to make sure she is safe. She has wings. She could probably outfly any threat, but if the threat has wings, I wouldn't be so certain. I have never seen her fight, though I am sure she is capable. Is it possible to see Benedict?"

Adam smiled. Copper expected him to say no, or at least to be unprepared, but instead, Adam turned to the carved wooden bookcase and slid back one of the slats to reveal a monitor, and within moments, Benedict was on-screen. The light in the room was dim. There would be no way to tell where he was or if he was in the house. Clever man.

"I take it you have news?" he asked, trying to corral his eagerness.

"Good afternoon to you. I wasn't at all sure you were awake to receive us," Copper remarked, slight amazement in her voice. She had been right. He was old.

"I had hopes you would be successful, and to answer your unasked question, I do not require to be asleep during the day. I do most of my work for those who have to so that I can spend my evenings doing other things."

Copper cleared her throat to ease her nervousness. "Well, your other thing is in the forest, in a very nice tree house. I can leave the map here for you. Naheed is in the forest, watching her. I take it you will be going there this evening to see if you can coax her into coming back to the world at large?"

"Yes, that is my intent. I asked my staff to field questions through me instead of Em. I am not sure if or when they can be answered, but we need to be organized about this. Thea was unprepared. Everyone was too stunned last eve to actually realize what they were seeing. Some dare to ask, others don't want to know. If you are willing to see we are undisturbed, that would be appreciated. I'll try to get her to come back to the country house, if that is acceptable to you, Emlyn."

"Yes. It is fairly out of the way. Though I have had a few phone calls, no visitors. If you have headed them off, I thank you for that." He almost sagged with relief.

"What are you going to do about the situation?" Adam asked, curious.

Em shrugged, shaking his head. "I'm not sure. It is up to her whether she returns to work as if nothing has changed. The businesses can run without her being there. She could telecommute in, if need be, to handle her regular paperwork, but I know she likes doing her job. She worked hard for that degree and respect. I don't want her upset by this. It wasn't her choice or her timing."

"No, it certainly wasn't, nor did I think she was in danger from her own kind. That worried me," answered Benedict. "As soon as it is dark, I'll go and retrieve her."

"Good," stated Copper. "I appreciate the fact that you didn't chastise Naheed. You were generous."

"I understand his desperation. We have all known those who were ill and we had no ability to cure or heal them. Suddenly, an angel arrives and your mind has to believe that she can create miracles."

"She did with you," muttered Emlyn softly.

"Yes, she did," added Benedict honestly as Em flushed lightly. Damn that hearing of his.

"Then we have a plan?" Copper asked. "I'll be there with a few others to supplement your cordon. I take it you want extreme privacy for this conversation?"

"As much as I can get. I don't want her spooked, nor do I want anyone staring. We are comfortable together."

"But you want us close enough if Casren comes back?" Adam asked bluntly.

"Yes. Close enough to clip his wings," Benedict replied with purpose.

* * *

Thea alighted on the small circular porch that wrapped around the tree house, just outside the double open doors. She folded her wings and adjusted the short little lavender knit halter dress she was wearing before allowing her wings to disappear. She had left a small night-light burning, and by that dim light, she could see Benedict sitting on the dark-green futon, eyes casually regarding her. She blinked and sighed, shaking her head slightly. She should have known.

"What are you doing here?" she asked, puzzlement in her voice.

"What are you doing here?" he asked, curious.

She had to admit, he looked good, and he was dressed for hiking in the woods, dark jeans, a T-shirt, and heavy boots. It was such a change from his business attire; it made her heart skip a beat.

"I came to stretch my wings and to write down all the questions that I have asked myself over the years, and what answers I have found, because inquiring minds will want to know."

"And I am so sorry for that."

She ducked into the shelter of the tree house, arms folded across her chest. She shrugged.

"I had held on so tightly with Alexander, but with Casren, I had no choice. They just appeared as if in greeting to him. So what is being said?" She wanted to know but didn't really want the answer.

He met her eyes, trying to ease her worry. "Everyone is very calm, very curious. We can post your questions and answers so that you don't have to take the brunt of their inquisitiveness. I'm not concerned about them right now. I am concerned about you."

"I never thought of turning my voice to the heavens, nor did I know that I had any enemies. Meeting my dad under those circumstances was illuminating, to say the least."

"You do have his eyes."

She managed a soft smile, walking toward him. She seated herself across his legs, straddling him. It was erotic, to say the least, to be this close to him, so sexually blatant. She brushed a stray strand of hair from his eyes and leaned in to kiss him. She kissed him lightly across the forehead, then the eyelids, down to his nose, and then to his lips. He kissed back, tasting the sweetness of her mouth. He didn't want this moment to stop.

"You have quite a little hideaway for yourself here. Not even Em knew about it."

She laughed, lightly tossing back her head, hair flowing about her face. "When he left for school, I had them build it for me. It's pretty nifty, and it hides not only me but other things as well." Thea cupped his face and kissed him again.

Benedict leaned back, regarding Thea with questioning eyes. "Why me, Anthea? Why do you want me?" he asked in earnest.

"Oh, you mean beside the fact that you are hot-looking, powerful? You can't be that naive, my dear Benedict. Are you familiar with Linus and the Great Pumpkin?"

Benedict raised a curious eyebrow and nodded. "Yes, I am."

She wasn't surprised. "Then you know that for the Great Pumpkin to come to your pumpkin patch, you had to have a special quality. What was it do you remember?"

"Sincerity," Benedict answered, sure of himself. "The pumpkin patch had to be sincere."

"Yes, you are sincere. You have a great soul, Benedict, and I want it to be mine."

"So you are the Great Pumpkin and I am the pumpkin patch?" he asked wryly.

Thea nodded as she gracefully rose and stepped back, allowing him to meet her gaze. With the hem in her hand she drew the dress over her head and tossed it to the floor. She stepped back into the moonlight that painted the forest in its silver light. Her wings sprang from her back as she stood unadorned, waiting for him to either speak or close the distance between them. She was a sight to behold, like a painting from an old master. He had to blink to make sure he could accept such a beauty awaited him. He rose gracefully from the futon, walked slowly, deliberately to the threshold of the doors. He knelt down on one knee before her, curled his arms around her waist, and kissed her navel. She smiled, running her hands through his hair. He inhaled her scent and that of the forest, more aroused than he had ever been, filled with emotions he wasn't sure he could contain. She tilted his face up to her, leaned down, and kissed it. She sunk down to her knees, embracing him. Benedict gently caressed the feather of her wings, and a small moan escaped her lips. Her hands slid over his stomach, dipping into his waistband, until she pulled his T-shirt free. He leaned back and allowed her to pull it up over his head. She gently tossed it aside as she leaned her body into his flesh. He could feel the hardness of her nipples, the feel of her nails along his back. He sighed contentedly as they kissed again. There was a ripple of magic in the air. It was the first time he had felt it caress him. He watched as her wings vanished. He felt her hands tug at his belt, then lower his zipper.

"I still have my boots on," he murmured.

"And way too many clothes to suit me," she added as she rose.

She looked down at him with a quirky, come-hither smile. He watched her walk into the dim light, gesturing him to follow. Benedict rose to his feet, kicked off his boots, and slid out of his pants and boxer briefs. He slowly approached her, his hand out to take hers. He followed her through a little archway into what could be called a bedroom.

"It is proof against light. You could stay here if you needed to," she murmured softly.

"It is a fine house in the trees you have, Anthea."

"It was my sanctuary more times than I can count. It has been my sanity when I thought I might not have any remaining."

Benedict seated himself on the narrow bed, lying back so that she could look at him. He lay there watching her as her eyes ran the length of his body. She stood for several more seconds, trying to convince herself that he was all hers. She slowly approached and then leaned over his body, gently caressing his firm arms, fingertips trailing down to his waist, across his abs, and then lower into the nest of course hair. His eager organ twitched; he was so hard his body ached. His gums began to throb, fangs wanting to taste her, but that was a bad idea. Thea straddled his body, resting her wet heat against the junction of his thighs. His jaw clenched, hand touching her hips to try to still any movement. She leaned down and proceeded to kiss him lightly again across his face, his throat, her dull teeth biting him along his neck. He arched into her, trying hard to let her lead the way.

"You like that?" she asked, a soft smile on her lips. She was trying to determine what it was that drove Benedict crazy with desire. Just being around her did that to him.

"No one has drank from me, touched my throat in ages," he murmured softly as she tugged on his earlobe.

She rose up, smiling warmly at him as she turned her attention to his chest, teeth nibbling on his nipples, tongue painting wet patterns on his skin. He groaned, feeling the heat of her body against him. She knelt upward, positioning herself over him. He allowed her to gently take the lead. She would take him into her when she was ready. He watched her bite her lip in uncertainty.

"Help me," she whispered as he thrust slowly upward. She was silky, hot, tight, and tried valiantly to block his entry. Thea gasped as he plunged forward, burying himself in her heat. Her snug passage enclosed around him, and her back bowed, wings flaring outward, the resulting breeze stirring their hair. He realized that the tree house was just large enough for her to spread her wings without damage. She met his hot gaze as she stretched her arms up and began to slowly move across him. He could feel her body shift and jerk, and he knew she had to move. She had no choice but to move and spur her desire on toward orgasm.

"Take your pleasure with my body, Anthea."

She leaned forward, hands on his chest, moans bubbling out of her mouth. Benedict watched in rapt fascination as her body flushed, glowing symbols painting designs across her wings. Power embraced him, feeding him more distinctly than blood. He cried out as she came, body throbbing around him, milking him. She leaned forward, heart thumping in her chest, arms around his shoulders, wings folding to vanish.

"Hold on," he whispered as he turned her over, still snug in her body. She raised her right leg over his thigh as she gazed lovingly up at him. She was panting at him, face flushed, eyes bright with passion.

"That was better than I imagined, but you didn't, did you?"

"Not yet. I wanted you to lead the way into our love."

Benedict watched as her breasts jiggled, nipples pink, a light sheen of sweat bathing her body. He began to thrust inward, still hard, still on edge, desperately seeking his release. She moaned his name, and he came deep within her, hips still delving deeply into her body. God, she felt like paradise, made just for him, he thought. His virgin angel, his Anthea, the woman he wanted to be his, his wife. The thought jarred him back to the moment, back to Thea. He leaned down and kissed her gently, turning them slightly on their side. He didn't want to leave her body; he wanted to stay entwined with her. She clung to him as if he were her life line. Her body was hot to the touch, almost fevered.

"You were very gentle with me," she whispered in his ear.

"I didn't want to be." He chuckled. "There is time yet for that. I came here to ask you to come back with me, and instead you enveloped me in a passion I didn't know I had. You have become my world. Cities mean nothing to me now, just you."

"You have a way with words, Benedict. I will cherish each one that you say to me, collect them in my mind always, to remember."

"Ah, pumpkin, that is sweet."

She pushed away, slightly glaring at him as he laughed.

"You don't like that term of endearment?" he asked as she slapped his chest lightly. His body trembled at her touch, and he was growing hard again. Never had he been this aroused by any human or blood woman before. It was magical. She met his gaze.

"You feel as if you are growing inside me," she whispered to him.

"I want you that much," he growled as he rolled her back over.

This time, however, he drew away from her, out of her warmth, and proceeded to kiss the length of her body. His tongue dipped into her navel and then toward her thighs. He kissed the fluff between her legs and then delved into her heat with his tongue. He could taste blood mingled with her juices. He felt her body rise to meet the rhythm of his licking, sucking, her hands gripping the side of the bed, cries filling the night air. He loved to hear his name from her lips.

"Benedict!" she shouted as he felt her come apart beneath him.

He laughed, raising her thighs and thrusting hard into her. His cries joined hers as she met him move for move, body almost stronger than his, and they came again, in unison. Darkness almost swallowed him. He grew dizzy as he collapsed on her.

"You may be the death of me yet, lovely one," he murmured as she laughed lightly.

"I thought you had more stamina than that," she cooed teasingly.

"It has been a long time, and I was harder than steel wanting you. The first time you touched me, I could have come. You like me kissing you?"

"I like you kissing me anywhere, my sin and sincerity."

Anthea had realized when she found Benedict waiting for her that she couldn't remain hidden. It had been a nice dream, hiding away from the world, but she wasn't one to run from a fight. Truthfully, she had come there to think and to work on trying to answer the questions she knew would come. She had a small flash drive from an old laptop she had secreted there. She had spent the day deciding what to do and where she should go from there. She wasn't one to hide, and now she didn't have to. A great weight had been lifted off her, and it didn't matter what people thought of her or if they knew. As long as Em still had her back and she still had Benedict, all was right with the world. They had lingered in each other's arms until, finally, Benedict had coaxed her to leave. It was time to go. They dressed, secured the tree house, and Benedict followed her to the ground using the sturdy ladder. The night sky was filled with twinkling stars and half a moon. He smiled as she touched his face.

"I want you to know you don't have to do this all at once. We can take baby steps, all right?"

She nodded, embracing him. To Benedict's pleasure, her arms were warm, but to his dismay, Thea had picked him slightly off the ground into her arms. He opened his eyes to question her, but before he could, she took three great leaps and her wings launched them into the air. His voice cried out, scattering a few of the night birds, his arms holding onto her tightly.

"You should have given me warning." His voice trembled slightly.

"You wouldn't allow me to do it if I did."

She laughed as Benedict tried not to look down. He closed his eyes instead, feeling the cold night air swirl around them. He could feel her body shift as she held him, and as he peeked out from beneath his eyelashes, he could see they were heading earthward. Benedict didn't open his eyes fully until she released him and his feet were on firm ground. He tumbled back and landed on his butt on the cool grass. She looked down at him, trying not to laugh at his discomfort. She tried to look contrite, but he wasn't buying that coy look.

"Now that was something to see," commented Marta from the rail of the country house. She glanced skyward and then down to where Benedict sat. She thought he looked pale. "Don't need a ticket, and you have the best seat in the house."

Benedict frowned at her as he got to his feet and dusted himself off. "You are amazing," he said as he took her chin in his fingers and kissed her roughly. "Not too many things scare me, but I would be willing to try it again sometime, with warning, if you please."

"I took unfair advantage, I'm sorry," she remarked, pouting cutely. She wasn't sorry; she was enjoying the fact that she had scared a very old blood.

"Are you well, Thea?" Em asked as he rushed to embrace her. Her wings had already been folded back and vanished.

"I'm okay. For once, I have no more secrets."

She extended her hand out to Benedict, who took it and kissed it gently. He glanced at Jackson, Marta, Lang, and Matt, who had all stood waiting.

"I hate to be a Debbie Downer, but Alexi has been trying to reach you."

Benedict frowned slightly as he walked toward where Marta stood by the rail.

"He says that he has information that you need to know. I can call him back if you would rather."

"Where did you tell him I was?"

Marta chuckled. "I told him you were chasing an angel," she muttered as she turned back and concentrated on the phone.

"Is something wrong?" Thea asked, concern in his voice.

"No, pumpkin. Everything is all right," he added as Lang and Jackson snickered. He glared at them as Marta handed him the phone.

Alexi had been one of Benedict's seconds; he now ran a city of his own in Benedict's network. It was more an empire than a network, but Benedict was modest in that way. Benedict stepped into the shadows for a moment of privacy, phone in hand.

"Boss, I'm glad I caught you. Sorry to call without an appointment."

"Alexi, you can call me anytime, you know that. What has gotten you so upset or riled up?"

His children had different names for him. Some called him boss, and others called him sir, father. There were a few that called him master. Benedict had told them they could call him by name. He heard Alexi take a deep breath as if to settle his worry.

"Someone from your new city put out a plea that it was up for grabs. Ruiz and Fontes were on their way to you. They didn't know that it had already been claimed by you, or else, they wouldn't even consider such an act of aggression. I caught Fontes. He was very grateful that I had stopped him from making a huge mistake. In fact, he wishes you much prosperity and hope you won't hold it against him that he might have considered challenging you. I couldn't reach Ruiz, but I understand from Raoul that he caught up with another troublemaker, Reed, and they are both on their way. They don't know that you have already taken the city, that you are claiming it as your own, and that the blood have given you their oath."

"How did they hear about the city? Do you know who made the plea?" Benedict asked, voice controlled.

"An invitation, I think Fontes said. I can find out who and when, if that would help?"

"I wouldn't want to kill Ruiz. He has possibilities as a loner, but Reed, she can be a handful. Thank you, Alexi. What you have already told me is useful. I know it wouldn't be one of our blood-born who issued an invitation. They know who I am, and the others would wait to see my stance, to see how dangerous I was before daring a challenge."

"And no one in their right mind would challenge you," Alexi confirmed.

"I appreciate your confidence. It is gratifying. I'll have the first watch keep an eye out, and we will go from there. How is your city prospering?"

"It is doing well. When you are settled, I would love to discuss options. I would love to hear how you are faring." Benedict looked out across the porch at Thea, who was petting Polly. "Better than I expected, Alexi. I have found love in the last place I would have expected. All my children will hear more about the woman I have chosen. She is one in a million, unique beyond price."

Alexi could hear the pride in Benedict's voice. This was a good thing. "I am so happy for you, boss. I will keep in touch. I will be sure to tell everyone else of your good fortune."

"It is beyond price, Alexi." Benedict handed the phone back to Marta, who smiled and winked at him.

"So Ruiz and Reed are on their way? I'll let the others know. You thinking of scaring the shit out of them?"

He chuckled lightly. "Reed, I wouldn't mind putting over my knee, but Thea might get the wrong idea."

Thea walked up and curled her arm around him possessively. "Is everything all right?" she asked, a slight edge in her voice.

"It is for now. I need more information before anything is done. I promise, the moment I know more. But you need your rest. You need time to put the pieces of your life back together."

"My life has always been a puzzle, but you are the last piece for it. I have you, that is all I need," she whispered in his ear.

Marta thought that was very sweet, and she knew it was earnestly meant. Benedict kissed her cheek. Benedict finding the love of his life made her think that maybe there was someone out there for her. She knew that women had played court to Benedict, but never had he fallen so swiftly and deeply in love.

"Ah, pumpkin, someone has gifted me you, and I don't think I could ever repay that kindness. Although I wasn't alone, sometimes you feel that way when your heart has nothing to cling to." Benedict kissed her forehead. "Good night, pumpkin."

She shook her head as he laughed, and watched them leave the patio, rounding the house, where they would leave her to her brother and his thoughts. Matt nodded to her politely.

"You need me for anything?"

"No, but you can tell the others in the forest that I am back. They can end their watch."

"You knew we were there?" he asked, mildly dismayed. He had hoped that they had gone unnoticed.

"Oh, you can hide, but not from the predators overhead. Tell them thank you."

"Copper was among them."

Thea opened and then closed her mouth, unable to comment.

"I thought that would be your reaction." He waved to them before leaving. The house was silent; only she and Em remained, with Polly chewing on a squeaky toy.

"Quite a few nights, huh?" he asked, unsure at how to proceed.

She sighed, seating herself on the patio. She stared heavenward. "If you had told me that I would meet demons and angels, I would have told you that you were crazy. I didn't even believe that Claire could possibly be right in her supposed vision."

"It was a generality. It could have been anyone. *The dark* is not very descriptive," Em remarked. "You appear content. I'm not sure if that is the right word, but you okay?"

Thea ran her hands up and down her arms as if chilled. "The choice was made for me. I would have rather the timing be different, but I don't have to explain now, because they saw for themselves." She pulled out the flash drive. "Here are the questions I asked myself and the answers that I have. They can be posted through Benedict. I know people want to ask all sorts of things."

"You mean like Naheed thinking you could heal?"

"I'm not a superhero. I really don't have all these magical powers."

"But you do have Benedict, who will ensure that you don't get hurt by other sorts of beings. He will watch your back."

"You can still do that, too, can't you?"

Em chuckled nodding. "Yeah, but I'm only human."

"You and RM are a match," she stated proudly.

"I know, and I see that now. She was impressed with you, but other than the fact that you have wings, that didn't color her judgment. I'm glad that I don't have any more secrets with her."

"I don't want what people think of me to change. I know things won't totally go back to normal, but I would like it to be as close as possible. I want to go to work tomorrow. I may only be able to work in the back, but I need to try."

"I understand," he said with a nod.

"How long do you think it will be before word of me spreads to the humans? I know some were present at the gathering, but they might be too afraid to say anything, considering who was present."

Em shook his head as he gestured to his sister. She stood and allowed him to hug her.

"I don't know, but we will take it one day at a time, all right?"

She nodded.

"And we will look to the skies for family or enemies. Your father was very handsome. You have his eyes."

"And wings, apparently."

Chapter 25

She and Em drove into the city together, both dressed for work, both acting as if it were just another day without all the drama. There would be enough later, Em was sure of it. He had asked RM to listen to the heartbeat of the city, to report on what might be said, on what people might do. It never occurred to him that they would send her gifts or flowers or that the clergy were eager to see her. As they approached their businesses, they had to round the block again, wondering how best to get her into work. They decided to go into the chapel. Em pulled up to the curb, turned off the car, and looked at Thea. There was a smattering of people mulling around the mortuary and chapel.

"You ready to make a run for it? You will be safe inside, and I can get everyone to leave."

She nodded as she grabbed her purse, opened the door, and darted around the car. There were voices raised, eyes following her as she leaped up the stairs in her heels and entered the chapel. She startled Pearl, who was arranging the flowers by the altar, and Zander, who was polishing up the pews.

"Morning, boss," they said as they watched her wave, heading toward the back door that would lead her from the chapel into a different kind of sanctuary. She was in and then out, followed by Em.

"Nothing to see here," he remarked with a chuckle as he followed his sister into the mortuary.

Thea passed reception and ducked into the back work room, where she only had corpses for company. She leaned against the worktable, flushed from running the gauntlet. She cleared her throat, shouldered her purse, and decided to get to work. Em said he would handle it, and she believed him. Thea pulled on her white work smock and turned to the corpses that were waiting for her. She ignored the voices beyond the workroom. She ignored the ringing phone, until she caught site of a familiar number. Sarah. Thea glanced at her watch. It was almost noon, and she could do with a break. She seated herself by her desk, in the harsh light of the fluorescence, and took the call.

"Thea here," she said, hopeful for just a normal conversation.

"Thea, it's Sarah. Something odd is going on."

She wondered what Sarah considered odd. Last time she said something was going on, she couldn't find two different shoes and thought it was a conspiracy.

"What might that be, Sarah?" she asked cautiously.

"Mal has friends you know, the other kind, not humans. You know what I mean."

"Yes, Sarah, I do," she replied with a sigh. Where was this going?

"They are saying that Caroline was killed by a demon and that at this big party for this new blood, there was an angel there. They are saying that you aren't human."

Thea was silent before she replied. "Okay, so are you asking me a question or just telling me what has been said or…?"

"Is all this true? I know that you know more about nonhumans than I do. I don't deal with them if I can help it."

Yes, Thea knew that.

"They say that you are the girlfriend of the new head vampire?"

"They don't like that name, Sarah, and you should try to be politically correct when the person in question can rip off your head and play with your spine."

Sarah cleared her throat and made her impatient noise.

"It is true that there is a new head blood, Benedict by name, and yes, he is mine. They don't really marry, so you might just call him my mate. That is as good a name as any. As for demons and angels, yes, Caroline was killed by a Demonkin. Yes, a demon and an angel did show up at the welcoming event for Benedict."

She guessed, by now, Sarah's eyes were wide, practically popping out of her head. She had to be pale as well.

"And are you human or not?" she asked, putting her figurative foot down.

"Would it make a difference in our friendship?" Thea asked bluntly.

"I can't answer that until I know what you are."

Thea glanced up at the door and found Em standing there, looking slightly frazzled.

"I am not human, Sarah. I never claimed to be, and everyone just figured that I was. I am an earthbound angel. The rumors are right. Although I was going to come out eventually, the revelation at the party sort of sealed my fate."

There was dead silence on the other end of the phone, and then she realized Sarah had hung up. Thea stared at the phone, heat rising to her face. She blinked back the tears that threatened. She cleared her throat, embarrassed.

"What's up?" she asked, voice sounding soft, hurt.

"Cleared up the array of people. Had to get the police to cordon us off. However, there is one of the monks from St. Mark's. He would like to have a word with you. Apparently, he saw the angel that picked up the weapon you had returned. You want to talk to him? He intimated that he might have a message for you."

Thea sighed, standing. She shrugged out of the lab coat and gently ran a comb through her hair. "Is there anywhere we can talk in private?"

"How about on the back patio? The day is lovely. I'll make sure that no one bothers you. And just to let you know, it wasn't only the police who tried to keep us in business. There were changelings as well."

She raised an eyebrow, as if disbelieving what her brother had said. He raised his hands to affirm he didn't have any answers either.

"All right, I'm not sure I can take too many more surprises," remarked Thea.

"You and I both," commented Em with a heavy sigh.

Brother Patrick stepped out into the sunshine garbed in a monk's robe. He looked terribly old-fashioned and out of place. He would have looked better in jeans and a tee, fit in better with the new world, but it suddenly occurred to her that maybe the arrival of an angel in his church might have been the cause for such humility. She stood and extended her hand to him. He kept his dark-brown eyes on her as she gestured for him to sit.

"Thank you for seeing me. I hadn't realized that there would be such a fuss. Apparently, in our city, news travels at the speed of light, mostly through the paranormals, but on occasion, it does get to the clergy. However, we did have a special visitor to affirm what is being said."

"Then what is it you want to know, Brother Patrick?" she asked, curious. The air was soft and fragrant today. The sky was empty of clouds and as blue as her eyes. It would be a lovely day to fly.

"I want to understand about these angels and demons. Can you tell me what exactly happened?"

"Well, I am sure you are aware of the legend that angels and demons are allowed a year on this earth. What they do while they are here, is up for anyone's guess. There are also humans who are part human and demon or angel. They are called Demonkin or Angelkin."

Patrick listened intently. "But you are not one of them."

"No. A Demonkin decided to use magic to communicate with his family but didn't realize that the spell would release a full demon."

Patrick frowned, in deep thought.

"I was told that I should ask for help from a heavenly source to send him back to the hell realm. Of all the places I thought might be the best place to pray, I thought of St. Mark's."

"But we aren't your church, are we?" Patrick asked with curiosity.

"No, but I had admired the beauty of it. It speaks to me. I can't tell you what it says, but it is there all the same. In those thirty minutes, I prayed for a weapon to defeat the demon, and my prayers were answered."

"But once you had the weapon in your possession and finished using it, you had to return it."

"I did, because I was pledged to do so. I laid it on the altar, knowing that something would come."

Patrick nodded, his gaze growing distant. "She came in a shower of light. She was only there for a blink of an eye, but long enough for us to see her. We were too stunned to move or to say anything to her, we just knelt and prayed. We knew then that there were angels among us. Rumor has it that you are a full angel, earthbound."

"I am so. I am kin to angels," she admitted bravely. "That doesn't make me any different than who I was before, except that I have wings. Did this glorious vision have anything to say?" She was hopeful.

"That there is an angel among us."

Thea nodded, shrugging.

"That you were sent for the good of man. I wasn't sure whom they meant at first, but it would be remiss of me if I didn't think of you first."

"Your thoughts didn't betray you, but I can't give you anything that you don't already have."

"We have affirmation. That is enough," added Patrick with a small smile. "That is all that we seek, to know the truth and that such exists. We have prayed for so long. We have read books, seen lovely windows that have angels and demons in a riot of color."

"And is it a blessing to know that it is true, or is it scary to know?" she asked, curious.

"It is what it is, and for that, I thank you. You are welcome anytime in St. Mark's."

Thea inclined her thanks. "And I'm not even going to have to prove to you who and what I am?"

"Not unless you want to," he added, standing.

She stood and shrugged out of her jacket. "For you, Brother Patrick," she remarked softly as her wings stretched out into the sunlight.

He lowered his head and whispered a prayer. "Glorious," he muttered. "And very cool."

"Isn't it, though?" she remarked with a slight smile.

* * *

It was almost dusk and quitting time. Thea had spent the long day working, trying to keep her mind off other things. It had quieted down considerably, and they were at least able to look out into the parking lot without a lot of eyes staring back. She never would have thought that Copper would back her, help her. It was a strange development indeed. Thea was leaning against the curtains, staring out into the growing dusk, when her phone rang. She glanced back at reception, the mortuary growing quiet. The chapel, however, filled with guests for an evening wedding. A new floral arrangement sat in the front entry. It was totally made up of white flowers, with added greenery. They were calling it the angel arrangement, flowers looking as if they had feathery wings. She smiled to herself. It was inventive, to say the least. Thea looked at her phone. It was Benedict. She smiled to herself, answering it, wanting and needing to hear his voice.

"Pumpkin, I was startled to hear that you went to work today."

"Adam still following me?" she asked wryly.

"Perhaps. You might be disappointed to lose his companionship. How have you fared?"

"Better than I thought, I guess. I am much better now that I hear your voice."

He chuckled. "You are going to turn my head with so many compliments. Can we see each other tonight?"

"I would love that, I need that. Let me get changed into comfortable clothes, grab something to eat, and I will be right over."

"Adam can drive you, if you like," he offered.

"Perhaps. Benedict, I love you. You know that, right? No matter what happens in this city, in this world, or with me, you will always have my love."

"Oh, my shining star, there is nothing more precious in this world than you or your love."

"I don't want it to make you weak, Benedict. I don't want to be used against you, and you have built too much for one person to destroy it all."

"Anthea, you will only strengthen it. Don't be long. I want you at my side."

"And I want you on your back," she said with a seductive giggle.

* * *

It never occurred to Clegg to look skyward to greet an arriving guest, but that was what happened; he had just turned around and almost stumbled into Anthea Black. She stood on the lawn dressed in sneakers, jeans, and a halter top. Over her arm lay a jacket, and behind her, fluttering in the light evening breeze, were two gorgeous feathered wings. He cleared his throat, nodding to her politely.

"I apologize, Ms. Black, I didn't hear you land. The main house mentioned that you would be by. May I walk you to the door?" Clegg watched in silent amazement as the wings vanished, Thea swinging her coat around her shoulders.

"That would be fine, unless you are needed here at the gate?" she asked.

"No, there are others that can take over for me." Clegg gestured toward the winding stone path. He settled in beside her, matching her pace and stride. It wasn't that Clegg didn't believe; it was just something you had to see, and now he had seen it. Luckily, his eyes hadn't bugged out and he didn't stammer like a school boy. The lights at the front of the house were ablaze, and the front door opened to reveal Benedict. There was a puzzled smile on his face.

"Security didn't see you drive up."

She chuckled, pointing to her back. "I took a shortcut. Hope you don't mind me flying in."

Benedict embraced her tightly, and they clung to each other for a long moment.

"Thank you for the escort," she said to Clegg.

"You are more than welcome," he added as he closed the door to the house behind them.

Benedict took the jacket from around her shoulders and hung it up on the nearby coatrack, ushering her not into the front entry of the house that was for guests but farther into his home, into the more private areas, like the kitchen.

"Can we get you anything to eat or drink?"

"How about something warm to drink, hot chocolate maybe?"

"With whipped cream?" asked a voice from behind the kitchen door.

Thea turned, meeting the eyes of a man she hadn't met before.

"Thea, this is Chef Tony Piketti. I was able to steal him away from his restaurant for special events."

"I'm not sure my arrival qualifies, but that does sound lovely. Where did you want to talk?"

"How about out by the pool? We have a small fire going. I'll try to explain and answer any questions you might have."

She nodded, taking his offered arm. He accompanied her out back, the patio lit by soft lanterns and a small brazier. She seated herself on the soft lounge, stretching out her legs, and she seemed to melt into it, relaxed. She met his gaze, staring at him, amazed that he was hers. She would not have believed it.

"So what exactly has happened?" she asked, concern plain in her voice.

"Firstly, I don't want you to worry about anything. You don't need any more stress than what has been put on you."

"Benedict, I am out of the box. There is no shoving me back in. And so here I am. You take me as you see me. Tell me."

"Well, when I first arrived, someone contacted a few other bloods and suggested that the city was up for grabs and they might want to take a run at Arkin Kane. None of the blood here would do that, so it had to be a changeling."

"Does this happen often?" she asked, uncertain.

"Not to him," called a voice from the kitchen. Thea wasn't sure whose voice it was.

"Anyway, I have a large network of people—"

"Empire," remarked the voice. "Call it what it is."

Benedict shook his head as Thea smiled softly.

"Whatever you want to call it, the men and women who were my seconds keep in touch with me. They have the responsibility of a city. I'm sort of like the president of the company, they are board members, and they knew that I was coming here, not for any particular purpose, but that I was taking a look-see. Alexi wanted me to know that he managed to stop one from pursuing a challenge for the city but there are others on their way."

"I have been a silent witness. I can't tell you if the challenges I saw were within the confines of tradition or what. Can you tell me what happens?"

"He should kill them," added Marta tartly as she pulled up a chair and sat down, handing Thea her hot chocolate. There were even little sprinkles on top. Thea took a sip, whipped cream topping her nose. It was Benedict who leaned over and kissed her.

"Sweet," he murmured as she flushed.

"We are watching for their arrival. They will send a formal challenge to me, and we will meet at our new residence in the city. I think you called it the Renard building. Once they realize who I am, I doubt the challenge will stand. I would rather know who coerced them to come."

"If it is a changeling or one of the Seven, do you have any power to do anything?" she asked.

"He should kill him or her," added Marta, and Thea tried to hide her smile.

"Don't mind her. I think she has been watching too many movies," added Lang in passing.

"I'll press that he or she is exiled from the city, not sure on the number of years yet, but I'm toying with a few ideas."

"You like to be sneaky."

He nodded with a wicked smile. "I like to be fair. You have to understand that now I am here, they are in a precarious position. Before, when Yardley was in charge, there probably wasn't a vast array of other changelings who wanted to bother with this city, but now that I am here and there is stability, that may change. They could be voted out, challenged out…the city is in for some changes."

"So do the other heads of the blood also come to support you when a challenge is issued?"

"Yes. Actually, any of the blood can come to watch. I have seen challenges that were standing-room only packed with spectators, and others were it was just the two combatants."

"And since I am your sweetie, I need to be there, right?"

He lifted her hand and kissed her gently. "You are my sweetie, pumpkin. That is going to be your choice, Anthea. I won't force you to be there."

She frowned slightly. "Where you go, I go, and I want to see you kick ass if necessary."

Marta chuckled. "Oh, he is good at kicking ass. In fact, we need to get him a T-shirt that says *kickass and doesn't bother with names*."

Benedict rolled his eyes. "I don't think there will be much to see, unless you enjoy seeing a changeling squirm. As soon as I know who did it, he or she will be summoned."

"Now that is what I call a relaxing evening," Thea added as she drained her hot chocolate. There was a moment or two of silence. "You said that you have a network or empire, whatever you want to call it. Do they know about you and me?"

"That is an excellent question. I made my stance known to everyone in the city, but I haven't released any sort of information to my family. I need to do that in case you need assistance. They need to know who you are and what you mean to me."

"What are you going to tell them?" she asked, curious, their eyes meeting.

"What do you want me to tell them? I wouldn't say anything that you are not comfortable with. You tell me."

Thea leaned back in the chair, eyes growing distant. "Well, I want them to know that you are mine. I'm not going to stand for calling you a boyfriend or fiancé. No, you are mine. I think *husband* fits the bill nicely, unless you disagree."

Benedict opened and then closed his mouth. Never in all the centuries did he think anyone would call him husband. He never thought of himself as the marrying kind, but now he couldn't think of being parted from Thea.

"I would be honored to be called that title from your lips," he said, voice sounding thick with emotion.

"Then you can call me *wife* if you like. I don't need a ceremony, unless you think it important. I was never one to want to be at the center of attention."

"You are now, but hopefully it won't last," added Marta. "You are just the in thing, like a pet rock."

"I applaud your optimism. Tell your people the truth. They need to know if they are going to make decisions on my behalf or come to my aid."

"As you wish."

Marta thought he was almost giddy with happiness; she had never seen him this way. It was refreshing.

"Just as an afterthought, I'm not going to be pissing any female bloods off by taking you off the market, am I? Just wanted to know if I need to sharpen my flaming sword."

Marta coughed, lightly amused.

"There has never been anyone but you," he confirmed.

"He is sweet, isn't he, Marta?" she gushed, and Marta rolled her eyes.

"Please, I'm heading toward sugar shock. But seriously, I am glad that you two have found each other. Benedict deserves to be happy. He has done so much for our race and others. It is time he had a piece of paradise for himself."

Paradise. She flushed slightly.

"Would it be an imposition if I decided to stay here with you? I have been thinking that Em needs to move on with RM, and if he is looking out for me, he can't look out for himself. Everyone deserves the right to have a life, and his is shorter than mine. I want him to be happy."

"You are a very thoughtful sibling." He trembled in excitement.

"I have thought of him as my brother for so long. We may not be blood, but I don't think that matters. If it isn't too much of a bother, I would like to consider this my home. I wouldn't do it right away, of course, but…"

"At your convenience and leisure, my darling. If you like, I can show you below in a bit more detail. You can stay with me, or you can have a room upstairs. I understand the east side of the house has a wonderful sunrise." Benedict stood, offering his hand to her, and she took it, standing. Marta felt for a moment as if she were intruding. It was Chrisanne who broke up the loving stares between the two. She cleared her throat, slightly embarrassed.

"It is Babette. She wants to know if you want her to send a small force to suitably impress and stop those at the city borders."

Benedict shook his head. "She worries about me as if she were my sister or mother. Tell her that I appreciate the offer. It is thoughtful. But I have the situation well in hand. My force here is the best, and if I didn't want to see them, there is no way they would gain access to the city."

Marta nodded, turning to leave when Benedict stopped her.

"Go ahead and let her know that I found true love. Answer her questions the best you can. It is faster than posting it for all my family to see. Babs's gossip moves faster than a forest fire. We may have company after that to meet you, but I would love for you to meet the men and women who are so much a part of who I am. And you are a part of that now."

Thea gently touched his face, caressing it as he curled his arm about her waist and walked her back toward the house. Marta glanced at Lang, who shrugged. Chrisanne peered out of the kitchen at the threshold.

"So what are you going to tell them?" he asked.

"The truth, I guess. They won't believe it, but he gave me permission. They will think it's a joke."

"Why don't you sit with Georgiana? She is serious as a heart attack and no one would dare laugh at her. She would make Babs have second thoughts about making a joke about either Benedict or Anthea."

Marta looked at Lang. It was a good idea. "You are evil, Chrisanne. A good idea. Go get her."

Lang followed Marta to the communications room. He peered over at the screen and found Babs waiting patiently to speak to her master, but instead, Marta seated herself. It wasn't that Babs didn't like Marta, but she was jealous of the power that she seemed have with Benedict.

"You did tell our master of my offer, Marta?" she asked, gently running her hands through her red hair, primping.

"Yes, I did, Babs, and he was most grateful, but I think he wants them in the city. He wants to know who tipped them off. You know, he can be whimsical that way."

Babs frowned slightly as Georgiana seated herself beside Marta. Geo, as she called herself, was a tall waiflike woman with braided blond hair, cool blue eyes, and nary a smile.

"Babette," said Geo coolly.

"Benedict wanted me to tell you that he has found the love of his life in this city, so I don't think he will be leaving here anytime soon. He seems to be profoundly happy."

Babs's eyes opened wide at the statement.

"Eventually, he might travel with his wife so that he can introduce her to his world at large, but right now, they have other plans."

"Wife?" It was a screech that caused Lang to wince.

"That was what he called her, isn't it, Lang?" Marta asked in confirmation.

"Yes, and she did call him her husband."

Babs was shaking her head, beyond flustered, with Geo trying to keep the amusement out of her expression.

"Who is this woman? Is she a blood or just a simple human who will turn to dust in a few years?" Babs asked pointedly.

"I'm not sure how to describe Anthea Black. What do you think, Geo?" Marta asked innocently.

"Well, Marta, she is a businesswoman, owns a few thriving businesses. She is very pretty, and she is an angel," Geo remarked.

Babs waved her hands at the two women, annoyed.

"No, Babette, she is an angel with wings and everything," restated Marta. "They are in love, and he wanted his children to know this in case she should need help or assistance."

Babs's gaze was narrow. Marta and Geo weren't giving her an inch; there was no way for her to tell if they were joking. Lang peered in over their shoulders and could see Babs's confusion.

"They are telling the truth, and you need to let everyone know that he is happy, they are each other's, and she is a child of myth. While you have been running your city, we have encountered both demons and angels. It is a story to be told, and maybe one day you will hear it."

"As you wish," remarked Babs, uncertain. "You will be sending this dictate out to everyone?"

"Yes, but you are one of the first not in this city to know. Feel honored." Geo signed off, managing a short sharp laugh.

"Well, she totally doubts us," added Marta.

"She shouldn't, because she will just piss him off. Expect more questions as soon as Babs gets the word out." Marta turned to Lang. "You thought that was funny?"

He shrugged. "I like to see her put in her place. She has always been dogging his step, thinking that he might turn around and want her. She would be wrong."

"Yes, she was."

* * *

Benedict had only just closed the door to his room when Thea pinned him to the door, her body pressing against his, her lips closing over his in hot, lusty passion.

"I think I have created a monster," he remarked as he tugged her hair, letting her catch her breath.

"I want you. Is that a bad thing?" she asked as she spun on her heels and waltzed over toward the bed.

"No, but you don't give a man a chance to do the seducing."

"We have plenty of time for that, Benedict, but if you insist, you are more than welcome to try to seduce me." She coyly sat on the bed, a small pout to her lips, fluttering her eyelashes at him.

"Fuck the seduction," he hissed under his breath. He pounced on her, grinding her into the softness of the mattress. His hands were tugging on her clothes, caressing her body, driving her to distraction a she lay beneath him partially dressed, flushed from need and want. He thrust his hands into her panties and found her wet and waiting for him.

"You undo me," he muttered into her throat, his fangs grazing the virgin skin.

She giggled and wiggled beneath him, tickled by his breath. He chuckled as he plunged fingers into her narrow channel. Her body arched.

"Give me what I want, Benedict," she demanded, tugging at his clothing. Soon he was bereft of shirt, his clothing awkwardly angled over his body as he drew her legs upward and rammed into her silky heat. As soon as they joined, it was as if the world spun on its axis. The overwhelming need quenched as they moved in rhythm to satisfy each other's needs. It was a powerful joining, Thea straining to make Benedict come, Benedict hoping to get Thea to beg. But it was no time for games; they just needed each other. A cry escaped her lips, and her back bowed as she came, shoving Benedict deeper into her body, power rippling over her, cascading over his body, draining him, as he could no longer hold back. The orgasm was ripped from him, their bodies trembling in the aftermath as he fell forward onto her, trying to turn slightly to her right so he didn't press the air from her lungs. They lay in each other's arms, Thea sweating, panting, Benedict with his eyes closed, trying to regain control of his emotions and the power that filled him.

"I think I will need a ride home," she said as he laughed and kissed her nose. "I couldn't get a wing up if I tried."

"Nor I another appendage of mine," retorted Benedict.

Chapter 26

It should have been a serious situation, but instead it seemed to Thea that everyone was enjoying themselves way too much. The call had come in from what Benedict's team called the first watch. That Reed and Ruiz had been spotted entering the city a day later. If they thought they had entered unseen, they would have thought wrong. The city was waiting with bated breath to see these two blood do something so entirely stupid. With their arrival, everyone knew that the invitation would be forthcoming if they found the city worth their effort. Thea was pretty sure that they would want the city. After all, Benedict had wanted it. No one seemed terribly worried, and Thea was trying to suppress her anxiety.

As soon as the two challengers entered the city, they began the process of assessing whether it would be worth their effort, and as Thea feared, the invitation was delivered to Benedict by Edden. Thea wondered why Edden, but then again, the SoulFires Tavern was popular. It surprised Thea that they hadn't actually done any competent intelligence work; they were cocky enough to believe they could take this upstart Arkin Kane. The blood of the city didn't correct them, didn't warn them. No, this was going to be something to watch. It hadn't mattered whether they were blood, changeling, or human. Everyone seemed interested in watching a fight. Thea hadn't been in attendance when the invitation had arrived; Edden delivered it promptly to security, who took it to Benedict. Edden had thought of just ripping it up, but tradition demanded it be delivered, and he was a bit upset that they thought he should do it. If they were so brazen, he figured, they should have done it themselves. The invitation was formal, as they always were, and the upstarts waited for an answer.

It wasn't the first invitation that Benedict had ever received, but it had been a long time indeed since anyone had challenged him. He had faced bloods, changelings, humans, and a fair number of fey in his time, and he had come out the victor. He might not have come out unscathed, but he had been successful either with body or with words.

Em had tried to calm his sister down, but she wasn't having any of it. It wasn't that she didn't think Benedict could handle Ruiz and Reed; she just wanted them to get on with their lives. She wanted and craved the normal routine. She wanted this to be over.

Benedict responded with a place and time, and it was delivered by Geo, who had been flexing her hands, itching to take on the upstarts. He then called his worried pumpkin, who answered the phone promptly.

"Anthea, don't tell me that you were sitting by the phone, waiting. Were you?" he asked, voice filled with amusement.

"No. I'll have you know I was pacing with Polly. Esther told me that the two idiots had arrived. Why didn't you call me and tell me yourself?" She was pouting, he was sure of it, and that just made him want to kiss her into submission all the more.

"I didn't want you to worry unnecessarily. Adam is on his way to pick you up. It will be over tonight, I promise."

She was silent on the other end.

"Thea, it is sweet for you to be worried over me. I haven't had anyone worry about me in a very long time. I find it delightful, even sexy."

"Me, worried about you? Oh, pashaw, I know you can take them. I just had started packing and needed a place to put all my boxes," she quipped, warming Benedict's heart.

"Well, bring the boxes over. I'm waiting for you to join me in my bed."

"Evil man," she muttered. "I don't like confrontation. I know that sounds odd, considering I faced a demon and will face accusations and curious eyes on me as the only earthbound angel I know on this planet, but I want us to get back the way we were. I want us back doing business. I don't want us watching our backs."

"Oh, Anthea, this is just a minor inconvenience. You have to see their faces when they find out it is me. Marta can't wait to see the horror in their expressions. It will be something to see, better than a movie."

She sighed, shaking her head. A knock on the door jarred her thoughts.

"I think Adam is here."

"Good. He will take you to Renard. I will meet them at the main entrance. The foyer has enough room to dance if the need arises."

Men.

"You aren't so much focused on the fight as on who called them to come, are you?" she asked.

"That, I do want to know, and there is no way in hell that they won't tell me."

She shivered slightly at the conviction in his voice.

He cleared it and softened. "It is going to be quite a crush tonight. Those who gave an oath to me who had been under Yardley will be there, and of course my people. You know how we love a good surprise. It is my business to keep them entertained, you know."

She sighed, shaking her head. "I'll keep that in mind."

"Oh, Thea, you were the biggest surprise of all to them. I love you."

She sighed, contented. "And I you as well. I'll be right there."

Em had let Adam in the front door; he sauntered in, trying to ignore the rather-loud conversation that she was having with Benedict.

"I take it your sister is a bit unsettled?"

Em shrugged, leaning against the countertop in the kitchen. "She isn't competitive, nor is she into contact sports like this is libel to be."

Adam shook his head as he saw Thea wave to him. She bounded up the stairs, and he figured she was going to either grab her purse or change. He could never tell with women or with angels.

"This won't be anything of the sort. You have to understand that once Ruiz and Reed find out whom they are facing, it will be a polite bow out."

"Are you sure about that?" Thea asked at the door to the kitchen. She was dressed in a gray pantsuit, a pretty blush-pink halter top beneath her jacket. She looked lovely this evening. She was even wearing sensible shoes.

"Will there be a medic there?" she asked, curious.

Adam walked to the front door and opened it for her. "You mean Robbins? He almost always attends these types of events. However, he has never been needed for our side."

She nodded, almost feeling comforted. Adam gently offered her his arm as they walked to the car. It was a limo. She was surprised that he wasn't driving his old and average trail car. He chuckled, noting her gaze.

"You are his consort, you should arrive in style."

She climbed into the back of thc limo, a spray of flowers waiting for her. The small note from Benedict said not to worry. She was trying hard not to.

It seemed like eternity until they arrived around back of the Renard building. She frowned, looking at Adam.

"Ruiz and Reed enter in through the front. He won't let them get past the front foyer. It will be short and sweet. We really want to know who called them to come."

"If you had to hazard a guess, who do you think it is?"

Adam shrugged, rubbing his face as they stepped out of the car. Jackson was there at the door to greet them. He gave her a brief kiss on the cheek, escorting her in. Yeah, Adam had his own idea but wouldn't voice it to her.

"I was going to ask you that. You know them better than I do," he remarked. Thea could hear brief snippets of conversation in the distance. She recognized Esther's voice, and Copper's. She could smell food and hear the clink of glasses. What did they think this was, a party or something? As if Adam had heard her thoughts.

"You have to show that you are unaffected by such a challenge, so you make it seem inconsequential. The boss takes these things very seriously. He doesn't want to have to hurt one or two of his own. He did, however, think about taking Reed over his knee for a good spanking."

Thea frowned; if he was going to be spanking anyone, it had better be her, followed by makeup sex.

"To answer your question, I would guess Lyle or Perry. Maybe Hector, if he was pushed."

"This wasn't something I had thought would happen, or we might have been prepared just to take the changeling," Adam remarked as they bypassed the steps, coming into the grand foyer. It looked better than it had.

Benedict stood off to her right. She drew a breath, the fluttering in her chest subsiding slightly. He stood in his signature color of gray slacks and a crisp white shirt, no tie. His sleeves were rolled up, and he looked ready to chastise. A stray thought ran across her mind. Being turned over his knee, she flushed slightly as he offered her a hand.

"Ah, my darling, come up onto the steps with the others." He kissed her gently on the lips, pulling her into an embrace. She melted into his arms.

"I was worried," she cooed.

"I know you are, but don't fret."

He turned her so that she could see Esther and Copper over to the right along the wall chatting away as if they were old friends. Around them on the steps stood the blood, Terence, Emily, Tasha, Margaux, and Asao, all dressed elegantly. To her left was security, Benedict's security. They all delivered a very graceful bow to her as she set her purse aside on the steps to her left, straightened her shoulders, and prepared to greet Ruiz and Reed. Benedict stood in the middle of the blood, his eyes locked on the front doors. Thea stood just a step behind him, looking out over the sea of people gathered. She swallowed and suppressed her fear. This wasn't anything like Yardley or the others trying to take the city; this seemed all very civilized.

There was noise at the front doors, Ruiz and Reed entering the foyer. Ruiz had caramel-colored skin, dark hair, and dark eyes. He looked fit. Reed was just a hand's length shorter, brunette hair coiled around her head, bright-red nails, and narrow, cool eyes. Ruiz was wearing camos, and Reed a more tailored suit, but with sensible shoes. They stopped just inside the doors and surveyed the situation. If Thea had been them, she would have nodded, bowed, and then turned to run like hell. This was not a situation you should find yourself in. Thea looked down at Benedict, waiting for him to say something, but instead, a tall female blood stepped between where they stood and the new arrivals.

"Welcome to our city, Ruiz and Reed."

They looked at each other, mildly taken aback that they were known. Thea figured that Benedict probably knew everyone; he was just that old and that clever.

"May I present the current master of the city—"

"We know who he is, bitch," said Ruiz. "Arkin Kane, we heard you came to take the city for your own, and there have been a few who have taken exception to that."

"I wouldn't call Geo a bitch," muttered Marta as she stood off to Thea's left up on the stairs. "She takes things very personally."

"Why don't you tell me who called you so I can thank them for the entertainment?" Benedict answered lightly.

Copper held her breath. She knew this was going to be bad, and it was. Lyle Wegman had called for them. She closed her eyes, trying to get ahold of her emotions. Lyle's future was now up to Benedict, and she wondered absently if he would choose his death. It wasn't Benedict who looked over at her. No, it was Asao, who gave her the sign to bring Lyle to the square. Copper nodded. She had chosen her side. She had chosen to align herself with Benedict and an earth-bound angel. It was the right thing to do, though others might not see it that way. Zara was rather fond of Lyle; he might not go without a fight. Esther watched Copper slip away. Thea shook her head, taking another sip of the champagne that Marta had given her. She hadn't known when there had been so much excitement in this city.

"Now, if you will allow me to finish," Geo remarked, voice tight. Thea thought she was highly strung. "I will complete the introductions."

"If your master makes you." Reed sighed, looking at her red-lacquered nails, appearing bored.

"May I present the master of the city, Arkin Kane, a.k.a. Benedict Macai." There was a smug smile on her face as she stepped back, arms folded across her chest, giving them a good look at the master of the city. There was an air of expectancy and silence that filled the chamber. Ruiz's eyes narrowed as he looked hard at Benedict. Reed was relying on Ruiz to make the move. Did they go or not? Boy, she was stupid.

"Benedict?" he asked softly under his breath.

"Yes?" Benedict asked, curious. "May I present the city elders, my second, Asao; Terence; Tasha; Emily; and Margaux. I would also like to present my consort, Anthea Black."

She wondered why he didn't introduce the others, but perhaps they liked it that way. To be unnamed was to be unknown.

"You are Benedict?" he asked, voice cracking slightly.

"Yes. If you hadn't been in such a hurry to get here and fight, Alexi or Raoul might have saved you the trip, but you are here now. What is your purpose here? Do you want to challenge me for the city?"

If it was possible, Thea thought Ruiz looked pale. Reed was chewing on her fingernail, gaze running back and forth along those who were gathered. Benedict was calm; he just waited for some response.

"If you don't mind answering me? There are other things I would like to be doing this evening, and if I am going to have to fight, I would like to get it over with. I wore an old suit, just in case."

Thea's lips twitched. He was enjoying their discomfort. It was probably the best revenge.

Ruiz managed to shake off the shock. He straightened himself uprightly and cleared his throat. "Our apologies, Benedict. We were unaware that you had taken this city as your own. You have so many under your rule it never occurred to us…it has been a while since you have surfaced and have been seen."

"Ruiz, I have always been somewhere, and my seconds have taken the cities in their name to make certain our race prospers and that there is no further animosity between our peoples. Peace above all else is paramount."

Ruiz nodded, managing a very deep bow. Reed, however, was a bit more skeptical.

"So you aren't going to challenge him for the city?" she asked, voice echoing across the foyer.

"I don't want to die tonight," Ruiz remarked dryly.

"So you decline to fight him. But what about the others? Do you want a place within their ranks?"

Ruiz looked pained by Reed's words. Thea waited to see what was going to happen. Really, she was more interested in seeing Lyle wheedle his way out of having set all this up. Thea watched as Reed stepped forward.

"Well, I don't want to challenge Benedict, but I'll take on his consort. She is, after all, a human, and I feel I would be a better match to him in this city."

You could have heard a pin drop in the foyer.

"Oh, you chose the wrong woman to pick on," commented Esther. Thea wondered just how much champagne she had had.

Terence and Margaux stepped forward.

"That can't happen," Terence remarked firmly.

"You and I can go a couple of rounds," offered Margaux. This was one evening she looked sensibly dressed and up-to-date. Maybe she didn't want to soil one of her gowns.

"That isn't what tradition and our laws demand. I have my right."

Thea stood and looked at Reed, and she smiled. In fact, she sort of chuckled. Benedict turned around to regard her, an odd expression on his face. Thea set the flute of champagne aside, shrugged out of her jacket, laying it on the steps. She dared a step down to Benedict's side.

"She wants to take me on?" she asked, bright-eyed.

"Yes, pumpkin, she does," Benedict responded carefully.

"Shouldn't she have the right to change her mind as well?" Thea asked, curious.

"Yes, she does," added Tasha smugly.

It was Thea who stepped down past Benedict to the bottom steps. "You want to fight with me?" she asked again bluntly.

"Yes. Why Benedict Macai would want a human for his consort is beyond me. You must be a hell of a good lay."

Thea laughed. "Before we do this little dance, you might want to understand what you are facing."

"Thea, you don't have to do this," cautioned Asao, concerned.

"Are there ways around this law? Obviously, she thinks that if she kills me, she can have Benedict. He, of course, would just kill her, and then he is left with nothing and she has lost her life. She has the right to decide how she wants to spend that commodity, with me or with him."

Reed walked up to stand about twenty feet away from Thea. "Would everyone behind me move back a step or two?" Reed watched as they did as she asked, her gaze narrow as she considered what was going to happen.

This was it, an affirmation of what she was, and for the first time, she wasn't nervous or scared. It was her choice, and Benedict didn't like it at all. Thea outstretched her arms, and her wings blossomed along her back. It wasn't just the wings, however; it was a transparent curtain of power that rippled the air and made both Reed and Ruiz fall back in fear. It shimmered before Benedict and his court. It created a silent whirlwind.

"You go, girl," Esther commented cheerfully.

Thea leveled her gaze at Reed. "Yes or no?" she asked, bringing her wings down across her back.

Reed and Ruiz both turned and ran out the door and into the night.

"Well, hell!" Benedict dared to lean down and kiss her on the left side of the throat just as Copper appeared at the front door with Lyle in tow. She wasn't the only one holding him. Arabella, one of the Seven, was there as well. He struggled to pull away from their grasp. He wasn't succeeding.

"What scared the hell out of them?" Arabella asked as she cast a glimpse at Thea. "Oh, pretend I didn't ask. Nice to see you, Thea. I never thought you were that scary, but I guess looks can be deceiving."

Thea nodded as she let her wings vanish behind her back. Benedict embraced her gently, and Asao laid a hand on her shoulder.

"You were bold, indeed," he commented proudly.

"Hey, I'm here. I might as well be here, right?" she asked. "No sense in hiding. You all had the nerve to come out. It is time I did so as well."

"Bravo," added Emily.

Benedict stepped past Thea and regarded Lyle, who ceased his struggle. He was slightly surprised that it was two women who had brought him in. Where were the men?

"Copper, Arabella, thank you so much for bringing Lyle to me. I presume that you know those two bloods who hightailed it out of here?" Benedict asked lightly.

Lyle straightened his clothes and tried to regain his composure. He cleared his throat and met Benedict's gaze. "Yardley was dead, and you were circling. I hadn't heard of Arkin Kane. I didn't know what you would mean to this city. None of the other blood would stand up and be counted, so I took it upon myself to try to fill this city with fresh blood, so to speak. I don't know those two specifically."

"No, the others you contacted knew better once they were informed that I was here. In days gone by, I would have killed you. I would have been done with you. But we are supposed to be more civilized. I have killed more men and women than I can count, and most of those fights, I didn't start. So I can give you to someone else to kill, but actually, I think what hurts most is to take everything away from you, all that is yours. You are exiled from this city and any other city that is under my family's control."

Copper's and Arabella's mouths hung open, Asao smiled, and Emily clapped. It was better than death. This would haunt him for the rest of his life. He would have nothing, and if he did, it would be far away from anywhere metropolitan. Lyle's face was pale, his body trembling as his legs gave out and he hit the floor.

"You have until dawn this day to leave the city. By the time I leave here, my family will know and be on the lookout for your arrival, wolf."

Lyle crab-crawled away from Benedict. Thea bet he was wishing Benedict had just killed him; it would be far easier.

Benedict turned his gaze on Copper and Arabella. "If you will make sure he doesn't take anything that isn't already his. I don't know how you want to work it since he was on your Council of Seven."

There was no verbal response; there was nothing for them to say and do but nod. Esther was beaming. She thought this was better than a reality show.

"You are awesome," she muttered, raising her flute to Benedict, who rolled his eyes. Within seconds, Lyle was out the door, followed by Copper and Arabella. Lyle might not make it out of the city; it would be kinder to kill him. That way, he couldn't sow discontent or encourage others to take their council.

"You sealed his fate," commented Terence. "He won't live come dawn."

"I suspect as much, but I won't have his blood on my hands. They have to clean up their own mess. Now, I believe the festivities are over. Ms. Black-Macai, can I escort you home? I should like to see all those boxes that you packed."

It was Tasha who put out a hand to stop Thea for just a moment. "What would you have done if she had insisted on fighting you?" Tasha asked, curious. "That weapon you had to face the demon with is gone."

Thea smiled at Tasha, and she didn't like that one bit. "Don't make the mistake that I am not armed, Tasha," she quipped as Benedict curled his arm around her and walked her back up the stairs, leaving with her jacket and purse, and leaving the blood-born and a very amused Esther behind.

When they reached the top of the gallery, Benedict turned her around and met her cool gaze.

"What? You can worry me but I can't worry you? She chose me out of everyone here because she thought I was weak, human weak. I'm not weak."

"I would have liked a few moments to talk you out of such a glorious display, or maybe just turn you over my knee and chastise you for such boldness, but you are right. You need to stand on your own two feet and fly with your wings."

She rolled her eyes, kissing him on the lips. "Why don't you come over to my place?" she remarked, wriggling her eyebrows. "Unless you need to chase Ruiz and Reed out of the city?"

"No. Georgiana and I think Terence, with Margaux at his side, might enjoy that more." He kissed her on the throat, and strangely enough, he didn't feel the lust for her blood. Benedict walked her to the back stairs, down to the lower level, passing Adam, who was scarfing down a sandwich.

"Over already?" he asked, mumbling between bites.

"Yes, and we won't be needing your services. I will be with Anthea if anyone needs anything, and I am counting on the fact that they won't."

"Gotcha, boss," he remarked, raising a glass of milk.

They stepped out into the night air, with Thea drawing a deep breath.

"Will your other children accept me as easily as they did?" she asked, concerned.

"You are impressive all on your own, and to be honest, Thea, it doesn't matter. We owe nothing to anyone else, just to each other. After all I have given them, they will be happy to see that I have found someone, that I have received something."

She leaned in and kissed him. She slipped her hand in his and pulled him into one of his many cars.

It had been a quiet drive back to the house, each distracted by their own thoughts. Benedict knew that there wouldn't be a formal challenge, but it had shocked him that Reed would think he would allow her to take on Thea. Or that if she won the challenge, he would want her. Benedict had been surprised that Thea gave Reed an out, showing off her magnificent wings. And it was true: now that Anthea was out, it was time she stopped regretting it and lived. Thea had even shocked herself by standing up to Reed, and it had been about time. It had freed something she felt had been tied up for a very long time.

Benedict patted her leg gently as they pulled up to the curb.

"I heard you wanted to take Reed and put her over your knee." He raised a curious eyebrow.

"Was I just as bad?" she asked coyly, laughing as she leaped out of the car.

Benedict followed her up the stone pathway to the doorstep. She touched her hand to the knob and froze. She felt a chill rise up her spine, the familiarity of something beyond. She turned sharply and placed her finger on Benedict's lips. He froze, waiting to understand what Thea was trying to tell him. She gestured to her back, making the symbol of wings.

"Let me go in first," she whispered in his ear. He nodded but didn't like the situation.

She had a bit more experience with her people than he did, but how effective would he be in a fight? He flexed his hands, preparing for anything. Thea opened the door, not finding an eager Polly. She hoped the pup was all right. She could see the wash of a warm glow from the living room, but there didn't seem to be a light on. As quietly as she could, she crept toward the threshold and peered into the room. There, standing by the cold hearth, was a woman bathed in the faint, soft golden glow. Thea had no idea where the light came from but realized that she, too, was giving off a soft light, as if she recognized the need for light, or maybe because she knew what this woman was. The woman was wearing a long white tunic with trousers beneath, her feet bare. Her dark hair lay in ringlets about her shoulders, barely brushing the golden torque that lay around her neck. Thea could feel Benedict at her side. She extended a hand to him to stop his forward movement. This woman didn't mean any harm, because in her face, Thea recognized her smile. It was hers. She had seen it a hundred times in the mirror, in her reflection.

The woman spoke. Her voice was soft, but commanding, as if you had to listen to her.

"Anthea Sheridan Black, Benedict Macai, greetings. I mean you no harm."

"It never hurts to be careful, Mother," answered Thea boldly.

She smiled, her eyes crinkling lightly, pleased to be so easily identified. She inclined her head, grateful. "You have your father's eyes and my smile. I am gratified to see that, child. You have grown into a lovely young woman. I am pleased to see it." The angel turned her gaze onto Benedict, who managed a graceful bow. This was turning out to be some evening. "Benedict, your mother, Sareet, is so happy that you have done well for yourself and your people. She knew you were strong."

Thea looked at Benedict, and she could see the astonishment in his gaze.

"My mother?" he asked in a soft whisper.

The angel nodded. "Angelkin. That was why you were so drawn to my daughter, and we agree, it is a fine match. We want to see you both happy. She is not of my choir or host, but I know of her."

Benedict had an odd expression on his face, as if he was trying to define his life by what she had just told him.

"I am happy, Mother. Why are you here?" Thea stood still as the angel walked silently forward until she reached out to touch Thea's hair. She fluffed it lightly with her fingertips.

"When I heard your voice asking for the weapon, it was I who delivered it to you. You used it well. Thank you for returning it so promptly."

"I gave my word. I should thank you for giving it to me, for your trust. I wasn't really sure how to ask or what to ask for," she answered honestly.

"I wanted to tell you that you have no reason to be afraid of your people. Everyone exists for a reason. You have purpose, even if others do not see it. Casren has no power over you. Your father and I will make sure that you are safe and continue on the path that is set."

"Was my sole purpose to deter demons, keep them at bay?" she asked softly.

"Not all Demonkin are evil, but some do tend to go the dark way. Knowledge itself is not evil. It is what is done with it that determines what people think of it. I would like to think that perhaps your sole purpose was to find someone to love, like Benedict here. Surely, your lives will be enhanced. We want you to be happy."

Thea sighed.

"I am sorry that we were not there when you came into your power, your wings."

"I could have used the help, or at least a manual, that is for sure," Thea said. "I am glad we got to meet. Can you tell me your name?"

"Desreial." With that, Thea's mother gently kissed her daughter on the forehead and, in a golden glow of light, vanished.

Thea and Benedict stood side by side, silent, each lost in their own thoughts. There was a quiet, peaceful silence that filled the front living room, both Thea and Benedict standing only in the light of the moon filtering in through the windows. She reached over and turned on the small lamp near an overstuffed wingback chair. She was now able to see him more clearly, but even though they were in the same room, she could tell he was ten lifetimes away from her. Thea could almost see him riffling through each moment in his life to determine whether being Angelkin had saved him. There was a slight twitch of his lip as her mind wandered back to when they had first met. Had he been lured to her by the kinship in their blood? Would they even be together if they weren't similar?

Benedict's hand cupped her chin. He had a soft smile on his kissable lips.

"I know what you are thinking."

"Do you?" she asked coyly. "How presumptuous of you."

He chuckled lightly. "You are thinking that I was drawn to you because we have similar blood, which, until now, I hadn't the faintest idea I had."

"The thought had crossed my mind, but it also calls the other way. Maybe that is why I am attracted to you."

"But what are the odds, Anthea, that we would meet here in this city?"

"Quite astounding, I am sure, my angel," she quipped as he chuckled, embracing her.

"You do know what this means, don't you?" He took a step closer to her, Thea's gaze lost in his. "It means I can taste you without having to worry about becoming ill or injured." He saw her eyes widen slightly, and she licked her lip in nervousness.

"Does it now?" she asked, voice barely above a whisper.

"That is, of course, if you want me to." His voice was low and seductive. "It would normally be part of our relationship, but because I thought we were different and that your blood might kill me…"

With a squeal, Thea ducked under his arm, ran around the corner, and went up the stairs. She was faster than a normal human, of course, but then again, so was Benedict. He followed closely behind her but was at a slight disadvantage since he wasn't sure which room was hers. He dashed into her room, eyes on the bed as she leaped out from behind the door. She grabbed him around the waist and twisted toward the bed. They bounced as she pinned him into the soft comforter. Her face was flushed, her hair wild about her face, a triumphant smile on her lips.

"Is this a challenge?" he asked, eyes glittering with passion.

"It's an angel smackdown," she remarked as he flipped her over onto the bed, his body pressing her into the soft linens.

"Let's make it an angel soft-as-down," he muttered as he kissed her hotly on the mouth, her arms encircling him.

"I guess, since you were brave enough to fly," she answered.

"You made me fly," he remarked. "You do just by being by my side."

She rolled her eyes at him. "But you won't make me do this unless I want to," she asked firmly.

"Correct," he muttered, nibbling on her earlobe.

"Then what's keeping you?" she asked slyly.

She gently turned her head, closed her eyes, and waited for her angel Benedict's kiss.

About the Author

The author lives with her family in the wilds of Florida, in between two coasts and nearby magical kingdoms. She writes urban fantasy, paranormal romance, and science fiction. She enjoys the company of large dogs with happy, wagging tails, old mystery movies, and, on the whole, would rather be writing.

CPSIA information can be obtained
at www.ICGtesting.com
Printed in the USA
BVHW070727080223
658054BV00001B/79